Wolff's Bane

H. J. Russell

The characters and events portrayed in this book are fictitious. Any similarity to real persons, living or dead, is coincidental and not intended by the author.

For Alex and Nina, who could always find the laughter.

"O wert thou, Love, but near me!
But near, near, near me,
How kindly thou wouldst cheer me,
And mingle sighs with mine, Love."
—— **Robert Burns**

Warning

This story contains information about sexual assault and/or violence which may be distressing to some audiences but is essential to the plot. Reader discretion is advised.

THE STING

***"Eating just one billionaire would do more to prevent climate change than going vegan or never driving a car for the rest of your life."* — Extinction Rebellion (XR) Instagram post, August 2022**

***

from:	Gary Singer < Gary.Singer@tacitnet.mi5.uk >
to:	Jamie.Douglas@tacitnet.mi5.uk
subject:	Operation Monkshood
security:	AES-256 encryption

Jamie,

Latest string from wobblyheads: target's joining climate protest in Manchester on Saturday. They're encouraging groups to block motorways, lock onto railings - usual eco-idiot stuff but gives you and Frazer the opportunity to make contact. Plan is you'll join activists at Neo Petroleum's HQ in Old Trafford. Make your way there on Fri and we'll meet in evening to go over the brief, instructions for operatives etc. Details to follow. Frazer may not

```
get this chance again for weeks so, needless to say,
this is not the time for fuckups!
  Gary
```

Jamie

Forty metres is high, but it seemed much higher as Jamie clung by his fingertips from the roof. He sucked in a deep breath, risked a glance at the sea of protesters below as a wave of riot police crashed through them, and prayed the specialist climbing team would arrive soon. Flattening himself against the tiles, he gripped with his toes and shifted position to ease the cramp in his legs.

He'd scaled a few buildings in his army career but never glued himself to one. On terra firma, it'd seemed like a good idea; a way to attract attention and help his partner Frazer inveigle himself into the group. Now Jamie was not so sure. Even if he survived, he was sure their MI5 handler would flay him alive for this crazy stunt. Or his missus ... in fact, Kathryn would fry his balls in batter if she learned about this.

"Help Frazer infiltrate a bunch of eco-freaks," Gary had said. "It's a babysitting job."

Except it wasn't.

Frazer had been recruited straight from Cambridge University and sounded like he'd been force-fed plums at Eton. He couldn't play the part of a rope-access technician in the construction industry or act like an eco-activist convincingly. Despite the detailed brief, he struggled to remember facts about his legend or formulate a coherent argument around the climate cause. Frazer was destined to be a desk spook, not a field officer, and Jamie couldn't believe the eejit had made it through training. He suspected the old school tie had been a factor.

When Gary had asked for a report on Frazer, Jamie had written 'I wouldn't breed from this officer.' Regardless, upstairs gave the operation the green light and Jamie was asked to prepare Frazer for his undercover stint and teach him to climb. He soon realised that if Frazer was to have a shred of credibility, he had to do something spectacular, which was the reason they were currently glued to a roof.

Jamie was an experienced climber and thought he'd factored in everything: equipment, materials, weather, windspeed. Everything except a nest of stripy wee bastards.

I bloody hate wasps.

As he lay with his cheek pressed against the cool slate, he heard sirens in the distance and the roar of the seething crowd below as the vehicles drew near. His right calf muscle was beginning to ache with the build-up of lactic acid and he shuffled. He lost his footing and scrambled to grip with his toes, the skin of his glued finger pads stretching painfully. Heart pounding against his ribcage, he fought down his panic and glanced up to reassure himself the rope was holding tight.

Where the hell are the polis?

He stole a glance at Frazer who was on a rope a few feet away. Clocking the younger man's agitation at the arrival of the curious wasps, Jamie realised he really was a lousy babysitter.

"You okay?" called Jamie.

"Splendid."

At least Frazer's sense of humour was still intact.

Then came the noise Jamie had been dreading; a low buzzing near his left ear. He twisted his head away but the fiend persisted. The humming stopped, and then restarted so loud he realised the creature was crawling over his balaclava towards his face. He flicked his head but the sound only increased in an angrier register. He turned his head to the other side, hoping to squish the wee bastard against the tiles. The drone continued against the fabric covering his other ear. Jamie shook his head violently and the insect flew off. Blowing out a hard breath, he tried to get a better purchase with his feet and steady his heart rate. Then several of its wee friends arrived.

Frazer swore again as more wasps crawled over the lightweight fabric of his climbing trousers.

"Don't move," shouted Jamie, flinching as he himself was stung on the neck.

Frazer thrashed and yelped as the wasps attacked him.

"STAY STILL" yelled Jamie, fearing his partner was going to dislodge himself. "The police are on their way."

Writhing now, Frazer howled, "I'm allergic."

Jamie watched in horror as Frazer flailed his limbs, ripping his glued hands from the tiles, and tumbled down the roof. Shrieking in fear and pain, he tipped over the edge and jolted to an abrupt halt on the end of his rope. Several tiles slipped off and there was the sound of screaming as they hit protesters below.

Jamie called to Frazer repeatedly but there was no response, just a choking sound.

FUUUUCKKKK!

***

Kathryn

Kathryn scurried round the cottage searching frantically for her car keys. Being tardy for work was never good, especially today.

Jamie had only been gone a few days and already it seemed everything had gone to hell in a handcart. Cursing, she rummaged in drawers, behind cushions, and in the pockets of her jacket as Meg watched with interest. The collie was used to the morning routine and sat patiently by the door.

"Of all the days," she muttered.

Less than a year into her job as a cyber-analyst at the headquarters of the United Kingdom's Security Service, MI5, Kathryn was still on probation. With her final review imminent and a new boss scrutinising her every move, arriving late was the last thing she needed.

Crouching, she tipped the contents of her handbag onto the hall rug. She spotted the keys amongst the detritus, snatched them up and swept everything back into the bag. Meg sauntered over and licked her ear, making Kathryn laugh.

Burying her face in the dog's black and white fur, she said, "I know, I miss him too."

After an hour's drive into central London, Kathryn entered the offices of Thames House with the dog trotting at her heels. The security guard greeted her and she handed him her mobile phone since no personal electronic devices were permitted inside the building. After putting her bag through the X-ray scanner, she and Meg passed through the metal detector.

She took the lift to the offices on the third floor where she worked in Declan Fitzpatrick's Digital Intelligence team. To enter, she and Meg had to traverse the 'tubes'. These glass and steel contraptions assessed the occupant's weight to make sure they were alone and not with someone holding a gun to their head. Or with a collie.

Kathryn's request to bring the dog into the office had initially been denied but, after appealing to her manager Julien, permission was granted after he'd argued Meg was an emotional support dog. However, Julien insisted the animal was insured and wore a high-viz bib but, after Meg shredded three, they compromised on an identity tag.

Kathryn was surprised to see her team leader Fitz already at his desk as she was normally in before him. Anxious, she glanced at her watch.

She'd first met Fitz on a joint operation between the Security Service and Counter Terrorism Unit where her cyber skills had been needed. During this deployment, he'd been so impressed by her hacking abilities that, despite her convictions for computer misuse, he'd pulled strings to recruit her. The job of the Digital Intelligence team was to collate, analyse and react to information gathered from cyberspace, agent handlers, electronic eavesdropping, and surveillance, and to support the operations teams on the ground.

Fitzpatrick probably wasn't his real surname, just as Douglas wasn't hers. On joining the Service, employees were instructed to adopt an alias to ensure they couldn't compromise anyone in their team or others employed by MI5. She and her husband Jamie Denton, also an MI5 officer, had chosen Douglas as their alias.

Noticing Fitz's crumpled shirt and the dark sleep bruises around his eyes, she thought he appeared older than his thirty years.

"Morning, you're early," she said.

He glanced up, "Actually I'm late, I haven't been home yet."

It wasn't unusual for analysts to spend the night at their desks if there was a major incident or an operation was coming to a close, and she'd done it herself on several occasions.

"Ah, one of those nights," she said. "Want caffeine?"

When he nodded a grateful acceptance, she settled Meg beneath her desk and made her way to the canteen on the ground floor. The building boasted excellent facilities since, for safety and security, the Service didn't want staff leaving unnecessarily. Conscious of her tardiness, she resisted the baked temptations on offer, collected a latte for herself and a double espresso for Fitz, and returned to her desk.

Handing Fitz his coffee, she suppressed a groan when she spotted their new boss Harriet Stockbridge approach with a clipboard. Harriet had been seconded from GCHQ after someone high up the food chain had attended a seminar on the Agile methodology and announced they wanted to use it within the Service. A heavyset woman in her early thirties, she wore heels and a navy pinstripe dress with a short hemline. In comparison to Kathryn's slim frame and delicate features, Harriet looked like a mountain troll.

Recruited from Oxford, Harriet was on an accelerated promotion scheme and had risen rapidly through the ranks. As ambitious as she was ruthless, she'd gained a reputation for climbing over the bodies on her way to the top. Determined to shake things up and make her mark at MI5, she'd introduced a series of new working practices which she claimed would result in 'synergies' and 'efficiency gains'.

As far as analysts' day-to-day work was concerned, this meant attending daily meetings in which they shared their progress, all while standing up. The process reminded Kathryn of a *Fast Show* comedy sketch called *Jesse's Diet* where old Jesse would emerge from an outdoor latrine and announce what he'd digested: 'This week, I have been mostly eating broccoli.'

Kathryn forced her lips into a smile and greeted her. *What fresh hell is this? And who uses a clipboard?*

Harriet cast an unkind eye over Kathryn's casual attire. Although there were few women in the technical teams, Harriet had made it clear there'd be no sisterhood. Instead, she exhibited that special kind of hatred that plain women reserve for their attractive counterparts.

"You haven't updated Synergistico with your progress on Operation Closet," said Harriet.

Another of Harriet's new toys, the Synergistico application was designed to manage the team's projects, accountability and communications. In Kathryn's opinion, it was one of worst computer programs she'd ever come across.

Kathryn apologised, adding, "This week, I have been mostly working on Operation Harbour."

Fitz snorted with laughter, spraying coffee over his monitor.

Harriet shot him an icy glance before turning her ire on Kathryn. With a pinched expression, she snapped, "Then I suggest you add notes to that effect. How else am I supposed to account for your time and deliver value to our clients?" When Kathryn nodded, she added, "I want a detailed breakdown of your work by lunchtime."

Maintaining her smile, Kathryn resolved to write a report containing every phrase she'd ever heard on *The Apprentice*.

Harriet said, "The stand-up meeting's in ten minutes, don't be late."

Kathryn and Fitz watched as she stomped back to her office in the opposite corner of the open-plan space, and they shared a wry smile. Before either could say anything, Julien appeared.

In his late forties with boyish good looks, Julien Tomkins was tall with a mop of dark hair flecked with silver. He'd been Lead Operations Officer on Kathryn's first assignment but, since his promotion, he now oversaw several operations including the one her husband was assigned to.

Julien greeted her in his plummy accent. "Good morning, Kathryn. I'd like a word in my office please." Then, without waiting, he spun on his heel and strode off.

Turning to Fitz, she whispered, "What's going on?"

Fitz offered a weak smile in reply. "Err ... you best ask Julien."

Kathryn's stomach hit the floor. *Oh God, has something happened to Jamie?*

She dashed after Julien. Had Jamie been hurt? Or worse? She shut down that thought, unable to let her mind go there.

Although Julien was running the show with Fitz providing cyber support, she'd been kept in the dark about the details on the orders of their director. Director A, as he was known, was uneasy that two of his staff were married, although she and Jamie occupied different roles in separate units. Kathryn, however, knew every backdoor and vulnerability in MI5's computer systems. After much soul-searching and, despite the risk to her career, she exploited this to keep unofficial tabs on what Jamie was up to. This was her husband after all, and old habits die hard.

She'd learned that A-Branch, the surveillance wing, had been monitoring a group of eco-activists with Fitz doing the digital legwork and Jamie and team tracking the group's movements. However, normal tactics had failed to yield results with these particular individuals, many of whom lived in the margins of society, and so a decision was made to place a covert operative amongst them. Her husband had left a few days ago and, although she'd spoken to him regularly on the phone, she'd no idea what he was up to and little information had appeared on MI5's systems.

Convinced Jamie was dead or in mortal danger, her heart thumped as she approached Julien's office, a spacious glass affair with an enviable view. Julien ushered her inside and closed the door.

Inviting her to sit, he said, "It's nothing to worry about, Jamie's fine. I've just spoken to our police liaison and they'll have him down in a flash."

Gawping at him, she said, "What do you mean 'they'll have him down'?"

"Follow me," he said, "It's better you find out from us than from the media."

Before she could quiz him further, he opened the door and marched towards the main briefing room. Kathryn trotted to keep up with him, her mouth dry.

What the hell's going on and why are the media involved?

The briefing area was packed and she slid into a seat at the rear next to some twitchy looking people she assumed were surveillance operators. Their hypervigilance, coupled with the fact they always sat at the back, meant she could usually tell them apart from the intelligence analysts and support staff. The wiry guy next to her threw her a look that said, 'What the hell are you doing here?' Neither had long to wait to find out.

The windowless room was equipped with a bank of large television screens, a lectern housing a dashboard that controlled the imagery, and an enormous digital wall clock.

Julien strode to the front and began the meeting in the standard way. "Good morning team. Please take a moment to update your devices and I'll begin the briefing on Operation Monkshood at 0815 hours."

Minutes later when everyone was settled, Julien proceeded to give background information about the operation, which she suspected was mainly for her benefit. She wondered if Director A was aware of her presence here, or if Julien had decided to ignore his orders. Unlikely, knowing Julien; he was all policy and procedure.

A Sky News bulletin appeared on the television about the protests taking place in Manchester. The reporter explained that, earlier that morning, climate activists had descended upon the city in droves, blocking major roads and causing disruption by lying down en masse. Some protestors had stormed the headquarters of Neo Petroleum following the company's recent announcement about the expansion of their petrochemical processing plant in Scotland. The mood had turned ugly when a handful of activists had climbed onto the roof of their building.

The image switched to a video feed from an on-scene helicopter hovering above the city. The screen filled with a close-up shot of an activist dangling precariously from a rope over the edge of the roof. Kathryn watched as the man was winched to safety by a team of specialist police climbers and handed over to paramedics.

With a grim expression, Julien said, "The man you see is Frazer. He's one of us. We understand he's suffered an allergic reaction. I'll update you as soon as we have news about his condition."

After Frazer's rescue, the camera focused on a second protester who, the reporter explained, had glued himself to the roof of the building. Dangerously close to the edge and apparently unable to move his hands, he was writhing around on the slates. Despite the balaclava, Kathryn realised it was Jamie and she gave a loud gasp. Everyone in the room turned to stare at her.

Julien addressed her. "Jamie's fine and they'll have him down in two ticks."

She watched as two officers in safety harnesses scrambled over the roof towards her husband, and then retreated. Jamie was thrashing his head around and yelling.

"He doesn't look fine!" she said.

Julien raised his palms and said, "I assure you he is. I've spoken to our liaison officer and they've a specialist team on-site." As they watched Jamie flick his head back and forth and become increasingly agitated, he added, "they just need to let the pest controller do his thing first."

"Pest controller?" she shrieked.

"Apparently there's a wasps' nest."

Kathryn shot to her feet, "Oh my God, he'll be stung to death."

The guy next to her placed a gentle hand on her arm and whispered, "No harm will come to him, he's one of ours."

Tell that to Frazer!

Open-mouthed, she looked from him and then to Julien who nodded. Reluctantly, she took her seat again, her cheeks burning. The next few minutes were excruciating as she watched a team of climbers lower themselves to where Jamie was suspended. One of them puffed what appeared to be smoke around the area while another doused Jamie's hands with liquid and then pried them off the roof. The news anchor explained it was common practice amongst protesters to glue themselves onto structures and police had to use acetone to free them.

When one of the climbers attempted to remove Jamie's balaclava, he flailed some more preventing them from rolling it past his eyes. He kept twisting away, concealing his face. Murmuring rippled through the briefing room as they watched him being hoisted until he was on the flat surface at the top of the roof. Several uniformed officers awaited and one of them grabbed him roughly by the scruff and hauled him from view into the building.

All eyes were upon Kathryn as Julien turned to her. "There, you can relax now, he's safe and sound."

Safe and sound? I'm going to bloody murder him!

The Result

"Those hippie potheads over at NASA CLAIM that 2021 was the hottest year on record ... Excuse me, I have to put the cat out (he's on fire again)."
— Quentin R. Bufogle, author

***

Jamie

Clenching his jaw, Jamie braced himself for the first blow. It came fast and heavy, thudding into his ribs and he gasped for air as he folded under the onslaught.

"Bunch a' fuckin' clowns, the lot of you," yelled one of the constabulary's finest. He grabbed Jamie's jacket and hurled him into the back of the police van. It stank of Lysol and piss.

Wincing, Jamie exhaled a long breath knowing he'd gotten off lightly; he'd dished out far worse as a copper. The stings from the wasps were more painful than the beating, and his swollen neck and hands throbbed.

"How's my mate?" he asked, taking a seat. He'd had no news of Frazer since he was carted off in an ambulance.

"He'll live," muttered the officer.

As the police dealt with the next arrestee, Jamie darted a glance at the protesters beside him, and his heart skipped a beat when he spotted Frazer's target sitting on the bench opposite.

Several of the activists were dressed in black and Jamie guessed they'd taken part in a 'die in'. From his vantage point earlier, he'd watched as hundreds had lain down on the roads causing traffic chaos.

Bloody idiots!

Diagonally across from him was a young lad, his dark clothing in stark contrast to his deathly pale face, except for a stream of blood dripping from a nasty gash in his head. Two middle-aged women with short bottle-red hair sat next to him. They appeared more relaxed about their situation and they offered a smile. To his left was a bear of a man wearing combat fatigues who also appeared to have been on the end of the officers' views on non-violent direct action.

Jamie cut a glance at the target. He knew from the brief he was thirty-five, the same age as himself. Tall and athletically built, he sported a goatee and long hair and was clad in black. He appeared confident and not in the least daunted by the situation. Jamie wasn't surprised given the guy was a seasoned campaigner with a chargesheet as long as his arm.

Goatee gave him a brief nod and said, "Alright?"

Rubbing the pads of his fingertips which were stinging after being doused in chemicals, Jamie replied, "Aye, never better."

"What they nick you for?" He spoke with a thick Manchester accent.

With a dark chuckle, Jamie said, "Just for sticking around."

Goatee laughed. "Where were you?"

"Neo Petroleum's roof."

He shot him a look of admiration. "Wow, was that you? Seriously impressive man!"

The others in the van murmured their approval.

"You?" asked Jamie.

"Locked to the railings at the entrance."

Jamie grinned. "Sweet."

Shit! Frazer should be having this conversation, not me.

They were interrupted when two officers graciously helped another protester into the van, a pretty young woman with long blonde hair and large breasts. She appeared to know the target.

Jamie shouted, "Oi, I want ma fuckin' gear back. I need it for work."

Muttering obscenities, the officers slammed shut the doors of the van, plunging the occupants into semi-darkness. As the vehicle's engine roared to life, goatee introduced himself as Ethan. Few on these marches ever gave their full names, including Jamie.

Ethan asked what he used his equipment for and Jamie explained he was a rope-access technician who spent his working life scaling cranes and skyscrapers. Jamie had helped Frazer rehearse his legend well, aware his colleague's life may one day depend on it. When Ethan asked if he was part of a group, he told him he and Frazer were acting on their own. The van turned a sharp corner and they lurched in their seats.

"Done this kinda thing before?" asked Ethan.

"Aye, been on a few of these," said Jamie. "Last one was in Edinburgh." He said on a laugh, "They'd quite a time of it getting me down off the Scott Monument."

"Didn't think you were from these parts."

"Glasgow originally, Salford now."

"My deepest condolences," said Ethan. He regarded Jamie for a few moments, as if deciding his next move then added, "I'm part of a group called the Climate Warriors. If you're interested, you'll find us at the Ubuntu Centre."

Jamie had learned of the community centre in Salford from the initial intelligence gathered about the group. The dossier described the place as a 'hub of left-wing political activism' and home to one of the city's few vegan cafes known as the Anarchist Coffee Pot.

More pot than coffee.

Jamie nodded. "Aye, might do."

The van screeched to a halt and the rear doors flew open.

"Show time," muttered Ethan.

Result!

Except it should have been Frazer's.

***

Kathryn

Kathryn returned to her desk and Fitz glanced up from his screen.

"You alright?" he asked.

She summed up what'd happened although she suspected Fitz knew more about Jamie's operation than she did. He suggested she took the rest of the day off but she insisted work would help take her mind off the situation. In any case, she didn't want to be labelled a slacker by Harriet.

After booting up her machines, she launched the BBC News app, only to see images of Jamie and Frazer splashed over her screen. She checked her email and wished she hadn't when she saw a meeting invitation from Vetting. She scanned the message for details but there was nothing to suggest the purpose of it. Was this just an informal chat ahead of her probation review in a few weeks' time or something else? Her heart sank. Previous encounters with Vetting had been unpleasant, and their style was more interrogation than informal discussion.

Was she in trouble and, if so, for what? Since joining the Service, she'd made an effort to put her shady past behind her and stay on the right side of the law.

Except the once.

The memory of it pricked at her conscience and she pushed it aside. Surely Vetting's interest had nothing to do with what she'd done in Glasgow?

Maybe it was something to do with her quashed convictions for computer misuse? Since joining MI5, she'd been careful to adhere to the strict legal and procedural framework which governed her role. She'd also steered clear of any hacktivist activity, including the Grey Nemesis group to which she'd belonged up until her arrest. She had, however, kept in contact with one member: Scotty, her cyber-buddy whom she'd known for years. After all, if it wasn't for Scotty watching out for her on her last job, she and Jamie would've frozen to death on a Scottish moor. Had Vetting discovered they were still in touch?

As a cybersecurity expert and ex-hacker, Kathryn was skilled at navigating the digital ether without leaving a trace. However, she also knew the Intelligence Services employed some of the best in this field, many hand-picked from the top universities, and they used military-grade technology to spy. Had one of her colleagues detected a speck of her digital dust? And, if they knew about Scotty, she'd be in serious trouble; serious enough to finish her career.

An image of her stepfather's terror flashed before her eyes and she shuddered. Flashbacks were becoming a frequent occurrence and few days passed without this scene replaying in her mind. Rubbing her temples, she blinked it away. If Vetting had learned about what she'd done, her life would be ruined. Hers and Jamie's.

Sipping her coffee which had gone cold, she stared at the meeting invitation knowing she'd have to wait two whole days to find out the reason for their interest in her.

Wondering if her past had finally caught up with her, she gnawed on her fingernails.

***

Jamie

from:	Gary Singer < Gary.Singer@tacitnet.mi5.uk >
to:	Jamie.Douglas@tacitnet.mi5.uk
subject:	Operation Monkshood
security:	AES-256 encryption

Jamie,

So what part of 'keep a low profile' and 'you're just there to help' did you not understand? You made the 6 o'clock news FFS. Julien's doing his nut! Keith said you'd be trouble but until now I was prepared to give you the benefit of the doubt. Your only saving grace is there was no compromise but I DO NOT WANT A REPEAT, OK? Operators are supposed to get authorisation before breaking the law.

By the time you read this you should've been bailed. We'll have a debrief after court. Don't be late.

Gary.

P.S. Frazer's okay but still in hospital.

***

After being photographed and fingerprinted at a police station, Jamie spent an uncomfortable couple of nights in the cells along with several other 'enviro-idiots' as the local cops referred to them. Jamie knew Fitz would've linked his fingerprints to his legend, James Douglas, and there'd be a marker on his police file. When discovered by the custody sergeant, this would filter up the chain of command until a discreet phone call was made to an ACC. But despite the secrecy, he'd been a detective long enough to know the station would be rife with rumours and speculation about who he was and why there was a block on his record.

On Monday morning, he and several other protesters appeared in front of a magistrate and were charged with mobbing and rioting. Once freed on bail, Jamie went in search of his handler.

Gary had texted directions to where he was parked and Jamie slipped into the passenger seat of the silver Audi. A similar age to himself, Jamie had first encountered Gary during a previous undercover deployment when he and his colleague Keith had interrogated him. He remembered the grilling well and knew his polished appearance and tailored suit hid a steely side.

"God, you stink," said Gary wrinkling his nose as Jamie shut the door.

"It's lovely to see you too darling," said Jamie. "Got anything to eat?"

Scowling, Gary leaned over to the back seat and produced a Tupperware box which he passed to Jamie. "The wife made them." He started the car and pulled out into the traffic.

Jamie opened the box and bit into a brown bread sandwich. As he chewed, he peered suspiciously at the remainder of it and mumbled "What the fuck's this?"

"Humous on rye."

Jamie threw him an incredulous look. "Humous? I'm bloody starving. I'm knackered. And, apparently, I smell ... and you feed me humous?" Tossing the remainder of the sandwich into the Tupperware, he pointed over to the right, "There's a McDonald's over there."

Gary grumbled, "You're supposed to be undercover."

"I'm not a tofu-eating twat. I need a burger."

Exhaling a long breath, Gary steered in the direction of the golden arches muttering, "You're supposed to live your cover."

Jamie asked about Frazer, and Gary explained his hands were badly injured and he'd require skin grafts. Jamie realised there was no way Frazer could continue on the job and his heart sank, knowing what would be asked of him. It also explained why Gary wasn't hauling him over the coals.

They parked and Jamie jumped out. "Want anything?"

"I'll come," said Gary unfastening his seatbelt.

"Not dressed like that you won't. You look like my solicitor, not one of my mates. Live your cover, remember."

Shaking his head, Gary sighed, "Fine. Get me a beanburger."

Snorting with amusement, Jamie headed into the restaurant, only to return a few minutes later with a cardboard tray of coffee and a paper bag full of food. After passing Gary his, Jamie bit into his burger and moaned out his pleasure.

Gary grimaced. "You do realise that's mechanically-recovered and pumped full of antibiotics, hormones, and chemicals?"

Through a mouthful, Jamie mumbled, "Mmm, food of the gods."

As they ate, he told Gary about Ethan's invite to the group.

Gary wiped his hands and his expression turned serious. "You know what I'm going to ask?"

"Aye, you want me to take Frazer's place."

"It's a request, not an order. We wouldn't normally ask a married officer to undertake a job like this, since it might go on for months."

Jamie took a gulp of coffee and stared at the car park. The last thing he wanted was to leave Kathryn, and the thought it might be for a long stretch filled him with despair. His marriage was the most important thing to him; more than the job. However, he and Kathryn had discussed the possibility of this happening and they'd accepted that a lengthy deployment was inevitable during training.

And in terms of the alternatives his colleagues had been offered infiltrating far-right groups and Islamist extremists, this operation wasn't half bad. Only last week, a surveillance operator had narrowly avoided being beheaded. By comparison, dealing with a group of hairy arm-pitted environmentalists was preferable, even if it was likely to drag on for some time.

Then there were the financial considerations. The salary of an MI5 surveillance operator wasn't great, and he was earning less than when he was a copper. Money — and the fear of not having enough to provide for a family — was a constant worry, and something that had never left him after seeing his mother struggle to make ends meet. Even before as a well-paid detective sergeant, he'd fretted about income, savings and pensions.

Suspecting it would be career suicide to refuse the request, Jamie knew he'd little choice.

Turning to Gary, he said, "Spying on a bunch of crusties isn't the assignment I imagined being given, but I guess it could be a lot worse ... even if I do have to eat bloody humous."

Gary chuckled, "Cheeky bastard."

***

Kathryn

Kathryn had spent two anxious evenings alone agonising about her upcoming meeting with Vetting. On Monday morning, she explained to Fitz she'd an appointment with them and he asked who she was meeting.

"Robin Prince," she said.

"Ah, the Prince of Darkness himself. You got garlic?" Then, spotting the expression on her face, he added, "Hey, don't let him rile you."

"What do you know about him?"

Fitz paused before answering. "Hmm, let's just say he's enthusiastic."

"Well, that's just great," she muttered.

With a sense of foreboding, she made her way to Vetting's lair deep in the bowels of the building. She found Robin's office tucked away at the end of a long corridor. She knocked and entered, half expecting to see a coffin in the corner. What she got was a hunk in his early forties with jet-black hair and a chiselled jaw.

"Take a seat please," said the hunk without taking his eyes from his computer screen.

Kathryn slid into the chair opposite his scrupulously tidy desk, realising how messy her own was in comparison. During a normal workday, hers usually featured towers of papers and files, although security policy dictated these were locked away each evening. 'Empty desk, empty mind' was her motto. She inspected her fingernails and darted glances at him as he continued to ignore her.

Robin's role was to ensure that employees could be trusted with sensitive government information. The process of acquiring 'developed vetting' or DV status was a lengthy one that took place during recruitment, and continued during an intelligence officer's career. The checks were obtrusive and involved scrutinising friends, family, finances, employment, convictions, sexual preferences and predilections. There was little Vetting didn't know about MI5's staff, and the thought of this made her uneasy.

Like other recruits, after an initial training period, she and Jamie had been placed on probation for a year. In her husband's case, she suspected this was a mere formality, given his background in the military and police. She was sure he was being prepared for greater things than his current surveillance role. About herself, she was less certain, and now less so given the sudden interest in her.

As Robin continued to tap on his keyboard, she regarded him with growing suspicion. Maybe this was a tactic, to beguile prey with his good looks.

During her onboarding, Robin and his team had ripped apart every aspect of her life. Despite Fitz and Julien's support of her application, Vetting had raised doubts about her suitability because of her convictions for computer misuse. Kathryn discovered Robin had blocked her appointment, citing reservations about her honesty and integrity, and had refused to grant her the 'DV' status required for her role.

Director A had then waded in, insisting her past did not preclude her from joining their ranks. Finally, the matter was raised with the Director General who cast aside Vetting's objections and rubber-stamped her appointment. However, judging from the pinched expression on Robin's face, this decision still rankled.

Robin clicked his biro, opened the manilla folder in front of him and pulled out a photograph. Recognising the picture of her late stepfather Phil, she tried to hide her swirl of emotions, a mixture of fear, anger and disgust. Conscious of Robin's scrutiny, she met his gaze and raised an inquiring eyebrow.

"I'm sorry for your loss," he said glibly.

She nodded. *I'm not. You know the bastard killed my mother.*

"I'd like to ask you a few questions about your trip to Scotland last year."

Kathryn's heart beat furiously in her chest as she fought to maintain a neutral expression. She cleared her throat and said, "Certainly." *Ah, so this is where it's going. Surely, he can't know about Glasgow.*

"Your stepfather passed away in October last year," he said, sliding a copy of Phil's death certificate towards her. His aquamarine eyes bored into her.

She glanced at the document which stated the cause of death was heart failure. What the certificate didn't show was the fact she'd caused it by hacking his pacemaker. Hoping to God her heart was not about to fail too, she feigned disinterest and met Robin's steely gaze.

"That's correct, but what has this got to do with my trip?" *I had to stop him. He deserved what he got!*

"I was hoping you could tell me. It's odd he died at the same time you were in Glasgow."

Lifting one shoulder, she muttered, "Coincidence. He'd chronic heart disease, and I just happened to be in Scotland finalising the sale of my grandmother's house." *You can't prove anything.*

Saying nothing, he stared at her and clicked his pen repeatedly. Then, after what seemed like an age, he said, "That may be, but I still need you to account for all of your movements that weekend, including everyone you had contact with."

"I can try, but it was months ago." *Are you for real?*

Fixing her with his keen eyes, he said, "Minute by minute." Then, passing her a sheaf of papers, he added, "I need every last detail." More clicking of the pen.

Swallowing, she glanced at the forms, surprised to see requests for basic information about herself and her family that she knew they had already. As she scanned through the documents, Robin beat out a tattoo on the desk with his biro.

"I believe you know most of this already," she said, "my next of kin also works for MI5."

"We refer to ourselves these days as the Security Service." With a tight smile, he resumed his irritating clicking. "And I want the information on my desk first thing tomorrow morning."

Nodding, she wondered if his next of kin was Satan. Forcing her lips into a smile, she thanked him and left. After closing the door behind her, she fled to the toilet and sank to the floor against the wall of the cubicle.

Oh God, what the hell does he know?

The Review

"Adults keep saying: 'We owe it to the young people to give them hope.' But I don't want your hope ... I want you to panic. I want you to feel the fear I feel every day. And then I want you to act. I want you to act as you would in a crisis. I want you to act as if the house is on fire. Because it is."
— Greta Thunberg at the World Economic Forum, 2019

***

Kathryn

Kathryn couldn't sleep.

She lay in the semi-darkness and listened to the sound of her husband's gentle breathing beside her. The glow from the bedside clock illuminated his face and she drank in the sight of him. He looked so peaceful and she feasted her eyes on his features; the high-chiselled cheekbones and soft flawless lips which had been on her only a few hours ago. She resisted the urge to wake him for seconds.

The fact she even had a husband still surprised her. She'd never imagined having a partner, and if someone had told her she'd marry Jamie Denton, the detective who'd arrested her, she'd have thought them insane. Yet here he was next to her, the person she loved more than anyone else. She snuggled into his sleeping frame and wallowed in the intimacy.

God, I'm going to miss these precious moments.

Following his stunt on Neo Petroleum's roof, Jamie had broken the news this would be a long-term deployment. She'd known it was coming, had been dreading it, but undercover work was an integral part of the Development Programme through which he was being fast-tracked, and she'd worked for MI5 long enough to know it could be far worse. Field officers risked their lives on a daily basis investigating and infiltrating groups of violent criminals and extremists who posed a mass threat to life. By comparison, a bunch of eco-protesters seemed a tame option. Perhaps Jamie's near-death experience on their previous job had been a factor in offering him this one?

But it was not just the thought of him being absent for long stretches that was keeping her awake; it was the meeting with Robin. What had sparked Vetting's interest in her? Was it part of the probationary review process, or a routine investigation prior to Jamie's deployment? Whatever the reason, surely it was just a fishing exercise on Robin's part since she was certain there was nothing to connect her to what'd happened in Glasgow? Doubt gnawed at her.

As she stared at the ceiling, she replayed the events leading up to her step-father's death and the justification for her actions. After learning of Phil's early release from prison due to a heart condition, she'd kept tabs on him. Her vigilance had paid off when she discovered he'd been cultivating a relationship with a woman who'd a nine-year-old daughter; the same age she'd been when Phil had sexually abused her. When further digging revealed he was about to move in with this woman and her child, she'd decided to act. Swiftly. Given her own experience with the authorities, she hadn't contacted the police or social work certain that, by the time they intervened, the damage would've already been done. She'd had to stop him herself, once and for all.

She'd accessed his medical files and found he'd been fitted with a remotely-managed pacemaker. After that, it was a simple case of tracking Phil down, luring him to a cafe and hacking the device. His heart had failed in front of her, and she'd never forget the look of terror in his eyes when he realised who she was and what she'd done. It haunted her still.

She'd been meticulous in her planning, taking every precaution to cover her tracks and any trace of what she'd done. In the aftermath, she'd felt elation and relief at having gotten away with it and – if she was being honest with herself – no small measure of satisfaction that he'd got what he deserved.

Although she'd no regrets about taking his life to protect another, she'd been carrying the burden of guilt around ever since. She gazed at Jamie. No, she couldn't tell him, couldn't bear to see the disgust and disappointment in his eyes when he realised what she'd done.

Finally, she fell into a fitful sleep filled with images of her step-father collapsing in front of her, and her husband's look of horror when he discovered her crime.

***

"I'll be home as often as I can and I'll try and call you every day," mumbled Jamie between kisses.

The dreaded morning had arrived and Kathryn clung to him like a limpet, reluctant to let him go. It was early and they were standing in the hallway of their cottage, a rucksack at his feet along with Meg who whined. Jamie already looked different, with his scruffy beard and casual clothes. He held her tight against him and she inhaled his scent, wishing she could somehow bottle and preserve it.

"I love you so much," she whispered.

Brushing a tear from her face with his thumb, he said, "I love you too, baby. Please don't cry. I can't go if you're crying."

She wiped her eyes with the back of her hand and forced a watery smile.

"Please be careful. No more crazy stunts."

He answered with a final desperate kiss, then released his hold and caressed her cheek. She noticed he'd removed his wedding ring and, although she knew it was all part of his legend, its absence shocked her. She stifled a sob as he ruffled Meg's fur before grabbing his things and going. The urge to stop him from leaving was powerful and she railed against it, reminding herself it was temporary.

Then, with a final wave, he was gone. She closed the door and slid down the wall as great heaving sobs wracked her body.

***

Later, Kathryn drove slowly through the London traffic with a heavy heart. Her eyes were red and puffy from crying but she'd taken extra care with her appearance and donned a smart blouse and trouser suit, ahead of her probation review meeting. As if the day couldn't get any worse.

Mid-morning, she made her way to the Human Resources Department in Thames House and found the allocated room. The office door was open and, to her irritation, Robin was inside talking to Julien who wore a tight expression.

Kathryn paused and gave a heavy sigh. What was Vetting's role in this? She'd understood this meeting to be a routine one between herself, Julien and Personnel to review her performance over the last year and sign off her appointment. She would then be 'badged'; the term the Service used when an employee became a permanent member of staff. To her knowledge, Vetting hadn't been involved in Jamie's recent review.

With a sinking feeling, she turned and headed for the water cooler to gather her resolve. As she made her way back, she heard raised voices and Julien protest this was "highly irregular." Robin's rejoinder was cut short by her entrance and he avoided eye contact. Julien glowered at Robin, then rearranged his expression into a smile and nodded to her.

A woman she'd never met stood and introduced herself as Lena, a personnel officer. She wore an expensive business suit and exuded a crisp air of efficiency. With a practised corporate smile, she invited Kathryn to take a seat opposite them.

Kathryn's heel rat-a-tatted on the floor and she clasped her hands to keep from fidgeting. Lena explained that the purpose of the meeting was to review her progress, and then for each side to raise any concerns they may have, and set targets for the future. Lena invited Julien to begin the discussion.

Julien offered Kathryn a reassuring smile and opened a thin folder. He said, "Before I begin, I'd like to remind everyone about the events that led to Kathryn joining our ranks because I believe we should keep these at the forefront of our mind." He then outlined the unusual circumstances in which she'd been recruited after being offered a deal to avoid prison in return for her cyber-skills to investigate a religious organisation on MI5's grid.

Turning to Kathryn, he said, "Not only did you take up the challenge, you gave it your all. Despite the danger, you and Jamie triumphed and at great personal risk." With a pointed look at Robin, he added, "They nearly lost their lives."

Julien then summarised her progress since joining Fitz's team, and how impressed they were with her performance. He read from a glowing list of feedback, "Diligent, conscientious, imaginative, determined, skilled ... I could go on but you get the gist. We have absolutely no doubts about your ability to do the job. In fact, I'd go as far as to say you're one of the best digital analysts we have, and I recommend you're badged." He offered her a warm smile and closed the file.

Encouraged by his words, she blushed and mouthed her thanks. Lena then opened her own notes which appeared to consist of spreadsheets punctuated with colourful pie charts, bar graphs and frequency tables. She commended Kathryn on her timekeeping and attendance record, remarking she hadn't taken a single sick day. She also read out the report from her university supervisor which outlined the progress she'd made in her part-time studies in cybersecurity.

Lena asked if the job was different to the one she'd imagined and Kathryn said, "It's much better. The work we do is so important, it's a reward in itself."

Lena asked how she was coping with life as the wife of an MI5 officer adding, "I understand your husband has just begun a long-term deployment as a covert operator. That must be difficult for you both."

Kathryn repeated the answer she'd practised. "It's not easy being apart but we both knew what the job entailed when we joined." Her words sounded hollow even to her own ears.

Lena rewarded her with an understanding smile. "You've an excellent record of performance and an admirable work ethic. I also have no reservations about recommending your appointment to the Security Service."

All eyes then turned to Robin who opened the thick file in front of him. Kathryn almost expected a forked tongue to slither out between his pursed lips. She watched as he sifted through reams of paper, wondering what possible information he had on her to fill such documents. Then, after what seemed an interminable length of time, Robin addressed her.

"I have no reservations about your ability to hack computers."

Julien butted in, "It's called digital analysis."

Ignoring him, Robin continued, "However, a probationary review is also about establishing whether an employee is suitable for a role."

Here we go.

She watched as Robin lifted his pen and began to click it. "And that's where I have concerns."

"And what possible reservations can you have?" snapped Julien, "For God's sakes man, she nearly died on her first deployment."

Returning a hard stare, Robin retorted, "Indeed, and without detracting from that, it's important to point out that all our agents put their lives on the line for their country." He turned his unkind eyes back to Kathryn, "As you said, you both knew what the job entailed."

Julien shook his head and muttered under his breath.

"As intelligence officers, we must be beyond reproach and it's my duty to ensure this." Robin removed a document from his file. "Let's not forget that you came to us as a convicted criminal."

Kathryn flinched, wondering if the stain of this would ever fade.

Julien bit out, "Old news. We're well aware of this and her skill set is exactly the reason we hired her and why she's so damned good at her job." Lena made to interrupt but Julien cut across her and glared at Robin. In a loud voice, he asked, "What exactly is your point?"

Kathryn had rarely seen Julien look so livid. As the two men glowered at one another, she felt like a mouse caught between two cats while the dog looked on.

Lena calmly said, "Let's hear what Robin has to say."

Robin turned to Kathryn. "I don't dispute you're good at your job. It's more a question of integrity."

"Which she has in spades!" snapped Julien.

Lena fixed Julien with a hard stare and asked Robin to continue. He turned his icy glare back to Kathryn.

"You're aware of my concerns about the timing of your stepfather's passing despite your insistence that it was mere coincidence you were in Glasgow on the same day." He paused and flicked his thumb through the paperwork she'd completed. "But you've failed to convince me that you'd nothing to do with his death."

Kathryn gasped, and Julien shot to his feet and roared, "Good God man, that's one hell of an accusation. On what possible basis do you make it?"

"Sit down please," said Lena. Clearly rattled by the turn in the conversation, she turned to Kathryn and said, "Would you like to respond to that?"

Guilt blossomed like a poisonous flower and Kathryn felt her face flush pink. With a trembling hand she reached for her water and took a sip to quell the gorge rising in her throat.

"I never ... I never laid a finger on him." Tears welled in her eyes and she pressed a hand to her mouth.

Robin shot back, "No, you're much too clever for that."

Julien slammed a palm onto the desk, the sound of it making them all jump. "That's enough!" He glared at Lena, "Are you seriously going to allow this to continue? This is a probationary review not an interrogation." When she returned a shocked stare, he surged to his feet, "Kathryn, follow me. This meeting is over and we're leaving."

As Kathryn scooped up her things, Robin spat out, "You had the means, motive and opportunity. You really expect us to believe you didn't use your skills to kill the man who murdered your mother?"

Lena gasped as Julien spun round to face Robin. His expression was one of fury and his fist was balled at his side.

Robin pushed to his feet and hissed, "If an officer's bent, it's my responsibility to weed them out. I'm recommending immediate suspension pending a full investigation."

Julien growled, "You haven't heard the last of this."

Turning to Kathryn, Julien placed a gentle hand on her upper arm and ushered her from the room. He closed the door and asked if she was all right. She nodded but the tears she'd been battling fell in a steady stream. He searched his pockets and handed her a starched handkerchief and apologised for what she'd just endured. He then guided her towards the lift and pressed the button.

As they waited, Julien said, "I can only apologise. The man's a zealot. I had no idea he was going to be involved or what he was going to say. I'm as shocked as you, and I assure you I'll be raising this at the highest level."

She sniffed and nodded. Inside the lift, he looked uncomfortable in the face of her tears and he shuffled his feet. "Take the rest of the day off Kathryn. We'll talk again tomorrow when we've both calmed down."

The lift doors opened and they stepped out.

Before parting, he said. "It's true what I said Kathryn—you're one of the best we have."

His words did little to allay her fear. Her past was like a shadow that kept pace with her—there was simply no running from it or from the truth of what she'd done.

THE WARRIORS

***"Who told you the earth was warming … Chicken Little?"* – US-energy firm 'Southern Company' spent $62.1m between 1993 and 2004 to deny the impact of fossil fuel combustion on the climate crisis**

***

Jamie

from:	Gary Singer < Gary.Singer@tacitnet.mi5.uk >
to:	Jamie.Douglas@tacitnet.mi5.uk
subject:	Operation Monkshood
security:	AES-256 encryption

Jamie,

I've arranged digs for you in Salford while you're undercover (details attached). Pick up the keys from newsagent on corner. It's basic as hell but the sort of place your legend might end up after splitting from his wife. Neighbours are clean skins. There's a young couple with a baby in the flat at the rear

- the guy's called Sean. He's got previous for drug offences and there've been a few domestics reported.

Will RV Tuesday evening, details to follow. Keep a low profile this time, I don't want another clusterfuck!

Gary

***

Jamie slumped onto the single bed and cast a despairing eye over the bedsit. It was worse than he'd imagined. He knew Gary had rented it partly because of its proximity to the Ubuntu Centre in Salford where he expected to spend some of his time.

Part of a brick-built terrace, it shared a cramped entrance leading to four flats, two on each floor. His was at the front, at street level, ensuring he experienced noise from the road, passers-by and other residents. He heard the main door slam followed by shouts from a group of teenagers loitering outside beneath a sodium lamp. He could make out their shapes through the grubby net curtain which did little to disguise the filthy windows.

Looking at the scuffed walls, threadbare carpet and mildewed ceiling, he sighed. A stud wall with an arched doorway ran the length of the back wall to provide a narrow galley kitchen. At one end was a stainless steel sink with a dripping cold water tap and an instant hot water handwash unit; at the other, a mouldy fridge and a two-ring electric hob. The flat reeked of damp and desperation and reminded him all too painfully of the council flat he'd lived in with his mother and sister after his father's suicide.

He glanced at his watch to determine how long he'd need to wait before he could phone Kathryn when she finished work. More than anything right now, he needed to hear the sound of her voice.

Four hours and twenty minutes.

The single overhead bare bulb went out, plunging the room into semi-darkness. Cursing, Jamie flicked the light switch without success. Using his phone torch, he checked the fuse box above the door. The pay-as-you-go electricity meter flashed, signalling it was out of credit. He swore again.

He eyed the two-bar electric fire with suspicion, knowing it would eat through any credit on the prepayment meter. Deciding to go in search of the nearest convenience store to purchase tokens, food and cleaning materials, he grabbed his jacket and keys.

Locking his door, he almost collided with a youth dressed in baggy joggers, an oversized grey hoodie and a baseball cap worn backwards. Jamie reckoned him to be in his early twenties, too old in his opinion for the skateboard slung under his arm. They exchanged a nod and the lad asked if he'd just moved in. Speaking in a strong Mancunian accent, he introduced himself as Sean and said he lived in the flat at the rear.

Ah, so you're the wee bastard that knocks your missus about.

Pointing to Jamie's flat, Sean said, "Hope your tight wad landlord replaced the mattress. The previous guy died of an overdose on it."

Jamie felt sick.

He followed Sean out onto the street and watched as he joined the group of teenagers. Dressed in a similar fashion, they greeted Sean with fist bumps and in a language Jamie couldn't fathom, but it was clear Sean was the alpha amongst them.

As Jamie trudged towards the corner shop, he checked his watch again.

Four hours and twelve minutes.

***

Kathryn

Next day, Kathryn got the summons to Julien's office where she found him hunched over his desk. He asked her to close the door and invited her to sit opposite. After inquiring how she was feeling, he rested his elbows on the desk, steepled his hands together and regarded her.

He began by reminding her about the positives from the probationary review meeting and her excellent record of performance. Then he explained that he'd raised a formal complaint about how the meeting had been handled.

Here we go, it's shit sandwich time: a positive slice, a shit filling, then another positive.

"Have I still got a job?"

Julien appeared taken aback. "Of course you do. This is just a blip and you needn't worry about it or let it detract from the important work you're doing."

"Robin made it pretty clear he wants me gone."

"He's simply taken a hard-line interpretation of the Service's procedure manual."

"So, I'm suspended?"

Shaking his head, he explained that the compromise they'd agreed upon was to extend her probationary period by six months. During this time, Fitz would continue to supervise her until the final review, at which point she'd be badged pending no further objections on the part of Vetting.

Her anger flared and she snapped, "To give Robin enough time to fit me up so he can kick me out."

Julien cocked an eyebrow. "To give me enough time to put together a counter case."

Unconvinced, she muttered, "Vetting are a law unto themselves."

"Continue doing what you're doing, keep your head down and this will pass. He'll soon find someone else to persecute." When her shoulders slumped, he added, "May I remind you of your excellent record of achievement?"

Yep, shit sandwich. Must teach the recipe on the management course.

After listing her accomplishments, he steered the conversation to safer ground and the subject of her next assignment. He picked up the phone and asked Fitz to join them and, as they waited, Julien inquired after Jamie.

She explained he was already homesick, adding, "I haven't told him about Vetting, he's got enough to think about."

Julien nodded, "Understood."

Fitz appeared, greeted them and pulled up a seat.

Julien unlocked his drawer and produced a manilla folder which he handed to Kathryn. "A little challenge you might enjoy."

Code-named 'Alabaster', it was a dossier containing a bio of a Russian national named Dimitri Balakin. She scanned the brief as Julien summarised its contents. Balakin was a 35-year-old diplomat based at the embassy in Kensington Palace Gardens in London. Wearing a suit and tie, the photograph revealed an athletic-looking man with a boyish face and raffish dark hair.

"Balakin's a recent arrival on our shores," said Julien. "He's drawn our attention because of his likely connections to the SVR, who are MI6's counterparts. We suspect he's no more a diplomat than you or I, and we want to know what he's up to. The file contains the basics but I need you to dig deeper."

"What am I looking for?"

"Anything remotely suspicious. Usually, their intelligence officers are here looking to further their careers. It might be he's trying to recruit someone in parliament or a senior business leader, although they know it's risky and we'll be onto them. Sometimes it's industrial espionage. Last year, we had a chap trying to get his hands on military tech, so if he starts sniffing round a defence contractor, we need to know."

Fitz said, "This'll likely be a slow burn. He'll take his time."

Julien nodded. "The Russians are clever, real masters of our tradecraft, that's why it'll be a challenge." He gazed wistfully out of the window, adding, "Not long after I joined the Service, one of the surveillance chaps told me that dealing with the Russians was like trying to grasp your shadow." He turned his gaze back to her, "No doubt our friend Balakin here is up to no good, but you might have a devil of a time finding out what it is."

She said, "I look forward to the challenge."

Julien fixed her with a stern look. "But stick to the rules Kathryn. No going off-piste. Do not give Robin any ammunition to use against you."

Nodding, she tried to hide her annoyance at the fact their work was so highly regulated with more policies and procedures than you could shake a stick at.

Julien stood, signalling the end of the meeting, and she and Fitz headed back to their desks.

Fitz said in a low voice, "Julien told me what happened with Vetting. You know it doesn't mean shit."

She mouthed, "Thank you."

He chuckled, "Want me to have our secret branch of assassins terminate the Prince of Darkness?"

On a mirthless laugh, she said, "Robin seems to believe I'm capable of carrying out a hit all by myself. Maybe I should request a transfer to that department."

Fitz quipped, "Apply to X Branch, Deniable Ops."

***

Jamie

The following evening, dressed in scruffy jeans and a black hoodie, Jamie made his way to the Ubuntu Centre. Built in the late eighties, the Centre was a soulless community hall tacked onto the side of a rundown shopping centre. Outside, Jamie passed a couple of spoon-burners begging change. They slurred a greeting as he dropped some coins into their Styrofoam cup.

Inside the foyer was a large notice board plastered with fliers for baby and toddler groups, exercise classes and social clubs. Behind an advert for yoga, he spotted a Climate Warriors poster featuring their logo, an image of planet Earth overlayed with the hands of a clock pointing to one minute to midnight. Jamie took a deep breath and headed for the meeting room at the end of a corridor.

The door was ajar and he heard voices from within. A handful of young people sat on plastic chairs listening to Ethan Price, the guy he'd met at the climate protest. All, however, were known to the Security Service and featured in the brief Jamie had been given.

Ethan was Jamie's primary target. A college drop-out who'd failed as an organic farmer, he'd first come to the attention of the authorities in 2010 when, as a member of Greenpeace, he'd entered the site of a coal-fired power station in Kent along with a number of other activists. They'd shut down the conveyor belts and climbed the 200-metre-tall chimney stack bringing generation to a halt. The case had gone to court but none were convicted after the jury decided their action was a justified response to the climate crisis.

Following numerous other protests, Ethan had parted company with Greenpeace after falling out with the organisers over their peaceful protest stance. He'd then formed a group of his own called the Climate Warriors. Officially, its members claimed to align themselves with Extinction Rebellion but in a recent stunt, they'd deviated from XR's non-violent direct-action values when they'd targeted a company who drilled oil fields in the North Sea. Ethan and the group had stormed the company's AGM and sprayed oil over the conference facilities causing extensive damage. They'd only avoided a prison sentence when the company unexpectedly dropped all charges after a mysterious benefactor stepped in and agreed to pay compensation.

Spotting Jamie, Ethan stopped talking and welcomed him to the group with an expansive smile. He was clad in a black shirt and jeans, with dark-blonde hair that reached past his collar. His six-foot frame was fit and lean, and he could have stepped from the pages of a magazine.

"It's Jamie, right?" he said, shaking his hand. "Good to see you mate." Ethan turned to the others. "This is the nutter I was telling you about, the one who glued himself to the roof."

That earned Jamie a round of applause. Ethan beckoned them forward and, one by one, they introduced themselves.

Jamie recalled Meadow from the protest. A tall woman in her late twenties with straggly blonde hair, a curvaceous figure and penetrating green eyes, she was striking in appearance. Another seasoned activist, she was well-connected amongst the climate protest groups but had, so far, avoided getting into any serious trouble. A warm smile lit up her face as she shook his hand.

Next was Rose who'd long dark locks and a solid dependable figure. She'd a pretty face and large breasts which swung freely beneath a tie-dyed kaftan which appeared to have been scavenged from a charity shop discount rail. She offered Jamie a wary smile that failed to reach her suspicious brown eyes.

The youngest of the group was a gamine young woman with hair so short it was almost shaved, except for a shocking pink clump on top. She introduced herself as Yaz, explaining it was short for Yasmine. Thin as a rake and clad in black, she was a mere waif of a girl. Jamie shook her hand and tried to look beyond the nose ring and black eyeliner.

Ethan beckoned the remaining member of the group over, a lad in his early twenties. Leon was black with short spiky hair and a scruffy beard. Two small hooped earrings dangled from his left ear. He shook Jamie's hand with a shy smile.

The door burst open behind them and another young lad sauntered in apologising for his tardiness.

"And this is Alex," said Ethan, "he'd be late for his own funeral."

Jamie recalled Alex was from a wealthy family. His mother was a senior partner in a legal firm in Manchester. He wore a hoodie emblazoned with a cannabis leaf on one side and the Jamaican flag on the other, and had dreadlocks that appeared to support their own ecosystem. Seriously, all the lad needed was Bob Marley music.

Grinning and glassy-eyed, Alex said, "Yeah-man" and offered Jamie a fist bump which made him laugh.

In another life, I'd be doing you for possession mate.

After the introductions, Jamie took a seat at the back beside Alex and Leon. Although their web site described them as an environmental collective with no hierarchy, Ethan was clearly the group's unofficial leader. Older than the others, Jamie suspected his years of experience and long charge sheet earned him kudos in activist circles.

"You join us at an interesting time," said Ethan. "We were discussing another protest in London later this month."

Jamie asked if that was the event being coordinated by Extinction Rebellion, and Ethan confirmed it was and that they planned to take part. There then followed a heated and protracted discussion about how best to participate given the theme of economic rebellion. Their discussion was as much about the morals and ethics of what they were planning as the logistics. Jamie listened, not wanting to appear too keen.

"And how do we get there? We've no funds," said Rose.

Ethan dismissed her concerns with a wave. "Leave that to me."

Jamie wondered where they got their money from as few of them worked, save for some low-paid, part-time jobs.

Rose looked unhappy but joined Ethan at the front. "We should target the banks," she said. "They're the ones financing fossil fuel projects. We need to send them a message."

There were murmurs of agreement and Leon and Alex shrugged. Jamie was surprised when Ethan asked for his opinion, something which appeared to annoy Rose.

Jamie looked from one to the other. "Aye, whatever you think."

"What sort of message?" asked Ethan.

"We could sit outside covered in oil holding banners," said Rose.

"Been done," said Ethan with another dismissive wave.

Before Rose could protest, Meadow piped up. "We could hand out fake money to passers-by. It'd be very symbolic." She spoke in a soft melodious voice.

"No one's going to remember that," said Ethan, "and the press won't take any notice. We need something with more impact, something dramatic."

Meadow appeared wounded by his dismissive tone.

Ethan looked at Jamie, "We need something memorable, like your stunt."

All eyes turned to Jamie. A voice in his head reminded him he was only there to observe and gather evidence.

Suppressing a chuckle, Jamie said, "Aye, just point me at their roof and I'll climb it."

That earned him another round of applause.

Shit! Gary's gonna skin me alive.

***

After Ethan wound up the meeting, Jamie joined the group at a local pub, a seedy joint with mismatched furniture and a sticky carpet. Ethan bought a round of drinks and they sat at a large table in the corner.

Despite his dry mouth, Jamie was careful not to drink too much, opting for beer in a coloured glass bottle so it wasn't obvious how much he'd consumed. He'd felt more confident about gluing himself to a roof than maintaining the pretence of a new legend. It reminded him of his first few days undercover in Hell's Glen, but there he'd had Kathryn by his side and a reason to be strong. They'd gotten through the ordeal together. Here he was on his own, and the prospect made him anxious.

Jamie sat opposte Rose who regarded him warily. She quizzed him on how he'd ended up in Salford and why he'd joined the protest, and he repeated his cover story about separating from his wife and finding work in the area. As he gave a spiel about his worries for the planet and humanity, he was aware of the group's careful scrutiny. Would they see right through him? He resisted the urge to look away – an instinctive and revealing tell when someone's lying – and made an effort to maintain firm eye contact.

Meeting Rose's watchful eyes, he asked, "So what's your excuse?"

She offered him a half smile. "People are dying and they'll continue to die, and it'll be the poorest who suffer most, not those who've caused the problem."

Feigning ignorance, Jamie asked the two founding members of the group, Rose and Meadow, how they'd met, and they explained their mothers had been at Greenham Common Peace Camp. Rose later met Ethan after joining Greenpeace, and introduced him to the group. Ethan in turn brought in Yasmine who'd been part of the Extinction Rebellion movement from its inception, and the lads had followed. Other members had come and gone over the years but this core remained.

Jamie listened intently, and it confirmed the information in the brief was correct. Discussion switched to the different tactics used by groups such as Greenpeace and XR, and it became apparent that what bound the Climate Warriors together was a shared sense of frustration that little had changed despite years of campaigning and protesting.

Yasmine said, "Politicians say the right things but it's all hot air. We saw it at COP26."

Jamie recalled the group had demonstrated at the UN Climate Change Conference in Glasgow in 2021, and that Rose and Ethan had been arrested.

When Jamie offered to buy the next round, Leon joined him at the bar. As they waited to be served, Jamie said, "You're a long way from home. How d'you end up in Salford?"

Leon's eyes twinkled with mirth. "You 'aksing' me that coz I'm black? You think I'm from Africa or somefink?"

Laughing, Jamie said, "Nah, I had you pegged as London, not Lagos." He knew Leon had spent years in and out of foster care as a result of his mother's addiction problems.

With a deep rumbling laugh, Leon said, "Yeh, Hackney man." Then flashing a wry grin and in an over-the-top American accent, "Hey, I know what you're thinking. What's a homie doing in a climate group, shouldn't he be running with his gang?"

Jamie put up his hands in mock surrender. "You're the one stereotyping, not me."

Leon had a smiler's mouth and a warm laugh. He said, "Am just pulling your leg mate. But it's all stabbings and county lines down there. I needed a change of scene."

"And of all the places to admire the scenery, you picked Salford?"

"Salford's not so bad. At least no one stabs you for being from the wrong postcode."

The barman took their order and, as they waited for their drinks, Leon said, "So what brings a sweaty sock to the fair city of Salford?"

"For the scenery." He joined in with Leon's laughter.

Jamie nursed his beer so he could keep a clear head. How this first meeting went was crucial and would set the tone for all future interactions. He knew his legend off-pat but one slip and he was certain they'd see through him. Especially Rose.

After joining the Security Service, Jamie had undergone intensive training, including a course on deep infiltration. Part of this was termed 'de-policing' which involved making undercover operatives aware of ingrained mannerisms and methods of speaking that screamed 'cop'. With Jamie's police and military background, he'd picked up a few habits requiring correction. Many were second-nature to him, such as always turning on the car ignition with the driver's door open; a technique he'd learned in Special Forces to minimise the damage done to occupants by a car bomb. Being aware of these non-verbal signals was every bit as important as remembering his cover story.

When Alex and Leon announced they were leaving, Jamie took that as his cue to go, saying he'd to get up early for work. Ethan asked for his mobile number and said he'd be in touch.

With a wave to the others, Jamie stepped out into the cold night air and trudged back to the bedsit. Realising he'd hardly eaten and that the little alcohol he'd drunk had gone straight to his head, he felt hungry but not enough to face cooking in that squalid kitchen. Suddenly gripped with home sickness at the prospect of spending the night there, he needed to hear Kathryn's voice.

He spied a chip shop on the corner of Romney Street, the smell of which made his stomach growl, and darted inside. Minutes later he emerged holding a warm bag of fish and chips. He entered the communal door leading to the flats and heard a commotion coming from the rear of the building. He stopped and listened. A man and woman were arguing above the piercing cry of a baby.

The woman shouted, "You won't take any responsibility."

"Don't talk to me about responsibility, I never wanted a kid in the first place." The sound of a scuffle then a roar, "You fuckin' bitch."

There was a cry and the sickening sound of a blow.

The man yelled, "Now see what you've made me do."

The baby gave a blood-curdling scream then fell silent.

Jamie flipped.

The Incident

***"In the lifetime of our children, most will face existential risk — half of the people in the world could die (approximately 4 billion) and as much as 90% of species will be at risk of extinction."* Gail Bradbrook, co-founder Extinction Rebellion (XR); Money Rebellion, June 2020**

***

Kathryn

Glancing at the clock in the living room for the umpteenth time, Kathryn wondered why Jamie hadn't phoned. He'd only been gone a few days and already she was worried. He'd sounded down when he'd phoned the previous evening, the emotion cracking in his voice when he told her he loved her. When he described his living conditions and the squalid bedsit, she'd choked back tears.

To help pass the time, she took Meg a walk. On the way home, she greeted their neighbours' son who was emptying the bin. His cottage was directly opposite and Kathryn often encountered him as she came and went with the dog. In his late twenties, Darren still lived at home, although his parents spent several months of the year working in Dubai. He was painfully shy and she'd rarely spoken to him. On seeing Kathryn, he gave a brief nod and darted back inside the house.

After another hour of worrying, she contacted Gary on the number Jamie had given her for emergencies. He sounded surprised to hear her voice and informed her Jamie had been involved in an incident and was currently being held at the local police station. His arrest had been flagged immediately on MI5's systems and Gary alerted.

"What kind of incident and why didn't you tell me?" she scolded.

"I can't say but it's nothing to worry about."

"Don't patronise me," she yelled, "of course I'm worried."

When Gary refused to say more, she cut the call. Cursing, she went to the spare room and fired up her laptop. Deliberating, she stared at the screen for several minutes. Then, aware it wasn't the smartest move, she pushed all thoughts of her career, Vetting and liberty aside, and hacked into the computers of Greater Manchester Police.

It didn't take long to locate the incident report which showed officers had been called to a domestic disturbance at a property in Salford and arrested a man called James Douglas. Suspected of assault, he was being questioned while detectives and a social worker waited to speak to a woman who lived at a neighbouring flat. The woman was badly injured and being treated in hospital, along with her partner, a man named Sean Gibbons.

Kathryn then penetrated the Police National Computer and perused Sean's record to discover he'd a long history of abusing his girlfriend and another before her. Police had been called to this address three times in six months after neighbours reported hearing arguments, but each time the charges had been dropped and Sean had returned. Kathryn flicked through a disturbing gallery of photographs of his bruised and battered partner.

She also found archived case files relating to Sean's own childhood and the abuse he'd suffered at the hands of an alcoholic father. However, after seeing the injuries Sean had inflicted on his girlfriend, she'd little sympathy for him. More worrying was the file also showed their child was on the Social Work's At-Risk register.

The phone rang and she leapt to answer it. Gary informed her Jamie was being released without charge.

"Is the baby okay?" she asked.

If Gary was surprised that she knew about the incident, he hid it. "The kid's unharmed."

"And is the girlfriend pressing charges?"

Gary gave a long sigh. "She's too scared. No doubt as soon as Sean's out of hospital, he'll be back to finish the job. God help her."

God won't help her, but I know people who will.

After apologising for her earlier abruptness, Kathryn thanked him and ended the call.

Glancing again at the photographs of the woman's injuries, she recalled the times she'd seen similar bruises on her mother. Phil had regularly beaten her mum black and blue, and had been sly enough to focus his blows on her body and limbs where the evidence could be concealed beneath clothing. On one occasion, however, he'd hit her so hard he'd broken her cheekbone and she'd required surgery. This had resulted in Kathryn being placed on the At-Risk register; not that it'd made a damn bit of difference. She'd no faith in the authorities; her own experience had shown their ineptitude and unwillingness to act.

Wanting to protect this woman and her child, she launched TOR, her gateway to the dark web and home to some useful vigilantes. Kathryn was as familiar with this world as she was with the surface net, having spent most of her young adult life lurking in its shadows. It was like coming home. TOR, short for The Onion Router, allowed millions of people to browse the internet anonymously and securely. For Kathryn, it was her invisibility cloak.

As she got to work, she thought about her previous life with the Grey Nemesis hacktivist community when she'd explored every dark corner of this world. It was a place of extraordinary, unfettered creativity where some of the most ground-breaking ideas took shape. Unfortunately, it was also where some of the very worst aspects of human nature could be found. Over the years, the dark net had changed as much as the regular one and, although its pages weren't indexed by Google and companies like Amazon didn't trade here, it had its equivalents.

Under the leadership of a genius hacker called Grey Lady, Grey Nemesis had used the dark web to target unscrupulous companies and individuals and dispense cyber justice. Over the years, Kathryn and her buddies had raided the coffers of corrupt banks and financial companies, attacked servers belonging to billionaires who'd rigged cryptocurrency markets, and perpetrated 'life ruins' on individuals who'd caused harm to children. She'd always derived most satisfaction from targeting paedophiles and child pornographers. That was until Jamie arrested her, after a fellow hacker called Pandora betrayed her and the Grey Nemesis collective.

Kathryn navigated to an obscure Star Trek chat room and found her mate Scotty under the guise of his new cyber handle *IntoDarkness*. Seeing his new pseudonym filled her with sadness as she understood how much it'd cost him to adopt it. When a hacker gave up an alias and started afresh, they lost all their contacts and the trust built up with them. She'd considered it herself but *Moniker* was more than a pseudonym; it was her entire identity. In cyberspace, she became a different person. Gone was her social awkwardness and self-doubt. Moniker was powerful and confident. And respected.

Scotty was in the midst of a flame war with a fellow trekkie about the merits of the original Star Trek series versus Deep Space Nine. The original poster, or 'OP', had risked life and limb by daring to suggest the latter was superior. Reading Scotty's reply, she laughed aloud.

[IntoDarkness] *You are a noxious fiend and a degenerate swine with acne and halitosis. I despise your mother for giving birth to you, and your father for the fact his orgasm produced your fugly face. You are a poisonous snake who deserves to be nailed to a tree, sliced down your corpulent length and for your slimy innards to be wrenched from your still-warm corpse. And you're fat.*

Still chuckling, she interrupted his rant and invited Scotty to a private chat room where she typed a message.

[Moniker] *You busy?*

[IntoDarkness] *Not unless you count dealing with fucktards busy*

[Moniker] *There are a lot of them about, and I've a dangerous one who needs sorting*

[IntoDarkness] *Aye aye Captain*

Kathryn explained about the Sean situation and asked if Scotty knew of any vigilantes based in the area who might be willing to help. Grey Nemesis had worked with several such groups in the past.

[IntoDarkness] *There's a new bunch on the dark web run by an ex-cop. They'll fit him up for a long stretch*

[Moniker] *How much will they want paying?*

[IntoDarkness] *Lucky for you my crypto's doing well*

Before Grey Nemesis had disbanded, Scotty had been their cryptocurrency expert, and he'd owned a Bitcoin rack which he used to mine for new coins. He'd once described it as the digital equivalent of the California Gold Rush where prospectors like himself use sophisticated hardware to earn new crypto tokens. Although he'd never revealed how much, she suspected he'd made a killing which was one of the reasons he'd evaded capture by the Feds for so long.

[Moniker] *That's so generous but I can't possibly accept*

[IntoDarkness] *Yes u can and after what you've just told me, I'll happily finance putting the dickshit in jail*

[Moniker] *You're the best!*

Scotty replied with a smiley emoji which was about as gushy as he got. After bundling up the information and sending it to him, she ended the chat and poured a glass of wine. Between Jamie's actions and her moonlighting as Moniker, she felt a greater sense of achievement than she ever got from the day job. At least there were no stupid policies and procedures on the dark net.

But the job had allowed her to reinvent herself and without it, what else would she do?

***

Jamie

from: Gary Singer < Gary.Singer@tacitnet.mi5.uk >
to: Jamie.Douglas@tacitnet.mi5.uk
subject: WTF?
security: AES-256 encryption

For chrissakes Jamie, you hospitalised him!

We need to talk. RV tomorrow 2 p.m. (details attached).

Gary.

***

Gary yelled, "You could've compromised the entire operation."

Rubbing the swollen knuckles on his right hand, Jamie grumbled, "He got off lightly, the bastard deserved it."

It was the morning after the Sean incident, and they were sitting in Gary's Audi at the back of a row of empty warehouses in an industrial estate. Jamie suspected his handler had picked the spot so he could give him a bollocking without being overheard.

Jamie explained that, concerned for the woman and baby's safety, he'd kicked down the door of Sean's flat and given him a beating. A neighbour had reported the incident and he'd been lifted and taken to the local police station. Later, the girlfriend had corroborated Jamie's story and he'd been released without charge.

Gary shouted, "What you did was reckless. You can't break the law unless it's necessary for your cover, and then only for minor offences. Anything else has to be sanctioned beforehand."

Shooting him an incredulous glare, Jamie said, "Screw that! I didn't join the Service to stand by while a woman and baby were attacked."

Gary gave a loud sigh of defeat then, after a pause, said, "And call your missus, she's been on my case. Dealing with one of you is bad enough."

Jamie felt a stab of guilt at not having called her. "Is Kathryn alright?"

"Fine, just worried when you didn't phone last night. She hacked into the police computers to find out what was going on. She knew more than I did."

Jamie shook his head and chuffed, "Aye, I can believe it."

"Just tell her to be careful, okay?"

"Aye, I will." Jamie gazed out of the window at a passing van and said, "But there was no compromise, and Ethan's just texted me so you can intercept his comms."

"Fitz is already on it. He says it's a burner so there's no chance of tracing it. He'll have tossed the phone by now."

"So, what next?" asked Jamie.

"Well, you can't go back to that bedsit. I'll need to move you."

"Thank Christ for that! You seen the state of that place? Just because I'm Scottish doesn't make me a savage you know. The next flat needs to be habitable."

Rolling his eyes, Gary asked, "Anything else – veranda, swimming pool, sea view?"

"And you owe me a fish supper."

Gary put his head in his hands and laugh-moaned.

THE SQUAT

"Despite the public outcry around the use of covert human intelligence sources to infiltrate peaceful protest groups, it appears this practice is ongoing." — **Geraint Davies, chair of the all-party parliamentary group on democracy and the constitution (2021)**

***

Jamie

3 months later - Salford, England

from:	Jamie Douglas < Jamie.Douglas@tacitnet.mi5.uk >
to:	Gary.Singer@tacitnet.mi5.uk
subject:	Operation Monkshood - Extraction?
security:	AES-256 encryption

I'm wasting my time here. It's been months and apart from a few lively protests and arrests on minor charges, there's nothing here. Why r we wasting time on a harmless bunch of activists when it could be better spent elsewhere?

When r u extracting me?

***

"This'll want a warm, sunny spot," said Jamie to Meadow placing the yucca plant on the table.

He was helping the group move into their new squat after they'd been threatened with eviction from their last place. Rather than wait for the bailiffs to turf them out, Ethan decided to look for a new base which could accommodate them all. To his surprise, this included Jamie. The invitation had come as a relief, especially after months spent in another squalid bedsit, plus it was a chance to burrow deeper now they were beginning to trust him.

The Climate Warriors were a clannish lot, he discovered, suspicious of interlopers. But, in the months since that first meeting, Jamie had made himself useful, becoming their driver and quartermaster, and ferrying equipment around the country. He'd rented a lockup nearby which was full of tents, sleeping bags, placards, chains and ropes for the protests, and he'd rapidly become the go-to-guy for everything and anything they needed.

He'd also helped find this new place; a building tucked at the back of a derelict industrial estate on the outskirts of Salford which had once been home to a gym. *Trimfit* was emblazoned across the entrance although the equipment was long gone, leaving a cavernous hall surrounded by offices and treatment rooms. A seating area with old sofas, a small kitchen and changing rooms with showers offered luxury compared to their last squat. And, since the courts treated squatting in commercial property as a civil matter, it made it difficult for the building's legitimate owners to move them on. So far, no one had come calling and the utilities were still connected; something Gary would ensure remained the case.

It was moving day but, to complicate matters, most of the group were in Glasgow where environmental activists from across the UK had gathered to protest. Ethan was keen to attend the event but Jamie dared not risk it since it was too close to his old beat. Instead, he invented an excuse not to go — a twisted knee he claimed was the result of a fall. He just had to remember to limp.

And keep Meadow at bay.

Her infatuation with him was a complication he hadn't anticipated. He'd tried letting her down gently on several occasions but she was persistent, and he was beginning to regret his decision to move into the squat.

Meadow placed the plant in the sitting area and began unpacking the kitchen. Jamie rested his walking stick against the counter and split open a box containing saucepans. As he removed them, Meadow sidled up to him.

She said, "Here, let me."

Her fingers brushed against his. Jamie moved away but she reached for his hand and pulled him towards her. Before he could retract, she stretched up to kiss him. Twisting his head away, he tried taking a step back only to find himself trapped against the kitchen units.

"Whoa," he said, placing his hands on her shoulders and gently pushing her away.

He cursed himself for getting into a situation where he was alone with her. He'd never considered himself attractive, not since an IED in Iraq tore a hole in his face. And, although he'd had cosmetic surgery and the scar had faded, the emotional ones had not.

Seeing the hurt in her gaze, he mumbled, "Sorry ... it's ... uhm ..."

She bit her lower lip and tears blossomed in her green eyes.

Ah, Jesus!

Resisting the urge to comfort her, he whispered, "Meadow, it's not you ... uhh ... my head's just not in the right place since my marriage broke up." He raked a hand through his unkempt hair as he risked a glance at her.

She gave an embarrassed smile and mumbled, "I thought by now you might be ready to move on."

He shook his head and fought to keep his longing for Kathryn from his voice. Homesickness lay like a deadweight in his gut. "I'm not."

"You never talk about your wife," she said.

He shrugged. "There's not much to say. We were married for a while then, when I started working away for long stretches, she'd had enough of being on her own and we separated."

Fixing him with her watery gaze, her voice wavered. "You still love her though?"

Looking away, he exhaled a hard breath. His marriage was the last thing he wanted to talk about, especially with Meadow. It wasn't that he disliked her, she seemed like a genuinely good person but she was a target. In any case, he'd no interest in her in that way; he'd no interest in any woman other than his wife.

Leaning his weight on the walking stick, he limped to the ratty old sofa in the corner of the room. The squat was cleaner now that he and Meadow had scrubbed it but the soft furnishings had stubbornly resisted their efforts. He perched on the edge of the couch, keen to put distance between them. Glancing at the clock, he hoped the others would return soon.

An uncomfortable silence descended.

Meadow looked at him expectantly and he said, "Yes dammit, I still love my wife ... and since that's the case, I'm not looking for anything else right now."

She sat next to him and turned her gaze on him. "Want to talk about it? Might help."

It was the last thing he wanted to do. He missed Kathryn so much it hurt. "What about you?" he asked, trying to ignore the gaping hole in his gut.

She ran her fingers through her long blonde hair. "Ethan and I split up shortly before you arrived on the scene."

He'd long wondered about their relationship but this was a surprise. "How long were you together?"

She looked into the middle distance. "Almost three years. We're still fond of each other but he's into polyamory and I'm not." After a pause, she added, "I really tried but I couldn't handle it." Spotting Jamie's bemused expression, she said, "Ethan doesn't believe in committing to just one person. He says it's too much like ownership. I was free to take other partners too but ... well ... in the end I couldn't deal with him being with other women."

"Ah," he said, realising this explained why Ethan was openly affectionate towards both Rose and Yasmine and why the women seemed to tolerate his behaviour. Until now, Jamie had been uncertain about who was sleeping with whom.

Seeing how sad and vulnerable Meadow appeared, he felt a bloom of guilt. He pushed it aside; he wasn't going there. "Aye, I can understand why that must've been difficult."

Turning to meet his eye, she said, "Do you believe in being exclusive?"

He plucked at a loose thread on his jeans. "Uhm, well I'm not into poly-what's-its-name if that's what you mean."

Jesus, where are the others? They should be back by now.

She threw him a disappointed look. "Call me old-fashioned, but I do and when I'm with someone, it's as if no one else exists."

That he could relate to, and the gaping hole in his gut yawned. Leaning on the stick, he eased himself to his feet. "I'll bring the supplies in, they'll be back soon." Again, he met her hurt stare.

Jamie hobbled downstairs to his transit van which was parked in the lot next to the squat. The outside walls of the building were plastered in graffiti, broken glass littered the tarmac, and he spotted a fat rat feasting on a discarded takeaway meal. He opened the rear doors of the van and retrieved a couple of fruit trays filled with food. As he limped back upstairs, Meadow reappeared.

"Want some help?" she said. Again, he saw the want in her eyes.

They unpacked the provisions onto the kitchen countertop. The morning's skip diving had been lucrative, providing an abundance of meat and vegetables. Most of the group were 'freegans', eating meat and dairy only when it was being discarded because, they reasoned, the damage had already been done. Jamie ate whatever was put in front of him, but he missed steak, especially the way Kathryn cooked it. He pushed the memory aside, his longing for her too much to bear.

While Meadow prepared a casserole, he peeled potatoes. They worked in silence, the atmosphere leaden between them. He glanced at the clock again, wondering what was taking Ethan and the others so long. He checked his phone but there were no messages. After putting the pot onto boil, he retreated to the sofa and stretched out the leg with the strapped-up knee.

Meadow stopped chopping and asked, “Still sore?”

He shrugged. “Getting better. I’ve taken painkillers.”

Pulling a face, she offered to make a tisane to combat the inflammation. He suppressed a sigh at the thought of the concoction she was going to brew, having tasted a few that’d previously made him gag. Despairingly, he watched as she retrieved her wooden case full of herbal remedies from a packing crate. After rifling through it, she produced several glass vials, and a pestle and mortar.

Sprinkling a little of each into a teapot, she listed the ingredients. “Ginger, turmeric, green tea, white willow bark ...” After adding boiling water, she strained the mixture into a mug and handed it to him.

Catching a whiff of the potion, he felt nauseous. Pasting a smile onto his face, he took a sip and repressed the urge to retch.

Ugh, disgusting.

“Delicious,” he said.

As she turned towards the kitchen, he tipped half of the liquid into the plant pot, wondering what the yucca would make of it. A tongue-in-cheek housewarming gift from Gary in his last bedsit, he hadn’t the heart to throw it out. Carrying a brew of her own, Meadow joined him on the sofa and smiled.

After another bitter mouthful, he asked, “Where did you learn this stuff?”

“I grew up surrounded by women at Greenham Common who taught me the healing power of nature. I’ve never swallowed a pill in my life.” Silence fell as they sipped their tea. After a few minutes, she broke it and said, “I could do Reiki if you like?” When he raised a questioning eyebrow, she added, “It’s an alternative therapy that channels universal energy to promote healing.”

Oh, for fuck’s sake.

Rearranging his face to hide his scepticism, he raised his mug. “Thanks, but the tea’s working wonders.”

Meadow returned a smile laced with undisguised yearning. She whispered, “I can wait ... you know...”

He opened his mouth to speak, then closed it, not trusting himself to say the right thing.

Where the hell are the others?

He busied himself with his phone, conscious of her gaze. Just as he was about to call Ethan, he heard a vehicle pull up outside followed by the slamming of doors.

Stifling a sigh of relief, Jamie eased himself to his feet as the others appeared.

"Good to see you mate," said Ethan shaking Jamie's hand. Then he cast an eye around the squat and said, "Love what you've done with the place!"

Leon greeted Jamie with a warm expansive smile, and Alex his usual fist pump which made Jamie chuckle.

Ethan kissed Meadow on the cheek, and she shot an uncomfortable glance in Jamie's direction. Ethan gave her a quizzical look. When Alex and Leon made a beeline for the stove, Meadow laughed and slapped their thieving hands away.

Jamie said, "How was it? You made the national news."

Groaning, Ethan plopped onto the sofa and blew out a breath. "The die-in got lots of media coverage and Alex managed to get himself lifted. That's why we're so late."

The Climate Warriors had joined other environmental activists at the Kelvingrove Art Gallery and Museum in Glasgow where they'd lain down beneath a dinosaur skeleton and pretended to be dead to raise awareness about the risk of extinction.

Jamie congratulated Alex who grinned from ear to ear, and Meadow gave him a hug. They'd been ribbing Alex for months as the only one amongst them to avoid arrest at recent demos. Leon, by comparison, was expressly forbidden from getting himself arrested by XR's Welfare team because of concerns about how unfairly black and ethnic minorities were treated by the justice system. Instead, Leon had been spending time with Jamie learning how to climb.

"Did the filth give you a hard time?" asked Jamie chuckling at the smile plastered on Alex's face.

"Nah, it was fine," said Alex with a dismissive wave.

Alex and the others disappeared off towards the showers, leaving only Ethan. While Meadow cooked, Jamie cracked open beer and he and Ethan chatted.

"We could have done with you this weekend," said Ethan. "It was a bloody shambles, and it made me realise how much we depend on you."

Jamie nodded at the compliment. Ethan's remarks and invite to join them in the squat indicated they were beginning to trust him. Until now they'd been wary, especially Rose who'd once joked that Jamie fitted the stereotype of an undercover police officer perfectly; turning up out of nowhere, working away all the time, and making himself useful. She'd even nicknamed him Inspector Douglas which had almost given him heart failure, but fortunately it hadn't stuck.

Soddin' typical, thought Jamie, they start trusting me just before I'm extracted. He expected the order to move to the closing phase any day from Gary.

"Something smells nice," said Ethan, wandering into the kitchen and wrapping his arms around Meadow's waist.

She glanced at Jamie and tried to shrug him off just as Rose appeared combing her wet hair. Rose shot Ethan a dirty look that confirmed Jamie's suspicion she was no happier than Meadow about polyamory. As he watched the interplay, he pondered on how Ethan had convinced the women to accept the arrangement. Unlike the others, Ethan didn't work or study; he was a fulltime activist who could offer only a life of squats and protests.

During dinner, they squabbled over trivial matters and teased Alex about his arrest. It was good-natured, and reminded Jamie of happy family meals when his parents had been together. All that had ended abruptly after Jamie's father lost his job, sank into a deep depression and took his own life.

As conversation drifted to the campaign, Ethan kept glancing at his phone. Debate then raged over how effective the protest had been in communicating their message to the public.

Bemoaning the lack of arrests, Ethan said, "We need thousands arrested and hundreds imprisoned, otherwise no one'll take a blind bit of notice. The authorities have got wise to our tactics."

It was clear the others shared his sense of frustration.

"So, what's next?" asked Jamie.

Ethan glanced at his phone again and grumbled, "More of the same, not that it's making a damn bit of difference."

The topic turned to 'woke washing' which Rose explained was a cynical tactic used by the fossil fuel industry to delay curbing emissions. She said, "They've moved beyond denying that climate change exists to downplaying the urgency of the crisis. They spend a fortune on propaganda to convince us of all the great work they do and how they're tackling the issues."

There was murmured agreement.

Alex said, "They don't want action; they want to kick the can down the road."

Ethan leapt when his phone rang and he darted outside to take the call. Jamie waited a few moments before excusing himself, and then headed in the direction of the toilets. Taking a detour, he tiptoed to the foot of the stairwell where he strained to hear Ethan's side of the conversation.

"I'll fix it ... yes, I know who he is."

Jamie swallowed hard, pondering on who Ethan was referring to. Was it himself? Had his true identity been discovered?

Ethan continued. "I need more money." Then, after a pause, "But things have moved on, and he wants to do it."

Jamie's heart thumped in his chest as a dozen possibilities flashed through his mind to explain these words, but the only one that made sense was that he was compromised. And what did he mean by "he wants to do it"?

Ethan ended the call and Jamie shot back upstairs and into the toilets. When he re-joined the others, Ethan was back grinning from ear to ear.

"I've good news," said Ethan, "We're going to the International Climate Camp."

Yasmine squealed and threw her arms around him and Ethan chuckled, while Rose looked on with incredulity.

"We're really going to Germany?" asked Leon.

Ethan nodded.

Rose raised a sceptical eyebrow. "Where's the money coming from? We can barely afford a trip to London, never mind Berlin."

Peeling Yasmine off him, Ethan darted a glance at Jamie before glaring at Rose. "From a friend, someone sympathetic to the cause."

When Ethan pulled Yasmine in for a dirty kiss, Rose walked away.

As the others whooped with excitement at the news, Jamie's heart sank at the realisation his chance of extraction seemed a lot less likely. Who had Ethan been talking to? Was this the same person bankrolling the trip and, if so, why? And, more importantly, had his cover been compromised?

This changed everything.

The Office

***Since 2019 more than 3,500 people taking part in XR protests have been arrested, almost all for minor public order offences such as obstructing the highway. And away from the glare of the media, more than 2,000 have been prosecuted and taken to court* — Extinction Rebellion (XR) 2021**

***

Kathryn

It was Friday afternoon, the end of another long week, and Kathryn, Fitz and a dozen of their colleagues were gathered in the office to celebrate Bryan's birthday. The youngest member of the team, Bryan had a mop of unruly blonde hair and a cheeky grin. As he blew out the candles on his cake, Kathryn joined in singing a dreadful rendition of *Happy Birthday*.

After devouring the cake, people drifted back to their desks.

"Got any plans?" she asked Fitz, knowing what his answer would be since his weekends were always the same.

Fitz gave a rueful smile. "Usual. Pub tonight, parents visiting on Saturday. You?"

She could tell from his expression he instantly regretted the question. With a matching smile, she replied, "Usual. Just me and Meg."

Her Jamie-shaped pit of emptiness gaped wider.

She was last to leave, and she drove slowly through the heavy traffic with Meg in the rear. Tears pricked at the corners of her eyes at the thought of another weekend on her own, and she reminded herself it was only temporary. Jamie had said he expected things to come to a conclusion soon. She wondered what he was doing and who he was with at this moment.

At the cottage, she changed out of her work clothes and headed to the common with the dog, hoping a walk might lift her spirits. She spent twenty minutes tiring the collie out with the ball launcher before returning home.

After feeding Meg, she retrieved a meal-for-one from the freezer and left it on the counter to defrost. Scrutinising the packet, she realised that, since Jamie had left, she hadn't cooked a proper meal in weeks and her appetite suddenly vanished. She poured a glass of wine and ran a bath filled with scented suds.

She trudged to the bedroom and began peeling off her jumper and jeans. As she approached the bedroom window to draw the curtains against the night, she spotted her neighbour Darren framed in the window opposite, wearing only a pair of y-fronts. Their eyes met and she yanked the curtains closed. After checking all the windows and doors were locked, she returned to the bathroom and snibbed the door before undressing.

Lying in the bath, she wondered just how long he'd been watching her.

***

Jamie

Jamie slid into the passenger seat of Gary's Audi holding a cardboard tray laden with coffee and doughnuts.

They'd been meeting weekly in various haunts around Salford since the operation began. Jamie had suggested today's location in the far corner of Burger King's car park after reasoning it was one of the least likely places to encounter the Climate Warriors. They looked an unlikely pair, with Gary in a crisp suit and Jamie in climbing gear.

"Alright cupcake?" said Jamie, passing his handler a coffee and a glazed doughnut.

Pulling a face, Gary said, "Have you any idea what this'll do to my glucose levels?"

Jamie put his hand out for it. "I'll eat it if you don't want it. I'm craving sugar."

Gary quickly bit into the treat making Jamie chuckle.

"You need sweetening," muttered Jamie, passing Gary several packets of sugar and a wooden stirrer.

Shaking his head, Gary stuffed the remainder of the doughnut into his mouth.

"Aye, I had you figured as a Julie Andrews," said Jamie. When this was met with a blank stare, he added, "White Nun." Then, at Gary's bemused expression, "Coffee, white, no sugar." Jamie stirred two packets into his own brew and said, "Whereas I'm standard-issue Nato, white and two."

"I can hear your arteries hardening," mumbled Gary, wiping his hands on a napkin. "So, what you got for me."

Jamie updated him on Ethan's phone call and the group's invitation to the ICC.

"Fitz traced it," said Gary, "but it was to another burner. We don't know who it belongs to, only that it was located in the Manchester area."

"Great, so we still don't have a scooby-doo who's bank-rolling them?"

"We've an idea," said Gary taking a sip of coffee. "Alexander's mother has been making regular cash withdrawals from various business accounts. The amounts are random and below the money laundering threshold but Fitz reckons she might be their benefactor."

Jamie recalled from his brief that Alex's mother, as well as running a successful law practice, was a partner in a property development company based in London. He said, "But Alex never has any money. Why would his mother give cash to Ethan and not to her son?"

Gary shrugged. “That’s your job to find out.” He took a document from his leather folio and passed it to Jamie. “But that’s not all. Turns out Ethan’s been in contact with a number of interesting extremists in Europe.”

Flicking through pages of transcript of Ethan’s communications, Jamie cursed. Dozens of known nutjobs were listed along with their rap sheets, the content of which made the hair on the back of Jamie’s neck stand up.

The Wolff

"Ice storm rolls from Texas to Tennessee – I'm in Los Angeles and it's freezing. Global warming is a total, and very expensive, hoax!" **— Donald J. Trump (@realDonaldTrump) December 6, 2013**

***

Kathryn

As Kathryn padded towards the kitchen, she heard crunching on the gravel outside and she froze. She wasn't expecting visitors, especially at this time of night, and her husband wasn't due home for another week.

Meg began to bark at the front door, and Kathryn tip-toed into the hallway. The footsteps approached and she could make out a dark shape through the rippled glass in the door. With her heart thumping against her ribcage, Kathryn crept towards the panic button located by the door. The figure drew nearer.

There was a jangle of keys and a bearded man with long hair whom she barely recognised entered. She gasped in delight at the sight, and then launched herself at him and he caught her in his arms.

"Oh baby, I've missed you so much," said Jamie, between feverish kisses.

"Not as much as I've missed you, you great hairy hippie."

Meg wound herself around their legs and whined.

Laughing, Jamie rubbed his beard against Kathryn's face making her squeal. "What kind of welcome is that to give your husband?" he chuckled.

Kissing him, she mumbled, "Come and I'll welcome you properly." She tugged him by the hand towards the bedroom.

"Baby, I really need a shower." He pulled her against his chest. "Join me."

Mashing her lips to his, she walked him backward to the foot of the stairs. He scooped her up and she wound her legs around his waist as he climbed the staircase. Inside the bathroom, he lowered her to her feet and, eyes glinting, flicked on the shower.

They undressed one another, their bodies a tangle of lips, tongues and fingers. She fumbled with his belt and laughed. Cupping her buttocks, he lifted her into the steam-filled cabinet and pressed her against the tiled wall. She slid her hand down to guide him and he slammed into her with a grunt. Hanging onto him for dear life, she moaned deep into his throat as he took her. Hard and fast and merciless. He kept up the pace until a climax tore through her, and then he followed her over the edge. Afterwards, panting heavily, they clung to one another until the water ran cold.

As they dried each other, she trailed her fingers over his sculpted torso as if it was the first time she'd seen his body.

"You've lost weight," she said. "Are you eating properly?"

"I was needing to lose a few pounds. Too much of your good home cooking, Mrs Denton." He flexed his muscles, making her giggle.

Desire coursed through her, and her caress dropped lower. Grinning, he carried her to the bedroom where he made love to her slowly like they were giving prizes for it.

Later, exhausted but sated for the time being, they gazed at one another for the longest time. Sifting her fingers through his damp hair and beard, she marvelled at how different he looked to the man she'd married. He was still handsome though, just in a raw, untamed way.

"This is a lovely surprise," she whispered, "I didn't expect you so soon."

"I'm off to Germany soon, I had to see you." Jamie explained about the group's invite to the International Climate Camp in Berlin.

She bit her bottom lip. "I thought things were coming to a close. How much longer will this go on? It's been months."

"Hard to say. All my intel up until now confirms they're a harmless, well-meaning lot. Most of the activists I've met are."

"So, why aren't they extracting you?"

"There've been a few interesting developments."

Jamie explained Ethan had been communicating with several extremist groups across Europe, and that Alex's mother appeared to be funding the Climate Warriors.

He said, "Ethan's disillusioned with peaceful tactics and he's been making noises about ramping things up. The people he's contacted are the type of nutjobs who carry out kidnapping and sabotage for the sake of saving a few trees. Julien's worried he's planning something big on UK soil."

She knew Jamie may not be party to all the intelligence surrounding his operation, a deliberate tactic to avoid influencing a covert operative. The fact he'd been told this much meant MI5 were concerned, and MI6 would also be involved.

He stroked her cheek. "They're starting to trust me and the trip should give me the opportunity to find out what they're up to and who they're in contact with."

She twirled his gold stud earring; another addition to his cover. "I worry about you all the time," she said.

"I know you do but this'll soon be over."

She fixed him with her gaze. "Until the next job."

Propping himself up on his elbow, he cupped her face. "I just need to see this through and then we can get back to how things were. I know it's hard, but it won't be forever."

He leaned in and kissed her. The kiss deepened and they made love again.

After, when thoroughly spent, he whispered, "I love you so much Kathryn. As long as I'm with you, I don't care what I do."

Tugging gently on his beard, she giggled. "Maybe you could be a tree herder?"

He tickled her until she begged him to stop. Then, reluctantly, she disentangled herself from him and pulled on her robe.

"You hungry?" she asked, "I could cook us a steak." Then, with an impish grin, she added, "or is meat murder to you tofu-tastic ecofreaks?"

Laughing, he chased her into the kitchen.

THE HOLIDAY

"The right has orchestrated a massive public relations campaign to discredit climate science and now a good number of Americans don't believe global warming is really happening." **– Professor Noam Chomsky [2011]**

***

Kathryn

Despite the breath-taking beauty of the landscape, Kathryn felt a sense of trepidation as Jamie manoeuvred the Landrover along the narrow roads towards the Silver Sands. It was a warm summer day and the surrounding mountains had yet to wear their cap of snow. Neither had been back to the area since their undercover operation together in nearby Knoydart; a job which had almost cost them their lives.

Jamie had taken ten days leave from his current role, telling the Climate Warriors he'd a job up north. Kathryn had also requested vacation, and Harriet had kicked up a fuss about the short notice but relented. Gary had instructed Jamie to remain in the country so they'd spent two nights in a dog-friendly hotel in the Lake District before making the long journey to Morar on the west coast of Scotland to visit Keith. Recently retired from the Service, Keith had been their handler on the Knoydart job, and they'd kept in touch since.

As sheep-studded fields and farm cottages flashed by the window, Kathryn thought about their time with the religious community in nearby Hell's Glen. It was there she and Jamie had fallen in love, despite the unlikely circumstances, and she treasured the memories. Even Meg seemed excited about returning and panted in the back.

Watching her husband drive, she worried about how he might feel, considering how close to death he'd come after the shooting. The therapy he'd been receiving from the Service's Welfare team had helped his PTSD, and he claimed not to have experienced a night terror in months. However, he appeared to be struggling with the transition from his undercover world to the real one. He seemed distant somehow, as if his thoughts were elsewhere.

His voice pulled her from her reverie. "You thinking what I'm thinking?" he said, his eyes fixed firmly on the road. He reached over and grasped her hand.

"Feels strange being back."

"Aye, and this time as a proper married couple." He chuckled, "but I was remembering a particular event."

She blushed at the memory of their passionate night in Keith's guest room when they'd first made love.

Jamie laughed and squeezed her hand. "Special memories Mrs Denton."

He swung the vehicle into the gravel driveway next to Keith's white cottage which was pretty as a box of shortbread. Kathryn opened the car door and Meg shot out in a streak of black and white and darted towards the entrance.

"I hope we don't meet anyone we know," said Kathryn glancing around.

At that moment, Keith appeared with Meg at his heels and said on a laugh, "Hey, I hope you're not including me."

He pulled each of them into a bear hug while Meg ran crazy circles of happiness around them.

"C'mon," said Keith, "Debra's desperate to see you both."

***

Jamie

Jamie rolled over in bed and reached for Kathryn only to find her gone. Remembering she'd risen early to paint, he groaned. This trip was like a second honeymoon and, despite his tiredness after a long session of lovemaking the night before, he was up for more. He flopped back onto the pillows and stared up at the ceiling.

Although his and Kathryn's relationship seemed as strong as ever, he was anxious a long-term separation would take its toll. The current situation was unfair on them both and he needed this undercover operation to end quickly, with a satisfactory result.

Their experience in Hell's Glen had changed him, and not just in terms of falling in love but in other smaller ways. He hardly drank now, and the only time he frequented a pub was with Kathryn, or as part of his cover. He was content to be home with his wife. She was enough.

The experience had changed Kathryn even more profoundly. When they'd first met, she couldn't bear any form of physical contact, with a mere touch triggering a panic attack. Yet in the space of only a few months, with therapy, love and patience, she'd been utterly transformed. He smiled when he thought about how eager she now was in the bedroom. He loved his wife and their new life together, and pondered on just why in hell he was putting it in jeopardy.

His thoughts turned to the Climate Warriors, and he wondered what they were up to. He'd grown fond of them, perhaps too fond, and he worried about their leader's influence on them. Ethan inspired awe and was smart enough to be aware of the effect of his charisma. Jamie realised how calculating he was; everything Ethan said and did was planned, even when he chose to be humble.

Meadow was open-hearted and easily led. Raised in a commune of women, she seemed unable to forge a life outside of the protest movement, making her vulnerable to exploitation by the likes of Ethan. She deserved better, as did Rose and

Yasmine having to share a lover. Jamie would never accept such a situation and the mere thought of sharing his wife with another man ignited a fiery jealousy.

He worried about the lads too, certain each had the potential to make more of their lives than the one Ethan offered. Alex eschewed the wealth and privilege his background offered, rather than using it as a foundation on which to make a real difference. Leon's circumstances were the opposite. The lad had a hollow space in his heart where a father's love ought to have been, and he was striving to fill it with this false family.

The ringing of Jamie's mobile interrupted his musing.

***

Kathryn

Kathryn had spent the morning on the beach with Keith painting, leaving Jamie to catch up on some much-needed sleep. In the lee of a sand dune, they'd set up director's chairs and easels amid the beachgrass. Sunlight glinted off the sea and the long grasses at the edge of the sand whispered in the gentle breeze.

Meg lay at her feet while Keith showed her how to mix sand with her paints to add texture to her work. The effect was striking. As part of her undercover legend, she'd often sketched and painted and had enjoyed it so much she'd been taking classes ever since. Glancing over at Keith's work, she realised she'd a way to go before she was as accomplished.

She poured them each a coffee from a thermos flask. Handing it to him, she asked, "Are you enjoying your retirement? Not too quiet after all the excitement of Five?"

Grinning, Keith said, "I love it, and Debra's here every other weekend or I'm at hers in Edinburgh."

Keith's partner had been the lawyer appointed by the Service to defend Jamie after he'd been wrongfully arrested during their undercover deployment. Debra ran a busy criminal law practice in Edinburgh but their relationship appeared to be thriving despite the distance and the demands of her job, a fact Kathryn took heart from.

Keith looked out towards the sea, adding, "To be honest, I needed the solace. The job was great but it took its toll, and then with the divorce and everything..." After a long pause, he turned to her and chuckled. "And you, Mrs Denton? Who'd have thought you pair would've got hitched, eh? I remember Julien worrying you'd murder each other."

She burst out laughing. "That was a real possibility at the start." When their amusement subsided, she said, "But I'm enjoying married life. I hate it when Jamie's away."

Keith nodded and gazed pensively out towards the shore again. "It was difficult for my wife too. She more or less raised the boys on her own, and even when I was home my head was somewhere else. It was hard to switch back into domestic life."

She chewed her bottom lip as Keith's words resonated loudly. She asked him about his undercover work.

"I only did a couple of jobs but they were for long stretches. One lasted almost three years." He took a gulp of coffee and added, "I shouldn't have taken it. I missed my kids growing up." After another beat, he looked at his feet and said, "And stupidly and to my shame, I gave into temptation and had a relationship with one of my targets, something I bitterly regret to this day."

She twiddled her wedding ring.

He poured his coffee dregs onto the sand. "That was the beginning of the end of my marriage. What we do is important, but it should never be at the expense of your own family."

Before Kathryn could say anything, Meg leapt up as Jamie appeared holding a phone to his ear.

Jamie said, "Sure, I'll let you know when I'm on my way. Aye, I'll pass you over to him now, he'll want to say hello." Offering the phone to Keith, he said, "Gary wants a word."

Kathryn felt a tightening in her chest knowing there must be a reason Jamie's handler had called during their holiday. The rueful smile Jamie offered her confirmed her suspicions.

Glancing at her unfinished painting, he said, "Hey, that's really good."

She put down her brush. "What did Gary want?"

He extended his hand and pulled her from the chair. "Baby, we need to talk."

The tightening sensation intensified. Leaving Keith to chat, Jamie guided her along the beach. As she trudged beside him, she noticed that the light which had been so ideal for painting a moment ago now seemed cold and flat.

When they were out of earshot, he turned, wrapped her in his arms and said, "I'm sorry, but I need to leave sooner than planned."

She groaned. "How soon?"

"Today. There's been developments and I need to get back."

Tears welled in her eyes as he dipped his head to kiss her.

Breaking away, he murmured. "I promise, as soon as this is over, we'll come back."

Clinging to him, she wept.

The Camp

"It is not surprising that in snowflake Britain, the snowflakes are melting." **— Sir John Hayes, Chair of the 'Common Sense Group' of Tory MPs, commenting on the UK's record-breaking heatwave in July 2022**

***

Jamie

2 weeks later, International Climate Camp (ICC), Germany

"Greta Thunberg's arrived," squealed Meadow sprinting into the mess tent.

There'd been a buzz in the camp about the Swedish environmentalist's eagerly anticipated speech that would launch the start of the ICC. Security was tight in the camp and the German authorities were out in force.

"What time's she speaking?" Jamie asked.

The group had arrived the previous day after a long, slow journey in Jamie's van which had been packed full of equipment. The camp was well organised and they'd been allocated a large pitch where they'd erected a catering marquee surrounded by their sleeping tents. Jamie had brought his own two-man tent which he'd pitched as far from the others as he could without causing offence, fearful he'd have a night terror or talk in his sleep. Communal sleeping was every undercover operative's nightmare for that reason and one of the things he feared most.

The ICC was host to thousands of environmental protestors from across Europe and the site they'd chosen near Berlin was enormous, spanning several hundred acres. It reminded Jamie of a music festival with its stages, stalls, teepee villages, campsites and row upon row of compost toilets. As well as multiple vegan catering stalls, there was a nature reserve, a spiritual sanctuary and a nude hot tub.

"Greta's giving her address at two," said Meadow, "I can't wait."

Jamie chuckled as he watched her bounce from foot to foot like a child expecting Santa Claus.

Over lunch, they chatted about the workshops and meetings they planned to attend. Jamie scanned the packed programme of events which listed everything from talks on climate change, to training on non-violent direct-action methods of protest.

Ethan asked what Jamie planned on attending and he told him he was interested in the Money Rebellion talk. This triggered a fierce discussion on how capitalism incentivised industries to cause ecological destruction. Jamie had heard the arguments before but this didn't prevent Ethan from proselytising.

Thumping the table with his fist, Ethan said, "The constant competition and need for efficiency, productivity, and profit is the root of the problem."

"And the flipside," agreed Yaz, "is the consumption it drives."

"Yet capitalism's done more to raise living standards than any other system," countered Alex.

That earned him a glare from Ethan.

Leon said, "I didn't have much growing up but I'm glad I lived in the West and not communist Russia."

Ethan looked outraged. "Jesus, next you'll be telling me you vote Tory."

Jamie leaned back and looked on with amusement as the lads provoked Ethan into a furious rant. Leon suggested the Conservative Party had proven green credentials, and he shot Jamie a sly wink.

Looking for an ally, Ethan said, "You're not saying much Jamie. What d'you think?"

All eyes were on him and he fixed Ethan with a cool gaze. Jamie Douglas, his easy-going legend, was normally content to sit on the side-lines and listen to debate, but it was clear Ethan and the group expected an answer. Months ago, if asked his opinion, Jamie would've regurgitated the information from his brief. Now he spoke with conviction. "I think industry takes a short-term view with little heed to the future, so it falls on governments to curb pollution and environmental destruction. And if the state won't intervene then it's up to the likes of us to put pressure on them until they do."

Have I gone native?

"Well said," remarked Ethan. "And you're right, nothing'll change unless we make a stand."

Jamie asked Ethan which seminars he planned to attend and he said there was one about creating a zero-carbon future that interested him.

Intending to shadow Ethan as much as possible, Jamie made a mental note to add that to his list. Jamie knew Ethan had been in communication with a German activist called 'K', and it was this worrying development that'd cut short his leave. Fitz had intercepted their messages which revealed the two planned to meet at the ICC. MI5 had been provided with a list of known extremists by the German authorities and they suspected his contact was Karsten Wolff, a radical who described himself as a 'green anarchist'.

Jamie had spent hours studying the brief on Wolff and he'd memorised his face along with a few others on Five's grid.

Knowing the ICC was probably teaming with the likes of Wolff, Jamie had been anxious from the moment he'd arrived. On a normal operation, backup was always nearby, just a phone call away. But not here.

Here, he was on his own.

***

Kathryn

from:	Kathryn Douglas <Kathryn.Douglas@tacitnet.mi5.uk>
to:	Harriet.Stockbridge@tacitnet.mi5.uk
subject:	Synergistico Vulnerability
security:	AES-256 encryption

Hi Harriet,

Just to let you know I found a serious vulnerability while testing the Synergistico application. Details attached but in summary there's a backdoor that could let a hacker penetrate our systems and gain access to sensitive data.

I've contacted the developers to request a change but it won't be a quick fix.

Hope this helps,

Kathryn

***

from:	Harriet Stockbridge < Harriet.Stockbridge@tacitnet.mi5.uk >
to:	Kathryn.Douglas@tacitnet.mi5.uk
subject:	Synergistico Vulnerability
security:	AES-256 encryption

All interdepartmental communications must come through me and follow the correct process. In future, kindly raise a change request containing the required details, appropriate severity code, with my name in the Approver field. Synergistico will then ensure the issue comes to my attention and is actioned in the proper manner, where I deem it necessary. In the meantime, I've instructed the developers not to spend any time on this.

Furthermore, I note that you have not been assigned the task of testing that app. If you do not have enough work to do, let me know so I can assign you additional tickets.

I am concerned that you are struggling to embrace changes designed to bring about improvements within the Service, so I would like to offer you additional training to help you adapt.

H.

Dr. Harriet Stockbridge MSc. PhD (Oxon) ICP-SYS
Director of Agile Development Programmes

***

Kathryn pressed her hands to her lips and re-read Harriet's reply. As if sensing her distress, Meg shifted beneath her desk and whined.

She'd been trying to be helpful; to go above and beyond what was expected, especially given her precarious situation with Vetting. She'd heard nothing from Robin since the bad-tempered review meeting, but the threat loomed over her like the sword of Damocles. In raising this vulnerability issue, had she just handed Robin the means to end her career? Or worse?

Chewing her fingernails, she glanced at Harriet's office in the far corner, but her door was closed and the blinds shut. Was she already reporting her to Vetting?

Fitz had the day off and she sorely missed his counsel. Certain he'd advise her to speak to Julien, she checked their boss's calendar but he was chock-a-block with meetings that ran late into the evening. And, conscious of how stressed

Julien seemed, she was reluctant to add to his worries. But, surely highlighting vulnerabilities in MI5's systems was an integral part of her role; after all she was a cybersecurity analyst.

Harriet's message, however, had made it clear Kathryn was not to circumvent the chain of command, and she feared that, were she to involve Julien, Harriet would instigate formal disciplinary procedures. A written warning would be akin to handing Robin her head on a platter. Reluctantly, Kathryn closed the message and moved it to her burgeoning 'Cover Your Arse' folder.

She drove home through heavy traffic, her mood as damp and miserable as the weather beyond the windscreen. Leaving her phone in the cottage, she took the dog for a walk in the hope the fresh air and exercise would lift her spirits. When she reached the grassy common, she unhooked Meg's lead and used the ball launcher to throw a tennis ball across the slopes. As she waited for the collie to fetch it, she savoured the earthy scent of the summer rain and thought about her husband. She desperately needed to hear his voice and know he was safe. She whistled for Meg but, to her dismay, the dog refused to come back. Dusk had fallen by the time Kathryn left.

Picking her way over the slippery path, she pulled the collar of her thin coat against the rain. As she approached the gate leading into the lane, a shape emerged from the trees and Kathryn's heart skipped a beat. Meg barked ferociously and strained against her leash.

It was her neighbour, Darren. She laughed in relief and tried to calm herself and the dog.

Darren's eyes roved over her and settled on her chest. "I haven't seen Jamie for a while."

Taking a step back, she said, "He's working up north." She turned away.

He gave a nervous cough. "You must get lonely."

She met his gaze and swallowed hard, recognising that look and the intention behind it. There was no one else around and the darkness seemed to creep in around her. Every instinct told her to flee but she felt rooted to the spot. Her breathing quickened and she braced herself.

Is he going to attack me?

Darren was short and squat but strong enough to overpower her unless she fought dirty. Desperately trying to remember her self-defence training, she placed the flimsy ball launcher under her arm and grasped for the bundle of keys in her pocket. Meg snarled at him, her hackles raised.

Kathryn croaked, "I expect him back any minute, in fact I must get home." She backed away, dragging Meg with her.

After putting distance between them, she turned and hurried along the lane. A streetlight was out, and she almost lost her footing in the mud. Hearing footsteps behind her, she hastened her pace, half expecting to feel his hand around her throat at any moment. It was a short distance to the cottage but the walk felt like the longest of her life. Heart pounding, she darted to her door and fumbled with her keys. Only when she was safely inside did she risk a glance back.

Darren watched her from the shadows beneath the broken streetlamp.

Kathryn double-locked the front door, closed the curtains, and checked all the doors and windows were secure. Pulse still racing, she darted upstairs into the spare room which overlooked the lane, but there was no sign of him. From her bedroom, she peered into his property and saw him enter his home office and sit at the desk.

As she watched Darren on the computer, she thought about phoning the police. But what would she say? A man had acted odd and followed her? It was hardly a crime. She didn't want to worry Jamie while he was away as there was nothing he could do in any case. She needed to sort this out herself.

Knowing she'd have to be careful not to get caught, she powered on her laptop. Bought with her first salary cheques, it was state of the art with more memory than she could shake a USB stick at.

As it whirred to life, she recalled what'd happened to her as a child and the effect her stepfather's abuse had had on her adult life. She'd clipped her own wings and retreated into cyberspace and, although Jamie had wrenched her back into the real world, the trauma continued to have a profound effect. She constantly checked over her shoulder when she was alone outside, looking for escape routes and exits, and she wore modest outfits and shoes she could run away in. It angered Kathryn that it was women who'd to change how they dressed and moved around to make themselves feel safe, stripping away their freedom, both socially and mentally.

Hacking Darren's internet connection was a walk in the cyber park. She began by scanning for local WIFI connections and almost laughed when she spotted one called 'Darrensnet'. The idiot was still using his router's default password so she was inside his network in a flash, covering her tracks in the process.

After launching software to scan the contents of his machine, she made a mug of tea and settled down to her task. It reminded her of many similar evenings spent with her Grey Nemesis buddies and she felt a pang of nostalgia.

The warm feeling didn't last. The contents of Darren's computer were as chilling as they were disturbing.

***

Jamie

After listening to Greta's rousing speech, Jamie returned to camp and helped the Climate Warriors set up equipment for their workshops. Meadow was offering sessions on Reiki and Herbal Medicine, while Rose ran a workshop called 'Repair what you wear' on mending and repurposing clothes. Jamie and Leon had advertised climbing lessons for later in the week, and within an hour of posting them, every slot had been filled.

Despite the apocalyptic theme of the ICC, there was an atmosphere of optimism in the camp which was almost palpable. Everywhere Jamie turned, people greeted and welcomed him, often with offers of free food and refreshments. He'd begun to feel more relaxed, helped in part by copious amounts of vegan wine. The ICC, he decided, was miles better than any music festival.

When it was time for the lecture on creating a zero-carbon future, Jamie accompanied Ethan to the packed marquee. Ethan surfed on his phone while they waited but Jamie couldn't see the screen clearly enough to know what he was up to. Initially, Jamie had found it difficult to get to know the driving force behind the group. Ethan's passion for the climate campaign was not in question and he devoted himself to it but Jamie couldn't help thinking the cause could just as easily be animal rights or political. Ethan needed a bandwagon like some people need religion.

Jamie's reverie was broken by a burst of applause as Karsten Wolff was announced as the next speaker. Jamie recognised him immediately from his profile picture as he strode onto the stage and took his place at the lectern. Tall and muscular with dark hair and a fashionable scruff on his face, Wolff looked like a film star, and Jamie noticed the enthusiasm with which many of the women welcomed him. Confident and assured, he appeared at ease as he thanked the large assembly, flashing a perfect Hollywood smile.

He began quietly, speaking perfect English with a soft German accent. He recounted the aims of the Paris Climate Agreement, a legally binding international treaty aimed at reducing greenhouse gas emissions to limit global temperature rises. The screen behind him flickered into life, displaying doomsday scenes of the effects of climate warming above agreed levels. Cataclysmic pictures of severe drought, glacial melting, rising sea levels, wildfires, superstorms and coral reef destruction appeared on a reel. The audience fell silent.

Wolff spoke eloquently about the 'carbon budget' which, he explained, was the amount of carbon that could be burnt without raising global temperatures. He cited a speech by Greta Thunberg criticising governments for putting their efforts into creative accounting and 'green washing', rather than reducing CO2 emissions. There were cheers at mention of her name.

Following a scathing account of the aviation industry's contribution to global warming, an image of a vast coal mine in Poland filled the screen as Wolff talked about the continued reliance on fossil fuels. His voice became more powerful as he explained companies were still investing billions of dollars in exploration, although the world had fifteen times the amount of fossil fuel that could be burnt while remaining within the carbon budget.

After a dramatic pause, he pointed to the screen and said, "Meanwhile, governments continue to subsidise this industry. Imagine what we could do if these subsidies were diverted to renewable energy sources?"

Another pause, and then louder, "And in cases where renewable energy subsidies have been levied, they've been wasted on big biomass which causes more deforestation, more pollution and more climate change. We're effectively subsidising ecocide."

As muttered agreement rippled through the crowd, his voice reached a crescendo. "If we continue at current levels, we'll have blown the carbon budget by 2030. Increasing temperatures will cause glaciers and ice caps to melt, sea levels to rise and engulf low areas. Deserts will grow and storms will become more violent, leaving vast areas uninhabitable. Entire species will become extinct."

Pictures of dying polar bears and koalas appeared, followed by a disturbing video of a family fleeing a Californian wildfire which caused gasps from the delegates. He added, "Human populations will either die or be forced to migrate, which will cause major political unrest."

Wolff thumped a fist on the lectern and shouted, "We need stronger action to bring about immediate change and stop emissions today. And we need governments to stop subsidising the fossil fuel industry and divert this money into sustainable renewables. Before it's too late!"

The marquee erupted in applause and delegates stood and cheered. Amidst this rapture, Jamie wondered what the hell Wolff meant by 'stronger action'.

As a fire ball exploded on-screen, Wolff's voice dropped to a low register and he leaned towards the microphone.

With a fanatical stare, he said, "We're running out of time."

***

Kathryn

Kathryn stared at her discovery in disgust. Darren was an 'incel'.

A portmanteau of 'involuntary' and 'celibate', the term described a community of men who hate women. Hydra-like in nature, it consisted of a sprawling network of forums, web sites, blogs, video channels and chatrooms, all centred around a violent, misogynistic ideology. These views were nothing new but, thanks to the internet, the men who shared them were able to come together and flourish.

Several years ago, Darren had stumbled on an incel forum via a private gaming chatroom. Under the username 'LonelyVirgin', he'd begun by sharing the fact he'd had no luck with women and was frustrated at being unable to find a partner. He described himself as five-foot, fat and ugly, which one member said made him a 'heightcel'; an unacceptably short man.

Darren revealed he was still living at home but, with a low-paid job, he'd little prospect of that changing. The community immediately responded by telling him the odds were stacked against men like him. One member explained how women held all the cards, going as far as to suggest there was a female-centric conspiracy to keep men docile. Another outlined the 80/20 theory; the idea that the top 20% of men enjoy 80% of the sex. This post prompted a lament of the 'sexual marketplace' where, according to the incels, young women slept with attractive 'alpha fucks' only to settle for less desirable 'beta bucks' whom they could exploit financially. Reading the content, Kathryn shook her head in disbelief.

The community appeared to be full of sad, lonely and, in some cases, suicidal men in need of professional help. For guys like Darren, this was a seductive world in which nothing was their fault. They were the ones discriminated against — the underdogs, the victims — and their suffering had nothing to do with their failings and everything to do with women. What also became apparent from his posts was Darren's need to belong, and to carve out an identity. The community served this purpose, and he was welcomed into it.

Incels shared a language Kathryn initially found difficult to understand. She consulted a glossary to decipher terms such as 'foid', meaning a female humanoid since 'woman' conveyed too much of a sense of humanity. The community's vitriolic ideology was often masked behind a smokescreen of wit, mockery and sarcasm which made it impossible to tell whether the comments were meant or not. Ironically, most of Darren's posts appeared on a site that stated hate speech was not allowed.

She noted he avoided any factions within the community devoted to self-improvement. Instead, Darren believed he was a hopeless case and, reading his posts, she almost felt sorry for him. Most of the community offered support and encouragement but it had its fair share of trolls, including one who told him to 'go rope yourself'.

After his initial foray, Darren's account lay dormant for months and during this period, Kathryn suspected he was lurking; reading, listening, and absorbing the violent, anti-feminist world view espoused by the community. When he became active again, his posts had an edge to them that made her shudder. He described himself as having taken 'the red pill' — a reference to *The Matrix* film — when his blinkers finally fell away and he could see the world how it really was: a 'gynocracy'. He admitted relief at being able to share feelings that he knew were unacceptable outside this circle.

Needing something stronger than tea to fortify her, Kathryn poured a glass of wine before examining Darren's recent activity. On one site, he'd supported a motion to change the legal system so women were regarded as property, first of their fathers and then of their husbands. He touted the belief that the problem was not one of women having sex but having the choice of whom to have sex with. According to Darren, sex should be redistributed, and men should be able to keep women as sexual slaves, arguing that the practice had long been a part of human history. Kathryn recoiled at photographs of Yazidi women and girls being sold at market in Iraq, and the comments these images prompted.

Darren had developed a feverish obsession with sex and his posts were laced with righteous anger at being denied it. The community only stoked the flames of his rage, pushing the notion that women were hungry for it but chose only to sleep with alphas. When someone asked why he didn't just visit a prostitute, he responded, "Because it's fake, and why should I pay for what is rightfully mine."

At that point, Kathryn took a break and topped up her glass before reading his latest posts. By the time she'd finished, she wanted a scalding bath and to finish the bottle. In the course of only a few months, Daren had been radicalised. The first indication that his online rantings threatened to spill over into the real world was in a post entitled 'Why rape should be legalised' in which he justified this with pseudoscience and fake statistics. The post received a record number of likes.

As time went on, he became increasingly despising of women, describing them as sub-human and deserving of rape. He wrote, "women are not sentient beings and should have no human rights." He advocated sexual and physical violence as a form of punishment then later, torture and murder.

Reading Darren's latest vitriol, her blood turned to ice.

[LonelyVirgin]*Just stalked a bitch. Husband's away but she still won't share her pussy. Seeing her terror gave me a raging hard-on*

Trembling, she switched off her computer and then checked the doors and windows were locked. She part-set the burglar alarm, placed her phone on the nightstand and slipped a long Maglite torch under the bed.

She lay awake haunted by the disturbing things she'd read and the graphic images she'd seen.

THE KNIFE

***"Half of humanity is in the danger zone, from floods, droughts, extreme storms and wildfires. No nation is immune. Yet we continue to feed our fossil fuel addiction ... We have a choice. Collective action or collective suicide. It is in our hands."* — António Guterres, UN secretary general 2022**

***

Kathryn

The following morning, Kathryn trudged to the 'Who Moved My Cheese' training session that Harriet had arranged for her and Fitz to attend. Based on the best-selling book of the same name, the course was about adapting to change. Kathryn had cursed when she'd spotted the invite in her inbox, and apologised to Fitz who'd merely shrugged and muttered it was a morning off work and a free lunch.

The course was held in Thames House and they were joined by a dozen others from various departments. Kathryn wondered what dreadful infraction they'd committed to find themselves inside the seventh circle of hell. Penelope, their instructor, looked about fifteen and was enthusiastic to the point of being annoying. She'd long dark hair scraped back from her face with an Alice band, and wore a navy twin set with white piping.

"Ooh, let's all play a game," announced Penelope, bouncing on her toes.

Fitz looked at Kathryn and rolled his eyes. "Ooh, yes let's," he said in a low voice, so only she could hear.

Penelope used a piece of rope to outline a circle on the floor which she explained represented their comfort zone, and she asked everyone to step inside the circle. Kathryn stood next to Fitz away from the others.

Smiling, Penelope said, "I'm going to give you a number of scenarios, and for each I want you either to remain inside your comfort zone or step outside into the 'discomfort' area. After a few lame examples, she said, "Now, imagine you're about to parachute from an aeroplane."

Grinning, Kathryn remained inside the circle as Fitz leapt out. To her surprise, she found herself alone.

"Wonderful" bubbled Penelope. "Now, how uncomfortable did that feel?"

Fitz said under his breath, "Almost as uncomfortable as this effin' course," which made Kathryn snigger.

One of the delegates shared that he'd a fear of heights and there was murmured agreement.

"Excellent," said Penelope, clutching her hands together. "Ooh, now let's try another. Imagine you're trapped inside a crowded carriage on the London Underground."

Kathryn swapped places with Fitz.

She whispered, "Surely you wouldn't want to be in that situation."

"Hey, I spend most mornings with my face in a stranger's armpit. Why d'you think I take the tube?" Fitz made a comedy face that made her laugh.

Kathryn shuddered at the thought of being pressed against strange bodies. Since moving to the south east, she'd been on the underground once when it was quiet and that experience had been well outside of her comfort zone, even with Jamie beside her. She avoided public transport whenever possible.

After the session ended, Penelope handed them each a certificate and a paperback of 'Who Moved My Cheese' which Kathryn intended to feed to the recycling bin.

The caterers arrived bearing trays of sandwiches and cakes. There was a knock at the door and Kathryn stifled a groan when Harriet joined them. Kathryn exchanged a look with Fitz and headed for the food. After filling their plates, they chatted with the others.

After a few minutes, Fitz whispered, "Incoming."

Kathryn turned to find herself faced with Harriet who held a plate so laden with food it was in danger of breaking. Penelope loitered at her side.

Casting a disparaging look at Kathryn's modest attire, Harriet asked how she'd found the course and what she'd learned. Kathryn replied with a glib spiel about embracing change and enjoying the challenges it brings. Penelope beamed with approval. Kathryn avoided making eye contact with Fitz whose shoulders shook with mirth.

"I'm surprised they don't teach these soft skills to students," said Harriet. "There ought to be a foundational module taught at every university."

Penelope agreed and this led onto a discussion about people's educational background. Kathryn was surprised at the number who'd joined the Service straight from Oxford and Cambridge. Fitz revealed he'd studied electronic engineering at college before completing his degree at Buckinghamshire New University.

Harriet wrinkled her nose. "I've never heard of that establishment. Must be one of those new-fangled ones."

Penelope brayed like a donkey and Fitz bristled but said nothing.

Harriet's eyes landed on Kathryn. "And which university did you go to?" she asked.

She'd been dreading the question and felt every eye upon her. "Uhm, I didn't."

Her reply was met with an uncomfortable silence broken only when Fitz said, "Kathryn has a skill set no university can teach. She's amazing at —"

With a triumphant smile, Harriet cut him off with, "Goodness me, our standards really have slipped."

Speechless, Kathryn blushed a volcanic shade of red.

***

Jamie

Jamie mopped sweat from his brow as he stirred the lentil chilli he and Meadow had prepared. The task of cooking made him maudlin, reminding him of happy times spent with Kathryn in the kitchen when they'd chat over flaming pans and feed each other morsels. Often a prelude to lovemaking, he'd lost count of the dinners they'd burnt as a result. As he worked, he tried not to dwell upon the miles separating them.

Despite his attempts to shadow Ethan, he'd vanished in the company of Karsten Wolff after his speech. Jamie had used the opportunity to find a quiet spot at the edge of camp to send the photographs he'd taken, and call Gary to confirm Wolff was the group's likely contact.

Gary answered on the second ring with, "Well, this confirms our worst fears. You need to stick to that bastard like shit to a blanket."

Trouble was, as Jamie explained, there was still no blanket to be seen and the camp was too vast to go searching for his target.

After wrapping up the call, Jamie returned and plonked a case of vegan wine he'd bought earlier onto the table. Leon rewarded him with a lop-sided grin and hunted for tumblers.

As the group tucked into the food, they laughed and joked about the events and seminars they'd attended.

Yasmine had gone to a talk on tree planting and landscaping designed to maximise CO2 absorption, which didn't surprise Jamie since she and Rose ran the Salford back-garden eco-warriors project. They spent their free time planting insect-friendly gardens and tending allotments which supplied much of the group's staple diet. Between the organic gardening and skip-diving, they were almost self-sufficient in food, although rations were meagre. Leon told them about a meeting hosted by *Wretched of the Earth*, an environmental group that focused on ethnic voices. Alex had them in gales of laughter as he recounted his nude hot tub experience with a beautiful young woman.

As the wine flowed, Jamie became aware of Meadow stealing glances at him when she thought he wasn't looking. His attempts to let her down gently were clearly not having the desired effect.

Jamie had moderated his drinking but the rest of the group were half-cut when Ethan appeared with Karsten Wolff. They were accompanied by a man called Ferdinand Meyer who Jamie recognised from his dossier as another eco-anarchist. Tall and powerfully built like Wolff, Meyer had blonde hair and blue eyes that were wary and watchful.

An antipodean, Meyer had been part of the Fireproof Australia group, a break-away Extinction Rebellion faction. Set up after the 2019-20 Black Summer bushfires that killed hundreds, the group believed in civil resistance proportional to the existential threat they faced. However, when Meyer had wanted to ratchet up their action, the group had kicked him out, and he'd come to Europe.

Wolff shook Jamie's hand firmly and said, "I've been hearing all about you."

"Nothing good I hope," replied Jamie.

Wolff laughed. "Ethan has been telling me what a great contribution you've made to the group."

"I'm just the driver," said Jamie, handing Wolff and Meyer a glass of wine.

"Hardly, he tells us you're a logistics genius and an expert climber. They're very lucky to have you."

Ethan said, "We couldn't manage without Jamie, he's heaven-sent." Then turning to Meadow, he added, "and talking of angels, this is Meadow."

Jamie noticed the sweep of Wolff's gaze as he regarded Meadow who became flustered under his scrutiny. As he watched the interplay between them, Jamie felt angry as every protective instinct he possessed suddenly flared. Meadow seemed to notice and threw him a curious glance as Wolff engaged her in conversation.

Wolff and Meyer spent an hour chatting with them. Neither drank much, refusing Jamie's offer to replenish their glasses. Wolff kept topping up Meadow's while Ethan hung on the German's every word.

Meadow showed the two visitors around the camp and workshops, and Wolff asked if he could take photographs for the ICC's social media campaign. Jamie pulled his baseball cap lower and tried to avoid being included but Wolff insisted and rounded them up for a group shot. Meadow stood next to Jamie and slid her arm around his waist, thwarting his attempts to dodge behind Rose.

As soon as Wolff and Meyer left, Rose raised a challenging eyebrow and said to Ethan, "You lot seem very chummy."

With a self-satisfied smile, Ethan said, "There's something we need to discuss."

Rose shot back, "Which usually means you've made a decision and you're telling us what it is."

Raising his palms, he replied, "That's unfair. We always take decisions as a group."

Yasmine said, "Let's hear what he's got to say." She placed her hand over Ethan's which earned her a sneer from Rose.

When a stony silence set in, Jamie prompted, "So, what is it?"

Ethan leaned forward and in a low voice said, "Karsten wants to join us in the UK for a few weeks. He's got ideas ... you know ... for more effective actions we can try."

Rose pursed her lips. "I bet he's got plenty of ideas, and none of them legal. I know his type."

"Don't be like that Rose," said Ethan, "we could learn a lot from him."

This ignited another heated debate with Ethan arguing their current efforts were ineffective, and Rose vehemently disagreeing. Ethan looked for allies but Meadow also expressed reservations saying she knew little about Wolff and what she did know wasn't good.

Rose said, "How d'you know we can trust him?"

"He's well-respected in activist circles. I checked him out," said Ethan. "Anyway, it's only for a few weeks to help us plan actions that'll really make a difference."

"We are making a difference," thundered Rose.

More argument ensued and Jamie listened until he was fairly sure of each member of the group's position. He hoped he'd read them correctly considering what he was about to suggest to bring this operation to a swift and successful conclusion

He cut across the arguing. "All those in favour of having Karsten join us, raise a hand."

Rose glowered at him and kept her hands firmly on the table along with Meadow and Leon. Ethan, Alex and Yasmine voted in favour, leaving Jamie with the deciding vote. They all looked at him with pleading eyes and he groaned. He'd misjudged the opposition to Wolff.

Leon laughed, "You were the one who wanted a show of hands."

"Aye, serves me right," he chuckled, slowly raising his.

Rose shot him a curdling look. "You disappoint me, Jamie. I didn't think you of all people would vote for anarchy."

Jamie stopped himself from pointing out that anarchists don't vote.

"Oh that's unfair," said Ethan, "it has nothing to do with anarchy. Why do you always twist everything?"

Jamie raised both hands in surrender, "I believe there's no harm in finding out what Karsten has to offer. If we don't like it, we don't do it. It's as simple as that."

Ignoring him, Rose turned the full force of her ire on Ethan. "This used to be a collective. It's not anymore. And it has everything to do with you needing to take control. That's why men were never part of decision making at Greenham."

Ethan surged to his feet and glowered. "Oh, don't start banging on about bloody Greenham Common again, I'm sick of listening to it. We've taken a vote. Respect the democratic process and stop trying to make this about men versus women."

Taking Yasmine's hand, he pulled her to her feet. With a venomous look at Rose, he snarled, "Suggest you bunk with Meadow tonight." He then led Yasmine to the tent he shared with the two women.

Rose looked like her heart had been pierced with a blade. Tears filled her eyes and she fled. Meadow cursed and ran after her, leaving Jamie and the lads exchanging awkward looks.

"For fuck's sake," said Leon, "that was harsh. Rose didn't deserve that."

There was muttered agreement and Jamie took that as his cue to go to bed, leaving the lads to finish the wine. As he crawled into his sleeping bag, he could hear Ethan and Yaz making love even louder than usual. He hoped Rose was out of earshot.

He lay in the dark, his thoughts full of Kathryn and how much he missed her. As his black mood engulfed him, he tried reminding himself of the importance of his task and the fact people's lives depended on what he and his colleagues did. It didn't work; he knew in his heart that being separated from his wife was too great a price to pay. She came first. Always. And if that meant pursuing a different career, then so be it.

He desperately needed to bring this business to a swift end, which was why he'd voted as he did. With Karsten under his nose, he was certain it wouldn't be long before the group were either arrested or deemed not to be a threat. The thought of his friends in prison troubled him. Somewhere along the way, he'd stopped regarding them as targets and that troubled him more.

Eventually, he drifted off to sleep only to wake with a start. Disoriented and dazed, it took him a moment to realise where he was and the sound that'd woken him was the tent's zipper. He sat bolt upright, heart pounding. Scrabbling around for the long Maglite torch, he struggled out of the top of his sleeping bag and shone the beam on the opening. Meadow popped her head through the inner lining, shielding her eyes from the glare.

He exhaled a relieved breath and placed the torch down, still lit. "Christ, you nearly gave me heart failure. What's up?"

Crawling on all-fours, she launched herself at him, her boozy mouth searching for his. He fell backwards and she was on top of him, her hands in his hair, her mouth hungry. Startled, he rolled her over and pushed himself off, shocked to see she was clad only in her underwear.

"Whoa Meadow," he gasped as he positioned himself as far away from her as the tent allowed.

She shot him an incredulous look and propped herself up on her elbows. "Hey, what's wrong?"

He sat back on his haunches. "I'm married, that's what's wrong."

"You're separated. Oh, for chrissakes, it's only sex Jamie, it's no big deal."

Shaking his head, he said, "It is to me." When tears welled in her eyes, he said more gently, "I'm sorry, but you asked me once if I'm exclusive. Well, the answer's yes. With my wife."

She sat up and he tried hard not to let his eyes stray to her breasts straining against the sheer fabric of the bra.

"So, what was all that earlier?" she huffed. "I saw how you looked at me when I was talking to Karsten. So, you don't want me but you don't want anyone else to have me either."

He blew out a breath. "It's not like that at all."

She sniffed and wiped her eyes with the back of her hand. "So, what do you want Jamie?"

He rummaged around in his rucksack and passed her a t-shirt. "Here, put this on."

With an angry glare, she tossed the garment aside, and then reached behind her back and unclipped her pink lacy bra. Wide-eyed, he gazed at her body as she slowly peeled it off. He couldn't help it.

Oh fuck!

Tilting her head, she whispered, "I know you're attracted to me, so what's stopping you? Come on, where's the harm?"

Using both hands, she fondled herself making her nipples bead, and then she reached for his hand and guided it to her breast. He pulled away as if burnt.

Swallowing hard, he kept his eyes fixed on hers. "Err, Meadow, I appreciate the offer, I really do, but please put the t-shirt on." He offered her the garment again.

"Jesus Jamie, you're such a bloody prude." She pulled the t-shirt on over her head and glared at him. Then her anger vanished and her eyes brimmed with tears.

Reaching out a tentative hand, he caressed her cheek. "Hey, it's not you, it's me. I'm not ready to move on and it's not fair on you while that's the case. You're a friend Meadow and I don't want to do anything to damage that."

Weeping now, she lent her forehead against his chest and he stroked her hair. She gazed up at him with glassy green eyes and he caught his breath. Her seeking lips were inches from his.

She said, "Can I sleep here tonight?"

"Uhm, I'm not sure that's a good idea."

"Please Jamie, don't push me away. I just need you to hold me. Surely that's not too much to ask?"

Despite her pleading, he stood firm. "I'll take you back to your tent."

He didn't want to hurt Meadow, he was fond of her, but it was true, he was exclusive. Since meeting Kathryn, he'd been completely disinterested in other women and he knew that, no matter the temptation, he'd never do anything to harm their relationship. Thank God she couldn't see him right now; if she could, she'd cut off his balls and feed them to Meg.

After seeing Meadow to her tent, Jamie returned to his. As he lay in the dark, thoughts of his wife flitted through his mind and he wondered how Kathryn was coping on her own. Despite his exhaustion and the alcohol in his bloodstream, he was too unsettled to sleep and it took him ages to fall over. When he woke to the sound of the tent's zipper again, he expected to see Meadow.

What he didn't expect was a figure wielding a knife.

The MP

"There's one issue that will define the contours of this century more dramatically than any other, and that is the urgent threat of a changing climate." — Barack Obama 2014

***

Kathryn

Yawning, Kathryn glanced up from her monitor. Darkness had fallen outside. The office was empty except for a team of cleaners and the sleeping dog at her feet. She'd wanted to drive home in daylight, and she cursed at the thought of returning to an empty house watched by her creepy neighbour.

As she was about to pack up and leave, an alert popped up on her screen to notify her of activity on project Alabaster, the one she thought of as the 'Russian job'. The Intelligence Services used sophisticated artificial intelligence software to trawl the digital ether for data linked to targets on their grid, and the colour of this alert indicated it was important.

She clicked on the alert and the Russian diplomat's file filled her screen. MI5's dossier was comprehensive and contained translations of official documentation from the Russian authorities, including Dimitri Balakin's passport, driving licence, bank details, and information about his family and known associates. She scanned the details, although she was familiar with the contents.

Born in a Moscow suburb, Balakin had studied languages at university before joining the military. After a short spell in special forces, he'd gone to work for the Russian Ministry of Foreign Affairs, where he'd been employed for the last six years. However, Kathryn had found a document showing Balakin was actually in the employ of the Russian Foreign Intelligence Service, known as the SVR. This was a similar organisation to Britain's Secret Intelligence Service (SIS), more commonly known as MI6 or simply 'Six'. This was not a surprise, and it confirmed Julien's suspicions he was in fact a spy.

Before arriving in London, Balakin had been tenured at the Russian embassy in Germany. Kathryn had contacted her counterparts there to find out what intelligence they had on him but they'd yet to reply.

After exhausting the official documentation sources, Kathryn had examined Balakin's digital media profile and any press articles in which he appeared. He'd recently been seen at a number of trade delegations alongside Russian entrepreneurs, industrialists and exporters but, other than that, his public profile was sterile. He used his middle name — Mikhail — for anything personal, but he'd been inactive on social platforms for months.

Conscious of the late hour, Kathryn drilled deeper into the details of the alert to discover Balakin had been spotted in a London restaurant in the company of an attractive young woman called Carly Milliken. The girl was of little interest to MI5, but her father was another matter. A director of a company that manufactured portable solar panels used by the military, he was a definite red flag.

Got you!

***

Jamie

Jamie saw the flash of the blade before it thrust towards his gut. He twisted and landed against the side of the tent. And then the figure was on top of him, eyes wild between the slit of a black balaclava. He tried to drive the knife into Jamie's throat.

Through gritted teeth, Jamie grappled with the attacker's wrist, the blade mere centimetres from his neck. He could barely make out his assailant's shape in the twilight but he was strong; too strong, and Jamie knew he risked being overpowered in seconds.

Jamie bucked and bridged beneath him and then rolled. It bought him only milliseconds but enough to wrench the knife away and headbutt. Grunting loudly, the figure drove a fist into Jamie's face which sent him reeling backwards. Lights flashed behind his eyes and he fought to remain conscious. Cursing, he lashed out, his punch finding its mark, but mashing his knuckles in the process.

Shouts went up outside and his attacker dived from the tent and disappeared into the night. Jamie searched frantically for his torch and switched it on just as Leon's head ducked into the tent.

"What the fuck man?" said Leon, "are you okay?"

Jamie's heart pounded painfully against his rib cage as he caught his breath. Clutching his injured hand, he said, "Aye, I'm fine, someone just got the wrong tent."

Shielding his eyes from the beam, Leon looked unconvinced. Jamie angled the torch away, and they gasped at what they saw.

Glinting in the corner, was a large Bowie knife with a jagged blade.

***

Kathryn

After working late to dig into Balakin's new companion, Kathryn had sent a summary of her findings on project Alabaster to Julien and Fitz. Next morning, they met in Julien's office to discuss her findings. Although she was fond of Fitz, it rankled that he'd to oversee her work, something he seemed equally unhappy about.

Julien had dark circles ringing his eyes. He sipped coffee and listened intently as she outlined what she'd discovered.

Originally from the far north of Scotland, Carly's father, Ian, had joined the RAF and trained as a pilot. After several tours and an exemplary service record, he'd retired relatively young on a Wing Commander's pension, and segued into freelance work as a consultant. He was currently employed by a company called Renew Venture Technology (RVT) who held several contracts with the Ministry of Defence, including one for portable solar panels.

Kathryn displayed RVT's website on the screen in Julien's office. She explained the company's kit was so lightweight and durable that it could be carried in a rucksack, used for auxiliary power on vehicles, or chained together to create a solar field base, reducing the need for fuel convoys.

"In other words, it's not the sort of tech we want our Russian friends to get hold of," said Julien frowning.

Fitz asked about the rest of Carly's family and Kathryn told him they'd settled in Oxfordshire where Ian's wife ran an interior design company which employed their daughter. Carly owned a small flat ten minutes walk from the family home; a property her parents had helped her buy with a generous deposit. However, despite the financial leg-up, Carly's finances were in a desperate state.

The frown lines on Julien's brow deepened. "We'll need surveillance."

"I'll notify A4," said Fitz.

Julien rose and went back to his desk. Assuming the meeting was over, Kathryn closed her laptop and began bundling up her papers, but Julien returned with a manilla folder which he handed her.

"I need your help with something sensitive," said Julien.

The file was labelled 'FLYING CIRCUS. TOP SECRET – UK EYES ONLY'. She'd learned about such documents during training but this was the first time she'd seen one bearing the highest classification. Although she'd clearance, she glanced at Julien before opening it and he nodded. Inside was a face she recognised; the Scottish Conservative MP Alasdair Montrose. Known as 'Monty', he was a stalwart of the party and tipped to become a possible leadership candidate.

After graduating from St Andrew's University, Monty had worked in business before establishing his own company, and seeking election as an MP for the East Deeside constituency. After serving as a Parliamentary Private Secretary, he was appointed to the Scottish Office where he had responsibility for energy policy and regulation.

Monty was one of few Tory MPs in Scotland. Since Thatcher, Scottish Conservatives were as rare as sightings of the Loch Ness Monster, and she recalled that Monty had only survived the last election with a slim majority. The Scottish Nationalist Party were nipping at his heels.

Julien steepled his hands and observed Kathryn as she scanned the dossier. He said, "Monty's earmarked for a position on the Defence Select Committee which oversees the Ministry of Defence and armed forces."

Kathryn suspected that appointing Monty to the Committee was a cynical manoeuvre by the UK government to keep the Scottish MPs on-side, given the looming threat of another Independence Referendum. In debates about the possible breakup of the Union, defence was a big stick with which the unionists and nationalists beat one another. Responsibility for defence was not devolved to the Scottish Parliament and remained under Westminster's control along with the use of Scottish military bases such as Faslane, home to the UK's nuclear deterrent Trident. Appointing Monty was the government's way of underlining their belief that the status quo delivered greater security than having separate military forces.

Julien added, "Before he can be appointed to the committee, we need a thorough background check."

Kathryn wondered if being entrusted with such a task was Julien's way of reassuring her he paid no heed to Vetting's low opinion of her. She asked if he wanted her to look for anything in particular.

"We need to be certain he's squeaky clean. No mistresses, boyfriends, dodgy dealings or affiliations that could compromise him and his family, or embarrass the government." The lines on Julien's brow furrowed as he regarded her. "You can appreciate why this is sensitive, given how prominent a figure he is, and the Home Secretary has personally authorised his vetting."

Steepling his hands again, Julien fixed her with a stern look. "Needless to say, it's vital you operate strictly within the remit of the Security Service Act. No going off piste on this one."

Julien then spent the next five minutes lecturing her on all the things she mustn't do during her investigation, and about the need to remain politically neutral. As he prattled on, she thought of all the hacking methods she'd like to use that would yield better results, but it seemed most of these would be closed to her. It felt as though she'd to operate blindfolded with one hand tied behind her back. However, she dare not stray beyond the boundaries because she was, as her grandmother would've said, on a shoogly peg until her probation was signed off. She silently cursed Robin.

Julien wrapped up the meeting, saying, "You'll report only to myself and Fitz. Return the file to me each evening. It mustn't leave this office." He asked if she'd any questions.

"When do you need my report?"

"Ideally by the end of next week."

She nodded. *Left to my own devices, you'd probably have it by the end of the day.*

The Attack

"The penny dropped with me when I took over as CEO. I realised we need to say that we are causing a problem and we need to solve that problem."
— John Browne, BP CEO (1995 – 2007)

***

Jamie

News of the attack spread throughout the ICC, drawing activists from all corners to where the Climate Warriors were camped, and soon there was a large gathering outside of their tents. Despite the early hour, the heat was stifling and Jamie's t-shirt stuck to him.

He spent the morning reassuring well-wishers he was unharmed and playing down the incident as an unfortunate case of mistaken identity. Amongst the visitors was Wolff, accompanied by one of the official organisers who, despite Jamie's objections, insisted on reporting the attack to the local police.

While they waited for officers to arrive, Wolff offered Jamie the usual platitudes, and quizzed him about what'd happened.

"Can you identify him?" asked Wolff.

Jamie shook his head and regarded Wolff. The attack had happened so fast and it'd been too dark to determine the height and weight of the figure. All he knew for sure was his assailant was a strong male of a similar frame to himself. He sized Wolff up. Although akin in height and build, Wolff lacked Jamie's toned physique, honed from years in the army combined with running and the gym. He'd gotten a look at his attacker's eyes but whether they belonged to Wolff or not, he couldn't be sure.

He cast his gaze over Wolff's clothing noting he was wearing a long-sleeved top and jeans despite the heat of the morning. Was that significant and, if so, what was he concealing? Still, what Wolff lacked in definition, he made up for in bulk so it'd be a fair fight and Jamie stowed that fact away for the time being. There was no sign of his sidekick Meyer and Jamie wondered if that too was important.

His wool gathering was interrupted by the arrival of two police officers, a paramedic and another ICC official. Wolff disappeared into the crowd as soon as the authorities appeared. While Jamie's injured hand was bandaged, the officers took photographs, collected the knife in an evidence bag, and asked Jamie and the others for statements. Although they followed standard procedure, Jamie suspected the police weren't particularly interested in a fracas between a bunch of eco-protesters.

After the officers left and the crowd had dispersed, Jamie went in search of solitude; not easy in a packed camp. Knowing MI5 would immediately learn of the incident, he needed to call Gary and file a report. The heat was suffocating and he wanted a shower. He sat on a tree stump beneath an oak and gathered his thoughts. Had Wolff attacked him or was it his sidekick Meyer? Was his cover blown and, if so, how? Had Meadow heard him talk in his sleep before entering the tent? Glancing round to check he was alone, he phoned his handler.

Jamie waited until much later to phone Kathryn since he didn't want to call her at work. When he did finally get hold of her to explain what'd happened, she burst into tears.

"I'm fine baby," he said, "please don't cry."

"Someone tried to kill you Jamie, it's anything but fine. When's Gary getting you out?"

He braced himself before replying, "Uhm, he's not, at least not yet. Things are starting to get interesting." When she began to protest, he added, "I'll be home tomorrow, we can discuss it then."

Gary's first instinct had been to put Jamie's extraction plan into action and he only agreed to let him continue after Jamie insisted on seeing things through now that Wolff would join them in the UK. Jamie suspected the group's direct actions would escalate and alter in nature with Wolff in the mix, and he'd be in a better position to gather intelligence on his international network. He also hoped it would mean the operation would rapidly come to a close.

After talking Kathryn down from the ledge, Jamie placated her with the news that they could spend the weekend together. Hearing the emotion in her voice almost broke him, and the miles between them suddenly seemed vast.

Missing her was tearing him apart.

***

Kathryn

Next morning, Kathryn barged into Julien's office and demanded to know what was going on with Jamie's operation. He refused to tell her anything, arguing it was against the rules.

"It's called compartmentation," said Julien from behind his desk, "I can't disclose information to anyone who's not involved in the operation."

Hands on hips, she fumed, "Sod the rules! Someone tried to murder my husband. Either you tell me what's going on or I'll go looking myself."

Julien looked as if he was about to explode and call security. Instead, he took a deep breath, rubbed the back of his neck, and in a resigned tone said, "Sit down Kathryn."

He called Fitz and asked him to join them. When Fitz appeared, Julien closed the door, and explained he would share some details about what'd happened at the ICC, provided Director A didn't learn of it.

Fitz showed them the photographs Jamie had sent to his handler the previous day from the ICC and he pointed out Wolff and Meyer. Kathryn noticed Jamie had his arm around a woman with blonde hair in several of them. She pushed her jealous thoughts aside and listened to Fitz.

"Wolff's got a record as long as my arm," said Fitz. He displayed a chargesheet listing everything from the German equivalent of breaches of the Public Order Act to criminal damage and assault. "He's also on the radar of the security services in the Netherlands and France because of his association with this eco-terrorist group."

He tapped a key and the names and faces of several people appeared on-screen, all belonging to a group known as the *Eco Monkey Wrenchers*. Their logo showed a spanner being thrown into the moving parts of a machine. She wondered if they were Luddites.

Fitz said, "Many of the group, Wolff and Meyer included, are wanted in connection with various acts of sabotage on European soil."

He flicked through images showing the destruction of property, while reading aloud the details of each. "They burnt down the offices of a company they believed was polluting a river, set fire to buildings belonging to a logging firm, ploughed up a GM potato crop in France, and smashed up a car dealership in Cologne which sold luxury SUVs."

The list was long, the damage amounting to millions of euros. Fitz explained that Wolff and Meyer were implicated in several of these attacks and had gone to ground a year ago.

"This climate camp's the first sighting of them since," said Fitz.

She asked why they hadn't been arrested.

Julien said, "We've an agreement with our German counterparts. We don't want to apprehend just a few individuals; we want the entire network including every known associate and person aiding and abetting them. Once we have this information, then we'll act together and shut down the lot."

Fitz said, "We were able to intercept some comms in the area. Many were from burner phones that have since disappeared off the network, but this one caught our interest."

A message appeared. *Aborted. Advise?*

"It was sent on the final day of the camp before the device went dark," said Fitz. The message details showed that it had been sent via a cell tower close to the location of the ICC.

Without missing a beat, Julien asked, "Is this referring to the attack on Jamie?"

Fitz shrugged and shot Kathryn an apologetic look. "Who knows. It could be or it could be something else entirely."

Kathryn gawped at Julien. "If Wolff or Meyer were responsible, it means Jamie's cover is compromised and he's in danger. You've got to get him out."

Shaking his head, Julien said, "Gary broached the subject but your husband refuses. Jamie insists he's safe and wants to see this thing through."

Blowing out an exasperated breath, she huffed, "Of course he'd say that, it's Jamie we're talking about. But you've a duty of care and you need to extract him." She could feel tears threatening.

"Kathryn," said Julien in a calm voice, "He's on his way home where we can keep a close eye on both him and Wolff."

"Wolff? He's coming to the UK?" she gasped, wondering why Jamie hadn't mentioned anything last night.

Julien nodded, "I've already briefed A4. We'll be all over him as soon as he arrives on our shores. Jamie won't want to budge given recent developments, and I'm not minded to extract him just yet. We've invested a lot in this and we're under pressure to get a result." When she protested, he silenced her with a look and added, "If I thought he was in danger, I'd pull him out. You have my word."

Knowing she was onto a losing argument, she gave a reluctant nod.

Turning to Fitz, Julien said, "Do we know who that cryptic message was sent to?"

"Nope, only that it was to another unregistered phone in the UK."

Julien said, "A4 are going to be busy."

Kathryn wondered what else Jamie hadn't told her.

***

Back home that evening, it didn't take Kathryn long to find the incident report filed by the officers of the Landespolizei force for Berlin. Using translation software, she hacked into the German equivalent of the UK police HOLMES system to find statements, evidence submissions, and photographs relating to the attack on Jamie.

She opened the gallery of photographs attached to the report and flinched when she saw the size of the terrifying knife in the corner of Jamie's tent. Then something else caught her eye. It looked like lacy underwear. Unable to believe her eyes, she zoomed in on the image.

It was a bra.

She gasped in disbelief. Stunned and distraught, she opened the file containing the group's statements and ran the contents through the translation software. Jamie's statement made no mention of anyone else being present in his tent at the time of the offence. Meadow's, however, detailed how she'd visited his tent earlier that evening. Kathryn realised Meadow was the same woman he'd had his arm around in the photographs Fitz had shown her.

Covering her mouth with her hand, Kathryn wheeled her seat back from her computer and let out a tortured cry. The shock of Jamie's betrayal hit her like a physical force. Unable to move, unable to breathe, she gawped at her screen and the pink lacy evidence of his treachery.

Slowly she rose, clutching her sides. Surely, she was mistaken? She glanced at the incriminating photograph again and recalled her chat with Keith amongst the grasses on the beach. Whisperings of the temptations faced by undercover operatives. Like a fool, she'd never believed her husband would succumb to such impulses. She'd hoped beyond reason he'd be different, and she wondered how many other wives and partners had thought the same.

As the full extent of his duplicity dawned on her, she began to cry, quietly at first, until noisy sobs wracked her body. She'd known something had been gnawing at him for a while. When Jamie was home, it was as if he was far off in a distant land. He'd said as much, acknowledging he was all-at-sea when he returned, as the lines between his real and undercover lives blurred. Now she understood why—he was in a relationship with another woman—and the horror of this fact was unbearable. The agony and humiliation made her cry out, the pain visceral, like he'd reached into her chest cavity, wrenched out her heart and ripped it in two. How could he do this to her? He was the only man she'd ever trusted and it'd been a hard-won trust.

He'd destroyed everything.

Sobbing uncontrollably now, she lay on the bed on her side, hugging her knees to her chest. She buried her face in the pillow to muffle the sound of her desolation, not knowing how she'd get through the next few hours, never mind the next few days. As she rocked herself, Meg whimpered at the foot of the bed.

The hours passed slowly in a blur of shock and despair. Sleep evaded her. Only when the cold light of dawn stole through the curtains did she glance at the clock. Remembering that Jamie was on his way home today, she dragged herself from the bed. She couldn't face him. How could she? The person who'd betrayed her trust and broken her heart?

Right now, she hated him.

The Note

When the BP 'Beyond Petroleum' campaign launched, they were spending 200 million on the BP image scrub, while spending less than a quarter of that on the actual solar programmes." **— Kert Davies — founder and director of Climate Investigations Center 2022**

***

Jamie

Yawning, Jamie turned his key in the lock and entered the cottage. The rooms were in darkness and the place was eerily quiet. He called out a greeting but there was no sign of Kathryn or Meg and he figured she must be out with the dog. He flicked on the kitchen light and froze at the sight of what lay on the table: a suitcase and an envelope with his name on it.

He ripped it open and read the note, a cold sweat suddenly dripping down his back. Scrubbing a hand over his face, he slumped into a chair and examined the document attached to the note. It was an English translation of Meadow's statement and stapled to it was another sheet of paper with a photograph of the crime scene showing the lacy bra.

No. No. No. No. No!

He groaned as the realisation of what Kathryn must've thought swept over him. Of course she'd have hacked the German police computers — this was

Kathryn — it's what she did. And of course she'd conclude he and Meadow had been sleeping together. How could she not?

Putting his head in his hands, he swore sulphurously. Tortured by the thought of what she must be going through, he kicked the chair back and began to pace.

Damnit! Where would she have gone?

He re-read the note, its words cutting him like a knife. *'I'm leaving you. Please be gone by the time I return. K.'*

He needed to think. Fast. She didn't have close friends outside of work and he didn't think she'd contact her colleagues. She didn't have family either, only him. Then it struck him — he did. He grabbed his phone and called his sister. Kathryn wasn't in Glasgow and all he managed to achieve was worrying Lindsay. Promising to call back later, he hung up.

Knowing Kathryn must be hurting something terrible, he was disgusted that he was the cause of it. He didn't blame her for leaving or for jumping to the wrong conclusion; faced with the evidence, he'd have probably done the same. All he cared about was getting the opportunity to put it right. He glanced at the incriminating photograph again, aware that even if she did give him a chance to explain, she may never trust him again. Through his own torment and misery, he realised he was in danger of losing the single most important and precious person in his life, and the thought terrified him.

His head throbbed and he rubbed his temples. Pouring himself a glass of tap water, he gazed out over the common. Meg was with her — that meant something — it was time to think like a surveillance operator and bloody find her. He was a hunter of people after all.

He called Fitz who answered on the second ring.

"Fitz, it's Jamie. I need you to find my wife."

***

Kathryn

Sighing, Kathryn closed her laptop knowing Jamie would arrive any minute. Using his mobile phone signal, she'd tracked his every movement from Germany to Salford, and then to the lockup where he switched the transit van for his Landrover. She'd then monitored his journey home and from there to Milford-on-Sea on the south coast. She'd known he'd find her — it was what Jamie did — and there'd been little point in hiding her location.

The lodge was the first place she'd thought of when she decided to flee since it was dog-friendly and only a couple of hours drive from home. They'd spent a long weekend in this holiday resort last summer with Jamie's sister and her family, renting a unit with a hot tub. The memory of laughter and drinking champagne made her maudlin, and she regretted returning under the circumstances and tarnishing it.

A car pulled up outside, a door slammed and she heard the crunch of footsteps on gravel. There was a knock and Meg barked. Kathryn's stomach lurched as she approached the door. Before opening it, she took a deep breath and arranged her expression to give him the full force of her fury.

Their eyes met. The strain of the last few hours was etched on his face and his eyes were as red as hers.

"Oh baby," he said in a voice cracking with emotion, "I haven't done what you think."

She spun round and stalked into the open-plan kitchen where she leant against the units and glowered at him. To his surprise, Meg snarled at him. Ignoring the dog, he took tentative steps towards Kathryn, his expression unsure. Pausing, he searched her face for a reaction; she gave none.

He extended his palms and said, "Can we talk?"

She bit out, "There's nothing to say."

"Please Kathryn, there's everything to say."

She noticed his bandage. "What happened to your hand?"

“My hand’s fine, forget the hand. Please Kathryn.”

He sat on the couch and she perched on the chair opposite. She kept her eyes fixed on the floor, and fought back the tears that threatened to overwhelm her.

In a low voice, he said, “I know what you must have thought, how it must have looked, but I’m not sleeping with her.”

She glared at him and hissed, “You seriously expect me to believe that? What sort of fool do you take me for?”

He tried to take her hands but she pulled away. Meg settled at Kathryn’s feet and growled at him.

“I know how it looks,” he said, "but it’s the truth. She came onto me but I turned her down. I swear to God that’s what happened.” He looked at her beseechingly.

“And I suppose her bra just fell off?” She gave a snort of derision.

“Kathryn, I love you, I’d never...”

Her tears fell freely as he explained how the bra had come to be in the tent. He tried pulling Kathryn onto his lap but she shrugged him off, and Meg bared her teeth at him.

Ignoring the dog, he took her hand and said, “I’m so sorry I put you through this, for what you must have thought.”

She gazed at him through wet lashes, “I don’t believe you.”

Jamie reacted as if she’d struck him. “Jesus, this is so messed up,” he said. “I don’t blame you for thinking it, but I promise you I’ve not been with another woman. Since you and I met, there’s been no one else.” His voice caught. “There never will be.”

He sounded sincere, but the evidence ...

Taking a tissue, she blew her nose and shook her head. “I don’t know what to think. My heart says one thing, my head another.” She rose. “I need time to deal with this, to figure out what I’m going to do. It’s not something I can just forget about, and while I do, I don’t want to be around you.”

As she walked away, he called to her, “Please listen to your heart Kathryn.”

***

Jamie

Jamie spent a restless night in the spare room of the holiday lodge. Alone.

When he finally succumbed to a fitful sleep, his dreams were filled with images of Kathryn leaving him. He awoke in a cold sweat as the first rays of dawn stole through the thin curtains. When he went to fetch a drink of water from the kitchen, he realised Kathryn and Meg were gone and panic set in. Had she left him?

He searched her room to find her clothes still there and the car outside and gave a sigh of relief. Pulling on his clothes and trainers, he sprinted down to the pebbly beach. He spotted Kathryn and the dog in the distance and ran towards them, his heart bursting in his chest as he closed the gap. Meg saw him first and bounded to meet him. Would Kathryn even speak to him?

She turned and froze, her long blonde hair whipping round her face in the sea breeze. He made a fuss of the dog and walked towards her. Her hard look of disappointment would haunt him forever.

He paused a few feet from her but the distance seemed greater. She stared at him and the glint in her eyes terrified him. He'd rather she shouted and lashed out than face her steely blank gaze.

"What can I do to make things right?"

Staring out towards the horizon, she said in a deadpan voice, "I can't see how we can ever go back to the way we were."

Her words cut him deep.

Taking a step, he reached for her hand. "Baby, please!"

She recoiled from his touch as if burned by it and hissed, "Leave me alone."

Raking a hand through his hair and in a voice breaking with emotion, he said, "I can't leave with things as they are."

She stepped away. "Better you go Jamie. I don't want you here right now."

"Please don't push me away. I know we can fix this but not if we're living apart."

"I need to be by myself." She turned and walked away.

As he watched her go, Jamie felt like his world had just collapsed.

The Choice

***"More than 40 years ago, oil industry scientists warned that burning fossil fuels would cause climate change."* — 'Big Oil Versus the World' BBC2 2022**

***

Kathryn

Kathryn awoke screaming from a nightmare. Meg sprung onto the bed and licked her face and it took her a few moments to orient herself into wakefulness and realise she was home. Flopping onto the pillows, she tried to dispel the visions that had wrenched her from her slumber: the trial for murdering her step-father, a life sentence handed down by Robin and then, as she was dragged from court past her colleagues, seeing Jamie turn away in disgust and into Meadow's arms.

Then, remembering the grim reality to which she'd woken, she wept. A headache pounded behind her temples and she felt nauseous. The clock on the nightstand showed it was just after five a.m. Feeling too distraught to sleep, she swallowed two painkillers with a glass of water and battled to retain them in her stomach.

She deliberated about whether to take the day off work or not. Given her predicament with Robin and Harriet, she was reluctant to take any sickness absence. Instead, she dragged herself into the shower and then took Meg for a walk on the common. Autumn had commenced in earnest and the cold grey morning reflected her mood. On the way back, she noticed the neighbour's son watching her from an upstairs window. Ignoring him, she hurried past. Unable to face breakfast, she took Meg and made the journey to work in heavy Monday morning traffic.

The day was spent staring at her computer screen oblivious to everything and everyone around her. She struggled to concentrate and each time she tried to focus, her thoughts returned to Jamie's betrayal. Despite having talked, she felt more confused than when she'd first learned of his duplicity. Everything hinged on his insistence he hadn't slept with *that woman*.

The thought made her queasy and she made a dash for the toilet where she vomited up the tea she'd drank. As she hugged the porcelain bowl, she caught sight of her wedding ring which only made her cry.

She pondered on how she'd fare without Jamie in her life and the prospect terrified her. She desperately wanted to believe him, despite all evidence to the contrary. But if she couldn't and had to accept his transgression, could she ever forgive him and allow him back in her bed? Surely that was condoning his behaviour and it'd only be a matter of time until it happened again.

She'd witnessed what her real father's serial philandering had done to her mother who'd said of him, 'A leopard never changes its spots.' Her mother had finally kicked him out only to replace him with a man far worse. Was this part of marriage? From time to time would she have to accept that her husband would wander and she'd have to pick up the pieces of her shattered life?

She flushed the toilet and washed her face and hands. Staring at her reflection, she said aloud, "So is this my choice: put up or split up?"

The realisation made her vomit again.

After rinsing her mouth, she returned to her desk and tried to focus on work, without success. Fitz had been especially nice to her since Jamie had involved him in tracking her down and at lunchtime, he tried to coax her to the canteen with the rest of the team. She declined and remained at her desk, unable to face food or company.

Mid-afternoon, an email from Harriet appeared in her inbox chastising her for missing the stand-up. She burst into tears. Fitz appeared at her side with a sympathetic smile and ushered her towards the canteen.

"Want to talk about it?" he asked, handing her a mug of tea.

Blinking back tears, she said, "I guess you know what happened? What I saw in the police report?"

He ran his fingers through his straggly hair. "I'm really sorry Kathryn, I don't know what else to say."

"Jamie swears it's not how it looks ..." She angled her head away and fought back tears. "... but of course he'd say that."

Fitz paused, appearing to swallow what he wanted to say. "What're you going to do?"

She gave a long sigh. "I really don't know. Jamie's on his way back to Salford and I'm in London wondering what the hell he's playing at. I'm torn between wanting him around and needing time away from him. Until this damn operation of his is over, nothing'll get resolved between us."

Leaning towards her conspiratorially, Fitz whispered, "I've just sat in on surveillance of Wolff's arrival in Calais. He came in on a false passport on a ferry this morning."

When she asked if he was on his way to join Jamie and the Climate Warriors, Fitz said, "He is now, but he took an interesting detour."

He explained that Wolff had led a team of A4 surveillance operators on a merry dance through the London transport network, and then to an Indian restaurant in Brick Lane where he'd lunched with a woman called Margaret-Anne McCrae.

"The publicist?" asked Kathryn shooting him a look of surprise.

"The very one."

Kathryn had heard of Margaret-Anne McCrae, or MAM as she was known in the press. An investigative reporter turned PR consultant, she'd gained notoriety for reporting a series of salacious sex scandals in the tabloids.

"Why would Wolff meet her? Surely he's not hiring her to promote the climate cause?"

Fitz nodded. "Good question especially considering her client list. Her agency is in bed with the very institutions the protesters accuse of funding the fossil fuel industry." He shrugged and added, "Anyway, I thought you'd want to know Wolff's now on his way to Salford so maybe that'll help bring things to a head."

But all Kathryn could think about was whose bed Jamie was sleeping in.

***

Jamie

Jamie drove in an abyss of despair towards the lockup to switch his Land Rover for the transit van.

Parting from Kathryn had nearly broken him. She didn't want him around but he knew that without the opportunity to talk face-to-face, they'd never get past 'Meadow gate'. Left on her own, he worried about her mental state. And his own.

Cyberspace was Kathryn's safe place, where she retreated when the real world became too much for her. He worried that without him around, she'd spend almost every waking hour of her free time immersed in it as she used to do before they met.

After switching vehicles, Fitz called to tell him they'd discovered another tracker attached to his van which wasn't one of theirs.

Fitz said, "Reckon it was attached in Germany, so someone other than us is following your movements. We left it in situ but Julien had one of the A4 probationers drive the van all over London while you were away. She'd a lovely tour of the building sites so your cover's intact."

He thanked Fitz and set off, grateful his colleague had also filled the fuel tank. The news about the tracker only added to his feeling of despondency. Had Wolff fitted the tracker or the German authorities? Jamie was still no closer to knowing if Wolff or Meyer was his attacker or someone else. The thought of sharing the squat with the German made him uneasy; however, it was the very least of his worries as he drove north.

The journey to Salford gave him plenty of time to mull over recent events and his relationship. He replayed his conversations with Kathryn over and over in his mind, annoyed that, not only had he failed to convince her it'd all been a dreadful misunderstanding, but he was leaving without a clue as to what she was thinking.

She wanted time to process what'd happened and decide what to do, and he understood that but what if she chose to leave? The thought was unbearable and filled him with dread. But if she stayed, he worried their relationship would never be the same. His actions had eroded the trust she'd placed in him, and it had been a hard-won trust considering what she'd endured at the hands of her step-father. Would she now see her husband as yet another man who'd let her down?

Sure, the job was important but was his own home life and happiness to be the sacrifice? Before meeting Kathryn, he'd always thought he'd a clear sense of what he wanted, and a career in MI5 had been a life-long ambition. However, living the dream was proving to be a nightmare in terms of the effect it was having on their marriage. His priorities had changed; they'd changed the instant he'd fallen in love with her. Either the job would need to adapt or he'd have to find another because their relationship came first.

By the time Jamie pulled into the services at Birmingham, he'd come to a decision. He called his handler and requested immediate extraction.

"Hold on," said Gary, "stay put, I'm on my way."

While he waited, Jamie called his sister. Lindsay was one of few people who knew what Jamie did for a living, and she listened as he explained what'd happened. After a long, heartfelt chat, Lindsay suggested he acquiesced to Kathryn's wishes and gave her the time and space she needed. When he asked how the family were, she told him her daughter Heather had suffered a serious asthma attack. The news only added to his feelings of despair.

Gary appeared and slid into the passenger seat of the van bearing a McDonald's burger meal and a coke. The smell made Jamie's stomach rumble, reminding him he hadn't eaten.

After examining the burger, Jamie took a mouthful and said "Mmm, real meat." Guilt pricked his conscience for enjoying it.

"That's debateable."

"What's in yours?" asked Jamie. "Tofu? Humous?"

Gary chuckled, "Wanker!"

"Aye, I love you too," he replied through another delicious bite.

When they'd finished eating, Gary said, "Ok, talk to me Jamie. I understand things are difficult at home, so where's your head at?"

Jamie puffed out a breath and repeated what had happened. Gary listened without interruption.

"I know what we do's important," said Jamie, "but so is my marriage."

"I completely understand," said Gary producing a manilla folder. "And I'll extract you if you want but there's something I'd like you to see first before you decide." He passed Jamie a document.

Jamie couldn't believe his eyes.

***

Several hours later, wired on energy drinks, Jamie arrived at the squat in Salford to a warm welcome from his comrades. The atmosphere amongst the group was almost febrile, and Ethan was running around barking orders at them ahead of Wolff's arrival.

Jamie feigned enthusiasm and helped with preparations, careful to keep a distance between himself and Meadow. Rose seemed subdued.

Wolff appeared early evening bearing food and wine from a French supermarket. He embraced them one at a time, lingering on Meadow. They ate together but Jamie had no appetite and picked at his food. They chatted about press coverage of the ICC which had attracted world attention, and this led onto a discussion about climate demonstrations in which Ethan was keen to prove his activist credentials. The game of one-upmanship continued until Ethan and Wolff began rhyming off their charge sheets like qualifications on a CV.

Finally, Rose rolled her eyes and said, "Shall I fetch a ruler and we'll see whose is bigger?"

Ethan shot her a scowl of undisguised contempt. Wolff then quizzed Jamie about his work as a rope-access technician and the climbing stunts he'd pulled during protests. Jamie told him about his audacious stunt on the roof of Neo Petroleum and Ethan and Wolff swapped a look.

After dinner, Jamie excused himself and went out to his van to call Kathryn. He took a deep breath before dialling. She picked up on the second ring. He explained he couldn't talk for long and asked if he could come home soon so they could talk. This was met with a silence far worse than if she'd shouted.

"Please Kathryn, this is killing me."

"I need some time."

"Ok, I get that but I'll try phone you every day. We need to talk baby."

When she agreed, he ended the call, telling her how much he loved her.

"I'll speak to you tomorrow," was all she said before hanging up.

Jamie wiped the moisture from his eyes before re-joining the others.

Alex and Leon were playing ping pong on a table scavenged from the back of a warehouse, and Ethan and Wolff were deep in conversation on the sofa. Jamie joined the women in the kitchen where Rose handed him a glass of wine. He backed it and refilled his glass.

"You look tired," said Meadow sidling up to him, "is everything okay?"

"Fine," he snapped. He stalked off and joined the lads, feeling bad for taking his anger out on Meadow. He only had himself to blame.

Between games, Jamie tried to eavesdrop on Ethan and Wolff's conversation but they spoke in hushed tones and he could only hear snippets. After half an hour, Ethan and Wolff shook hands and got up.

Ethan called out, "Is everyone free tomorrow evening? There's something Karsten and I would like to discuss."

"Here we go," muttered Rose loud enough for all to hear.

After agreeing a time to meet, Jamie sloped off to bed with a sense of foreboding.

Just what the hell were Ethan and Wolff planning?

The Target

"This is the only issue that matters. It does not matter if your kids clean their teeth or have good food or that you have a good married relationship ... if we are not going to survive." **— Dr Helen Caldicott, Greenham Common Peace Camp**

***

Kathryn

Kathryn spent the evening at home with a bottle of wine, finding out everything she could about Meadow Conway. Clenching her teeth, she typed Meadow's details into the search engine, unable to dispel the mental images she'd conjured of this woman in bed with Jamie. She found a wealth of information on the surface web.

Daughter of Sarah Conway, a social worker from Tenby in Wales, Meadow had been born and raised in the Greenham Common Peace Camp. The camp was established in September 1981 after a Welsh group, Women for Life on Earth, arrived to protest against the storage of nuclear 'cruise' missiles at Greenham. Meadow's mother remained there with her daughter until the camp was disbanded in 2000.

Kathryn flicked through photographs showing Sarah engaged in a number of actions. In one she was secured to the base's chain-link fence, and in another standing on top of the Commander's car; the latter earning her a week in Holloway Prison.

Press cuttings revealed she'd 'webbed up' the local magistrates court, a stunt which involved throwing balls of wool between protesters to form a woven obstacle. She'd later stripped naked and covered herself in ketchup and soot to represent the planet on fire. During her trial, she was fined for singing in a Gilbert and Sullivan operatic style.

Kathryn found herself smiling at the women's clever antics and she couldn't help but be impressed by their bravery and tenacity. In the end, the women achieved their goals bloodlessly; namely, the removal of the weapons and the return of the Common to the people.

Sarah Conway returned to social work after leaving the camp but her daughter had bounced from one protest group to another, until reuniting with Rose Thompson, the daughter of another Greenham woman. Together, they'd established the Climate Warriors where they exploited their knowledge of the protest movement and their connections amongst activists.

Kathryn hacked into Meadow's police records, and then into her MI5 file which revealed she'd not been on the grid of the Security Service before. Not until now.

She pondered on how different Meadow's childhood was to her own. Raised by a village of women where men were allowed no involvement, Meadow had been isolated and insulated from the male population. Had the Greenham women's views on patriarchy influenced her attitude towards the institution of marriage, meaning she paid its boundaries no heed? Jamie had told Kathryn that Meadow was aware he was married but Kathryn couldn't square the fact that a true feminist would hurt and betray another woman. Breaking the sister code by stealing another's partner made no sense. Unless, of course, Jamie was the seducer. Looking at a recent photograph of Meadow, Kathryn could not hate her.

After another slug of wine, Kathryn turned her attention to Darren. She'd continued to monitor her neighbour's online activities and had grown increasingly concerned about the tone of his posts which suggested he was prepared to put his twisted ideas into practice. His latest on a popular incel forum sent a chill down her spine.

[LonelyVirgin] Its time my fantasies became reality. Gonna kill a bitch. Doesn't matter who but one's better than none

To her dismay, many in the community responded with praise and encouragement, with one particularly callous response:

[FuglyCreep] Rape her first so she dies knowing you were inside her

Kathryn felt sick to her stomach but knew she had to act, even if it meant losing her job.

Or her liberty.

***

Jamie

Jamie spent the next day moping about the squat. He passed the time emptying the contents of the van and organising the lockup. Where possible, he avoided being alone with Meadow. She appeared to have sparked Wolff's interest, something which Ethan seemed to encourage. Jamie wondered if using Meadow to lure Wolff had also been part of his plan.

Leon seemed to sense the change in Jamie's mood and asked if he needed help with stock-taking. Leon was normally at college studying film and photography but this week he was on study leave. Jamie found his company a welcome distraction, and the task of unloading the van and restocking the lockup took half the time.

By mid-afternoon they'd finished the job. Taking advantage of the mild weather, they sat outside the lockup eating chocolate bars left over from the ICC supplies.

"So, what d'ya think Ethan and Wolff are plotting?" asked Leon.

"God only knows," said Jamie, "but I doubt it involves dressing up as a flower."

Leon chuckled. "Occupying petrol station forecourts and tanker surfing maybe."

Or far worse, thought Jamie remembering the information Gary had shown him. Sharing that intelligence had been a low blow as Gary knew it was something Jamie couldn't ignore. He silently cursed his handler.

"Don't feel pressured into doing something you're uncomfortable with," said Jamie, "you've your future to think about."

"It is my future I'm thinking about. No point having a career if the world's uninhabitable."

Jamie acknowledged he'd a point. "D'you think Rose and the others will be up for it?"

"Your guess is as good as mine. She's really pissed off at Ethan. Reckons he's taking over her group, and now with Wolff in the picture, the power will shift even more."

"Think Rose will veto it?"

Leon gazed into the middle distance for a moment then turned to Jamie. "Hard to know. She loves Ethan but I reckon she's torn between wanting to stop the coup he's mounted and needing to do what's right for the cause."

It was a thoughtful answer and Jamie nodded in agreement. "And Yasmine?"

Leon's face betrayed his emotions. Jamie had long suspected Leon had feelings for Yaz despite her relationship with Ethan. For Jamie, the threesome was unfathomable and he guessed Leon regarded it in the same way.

With a slow disbelieving head shake, Leon sighed. "Yaz'll do whatever Ethan tells her to."

Regretting his question, Jamie said, "Want me to tie you to the roof of the van so you can practise your tanker surfing?"

Leon joined in with his laughter.

***

Kathryn

Kathryn had spent a sleepless night worrying about Darren's plans but, by the time the cold light of dawn stole through the curtains, she knew what she had to do. Rising early, she made a strong mug of tea and sat at her computer.

Sifting through Darren's messages, she knew she couldn't take these to the police. She'd obtained the content illegally which meant she risked losing her job and possible prosecution. Part of the problem was the authorities rarely took threats against women seriously in the real world, so she'd little confidence they'd act on these. Had they been made against a religious or racial group, the word 'terrorism' would be bandied about, but not in the case of misogyny.

Yet she had to do something before a woman was murdered — or herself — and fast. Scrolling through her communications with Scotty, she found details for the vigilante group he'd used to stitch up the wife beater, Sean. She found their site hidden in the murky depths of the dark web and made contact under a new name rather than using Moniker. She explained that the group had been recommended to her by IntoDarkness.

She received a quick reply from someone called *Dark Canary* who requested details of the target. Kathryn bundled up the most vitriolic of Darren's posts, including his latest threats, and inquired about options for dealing with him, together with the costs. Rather than asking Scotty to fund this, she intended to use her own cryptocurrency savings and hoped it would be enough.

By the time she'd showered and dried her hair, there was a response:

[Dark Canary] We'll take care of it and since you're a friend of Scotty, this one's on us

Surprised *Dark Canary* knew who *IntoDarkness* really was, she wondered how long they'd been doing business together.

When she inquired how the vigilante intended to deal with Darren, the reply surprised her.

***

She spent the morning in the office attempting to trace the MP Monty's finances for the report Julien had requested. The deadline was looming but every time she tried to apply herself to the task, she couldn't focus. She'd expected it to be straightforward but at this rate, meeting the due date was looking doubtful, given that Alasdair Montrose's financial affairs were far more complicated than anticipated.

The standard checks on Monty and his family had been done already and were documented in the brief, including identity verification, credit history, driver's history, and criminal records. After double-checking official sources, she trawled social media platforms and news articles relating to Monty, his family, his corporate affairs and role as an MP. A privately-educated, Oxbridge graduate with a Home Counties accent, Monty was a quintessential 'Surrey Highlander'.

Ten years ago, Monty had founded a company called 'Montrose Renewables' which, according to their web site, developed, constructed and operated large-scale, grid-connected green energy projects across the globe. Monty was pictured standing next to an enormous wind turbine, but they also built solar parks, offshore wind farms, and hydroelectric power plants. Companies House listed him as a director along with his wife Sophie, and eldest son Rory as Chief Financial Officer. His youngest son was still at university in Edinburgh studying languages and not involved in the business.

After checking their public accounts, she dug deeper into their business banking. She found little of note other than some eye-watering dividends paid from the company to its directors on top of modest salaries, something which was neither illegal nor unusual. Their accountancy firm's records also appeared in order and she could find nothing that would raise eyebrows at HMRC. However, when she examined his eldest son Rory's personal account, her curiosity was piqued. Large, regular payments were being made from this into a digital currency service.

She groaned so loud that Fitz peered at her over the top of his monitor. "What's up?" he asked.

"Bitcoin. That's what's up."

***

Jamie

After the group had eaten supper, Ethan invited them to take a seat in the old gymnasium. Jamie sat with Leon and Alex and watched as Wolff connected a laptop to a small USB projector so he could project images onto the white wall in front. Once everyone was settled, he displayed the same sleek presentation he'd shown at the ICC.

Wolff spoke quietly. "I commend the efforts of groups like yourselves. You work tirelessly and devote yourself to this cause. You put your safety on the line at every protest, and you suffer the consequences. Without people like you keeping the climate crisis at the forefront of the public's' mind, our planet would be in an even worse state."

He looked at them in turn. "You're probably wondering why I'm here?" When no one said anything, he continued, "As part of the wider rebellion, you've blockaded bridges and brought cities to a grinding halt." He counted each activity on his fingers as images of protestors lying in the middle of roads appeared on the wall behind him.

"You've staged die-ins and mock funeral marches, you've poured fake blood over the streets, and you've occupied the Scottish Parliament and glued yourselves to the gates of Downing Street. You've targeted the London Stock Exchange, the Treasury, the Department for Transport, and the Bank of England. You've disrupted airports, train stations, ferry ports. You've marched, you've swarmed, you've gone on strike, and you've climbed." Wolff looked directly at Jamie.

As a series of images portraying peaceful protests appeared, he said in a voice laced with exasperation, "Together, we've carried out almost every conceivable non-violent disruptive action we can think of." Then, after a long pause, "But has it made a damn bit of difference? Are the politicians listening? Are the public aware we face the very real threat of extinction?"

He gazed at the group. "No. No one cares. Except people like us. And that's why we must act." Slapping a palm onto the table, he said, "This is the moment we stop the human race sleep-walking to its own destruction. This is the time we send a stronger message, one that cannot be ignored, one that will make an immediate difference and buy the human race time to come to its senses. This is the point we call time on the fossil fuel industry."

An image appeared on-screen that Jamie immediately recognised.

Wolff said, "And we'll do it by bringing this place to its knees."

Oh fuck! This just got serious.

The Plant

"The scientific evidence remains inconclusive as to whether human activities affect global climate." **— Lee Raymond, Exxon Mobil CEO (1993 - 2005)**

***

Kathryn

Kathryn fidgeted as she waited for Julien to finish reading the information she'd given him. She was in his office with Fitz for their weekly meeting, and the table in front of them was littered with paperwork about Monty's business contracts. The wall-mounted screen displayed a list of his payment transactions.

Julien had on a fresh shirt but his crumpled suit and 5 o'clock shadow betrayed the fact he'd slept in the office again. When he finally glanced up, she took a deep breath and explained she needed more time to unravel the MP's financials which were proving to be complex. Although she'd already flagged her concerns and this wasn't a surprise, she felt nervous about his reaction on hearing the news. Would this affect her next performance review?

"There are a few things going on," she said, "and his company is not nearly as healthy as he's led the shareholders to believe. For the past few months, Monty's son Rory has been funnelling large sums of money into digital currency and NFTs."

Julien shot her a quizzical look. "And an NFT is?"

"It stands for non-fungible token which just means it's unique, one-of-a-kind. Think of it as a digital certificate of authenticity, like proof of part ownership of a valuable asset like a painting." She could picture Julien investing in high-end art, imagining a Raphael above his mantlepiece. When he looked baffled, she added, "The Nyan Cat graphic was auctioned as an NFT."

"Does that count as art?" said Julien pulling a face.

"As much as an unmade bed," scoffed Fitz. "But isn't it just an investment strategy? Lots of people I know dabble in Bitcoin and NFTs."

"Sure," said Kathryn, "but on this scale it reeks of tax evasion and money laundering. Plus, he's using a middleman."

Julien looked at them both wearily and sighed, "Having been born when dinosaurs roamed the earth, I know little about digital currency so explain it in simple terms."

She smiled. "Remember the financial crisis of 2008 when currencies like pounds and dollars hit the floor?" Julien nodded and she continued. "Banks were betting large with everyone else's money, then governments had to bail them out to stop the financial system and economy imploding."

Fitz muttered, "Leaving the tax payer to foot the bill."

"Exactly," said Kathryn, "rescuing the very institutions that caused the problem in the first place."

Julien frowned. "I hope you're not getting political Kathryn; we're supposed to be impartial."

"I'm simply stating a fact." She tapped a key to display her personal Crypto.co m home screen showing charts of popular digital currencies she'd invested modest funds in.

The lines on Julien's brow deepened. "I hope you've declared these investments."

Ignoring him, she said, "So, in the wake of this, along comes Bitcoin which is not in the hands of an elite few." When he raised a stern eyebrow, she added,

"Cryptocurrencies are decentralised so there are no banks, governments or middlemen involved."

"But you said Monty's using a middleman," said Julien.

"His son's using a third-party anonymity service to buy Bitcoin, which is unusual unless you're trying to hide something. So, between that and investing in NFTs, I reckon he's up to something."

"Which could leave Monty compromised and embarrass the government," said Julien.

She gave a sheepish look, "But I can't be certain. I'm no digital currency expert."

Julien said. "You've done an excellent job getting this far."

"The wobbly heads have forensic accounting specialists," said Fitz. "We'll send your findings to them. I'll take you through the process."

Kathryn knew he was referring to GCHQ in Cheltenham. Of course they'd have a bloody process; no doubt a vexatious bureaucratic one. In triplicate.

Fitz added, "Expect a glacially slow response."

"That fast?" she asked.

"Tectonic if you're lucky," said Julien. "In the meantime, I'll use it as an excuse to push back on the deadline." Leaning back in his chair, he stifled a yawn. "So, tell me, how are you getting on with our little Russian friend?"

She'd been expecting the question about Balakin and had come prepared. "I've something interesting to show you," she said, displaying Balakin's LinkedIn profile and contacts. "He's been growing his connections for some time and I've noticed a pattern."

The Russian's profile was straightforward and typical of a junior bureaucrat; however, the connections he'd established since arriving in the UK showed he'd expanded his professional network considerably to include Russian expats, language students and academics. As well as his London-based contacts, he was zeroing in on staff and students in the Russian Studies Centre at Edinburgh University's Department of European Languages and Culture.

Kathryn explained Balakin had been in contact with the university's Director of Studies about giving a talk at the faculty. He'd offered to speak about Russia's continued reliance on fossil fuels and the challenges of developing a new strategy for the energy sector. Kathryn summarised communications between Balakin and the Director.

Julien twiddled with his cufflinks as he listened. "Hmm, he's very specific about what he wants to talk about, isn't he. Do you think he's trying to hook someone in particular? Is there a guest list?"

Even when tired, his sharp mind never failed to impress her. Julien was fluent in four languages but too posh to cut it on the street. As a tactical leader, however, he saw connections others wouldn't and always seemed to be several moves ahead. She'd wager he was a master at chess.

She tapped a key and a spreadsheet appeared containing a long list of invitees. "There is and I looked for anyone on it connected to the energy sector. One person stands out from the rest."

Her fingers flew over the keyboard and a picture of a young woman with long dark hair appeared. She was buxom with thick glasses and looked to be in her late twenties. "Her name's Anna Sokolov. She's British, has lived in Scotland all her life but her father was Russian. She's an engineer but recently began a part-time master's degree in Russian Studies at Edinburgh."

The ridges on Julien's forehead deepened. "Who does she work for and on what?"

"That's the most interesting thing of all," said Kathryn, displaying a web site for a company called Grid Scale Systems headquartered in Livingston. "Anna works for GSS. They design and manufacture big battery technology."

Julien said, "Let me guess ... for the energy sector?"

She nodded. "The problem for renewable energy is the intermittent nature of it. Wind and solar generate huge amounts of energy but when the wind stops blowing or the sun stops shining, it's no good unless you can store it. That's where GSS comes in. Their batteries store the excess energy, then feed it into the grid when it's needed."

She launched a short video of the CEO speaking about their products. Wearing a hard hat and standing beneath an enormous wind turbine, he said, "Energy storage is the key to a zero-carbon future. Our technology enables green energy producers to balance oversupply when electricity is being generated, and shortage when the sun sets or the wind drops." The image switched to a vast solar farm, and he said, "No longer will solar power be restricted to daylight hours."

Kathryn then showed a photograph of a cavernous turbine building. "GSS have a site in Eaglesham near Glasgow with a super-size 300-megawatt lithium-ion battery that stores excess energy from the wind farm. And they've another here in the south east of England next to a solar farm. Anna works for their research and development department in Livingston."

Julien emitted a long low whistle. "Balakin's after their intellectual property. That's why he's here. And that's why he was targeting that other woman."

Kathryn had been conducting social media intercepts for some time on Carly Milliken. However, after Julien had a quiet word with Carly's father, the relationship between his daughter and Balakin ended immediately.

Julien slid a hand down over his unshaven face and onto his neck. "The Russians are way behind the West in terms of developing green technologies. If he gets his hands on this IP, it'll advance his country's capabilities by decades ... not to mention the fact this poses a direct threat to our national interest."

"Well done Kathryn," said Fitz.

"Indeed, excellent work," said Julien rising to his feet, "Keep digging, see what you can find on this new woman and I'll talk to Director A. Balakin is now your top priority."

***

Jamie

The room fell silent as the Climate Warriors gawped at the photograph of the Grangemouth oil refinery and petrochemical plant. With its enormous cooling towers and steel spires cloaked in clouds of vapour, it resembled a surrealist's vision of a dystopian city.

Rose gasped. "You've got to be kidding."

"Are you insane?" said Meadow.

The others made similar exclamations.

Wolff said, "Allow me to explain."

"Oh, please do," snapped Rose shooting him a hard glare. "This I've got to hear."

"Are we blockading it?" asked Alex.

"I'm in favour of a stronger approach," replied Wolff, "a showpiece act of civil disobedience the likes of which this country has never seen, where we overrun the plant and bring its operations to a halt." He let this information settle for a few moments, then added, "If we can occupy it for a few days, maybe even a week, and stop fuel production we'll get publicity on a massive scale."

"Plus we'll slash Scotland's CO2 emissions overnight," said Ethan.

When their words were met with stunned silence, Wolff raised his hands placatingly. "It's only a proposal, something for the group to consider. I'll understand if not everyone's comfortable with it."

Ethan gazed round the room and said, "Let's hear the details and then we can decide whether we're up for it or not."

Jamie observed the interplay between Wolff and Ethan. It struck him as staged and a sense of unease began to creep over him. Rose appeared equally unhappy about Wolff's proposal.

"Why Grangemouth?" she asked. "For a start, it's bloody miles away."

Wolff tapped a key and a colour-coded map of the North Sea oil pipeline appeared, similar in appearance to the map of the London Underground. "It's

Scotland's only crude oil refinery and it produces most of the country's fuels, including 70% of what goes to filling stations in the north. If we shut down Grangemouth, it'll cripple Britain's petroleum supply."

Ethan added, "Costing the economy about £50 million in lost production for every day it remains closed."

"The government certainly won't be able to ignore that," said Yasmine. There was muttered agreement.

"All we ask," said Ethan, "is you consider whether it's something you want to be involved in or not. It'll be the biggest action we've ever planned."

Wolff cast a serious eye over the group and said, "Admittedly, this comes with great risk and every likelihood of arrest and imprisonment. But the rewards could be enormous. If we pull this off, it could be the tipping point in our fight to prevent catastrophic climate change."

"And it might spark similar actions by others across the globe," said Ethan.

Wolff flicked the screen back to the image of Grangemouth's towers belching out vast clouds of gas. "I want us to make history. Only you can decide if you want to be a part of it."

As he continued to outline the plan, Jamie watched the reactions on the faces of the others, knowing Wolff had chosen his timing well. Fired up and full of enthusiasm following the International Climate Camp and after a series of protests which had failed to produce the publicity and arrests needed, the Climate Warriors were ripe for harvesting. All they needed was a nudge and Wolff knew that. With a neutral expression, Jamie observed Wolff and Ethan working their powers of persuasion.

As Leon had predicted, Yasmine seemed eager to please Ethan while Rose remained sceptical, demanding to know the details of how he intended to get campaigners inside and bring production safely to a halt.

Wolff said he'd been involved in several take-overs at power stations across Europe and the principles were the same. First, they'd recruit activists from across the country to break in and occupy the site in great numbers.

"And how exactly do you propose on getting hundreds into the plant?" asked Rose, appearing even more dubious.

Wolff explained that protestors would be split into groups, with each tasked with breaking in and blockading strategic points or immobilising key parts of the infrastructure. He said he'd reliable engineering contacts who could help identify the areas they'd need to target in order to halt production and cause maximum disruption. Then, once they'd control of the plant, climbers would scale a structure and daub messages on the outside to publicise what they were doing. The entire operation would be streamed live around the globe.

Jamie listened intently knowing he'd have to repeat everything to Gary later. Wolff and Ethan had clearly put a lot of thought into the plan and he wondered how long they'd been hatching this plot.

"You don't need to decide now," said Wolff. "Just consider it and talk about it as a group. We'll discuss it again tomorrow."

Jamie scanned the stunned faces of the group, trying to gauge their reaction. Looking at his friends, he hoped to God they'd see sense and send Wolff packing.

The Briefing

***"Fossil fuels are subsidised by $10 million per minute, which represents 6.5% of GDP"* — International Monetary Fund 2015**

***

Kathryn

Although Balakin wasn't due to give his talk at Edinburgh University for another week, Julien wasted no time in stepping up intelligence gathering, and Kathryn found herself invited to a briefing for Operation Alabaster.

Accompanied by Meg, she hurried to the meeting room, only to question whether she was in the right place given the motley crew assembled. At the back of the room, sat a twitchy guy in a ripped tracksuit, an elderly gentleman in a tweed suit, and a woman with a pregnant belly. Loitering at the side was an Asian man with a long beard wearing a grey salwar kameez.

Julien stood at the lectern and glanced up when she arrived. He said, "Come in Kathryn." He beckoned her forward and said, "Allow me to introduce you to Green Team." Turning to the others, he said, "Green Team, this is Kathryn, one of our cyber-intelligence analysts. Oh, and Meg, who's head of security."

This raised a chuckle as she took a seat beside Mr Twitchy Tracksuit. He ruffled the dog's ears and was rewarded with a lick. Although Kathryn had witnessed surveillance operators at work, this bunch weren't what she'd expected — blokes in stout walking boots and North Face jackets perhaps, but not this unlikely lot. Then she realised that was the point; no one would ever suspect them of being spies as they simply blended in with the population. The only common feature they shared was a nervous energy, which reminded her of her husband's 'always on' mode. Jamie had once told her operators were recruited for the hyper-vigilance and then trained to exploit it. She tried to push thoughts of him aside as Julien began the briefing.

"Good morning everyone. Welcome to Operation Alabaster."

After outlining Kathryn's findings about the Russian diplomat, he handed over to Mr Twitchy Tracksuit who turned out to be Carl, Green Team's leader. Carl explained their job today was to take a first look at their target, Dimitri Balakin, who'd been code-named RED KITE. They needed an up-to-date photograph of the Russian and details of his daily routine. He also warned them that RED KITE was likely to be highly experienced at counter-surveillance.

Julien said, "I don't want him spooked. I'd rather you lost him than compromise the operation."

"Remember," said Carl, "the Russians are the second best in the world at this."

His comment raised a few laughs and even Julien cracked a smile.

As he switched off the screen, Carl said, "Okay folks, grab your kit and let's go. Channel 6 today."

As the operators left, Julien approached Kathryn. "Blue team are currently on their way to Edinburgh for a first look at Sokolov. I'll expect you at the debrief tomorrow." He waited until everyone had gone before adding, "Director A's arranged for us to meet with a chap over at Six. Time you were introduced to our cousins."

Knowing he was referring to SIS — the UK's Secret Intelligence Service, or MI6 — Kathryn tried to hide her surprise.

She hoped to God she was right about Balakin.

***

Jamie

Jamie awoke with a start and dripping in sweat after experiencing his first night terror in months. He reached for Kathryn only to find she wasn't there, and then fell back on the mattress with a groan. It'd been the usual dream, the one in which he held his dying mate after an IED had ripped Matt open.

It was still early and the squat was silent. He brooded about his phone call with Kathryn the previous evening. She'd been distraught and he'd been stung by the bitterness in her tone when she'd hissed, "How can anything be resolved when I know you're there. With HER." In the end, all he could do was remind her he loved her. The distance between them was growing by the day.

Unable to fall back asleep, he dressed and made coffee. Hearing movement on the stairs, he glanced up to see Meadow wearing skimpy pyjamas. She joined him in the kitchen and he offered her a brew. Conscious of her proximity and her gaze, he met her eyes with trepidation.

In a low voice, she said, "We never did talk about what happened between us."

His anger and frustration boiled over and he snapped, "Nothing happened Meadow and nothing will." It came out more sharply than he'd intended and she appeared stung.

Matching his tone, she said, "Fine Jamie, I get it." She sloped off in the direction of her room like a wounded animal.

Jamie threw up his hands. "Aw Meadow, I didn't mean it to sound like ..."

Ignoring him, she slammed her bedroom door. Jamie thumped his fist on the worktop.

Fuck! I can't say or do anything right!

After pacing the floor in a futile attempt to calm down, Jamie scrubbed the kitchen and cleaned the fridge until the others rose, and then he busied himself with cooking breakfast. Meadow remained in her room until Rose went to fetch her, and he could tell she'd been crying. He felt like a complete shit for the way he'd treated her, but was determined there'd be no repeat of what'd happened in the tent.

Wolff spent the morning ingratiating himself with the group, with Ethan hanging on his coat tails. When it became clear Wolff was making time to speak to each of them in turn, Jamie made excuses and left. Alex followed him and together they escaped to the corner shop.

When they were out of earshot, Alex muttered, "Had to get the hell outa there, Ethan's being bait."

Jamie had known Alex long enough to have picked up his street slang. With his dreadlocks and piercings, it was easy to forget Alex was the son of a wealthy solicitor. More reserved than the others, it'd taken time to get to know him but Jamie had warmed to him and a friendship of sorts had developed. Alex worked a low-paid job to make ends meet after dropping out of law school following his father's death. It was a tale Jamie could relate to.

Jamie muttered, "Ethan's simply making sure Wolff's anus is thoroughly clean."

Alex laughed and fell in step with him. "Seriously man, he's like a different person when Wolff's around.

Alex was right; Jamie had watched the two of them at play, like a well-rehearsed double act. He glanced around to make sure they couldn't be overheard and asked, "So, what d'ya think about his big idea?"

Shaking his head, Alex said, "Couldn't believe it at first, but the more I think about it, the more it makes sense. Wolff's a dick but he's right about the fact that nothing else we've done has made a difference." He glanced at Jamie. "What about you?"

"You know me," said Jamie, "I'm happy to go with the flow."

"Yes, you like to nail your colours firmly to the fence. But, seriously man, which way are you leaning? I mean, this is really major."

Jamie knew he had to be careful. As an undercover operative, there were legal lines he couldn't cross, and inciting or encouraging someone to carry out a criminal act they wouldn't otherwise do was one such line. And morally, he couldn't justify luring people he now considered friends into a trap. He hoped the group would see Wolff's proposal for the crazy idea it was and reject it. That'd be the best outcome: Wolff and Ethan would be charged, the rest of the group would be left alone, and he could go home to his wife.

He chose his words carefully. "Aye, but there are loads of ways to make a difference without sticking your neck on the line. Wolff's gonnae have to work a bit harder to convince me. I'm not going to be anyone's sacrificial lamb, and neither should you."

"Seriously though," said Alex, "what else can we do? We've tried everything but it's nowhere near enough. Maybe Wolff's right and stronger action is exactly what's needed before it's too late."

This wasn't what Jamie wanted to hear but he didn't argue. His job was to observe and gather intelligence, and he had to let this unfold. He said, "I'll support the decision, whatever you choose."

Alex muttered something about 'knucks' and offered him a fist bump, a gesture that never failed to make Jamie laugh.

***

Ethan called another meeting of the group that evening in the squat. Slouched in the seating area, Jamie watched as Ethan and Wolff began their double act.

Wolff crossed a foot over his knee, laced his hands behind his head and stretched back on the couch with a smug grin. Ethan sat opposite, resting his hand on the back of Yasmine's neck. Ethan asked if they'd all had enough time to consider the proposal and when there was muttered agreement he suggested a vote.

"We'd like this to be a unanimous decision," said Wolff. "I'll abstain."

Ethan looked around and said, "Can I ask who's in favour?"

Only Ethan and Yaz raised their hands. Jamie held his breath and looked at the faces of the others. After a long pause, the lads slowly raised their hands, and Alex shot Jamie an apologetic look. Meadow's half-hearted and hesitant vote followed. The sense of approval bestowed by Wolff's benign smile was almost intoxicating.

The atmosphere crackled as the group turned to look at Rose.

C'mon Rose, see sense and say no.

"I've given it a lot of thought," she said, her eyes flicking to Ethan. "It's not the sort of action we'd normally get involved in or would condone. I understand we need to push the boundaries of non-violent direct action but this ... this is off the scale. I'm really not comfortable with it."

Jamie quietly exhaled.

Rose gazed at Ethan and said, "But if you decide it's something you really want to do, I'll support you."

Aw shit!

A cheer went up and Ethan leapt to his feet and embraced her. Rose wallowed in his praise; it was the first time Jamie had seen her smile in days. Wolff grinned like a predator watching its prey approach a trap.

Jamie glowered at Wolff who met his gaze with a steely one of his own. Wolff said, "So are you in or out?"

Everyone turned to stare at Jamie.

***

Kathryn

Kathryn glanced at the time on her computer, aware she'd an important job to do when she got home. She tidied her desk, locked away all sensitive files, and returned her collection of coffee cups to the kitchenette. Before shutting down her machines, she checked if there'd been a response from GCHQ about tracing Monty's cryptocurrency investments. Fitz had taken her through the tortuous process of raising the request but she'd heard nothing back, and she wondered why it was taking so long.

"C'mon Meg, time to go home," she said, coaxing the sleepy dog from under her desk.

She collected her phone and checked it to see if Jamie had called but there were no missed calls or messages. Her mood plummeted further. Although their conversations were strained, she still needed to hear his voice and to know he was safe. She considered texting him and hovered her thumb over her phone, then put it away. Jamie could wait. She wasn't going to make it easy for him ... no matter what she decided.

Since discovering his treachery, she'd run the full gamut of unpleasant and unexpected emotions. Feelings of shock and anger had given way to disbelief and an overwhelming sense of sadness. And it wasn't just her mental health that was suffering; it was wreaking havoc with her appetite and sleep patterns making it even more difficult to think straight.

But Jamie was right; without talking it through properly, nothing would be resolved. They were stuck in limbo until this damned operation of his reached its conclusion and they could finally discuss the situation calmly and openly. The problem was, she didn't feel ready to do that yet. The wound was too raw, too painful. She needed time to gather her thoughts and make sense of her feelings so she could come to a decision about their future.

She checked her phone again before starting the car. Still nothing. Exhausted and depressed, she drove home.

Back in the cottage, she paced up and down in the bedroom, peering through the slats of the blinds whenever she heard a car. *Dark Canary* had messaged her earlier about the date and time of their visit and she'd prepared what she needed. After an anxious wait, a black SUV with tinted windows pulled up outside Darren's house.

Two men in dark clothing and balaclavas got out and walked up to his front door. One rang the bell while the other, carrying a holdall, hid around the corner. Kathryn held her breath as Darren's blurry shape appeared behind the frosted glass. When Darren opened the door, the caller tasered him in the chest. Darren slumped to the floor and the two men forced their way inside and closed the door.

Kathryn darted to her computer. She'd already connected to the camera on Darren's laptop and, after a few minutes, she watched his bedroom pitch and sway as one of the men angled it so she could record the event. The picture showed Darren secured to a wooden armchair with cable ties around his wrists and ankles. His joggies and underwear were gathered around his knees and his penis lay on top of a wooden chopping board on his lap. Despite the stocking covering his head, she could make out the look of terror on his face.

One of the guys reached into the holdall and produced a machete.

Darren strained against his bindings and yelled, "Why are you doing this?"

Pointing to the computer screen with the machete, the man replied in a strong Glaswegian accent, "This is why, ya wee shite."

Taking her cue, Kathryn displayed a scrolling transcript of Darren's worst incel posts onto his laptop's screen so he could read them.

Darren groaned out a mixture of horror and incredulity as realisation dawned. "I've never hurt anyone," he whimpered.

Grabbing his hair, the vigilante snarled, "Not yet you haven't. And we're here to make sure you never do." He raised the machete high into the air.

The blade flashed down and Darren screamed.

The Plan

"The climate crisis accelerates. Anti-protest laws proliferate. These developments are not unrelated" **— Jeff Sparrow 2022**

***

Jamie

"I've one condition," said Jamie, glowering.

Wolff appeared surprised. "Sure, what?"

Jamie pointed to Leon. "I'll agree to take part, I'll even climb, but I don't want Leon on the end of a rope." When Leon protested, Jamie silenced him with a look, adding, "I don't want you anywhere near this mate. It's too risky. If you play a major part in this, the justice system will come down on you like a tonne of bricks."

"That's my choice to make," objected Leon.

Jamie nodded. "True but, if you want my involvement, there's no way I'm having your lengthy stretch in prison on my conscience. Those are my terms."

"He's right," said Rose.

Leon huffed out a breath, opened his mouth to argue, then closed it after seeing Jamie's determined expression. Shrugging, he said, "Fair enough. But I want to do something."

"And you will," said Jamie. "The climbing team will need support on the ground."

"You'll lead the climb then?" asked Ethan, sounding surprised.

Jamie nodded and the group applauded.

"Aw, this is hype man," chuckled Alex.

"Fantastic," said Wolff grinning, "but you understand you'll be arrested?"

"I expect to be."

Wolff rewarded him with a sly smile that made Jamie's blood turn to ice.

Christ, Gary's gonnae hand me my arse on a platter.

"This calls for a toast," said Ethan.

He produced a bottle of Scotch and fetched glasses. The whisky burned a path from Jamie's mouth to his stomach.

Ethan called the group to order, saying, "Time to make a start."

He projected a Google Maps image on the white wall of the squat which revealed the sheer scale of the Grangemouth site. The refinery and petrochemical plant spanned an area almost as large as the town of Grangemouth itself which lay to the west.

The River Forth formed the plant's northern boundary, its banks a patchwork of verdant nature reserve and brown mud flats. A channel snaking from the Forth gave sea vessels access to the docks which were lined with colourful shipping containers stacked like Lego bricks. The smaller River Avon cut through the eastern edge of the plant before meandering towards the historic town of Linlithgow.

Wolff pointed to where the Forties pipeline system delivered crude oil straight to the refinery from fields in the North Sea. Indicating the Kinneil Nature Reserve and mud flats, he said, "The RSPB visit this area several times a year to monitor the bird population."

"Could we get in via the reserve by boat?" asked Ethan pointing to the channel leading from the Forth into the docks. "Or here," he added, indicating the smaller Avon.

Jamie said, "We don't have any boats and I don't fancy our chances if we get stuck on those mudflats on low tide." He couldn't believe they were having this insane conversation.

"What about the train?" asked Rose. She pointed to a railway track that ran along the outer perimeter towards Falkirk in the west.

"Worth a look," agreed Wolff.

They scoured the map again. The oil refinery was set in a grid of crisscrossing access roads, its upper edge dotted with cylindrical storage tanks like draughts on a chequerboard. A main public route ran along the lower edge, dividing the refinery from the chemical plant in the south.

Pointing to the four major access roads, Wolff said, "The main entrance is at West Gate."

"What security's around it?" asked Jamie. *Not that you've a cat's chance in hell of getting near it.*

Ethan zoomed in on the image to display a barrier and booth. "We need to get a closer look."

"Can we fly a drone in?" asked Alex.

Wolff shook his head. "The airspace is controlled and we'd be arrested if we tried." He glanced around adding, "We need to carry out reconnaissance to identify access routes and strategic points, and photograph key infrastructure."

Ethan rubbed his hands together. "So who's up for a reccie at the weekend?"

There was muttered agreement and Jamie agreed to drive the group to Grangemouth. Ethan quizzed him about the local area and he admitted it'd been many years since he'd visited Grangemouth. He recommended they posed as tourists in the neighbouring towns of Falkirk and Linlithgow.

Jamie said, "There are plenty of cycle paths and walks with views of the plant."

Wolff then suggested they all paired up. He turned to Meadow and proposed they investigated the southern edge of the plant. She appeared torn and looked from Jamie to Wolff. When Jamie avoided her eye, she relented with a nod.

Ethan took Yasmine's hand. "In that case, we'll check out the western access."

A flicker of jealousy sparked in Rose's eyes.

Jamie asked Rose if she wanted to accompany him to Linlithgow on the eastern side, and she gave him a grateful smile.

"Guess Alex and I'll go north then," said Leon. "I'll take my camera."

Wolff said, "You can't just pitch up and start taking photographs. It'll look suspicious."

Leon glared at him. "I'm a photography student. Doh!"

"What if you're stopped and asked why you're taking pictures of Grangemouth?" snapped Wolff, "You could blow the whole operation before it's begun."

Leon's nostrils flared and he bit out, "I'll say I'm doing a project on bird populations in industrial landscapes."

Aye, good answer, thought Jamie but the allegiances and cracks were beginning to show. To diffuse the situation, he offered to source fake identity documents so the lads could pose as RSPB inspectors to access the nature reserve.

After the meeting ended, Jamie took a drive and called Gary to give him the latest intelligence. He always felt a profound sense of remorse after these calls as he was fond of the group, if not its leadership. He knew he shouldn't feel this way about his targets. He also worried about Wolff's influence on Meadow. She was in danger of being pulled from the realms of peaceful activism into another world where violence and terror ruled. They all were.

Jamie said nothing about leading the climb since he was sure the protest would never get that far. Gary had made it crystal clear he was forbidden from getting involved beyond observing and gathering pre-emptive evidence, and on no account was he to break the law without a justifiable reason.

Gary asked if a date for the action had been set.

"Not yet. Reckon it'll be a few weeks."

"As soon as you know —"

"— so will you. Day or night."

Jamie could call Gary at any time but if, for some reason he was unable to reach him, he could phone the main Operations Centre at Thames House, give his code name, and the message would be relayed. Initially, Gary had based himself at a covert office in Manchester used by the Security Service but with the group's focus on Grangemouth, Jamie was certain he'd relocate nearby.

Bracing himself, Jamie requested the fake RSPB identities for Leon and Alex. He held the phone away from his ear to avoid being deafened.

Gary squawked, "What part of the instructions for UC officers did you not understand?"

Thank God I never mentioned the climb.

***

Kathryn

The machete thunked into the chopping board a mere inch from Darren's penis. Squealing like a stuck pig, he cried out for his mother and urinated.

Machete man jerked the blade free of the wood and pressed the edge against Darren's throat. Piss dribbled over the chopping board and the vigilante cursed in disgust.

He growled, "We'll be watching you. We'll never stop watching you, and if you as much as harm a hair on a woman's head, we'll cut your dick off and feed it to you." Then, turning to look directly into the camera through the slit in his balaclava, he added, "And that goes for each and every one of you sick fucks."

To punctuate his message, he delivered a savage punch to Darren's ribs. Darren crumpled. Then, using the machete, the man cut the cable ties and kicked Darren off the chair. Whimpering, he crawled into the corner and clutched his knees to his chest. The two men left and Kathryn heard the car pull away, but it was several minutes before Darren moved. When he finally got to his feet, Kathryn ended the connection.

She then spent the rest of the evening posting the video footage on every poisonous incel platform she could find.

THE RECCIE

***"In 2018, fossil fuel companies spent only 1% of their budgets on green energy."* Tzeporah Berman, chair of the Fossil Fuel Non-Proliferation Treaty Initiative**

***

Kathryn

Next morning, Kathryn took a seat at the back of the briefing room as she and Green Team awaited Julien's arrival. The surveillance operators looked exhausted. Slumped over chairs, it was evident Balakin aka RED KITE had given them the run-around. The 'pregnant' woman had removed her fake belly and was rubbing her lower back like an expectant mother, while Carl (aka Mr Twitchy Tracksuit) appeared to be fast asleep.

When Julien strode to the lectern apologising for his tardiness, everyone sprang to life. He tapped the screen and audio filled the room.

"Welcome to Operation Alabaster," he said. "We have Blue Team on the line for a debrief. They're returning from Edinburgh."

As blue-team gave their 'Over the Air' update of their surveillance of GREY GOOSE, as Anna Sokolov had been code-named, Kathryn scanned the photographs and video they'd obtained of her commute to work and visit to a sandwich shop with a colleague. Described as a 'clean skin' — someone unknown to

MI5 who they'd little information on — Anna was clearly oblivious to the fact she was being watched.

As the meeting continued, Kathryn struggled to focus, her mind drifting to thoughts of Jamie. What was he up to and was he with HER? She tried to dispel images of Meadow but still they plagued her. Although she and Jamie talked almost every evening, small snatches of hushed conversation in which neither could discuss the real issue between them, she'd no idea about his life in the squat.

"What have you found Kathryn?"

Julien's question jolted her from her reverie, and she suddenly felt shy under the gaze of Green Team. She'd never been comfortable speaking publicly, and pulled at the sleeves on her jumper as Julien beckoned her to the lectern. Meg trotted at her heels as though sensing her anxiety.

Kathryn had spent the best part of the day digging into Anna Sokolov's life and that of her close friends and family. She displayed some of her findings on the large screen as only relevant information was ever shared with surveillance operators.

"Err ... Sokolov ... sorry ... uhm ... GREY GOOSE is heavily in debt to the tune of thousands." Kathryn coughed nervously, conscious of everyone staring at her. "She appears to have an online gambling addiction, and is on these sites for hours at a time, sometimes late into the night."

The line crackled and one of Blue Team's operators spoke. He'd a strong northern accent and she could hear the sound of traffic in the background. "Yes, after her colleague left the café, GREY GOOSE spent time on the Global Casino site."

Julien thanked Kathryn for her update and Blue Team for their work, wishing them a safe journey home. He then asked Carl for an update from Green Team.

Wiry and lithe, Carl bounded up to the lectern and grinned. "Ah, you've got to love the Russians," he chuckled, "what a busy time we've had."

His team chuffed in agreement as Carl described RED KITE's movements and routine. Photographs and video from their surveillance of Balakin accompanied his update. He explained the diplomat had left his flat at seven o'clock that morning and taken the tube to the embassy. After a trade meeting in Central

London, he'd lunched with his boss in a restaurant before meeting with another colleague at a local café, and then he'd returned home at five where Green Team had left him.

Carl said, "He's good at counter, used every trick in the book to avoid being tailed." Then, on a laugh, he added, "Never saw us mind."

"Excellent work Green Team," said Julien. "We'll reconvene tomorrow at 09:00 hours to plan the work in Edinburgh."

Carl gave a cheeky smile.

***

Jamie

Jamie's journey north from Salford took over four hours in the busy Friday evening traffic. Everyone had bundled into his van which he'd emptied of his rope-access equipment ahead of their trip to reconnoitre the area. Jamie hoped to God they weren't stopped, and he didn't encounter anyone from his old life as a copper in Glasgow.

It was dark by the time they reached the outskirts of Grangemouth but the vast plant was well-lit, and the photos hadn't done justice to the true scale of it.

"Bloody hell, the place is huge," said Alex, "it's like a city."

Leon pointed to a high-level flare which illuminated the night sky like a giant orange torch. He asked what it was and Wolff explained it was for disposing of hydrocarbon gases and releasing pressure in the plant.

Jamie said, "The locals call it 'Aurora Flarealis'".

To give them a glimpse of the complex, Jamie took a long circuitous route around Grangemouth and the plant's perimeter. Afterwards, he drove to nearby Falkirk and dropped off Ethan, Rose and Yasmine at a Travel Lodge. Leon looked gloomy as he watched them disappear into the lobby.

Jamie continued on to a small hotel where Wolff and Meadow were staying. He wondered if they were sharing a room. Remembering the hotel he and Kathryn had recently holidayed in, put him in a sombre mood as he made the onward journey to Linlithgow.

He'd visited the picturesque town before but had forgotten how charming it was. He chuckled at the lads' awed reaction on seeing the great hulking silhouette of Linlithgow Palace, birthplace of Mary Queen of Scots. Although a ruin, it was still imposing and dominated the town.

"Wow, it's beautiful," announced Leon. "Hey, what are the women like?"

Jamie chuckled, "Like the palace ... beautiful but formidable."

Like Kathryn.

They'd booked an Airbnb on the edge of town, a three-story apartment which had once been the servants' quarters in a Victorian mansion.

Alex whistled his approval as he strode through the property. "Yo, we've lucked out."

"I'm starvin'," said Jamie, "fancy a chippie?"

Leon laughed, "Great idea, I'm fed up eating vegan crap. Just don't tell the others."

Later, after they'd demolished fish suppers from the local takeaway, Jamie broke out a case of beer and they stretched out on the sofas.

Leon raised his bottle and toasted, "To climate justice."

"To the end of fossil fuels," said Alex.

Jamie said, "To a lenient judge and a short sentence."

It was a sobering thought and the lads blanched. Discussion turned to what would likely happen after they were arrested and where they might serve out a prison sentence. Leon said Ethan had been in touch with a lawyer who did pro bono work for Extinction Rebellion who'd offered her help.

Jamie took a slug of beer and asked Alex, "Ever considered returning to law school to finish your degree?"

"Aw man," groaned Alex, "you sound like my bleedin' mother."

"He's right," said Leon, "if I'd your brains and family connections, I'd jump at the chance."

Alex muttered, "I'd a really shitty time at uni. It's not something I want to repeat."

Jamie paused, choosing his words carefully. "It must have been tough … after losing your dad."

Alex nodded and looked away.

There was a long moment of silence which Leon eventually broke. "You'd make a brilliant lawyer. Think how many companies you could sue for polluting and damaging the environment."

Jamie added, "Or the number of idiots like us you could defend."

They all laughed.

"Nah, I'm happy doing what I'm doing," said Alex shaking his head.

Jamie wondered if he'd feel the same after finding himself on the wrong side of the law.

***

Kathryn

It was the little things Kathryn missed that surprised her most, like Jamie singing along to the radio while he did the washing up, the mug of tea he brought her most mornings, and the love hearts he drew on her frosted car windscreen. Sundays were the hardest and the most painful reminders of his absence, and she yearned for the return of those long lazy mornings filled with laughter and lovemaking.

To detract from the ache in her heart, she spent the weekend researching Margaret-Anne McCrae, the woman that Karsten Wolff had been seen lunching with in London. It wasn't a task she could undertake in the office, at least not without raising a red flag since she'd no reason to investigate people connected to Jamie's operation. Julien had ordered her not to interfere and she feared that, were she to do so, she'd face disciplinary action. She was not about to give Robin the satisfaction of firing her.

MAM, as McCrae was nicknamed, was the youngest daughter of a bank manager and his teacher wife. Educated at Cambridge, where she gained a first in English, she trained as a journalist. While working at one of the tabloids, she broke a story about a high-class prostitute who was simultaneously servicing the needs of two top newspaper editors, a cabinet minister, and a billionaire arms dealer. With the notoriety she gained as the investigative reporter, MAM had left her employment and established her own PR company called *McCrae & Associates*. After initially promoting kiss and tell stories featuring celebrities, she'd cleaned up the agency's image and now specialised in corporate media relations.

Kathryn found online images of MAM and her ex-husband at various press gatherings. Margaret-Anne was almost as wide as she was tall, with bobbed red hair the hue of which did not occur in nature. A recent photograph revealed she hadn't aged well, the sagging skin at her neck the texture of crepe. She'd mean little eyes, teeth like old piano keys, and doughy breasts which swelled over an ill-fitting bra. In another picture, she wore impossibly high heels and a brightly-coloured tunic dress which, on someone slender, might have been pleasing; on MAM it resembled a hospital gown.

Trawling the client list of *McCrae & Associates*, Kathryn looked for possible connections between the companies MAM represented and Karsten Wolff's interests. She spotted none; in fact, many of their clients — banks and fossil fuel companies — were the antithesis of what Wolff and the Climate Warriors stood for.

Puzzled, Kathryn turned her attention to the financial trail, where she spent several hours hacking into MAM's corporate and personal bank accounts and investments. A series of regular deposits into a lesser-used current account caught her eye, each transaction for under the threshold where banks must report the source of funds. There had been several of these in recent months totalling around a hundred thousand pounds. However, when Kathryn attempted to trace the origin of these transactions, she encountered a digital wall of cryptocurrency. She groaned so loud Meg jumped.

Petting the dog, she grumbled, "More shitcoin."

***

Jamie

Jamie awoke with the hangover from hell, having stayed up half the night drinking with Alex and Leon. He'd enjoyed the opportunity to let off steam but was regretting it now. After a greasy breakfast, they climbed into the van and collected the others.

They arrived at Wolff's hotel to find him and Meadow outside, hand in hand. As Jamie parked up, Wolff slid a protective arm around her waist and pulled her into him. Jamie clenched his jaw and struggled not to let his contempt show.

He's bloody using her.

After equipping everyone, Jamie deposited the pairs around Grangemouth before he and Rose headed for Linlithgow. Rose was quiet on the journey, and he asked if she was having second thoughts.

"No, not about the protest." After a few beats, she said, "It's Meadow I'm worried about."

This was the first time Rose had shared anything with him.

"You two have known each other a long time."

She gazed out the window as the countryside flashed by. "I've come across guys like Wolff before. They only care about the cause, not the people involved in it."

"You think he doesn't care about her?"

"I think Karsten Wolff's the type of man who'll stop at nothing to get what he wants and to hell with everyone else."

He was surprised at her candour. Up until now Rose had always been self-contained and wary.

Stopping at a red light, he glanced at her. "Why did you agree to be a part of this?"

Folding her arms, she muttered, "Because we need to ratchet up the pressure on the fossil fuel industry. Wolff's right about that."

"That the only reason?"

She turned to face him. "I need to be here for Meadow so I can pick up the pieces afterwards." She exhaled loudly and said, "I just wish she was with YOU, not HIM." She gave a mirthless laugh. "And I never thought I'd say that. I was sure you were a spy when you first pitched up."

He nearly had heart failure and guffawed to cover it. "So, what changed?"

Smiling, she said, "You've kind of grown on us."

"You make me sound like a fungus."

They were still laughing when they arrived at the bicycle hire shop where Jamie had reserved two mountain bikes. While he completed the paperwork, Rose shopped for a picnic lunch which she stashed in a small rucksack. After, they cycled through the town, then cut off onto a path which led towards Grangemouth.

Autumn had yet to assert itself and, although there was a chill in the breeze, it was dry and sunny. Following part of the John Muir Way, a coast-to-coast route across the Central Belt, they cycled over rough tracks towards the eastern edge of the plant. When it finally came into view, they stopped for a break and took in the dramatic vista below.

"I can't get over the size of the place, it's enormous," said Rose.

After continuing as far as they could by bike, they padlocked the cycles and went on foot. Using his camera phone, Jamie took photographs of the perimeter fencing and the plant beyond, making sure Rose appeared in the foreground of every snap in case they were stopped and questioned. There was little sign of a security presence within that part of the plant and few people milling around. After taking pictures, they returned to the bikes, spread out a rug and ate their picnic.

Rose said, "Mind if I ask you something personal?"

Mumbling through a mouthful of sandwich, he replied, "Sure, what?"

"What happened between you and Meadow? I thought you were getting on really well."

Jamie explained about his marriage, realising that the version he'd invented for his legend about being estranged from his wife wasn't so far from the truth. He described what'd happened in the tent.

Shooting him an incredulous look, she said, "You still think it was mistaken identity?"

He shrugged.

"Guess it explains why Meadow's thrown herself at Wolff."

"Ah don't put that on me," he said.

She gave him a sheepish look. "And Ethan hasn't exactly discouraged it."

"Fuck's sake! Really?

She shook her head. "I genuinely think Meadow likes you."

His appetite vanished and he chucked the rest of his sandwich in the bag. After a gulp of water, he ventured, "So, can I ask you something personal?" When she nodded, he added, "You can tell me to piss off and mind my own business though."

She gave a humourless laugh. "I know what you're going to ask. Why am I with Ethan? Why do I put up with three in a bed?"

He looked at her in askance.

"Sooner or later, Yaz will get fed up with him and move on. But I'll still be here."

With an apologetic smile, he said, "You must really love him."

She nodded, her eyes glassy. "Guess I must."

Her pain was almost palpable.

The Spook

***"There is no such thing as the greenhouse effect. The atmosphere behaves neither as a greenhouse nor as an insulating blanket ... preventing heat escaping from Earth."* — Professor Ian Plimer 2009**

***

Kathryn

Kathryn gathered her things in preparation for her visit to Vauxhall Cross and the headquarters of MI6, the UK's foreign intelligence agency. Director A had arranged for her and Julien to meet a man called Dominic Shaftesbury from the Russia Desk. For security reasons, they were being chauffeured there in a staff car.

Julien strode towards her desk pulling on his suit jacket. Crouching, he produced a gravy bone from his pocket and offered it to the dog. Having been snarled at on several occasions, he'd started giving her treats and the collie was gradually warming to him.

Clapping her, he said, "Bring Meg, it'll piss them off."

Kathryn laughed. "I thought we were all on the same side?"

"We are. Still like to piss each other off."

During the short journey, Julien read the *Telegraph* newspaper. She wasn't sure if him keeping quiet was to avoid their conversation being overheard by the driver. Although she'd worked for Julien for some time, she knew little about him as staff were not permitted to share personal information with each other; a rule which only fuelled gossip and speculation. Throw together a bunch of intelligent people with little social life and office drama becomes the primary focus.

Julien wore a wedding ring and she assumed he'd children because she'd once been in his car and it had been full of children's toys. Or was that a ploy? Always impeccably dressed in sharp suits and tailored shirts adorned with cuff links, she wondered what his wife was like and how his family fared given the long hours he worked.

The car took them to a door at the rear of the SIS building that looked as though it was used for goods deliveries. Meg's presence had the desired effect and disrupted the security checks which were as stringent as at Thames House. The personnel had to make several phone calls and scan a snarling Meg, before they were admitted.

With the confidence only a private education bestows, Julien led her through a maze of corridors and into the lobby. Emblazoned in large letters above the main desk was the motto 'Semper Occultus' which translated as 'Always Secret'. They took the lift to the fourth floor, where Meg's appearance raised eyebrows. She could have sworn she heard Julien chuckle.

A middle-aged woman behind the reception desk greeted them. "He's in 415, he's been expecting you."

... Mr Bond.

Kathryn stifled a giggle as they followed Moneypenny's directions down a long corridor. A slightly-built man in his late fifties with sharp features and wireframed glasses opened the door and ushered them into a large, light-filled office. His wispy fair hair was thinning and his pinstriped suit hung loosely on his frame.

Shaking Julien's hand, he said in a soft effeminate voice, "Always a pleasure to see our cousins in Five."

As he extended a hand to Kathryn, she froze.

Julien quickly intervened, "Kathryn doesn't shake hands." The moment felt awkward.

Dominic gave a knowing smile. "Ah yes, of course. Delightful to meet you, my dear. I've heard so much about you and Meg. Quite a stir it caused."

Did he really just call her 'dear'?

She wondered if it was the dog or her marriage that'd caused the stir. Had gossip about her and Jamie's relationship extended to the wider intelligence circle? Dominic stooped to clap the dog then immediately retracted his hand in response to Meg's low growl. Julien's lips twitched in amusement.

They took a seat at the conference table. The Intelligence Services operated a strict clear desk policy to ensure no confidential information was left lying around, and she was always struck by the lack of personal items and photographs. Five's offices and workspaces had the same spartan feel but coffee and pastries had been provided. She helped herself while the two men exchanged gossip about a mutual friend from Cambridge University.

Dominic steepled his hands under his chin and asked how he could help. Julien retrieved the Alabaster dossier from his leather folio and passed it to him. Reaching into his pocket, Dominic produced a glasses case and polished his spectacles before taking his time to browse the file. Julien summarised what they'd discovered and outlined his suspicions about Balakin.

Dominic said, "The Russians are nervous about the Paris Climate Agreement. They signed up to it but are concerned a shift to green energy will damage their economy which is heavily reliant on fossil fuels. They're huge energy exporters but, in the race to decarbonise and develop sustainable alternatives, they're way behind the West."

Indicating the Grid Scale Systems brochure, he added, "Stealing this technology will allow them to boost their renewable energy industry by several decades."

"At the expense of ours," muttered Julien.

"Indeed," said Dominic. He turned to Kathryn. "State-sponsored espionage and cyberwarfare are far greater threats to us than your common or garden suicide bomber, my dear."

Kathryn bristled.

Dominic scrutinised the picture of Balakin. "I'll ask around, see what I can find out about our friend here. He might be known to some of my contacts. In fact, I'm having luncheon with a chap tomorrow who may be able to shed some light."

"That would be enormously helpful," said Julien.

Dominic closed the file and slid it back. "I presume you've a plan to make sure this technology doesn't fall into his hands?"

Julien gave an enigmatic smile and tucked the dossier back into his folio. "Call me if you find anything," he said.

After thanking Dominic, they left and retraced their steps to the ground floor. As they crossed the marble foyer, Kathryn noticed several security personnel squeeze into what appeared to be a broom cupboard behind the reception area and close the door.

"Did you see that?" she asked Julien.

In a low voice, he explained that because all the foreign intelligence agencies spied upon each other, most of the building was constructed using wire mesh to protect it from electronic eavesdropping, and regular sweeps were carried out for listening devices. However, if personnel had limited access to briefing rooms or wanted to share sensitive information quickly, they could use secure cupboards. "We've a few in Thames House," he said.

On the car journey back, Julien placed his newspaper on the seat beside them and regarded her. "So, how did you think that went?"

She paused, unsure of whether to say what she thought or not. Rather than voicing the fact she wouldn't trust Dominic as far as she could throw him, she said, "He seemed like a nice old dear." She emphasised 'dear'.

Chuckling, Julien opened *The Telegraph*.

***

Jamie

That evening, Jamie and the group met for dinner at an Indian restaurant in Falkirk. The place was packed and, although they occupied a table in the corner, they were careful not to be overheard. Over steaming dishes of fragrant curry and naan, they discussed how they'd got on with reconnoitring the different locations around Grangemouth.

Alex and Leon had breezed into the plant in a car borrowed from a local XR activist who owed Ethan a favour. Leon said they'd got a good look at the security at West Gate which was manned by two guards: a butch woman in a hi-vis jacket wielding a clipboard and radio who greeted drivers and performed vehicle checks, and another middle-aged guard inside a small booth.

Jamie asked if his fake RSPB passes had worked and Alex reported that the guards had merely waved them through unchallenged. He and Leon had parked up and used binoculars to observe comings and goings over the course of the day and to take hundreds of photographs of the northern part of the plant. They'd even counted the birds in case they were challenged on the way out, which they weren't.

"Jamie's right," said Leon, "those mudflats are treacherous and there's no way can we can get access by boat."

"The good news," said Alex, "is the barriers at West Gate are in a poor state of repair and could easily be forced open. A van would do it."

Wolff grinned. "Sounds like we have our way in." Reaching over the table for Meadow's hand, he added, "We had a productive day too."

Meadow gazed at Wolff as he explained they'd taken a look at the security surrounding the plant. The on-site team appeared to consist of a handful of officers, with a couple of guys who zoomed about the plant in jeeps, and a few others in 4x4s doing perimeter checks. Wire fencing topped with a spool of barbed wire surrounded the site.

"But it's nothing we can't get through with a pair of wire cutters," said Wolff.

"With enough of us, we can sway the fence down," said Meadow, "same as we used to do at Greenham."

Ethan rolled his eyes.

Jamie shared his and Rose's findings about the eastern edge where trains carried goods and products to and from the refinery, docks and container yard. The trains ran at night from the plant, through Falkirk Grahamston Station, and onto Carlisle where they delivered petrol, diesel and kerosene to the North of England. Rose showed them the photographs they'd taken of the bogies which had ladders on the outside that gave access to a hatch on the roof.

Rose said, "We could jump onto the train when it slows through Falkirk. It'd take us right inside the plant."

Wolff studied the photographs while Rose told them how they'd also searched for a base they could use before the protest. She said, "There's a disused community centre in Linlithgow which the council are selling off. It's large enough to house us and the volunteers."

Ethan asked how they intended to get access.

"Leave it with me," said Jamie.

Another wee job for Gary.

After the plates were cleared and coffee served, Ethan described the western side of the plant which he and Yasmine had surveyed. They'd also met with a former process engineer who'd worked at the plant. Disgruntled after being made redundant following thirty years of service at the refinery, he'd agreed to help them.

"He was a mine of information and only too happy to share it," said Yasmine.

Ethan cut in with, "He confirmed our best way in is through West Gate, but he says there may be an armed security team on-site. There are also police patrols and response teams on standby."

Meadow blanched and Wolff took her hand and whispered, "I'm afraid that's the risk you take if you mount a protest inside an oil refinery."

The information wasn't a surprise to Jamie — Gary had told him about security — but Wolff didn't appear fazed by the news.

Discussion turned to employee shift patterns based on information the engineer had shared.

Yasmine said, "Contractors start their shift about 8 a.m. and refinery staff around 6 a.m. When the night and day shifts change, there's a handover."

"So the ideal time to storm the gates," said Ethan, "is before the changeover, around 5:30 a.m."

Rose asked if they could trust the engineer. Yasmine reassured her that he was so bitter about the way he and his colleagues had been treated, that he viewed the protest as a way to get back at the company.

Ethan's face lit up in a smile. "His green credentials may be questionable but he's agreed to join us on the day. He knows exactly what levers to pull and what buttons to press once we're inside."

Information such as this was like gold dust. Jamie needed to find out the engineer's name so he could alert Gary but, since Wolff and Ethan were as jumpy as cats on a hot tin roof, he'd have to bide his time.

Rose's earlier words about him being a spy rang loudly in his ears.

The Stand up

"The climate crisis is both the easiest and the hardest issue we have ever faced. The easiest because we know what we must do. We must stop the emissions of greenhouse gases. The hardest because our current economics are still totally dependent on burning fossil fuels, and thereby destroying ecosystems in order to create everlasting economic growth." **— Greta Thunberg 2019**

***

Kathryn

Kathryn and Fitz stood in Julien's office testing out the theory that the discomfort of standing would keep meetings short. Fitz leaned against the wall while Kathryn shifted her weight from foot to foot. Ten minutes in and Julien went to pull up a seat, then scowled and remained standing.

"Balakin's asked to meet Sokolov," said Kathryn. Realising her mistake, she quickly added, "I mean RED KITE and GREY GOOSE."

Julien dismissed her error with a wave of his hand saying, "In here, you can use their real names. Has Sokolov agreed to meet him?"

She nodded. "After his speech at the university."

Julien turned to Fitz. "That's less than a week away. We need some of our people on that guest list."

"Already on it," said Fitz, "two of Green Team will be in the audience, the rest will follow when they leave. We'll have eyes and ears the entire time."

"Excellent," replied Julien. "I'll have the techs bug Balakin's apartment while he's in Edinburgh."

Grinning, Fitz said, "Already on it."

Later, Kathryn left Meg to sleep under her desk and returned with Julien for another meeting with Dominic at MI6.

After showing them in, Dominic picked up his desk phone and spoke curtly to announce his guests had arrived. Shortly afterwards there was a knock and two caterers appeared with trays of coffee and cake. Kathryn wondered whether Six's budget was greater than Five's.

Once the staff left, Dominic announced he'd obtained information about Balakin he knew would interest them. With a smug grin, he said, "He's a raven."

"Goodness," said Julien spluttering coffee. "A proper one?"

Kathryn looked inquiringly from Dominic to Julien in the hope they'd enlighten her. When neither did, she said, "Uhm ... what's a raven?"

Dominic gave an avuncular smile. "He spies through seduction, my dear."

According to Dominic's source, Balakin had been active for some time which explained why he'd been moving so frequently between postings in numerous European countries.

"He disappears as soon as he has the information he wants," said Dominic, passing Julien a folder.

Julien flicked through the dossier which was full of photographs of Balakin smiling with his arm draped around various women.

Offering Julien a slice of sponge cake, Dominic asked, "So, have you plans to prevent him stealing the IP from GSS?"

Julien explained he did not want to alert Grid Scale Systems to the fact their technology was under threat for fear they'd react by locking it down and spooking Sokolov. He said, "We'll let it play out and then pick both of them up after the exchange has been made. Once we have the evidence, he'll be expelled and will be on the next flight home to Moscow."

Dominic raised an eyebrow. "Risky though?"

Julien gave a tight smile. "Nothing my team can't handle."

***

Jamie

Following their reccie in Grangemouth, the Climate Warriors returned to Salford and began planning the protest in detail. Wolff tasked each of them with a particular function, with Jamie responsible for organising the climb.

The floor of the squat was strewn with plans, photographs and maps tacked onto rolls of wallpaper which could be rolled up and hidden at a moment's notice. Notes were jotted on whiteboards which could quickly be erased, with little recorded digitally. Operational security was tight and Jamie was beginning to understand how Wolff had managed to remain under the radar of the authorities for so long. Until now.

It was Sunday evening and Ethan had called a meeting to discuss progress and the role each of them would play. With a mug of strong coffee, Jamie pulled up a seat beside Alex and Leon. Yaz and Ethan sat opposite, while Rose perched as far away as possible from them. She and Yaz had been clashing and their constant bickering was causing an unpleasant atmosphere.

Wolff sat on the sofa next to Meadow, one foot crossed over his knee. He leaned back and wrapped an arm behind her and she snuggled in beside him. They'd been sharing a bed since returning and had made no secret of it. Jamie could only watch as Wolff, like a snake, charmed Meadow and drew her closer towards his coils.

Ethan flicked on the projector to display an aerial map of Grangemouth and he asked Rose to begin. She got to her feet and gave a nervous cough, and her eyes flicked to Ethan.

"For this to work," she said, "we'll need at least a hundred volunteers. I've already put out feelers and the response has been ... actually it's been overwhelming so—."

Wolff cut in, "Surely you didn't reveal what we're planning?"

Rose cut him a hard glare. "Of course not, I'm not an idiot. All they know is we're asking for support on a showcase protest in Scotland." Wolff nodded and she continued. "A couple of days before the event, I'll send details of our location to those who've volunteered." Rose glanced at Jamie. "Jamie's found someone sympathetic to the cause who has keys to the empty community centre in Linlithgow."

Ethan rewarded them with a full-blown smile. "So, we've a base."

Wolff asked how many activists she thought might turn up and Rose estimated that, even after allowing for those who'd likely drop-out, she expected about two hundred to show.

Ethan whistled his approval. "This is going to be the biggest, most radical direct action by environmentalists the world's ever seen."

Alex said, "Isn't there a risk that with those numbers pitching up so close to Grangemouth, the police will guess what we're up to?"

"Good point," said Rose. "Which is why we'll host a fake workshop on sustainability to provide a credible cover story. We'll even advertise it on social media in the local area."

"Brilliant idea," said Wolff.

Ethan reached for her hand, which made Rose smile. She perched next to him and he slipped a hand around her waist. Yaz looked like she wanted to rip her throat out.

Leon then outlined the logistics of housing volunteers in the community centre and ferrying them to Grangemouth on the day of the protest. After rhyming off a list of the supplies they'd need, he switched places with Ethan at the front.

Pointing out West Gate on the map, Ethan said, "Our best way in is to breach the barriers here. We may be able to bluff our way in as Alex and Leon did but, if not, we'll crash through them in a van." He paused and swept his eyes over his audience. "As soon as we're in, the rest of the convoy will join us. While this is happening, other groups will cut through the perimeter fence and storm the plant." He indicated several entry points along the perimeter.

Turning to Meadow, he said, "Meadow will demonstrate how to use wire cutters and, if there are enough of us, sway down the fence." He paused then added, "Once everyone's inside, a human shield will form at each entrance to prevent the police from getting in."

Ethan turned the floor over to Alex who'd been tasked with organising the volunteers into groups, each with a specific role. Alex explained that people would only learn what was required on the eve of the protest, when they'd be issued with a coloured t-shirt indicating their function. After breaching the plant, a group would blockade strategic points or immobilise key parts of the infrastructure while another would take control of the Refinery's Operations Centre. Other groups would climb or be responsible for welfare.

Pointing to the Refinery Operations Centre on the map, Wolff explained this was the main control centre for the plant, and was staffed by process engineers. Although protected by bomb and blast-proof doors, the engineer had assured him these could be opened manually, and the difficulty would be bypassing the internal doors which required a passkey.

"Or we could just take an axe to them," said Wolff.

The sinking feeling in Jamie's gut increased, knowing the German wasn't joking. Wolff invited Meadow to speak and they exchanged a smile as they swapped positions.

Meadow explained her plans to feed and care for volunteers during the course of the protest. Indicating the main security office on the map, she explained it also housed a medical facility. When she'd finished, Ethan asked Jamie to talk about the climb.

Jamie got to his feet and pointed to three cooling towers which lay about a quarter of a mile from West Gate. Indicating one of the towers, he said, "This one's been redundant for years and that's the one we'll climb."

Meadow gasped. "Isn't that really dangerous?"

Conscious of the jealous glance Wolff shot him, Jamie said, "Not if we climb it from the inside."

Jamie explained the bottom of the cooling tower was open and they could walk inside it. He described how each tower contained a wooden lattice structure for condensing water which trickled into an eight-feet-deep pool beneath.

Jamie said, "The framework will allow us to scale the tower from inside, emerge at the top and abseil down the outside."

"Bloody hell," said Leon, "that sounds like one bastard of a climb."

"It won't be an easy one," acknowledged Jamie, "but it's do-able. Once we're on the outside, we'll be visible to every media and press outlet gathered on the main public road."

Ethan grinned. "And the authorities will be powerless to stop them broadcasting the images to the world."

Wolff took Jamie's place, his expression triumphant. "Well done everyone. It sounds like we have a plan. All that remains is to set the date."

Ethan displayed a calendar on-screen.

Wolff said, "We know the shifts change at 6 a.m. so I suggest we breach the plant at 5:30 a.m. on Friday October 27th, a month from now.

Ethan beamed. "God, we're actually going to do this."

Jamie watched as the group applauded and congratulated each other, noting the self-satisfied smile on Wolff's face.

Thank fuck none of them will set foot inside Grangemouth.

The Raven

***"Man has nothing to do with it* [climate change]. *The only connection is that man is here at the same time as the sun and the moon are doing things."* — Piers Corbyn, Astrophysicist, Founder of Weather Action 2022**

***

Kathryn

From the Operations Centre in Thames House, Kathryn watched the live broadcast of Balakin's speech to Russian scholars and alumni at Edinburgh University. She'd hacked into the feed earlier to allow Julien's team to see inside the lecture theatre, although they also had operators present at the venue.

Corinne and Helen from Green Team were posing as delegates from an IT outsourcing company with offices in Russia. They were equipped with covert radios and tiny body cameras so they could record the meeting between Balakin and Sokolov. Corinne had signaled that Sokolov had been spotted amongst the crowd, although their target stubbornly remained out of sight from the cameras inside the lecture hall.

Balakin talked about the challenges his country faced in evolving their old Soviet-style utility companies into modern industries, and in making the transition to green energy. From the start, he captured his audience's attention with his candour and wit.

As Kathryn listened, she reviewed the file on Anna Sokolov although she knew it by heart. Five foot tall and curvaceous, Anna had shoulder-length black hair and piercing blue eyes framed behind retro spectacles which did little to flatter her appearance. Kathryn's grandmother would've described her as 'a plain Jane'.

Anna had been raised by her mother after her parents split when she was four. She'd had little contact with her father until she turned eighteen and visited him in Saint Petersburg. His death from cancer two years ago had presumably sparked her interest in Russian Studies and she was by all accounts an exemplary student.

Kathryn turned her attention back to Balakin as he delivered his closing statement.

"If the Covid pandemic has taught us one thing it is that none of us are safe until all of us are, and that's why it's imperative our nations work together to prevent climate catastrophe."

The audience applauded and the Director of Russian Studies, a spritely middle-aged woman dressed in red with ash-blonde hair, bounded onto the stage and thanked him. Announcing refreshments would be served, she led Balakin from the stage.

Although the official broadcast had ended with Balakin's speech, Kathryn kept the visual link up to give the Operations Centre a clear view of the reception. She disabled the lights on the cameras so no one in the theatre would suspect the broadcast was continuing.

Inside the lecture hall, a team of caterers appeared with a lavish buffet. Amongst the gannets converging on the canapes were Corinne and Helen who positioned themselves close to Balakin and the Director of Studies. This gave the Operations Centre clear audio visuals, despite the hubbub. There was still no sign of Sokolov.

"Where the hell is she?" muttered Julien. "Has she lost her nerve?"

Several minutes passed and then Corinne gave a covert signal on her radio to indicate Sokolov's approach. Kathryn watched as Balakin turned to greet Anna with a smile so expansive that she must have felt like the only woman in the room. They shook hands, and he kept hold of hers as she complimented him on his speech.

After small talk, the Director of Studies extricated herself and made a bee-line for Helen and Corinne who spent the next few minutes discussing the rapid growth of software development in Russia. Helen's spiel was well-rehearsed and she made the director smile after quoting the industry adage, "Give the urgent projects to the Americans, give the big projects to the Indians, and give the impossible ones to the Russians."

When the director went off to mingle, the operators loaded their plates and inched closer to Balakin and Sokolov, giving the team in Thames House a better view.

Flashing her a perfect set of white teeth, Balakin said, "So tell me about you Anna."

Sokolov returned a shy smile and twirled a coil of her hair through her fingers as the Russian's gaze swept over her before settling on her eyes.

Fitz snorted with amusement and whispered in Kathryn's ear, "D'you think they're taught how to flirt?"

"You hoping for some tips?" she teased.

"Huh, the chance to practise would be a fine thing."

She offered him a rueful smile. This confirmed her suspicions Fitz didn't have a partner waiting for him at home. Like herself.

As the evening progressed, Balakin politely batted away others' attempts to interrupt his conversation with Sokolov. Helen and Corinne were less fortunate so by the time the audio was clear enough to eavesdrop again, he was winding up the conversation.

Kissing her hand, he said, "I look forward to seeing you tomorrow, Anna."

Kathryn and Fitz swapped an amused look.

"Damn," muttered Julien, "we don't know where they're going to meet."

Kathryn had rarely seen Julien look so stressed and she wondered how much pressure he was under from his superiors about this operation and the others he oversaw. Fortunately, he seemed to internalise it, rather than taking it out on his staff as some of his counterparts did, and she was grateful to work for him.

Fitz said, "Kathryn and I are using a Gloworm spy attack so we'll scrape the audio from that."

When Julien looked bemused, he explained Gloworm allowed them to eavesdrop using the light from LED power emanations. Julien shook his head and muttered that he was getting too old for this game.

Another busy weekend for Green Team, thought Kathryn.

***

Jamie

After the planning meeting ended, Jamie grabbed his keys and took a drive under the guise of getting fuel. He parked on a quiet side road and phoned Gary.

He summarised the plans and told him the date and time.

Gary gave a long, low whistle. "Their plan's quite impressive," he said. "Might even work if we weren't onto them."

"Aye, that's the scary thing," said Jamie. "But the good news is you'll have everyone together the night before the protest."

Gary said he'd work with their police liaison on a strategy for mass arrests, while all the activists were gathered in the community centre in Linlithgow. He also assured him that the technical team would go into the premises beforehand so Five had eyes and ears.

"They'll need to be careful," said Jamie, "Wolff's no fool, he'll be on the lookout for bugs."

Gary chuckled. "Trust me, with Tom on the case, he won't find a thing."

"Listen," said Jamie, "I need some time off ... to work things out at home."

There was an uncomfortably long pause and then Gary said, "I'm afraid that's not going to be possible, not with the protest imminent. I need you there."

"And I need to be with my wife."

"I'm sorry but the answer's no—"

Jamie cut the call and threw the phone into the footwell. He thumped his fists on the steering wheel and swore.

***

Kathryn

Kathryn arrived at the office early Monday morning after spending another week-end on her own. Jamie had called each evening but their uneasy conversation had left her feeling more despairing than if he hadn't bothered. To escape the loneliness she felt, she was glad to return to work.

The office was empty and she busied herself with reviewing transcripts and video footage from the weekend's surveillance of Balakin. Her prediction that Green Team would enjoy a busy time of it proved correct.

Sokolov had spent Saturday shopping in Edinburgh's Princes Street, and at the hairdressers. The photographs Green Team had taken revealed she'd gone to extraordinary lengths over her appearance. Gone were the vintage glasses and dowdy clothes, replaced by contact lenses and a flattering dress. In the evening, she'd met Balakin at an upmarket restaurant in the city's old town and afterwards they'd gone to a cocktail bar where they remained until the small hours. Later, they'd taken a taxi to her apartment where Balakin spent the night.

Kathryn sipped her coffee as she scanned a machine-generated transcript of the audio surveillance from Sokolov's flat, courtesy of the devices that MI5's technical team had installed. The section featuring their coupling made for hilarious reading as a result of the software's attempts to transcribe grunts, moans and cries of passion. It ran for several pages.

She was still chuckling when Fitz arrived. Hitching his chin at the transcript visible on her screen, he said, "Old Balakin's a fast worker. Didn't take him long to get her in the sack."

She smiled in reply, recalling her own very different experience. It had taken months of patient coaxing on Jamie's part before she'd overcome her fears and they'd made love. Remembering those times filled her with sadness; right now, she ached so much for his touch it was painful.

Returning her attention to the transcript, she noted Anna had agreed to accompany Balakin on an all-expenses-paid trip to London the following weekend.

Fast worker indeed.

Julien called a briefing first thing, and Kathryn was surprised to discover that Pia, the psychologist she'd encountered during her first operation with MI5, had joined them. It'd been months since she'd seen her and Pia greeted her warmly. Without her support, Kathryn was certain she wouldn't be working here today, nor married to Jamie, and she was grateful to her. When Pia asked how she was, Kathryn gave what she hoped was a neutral reply.

With a knowing smile, Pia whispered, "If you ever need to talk, my door's always open."

Hmm ... maybe not so neutral.

Kathryn took a seat beside Pia at the front of the room and Julien began. Blue Team's leader provided an over-the-air update since he and his unit were currently on the ground monitoring Balakin in London. He reported that the Russian had left for work early and was already at the embassy. Kathryn had furnished them with details of Balakin's diary for the week.

After Carl's update on Green Team's surveillance in Edinburgh, Julien introduced Pia and explained she was here to offer insight into the strategies Balakin was likely employing. It was unusual to include surveillance operators in detailed briefings since they were usually only given enough information to perform their role without biasing it. However, Julien had apparently decided what Pia was about to share was pertinent.

The psychologist stood at the lectern and launched a presentation which appeared on the overhead screen. An elegant woman in her early sixties, she'd short blonde hair and vibrant blue eyes, and spoke with a hint of a Scandinavian accent.

Peering at her audience over the rim of her glasses, she said, "Many of you will be familiar with the term 'sexpionage'. With a click, a scene from the movie *Red Sparrow* appeared. "Usually this involves women whom we refer to as 'sparrows' or 'swallows'. They target men, as any businessman who's visited Moscow knows. It's so prevalent we even produced a manual on the subject of honey traps."

Carl made a lewd comment about swallowing which raised a laugh.

A slide featuring Balakin appeared. "But our friend here is what's termed a 'raven'. He seduces women."

An image of a grim-looking building complex appeared, all concrete, angular and brutalist. "For those of you unfamiliar with this place," said Pia, "this is what's called the 'Institute' in Moscow where the majority of SVR spies are trained. Within this school of espionage is a special academy where they teach the art of seduction."

"So, he's a bit of a sexpert?" asked Carl.

Pia smiled. "Oh, he's skillful for sure, and he'll know how to use his mind and body to maximum effect." Flicking back to the photograph of Balakin, she added, "Our German counterparts ushered him out of Berlin after a woman he'd been involved with was discovered dead in her apartment." An image of a pretty brunette appeared. "It was most likely suicide but, of course we can't be certain. Prior to this, there was a similar incident in Budapest." Again, another tragic young woman's picture filled the screen.

On-screen, Sokolov's face appeared and, above low murmurs of disapproval, Pia went on. "This is a fairly typical pattern of behaviour. He's chosen his target well; a shy girl, not used to attention from men. She's been single for a while and on dating apps but there's no boyfriend and no long-term relationship we know about. She's a lonely woman who'll be highly susceptible to his charms."

Looking at Sokolov's picture, Kathryn felt a measure of sympathy for her.

Pia displayed screenshots of Anna's online profiles and said, "We didn't have to do too much digging because her social media is public, and this will have allowed him to build up a profile of her and invent himself as her perfect partner. She'll be flattered, grateful and malleable. In other words, she's a textbook target."

A photograph of Balakin and Sokolov leaving the cocktail bar appeared. His arm was draped lazily around her shoulders and she gazed up at him.

Pia continued. "He'll let the affair develop gradually until he wins her trust. During this time, he'll love-bomb her, showering her with gifts and affection unlike anything she's experienced before. He'll anticipate and fulfil her every need until she's completely in his thrall. And once he has her in a state of all-consuming and addictive love, she'll be blind to what he's really up to, even if she has the odd suspicion." Glancing up at the team from over the lectern, her gaze landed on Kathryn. "But make no mistake, this is emotional abuse. He's doing this to control her."

Her gaze returned to the room. "He's supremely confident too. Kathryn discovered he's already booked flights and made dinner reservations for a weekend in London, and he did this before he spent the night with her."

"Poor lass," said Carl.

"Indeed," said Pia. "Then, when he thinks the time is right, he'll make his play." She clicked and a list appeared. "He's got three options. Seduction alone may prove enough to manipulate her but, if it's not, he'll add bribery. This might not be blatant and the money may be offered in the form of a gift. However, considering the amount of debt she's in, she's vulnerable." She glanced up before adding, "However, if all else fails, he may resort to blackmail."

One of the operators gave a low whistle.

"While RED KITE was galivanting in Edinburgh, our tech team bugged his apartment. What's interesting is they found surveillance equipment in his flat similar to what we use. So, my guess is he plans to gather compromising photographs or video of them in bed which he can use as a lever if she refuses to comply."

Kathryn was struck by the matter-of-fact way these tactics were discussed. She'd heard of sexpionage, knew it went on, just not how prevalent it was. The strategy seemed to be a cornerstone of spy tradecraft, and she wondered if this is what her own husband was up to. Had he been encouraged or instructed to do this, or had he simply used his initiative? Was he seducing Meadow to infiltrate the Climate Warriors or was she just an unintended benefit; someone to keep him company? Kathryn cursed herself for being so naïve and for failing to realise this came with the territory.

The thought of Jamie with another woman made her nauseous and she swallowed the acid taste in her mouth. Pia caught her eye. Kathryn looked away and balled her fists, certain her cheeks were burning with the shame of everyone knowing about her husband's indiscretion. Pia asked if there were any questions.

Composing herself, Kathryn asked, "After GREY GOOSE has given him the information he wants, what'll happen?"

With a rueful smile, Pia said, "He'll vanish."

Like Jamie.

***

Jamie

Jamie awoke screaming from a night terror, the second one in days. Cold sweat trickled down his back and his heart pounded furiously in his chest. He reached for Kathryn only to find the space next to him empty, and it took him a few moments to orient himself and realise he was in the squat.

He cursed Wolff, cursed MI5, and cursed himself.

Kathryn's absence in those wee small hours felt like torture. He craved her comforting presence and the warmth of her body.

Jamie realised he did not belong here. He belonged with Kathryn in a different life, and he felt alone and empty without her. He was bound to her, not just as a husband but as a kindred spirit. Both had their demons but they'd faced them together, so being apart from her was like losing a limb. His nightmares were a recent occurrence and a reminder that the PTSD he'd suffered since returning from Iraq had never completely gone away.

Flopping back on the pillow, he stared up at the ceiling and replayed his conversations with Kathryn over in his head. He'd explained why he couldn't take leave although he desperately wanted to. His words had been met with a long silence which worried him more than if she'd hurled invective at him. She insisted she needed time but their relationship was deteriorating by the day.

Would she want him home again? Could he ever repair the damage?

He cursed some more.

The Cult

"Rabid environmentalism embraces the hallmarks of fundamentalist Christianity. The end of the world is nigh. Judgement day is at hand."
— Professor Ian Plimer

***

Kathryn

Julien never ceased to surprise Kathryn and today was no exception. Kathryn and Fitz were sat in his office discussing Pia's presentation.

Julien said, "I'm not willing to risk letting Balakin get within a hundred yards of the GSS technology."

She was astonished, given what he'd said to Dominic about allowing the Russian's plan to play out.

"The first rule of intelligence," said Julien, "is never share information with anyone you don't need to, and that includes Six."

"Are we going to warn the company their tech's a target?" asked Fitz.

Julien shook his head. "We'll swap it for fake IP so Balakin believes he's got what he wants. I've asked the wobblyheads to create dummy specifications that look genuine but are utterly useless." He took a sip of coffee. "Trying to make those work should keep our Russian friends occupied for months, if not years."

The plan was clever but Kathryn realised they were missing an opportunity. "Can we add something to the files?" she asked.

Julien raised a curious eyebrow. "Such as?"

"Software that'll give us access to every machine the Russians install it on, and every system those devices connect to."

That got Julien's attention and he paused to give it some thought. "Won't it be detected?" he asked.

She grinned. "Not my little trojan pony."

Julien and Fitz chuckled. She was going to enjoy this.

***

Jamie

Jamie had received an invitation from Pia asking to meet her at an office in nearby Manchester. The message gave no indication why she wished to talk to him face to face, and his gut twisted at the prospect. From his previous encounters with Pia and psychologists like her, he knew she missed nothing; it was as though she'd x-ray eyes that could see into his mind. This woman also had the power to end his career if she deemed him psychologically unfit. He needed to be on his guard.

Her instructions led him to a 1960s-style building which appeared to belong to a software company. The receptionist directed him to a small soulless office on the third floor where he found Pia waiting. Furnished sparsely with a couple of old plastic chairs, a coffee table and sideboard, the space had a gloomy air. Apt, thought Jamie.

Pia greeted him, made coffee and then sat opposite him. He pulled a couple of chocolate bars from his pocket and offered her one which she declined. He munched on one as she attempted to thaw him out with small talk, all the while scrutinising him over the rim of her cup. Jamie's foot bounced and he placed a hand on his knee to still it.

"How's Kathryn?" she asked.

No way was he going to discuss his marriage with a bloody psychologist, and he was certain his wife would have told her nothing. "Aye fine, all good." He scrunched up the wrapper and wiped his mouth. "So ... uhm ... why did you want to see me?"

Could she tell he'd been sinking into depression and experiencing flashbacks again?

"I'm worried about you."

Oh hell, she knows. I'm finished.

Focusing on keeping his voice and expression neutral, he said, "Oh, why's that?"

"I've been reading your reports and I'm seeing a pattern of behaviour that concerns me."

He snapped, "I'm absolutely fine, and it's nothing I can't handle."

She cocked her head to the side and regarded him for an uncomfortably long time. Finally, she said, "It's not *your* behaviour I'm concerned about, but it's interesting you thought that. Maybe that's something we should explore later."

Jamie shot her a tight smile and silently cursed himself. *Say nothing!*

"What does worry me," she continued, "is Ethan's behaviour and the way he runs the group."

She picked up a file from the coffee table and flicked through its pages, saying "You describe him as a charismatic leader who uses his charms to surround himself with vulnerable young supporters." She glanced up and added, "Present company excepted."

Jamie wondered if she meant he was too old or not vulnerable enough, but didn't ask.

She continued reading from her notes. "He's isolated them in the squat and cut them off from their family and friends, replacing their support network with himself. He's a lover to the women and a father figure to the men."

He nodded at her stark analysis.

"He ensures most of you are on a restricted diet and are deprived of sleep." She glanced at the scrunched-up wrapper. "But more worrying are the methods of coercive control he uses to bend the group to his will. He's using sex to reward and punish the women, either giving or denying it depending on their acquiescence."

Jamie thought about Rose. He could see where Pia was going with this, surprised he'd not arrived at the same conclusion when all the evidence was staring him in the face.

She said, "He also controls much of the information fed to the group, sharing only what serves his purposes, and the message is always one of imminent catastrophe."

Jamie countered with, "He might be right about the apocalypse part."

She shot him a quizzical look and he immediately regretted his remark.

He said, "But I know what you're getting at. They're a sort of cult, aren't they?"

Pia closed the folder, placed it on the table and peered at him over the top of her glasses. "There's no 'sort of' about it, they're the real deal and that's why I'm worried about the effect it could have on you living amongst them."

"But I'm not a vulnerable young person, you said so yourself."

She arched an eyebrow. "But you are vulnerable. The human mind is a lot more malleable than we like to think, especially if people are in a distressed state." Her eyes bored into him.

"I'm not under his spell, Pia."

Pursing her lips, she said, "Nevertheless, you'll have to be careful not to participate in the disciplining of your mind because, make no mistake, that's what's going on here. Ethan and Wolff are master manipulators and, regardless of whether they're right about the climate emergency or not, they're using the campaign for their own ends."

Although her analysis was troubling, he was relieved it wasn't his own behaviour under her magnifying glass.

Observing him closely, she said, "It's important you exercise your intellect with other forms of information, and surround yourself with a strong support network to counteract Ethan and Wolff's influence."

"Aye, I'll make sure of it."

I might get out of this meeting unscathed after all.

With a half-smile, she added, "So, perhaps you'd like to tell me what's happened between you and Kathryn?"

Jamie put his head in his hands and groaned.

***

Kathryn

Kathryn tried to focus on what Fitz was saying. A headache throbbed behind her temples and she felt queasy. She was sat in Julien's office after he'd tasked her and Fitz with devising a way of swapping GSS's intellectual property for fake IP without the company knowing. They'd spent hours brainstorming ideas before coming up with the solution they were currently putting to Julien.

Fitz said, "So we've two challenges." He scribbled a rough diagram on the whiteboard. "The first is gaining access to the protected files on the company's secure network. This network is separate to the regular office one and isn't connected to the internet so we can't penetrate it remotely. We'll need physical access."

"So, a job for the technical team?" asked Julien.

Fitz nodded. "The second challenge is knowing which files we need to target on the secure network, and identifying the ones to swap out. There could be hundreds of them." He drew a question mark beside his diagram.

"The tech team will have limited time," said Julien, "they'll want to be in and out in minutes."

Fitz sat and cast a series of grainy images onto the large screen. "Kathryn's hacked into the company's CCTV. What you're seeing is the inside of the GSS offices and their secure data centre."

In one window, an open-plan office appeared full of people working on computers, while another showed a room full of server racks. Using her laptop, Kathryn took control of a camera in one of the offices and zoomed in on an employee's monitor. It was clear enough they could read the text on the screen.

Julien chuffed, "Ironic you're using their own cameras to spy on them."

"Oh, it gets better," snickered Kathryn. She pointed to a man sat at his desk picking his nose. "The guy digging for diamonds here is Dr. Henry Metcalf. He's a polymer expert and the brains behind their big battery technology."

They watched as Metcalf wiped his index finger on his jeans and took a bite out of a Subway sandwich. Julien pulled a face.

Kathryn showed him a series of stills she'd captured of Metcalf's monitor and explained that, by examining these, she and Fitz had been able to piece together the file names relating to the battery technology and the paths to them on the secure network. She said, "We've narrowed down what we're looking for."

"Who are the other people you're watching?" asked Julien.

Fitz explained some were IT engineers who'd access to the GSS data centre and secure network. Kathryn focused on a woman sitting at her desk on the phone. Beside her computer tower lay a small USB stick.

Kathryn said, "Their IT department use Razor USB drives to access and patch the secure network. This means the tech team can't just plug in any old Razor because only ones with specific MAC addresses will work." When Julien looked baffled, she added, "Basically, we need to steal one of their USB sticks to put the fake IP on."

Julien frowned. "And how do you propose we do that?"

In response, she displayed a website for a company that provided plants to the corporate sector. She said, "GSS hire indoor plants for their office from this bunch. As part of the package, a team come in regularly to water, feed and prune them."

Fitz said, "One of Blue Team's going in tomorrow lunchtime posing as one of their staff. She's going to swap this engineer's USB stick for another which looks the same."

Julien looked unconvinced. "Why this particular engineer?"

"She's off to Lanzarote soon so hopefully won't spot the fact her USB no longer works. With it being lunchtime, she probably won't have locked the stick away but our operator will swap any others she sees, just in case. And if that doesn't work, Blue Team will pose as cleaners in the evening and try again."

Julien frowned. "Hmm, so, assuming you get the USB, what next?"

Kathryn said, "I'll crack its encryption so we can use it to access their secure server."

Fitz said, "As well as watching Metcalf, we've sent him and his team some phishing emails. They look harmless enough but when opened, they infect their machines and the corporate network with our malware.

Kathryn said, "Metcalf might have a brain the size of a planet but he's just clicked on my special Subway meal deal offer so we're inside their office network."

Julien rubbed his temples as if in pain. "Will that get us access to the IP?"

"No, that's on the separate secure network" said Fitz pointing to the whiteboard, "but it'll make our job easier. We can now record every keystroke Metcalf makes which will give us his credentials. If we're lucky, someone will insert a USB into an infected machine which will infect the stick. And if we're really lucky, they'll pop that into the secure network."

Kathryn added, "We still need physical access to the secure network but at least we'll know what we're looking for and which files to swap out."

Julien complained this stuff made his head hurt. "Okay, I trust you know what you're doing."

Outlining their plan had made Kathryn realise just how many moving parts, assumptions and uncertainties were involved. If they got one bit wrong, the entire strategy would collapse and the Russians would obtain the real IP.

***

Jamie

Jamie woke early after more troubled dreams. His sheets were twisted into a ball and drenched in sweat and he made a mental note to change them. Living in a squat was no excuse to smell, even if the thought of doing laundry seemed like too much effort. He was normally fastidious about his appearance, and had spent too long in the army to allow personal hygiene to slide. Pity some of the others didn't feel the same. Alex smelled like a wookiee's armpit.

After showering, he made coffee, a habit the others frowned upon, and stretched out on the sofa. He thought about Pia's analysis of how Ethan subtly controlled their eating habits. Since joining the group, Jamie had lost several pounds; not that it was a bad thing. Kathryn had once remarked how fit and toned he looked, giggling he'd 'muscles on muscles'. Remembering the lovemaking this had led to made him maudlin.

Surprisingly, it had helped to talk things over with Pia. She'd listened carefully, sharing the fact that Kathryn had spoken to her in confidence, without revealing what they'd discussed. This gave him hope that Kathryn also wanted to heal the rift. Pia's advice echoed that of his sister: be patient, give her time, but talk regularly and tell her how you feel.

He'd confessed to having night terrors and they'd discussed his PTSD. Pia reassured him this was normal in times of high stress, and gave him medication to alleviate the worst of it, but it made him sleepy and he'd stopped taking it.

Leaning over to grab his mug, something shiny wedged between the cushions caught his eye. He pulled out a mobile phone. He switched it on, realising it belonged to Yasmine. As part of Ethan's operational security, he changed the group's phones regularly for disposable burners, but Jamie had refused on the grounds his work as a rope-access technician relied upon people being able to contact him.

Glancing around the squat, he listened for signs of life. There were none. Yaz hadn't enabled any security on her phone and he was able to access her messages and contacts. Scrolling through the list, he found texts between her and 'Stuart Mc' who appeared to be the engineer who'd agreed to help them. The messages revealed they'd met in Falkirk during the group's recent visit to the Grangemouth site. Jamie took a screen shot of the details and sent it to Gary.

There was a noise and Jamie glanced up to see Wolff on the stairs. Stuffing Yaz's phone back between the cushions, he wondered just how long the German had been watching him.

THE SEDUCTION

The oil and gas industry has made £2.3bn a day in profit for the last 50 years ... The analysis, of World Bank data, finds that petrostates and fossil fuel companies have made a total of $52tn since 1970. **— Prof Aviel Verbruggen 2022**

***

Kathryn

London, three weeks later

Pia's predictions were correct and over the next few weeks, Balakin cultivated his relationship with Anna Sokolov, although there was nothing gradual about it. He took her to west-end theatres, the best restaurants in Edinburgh, and a luxury spa hotel near Peebles. The operators in A branch were working considerable overtime, and their surveillance showed just how adept at seduction Balakin was, so it was no surprise when he began to seed his plan.

Just weeks after attending her first Operation Alabaster briefing, Pia returned to summarise developments based on the latest intel. Kathryn listened to her presentation along with the rest of the team.

Referring to the conversations between Balakin and Sokolov, Pia highlighted a section of transcript on-screen and said, "Here RED KITE is talking about GSS, the company GREY GOOSE works for. He says, 'They don't appreciate you,

Anna. They ought to treat you better.' So already he's planting the idea in her mind that she's undervalued by her employer. He wants her to feel justified when he asks her to be disloyal to them."

Kathryn had a bad feeling about where this was leading.

Addressing the next section of transcript, she said, "A few weeks in, the relationship is blossoming and he begins to prepare the ground. They've spent every weekend together with him paying for everything, claiming it's what Russian men do. When they're together, he's loving and attentive; when they're apart, he messages her constantly. The relationship is intensely physical as well as emotional. And, just last weekend, he upped the stakes and declared his love for her."

She paused to let that sink in and several of the team groaned out their disapproval at the Russian's behaviour.

Pia continued. "Now that he's gained her trust and established a strong bond, we really see the manipulation begin." She displayed another extract from a conversation in which Sokolov complained she couldn't get time off work to enjoy a long weekend.

[BALAKIN] I know you love your job but GSS work you too hard and pay you too little. You owe them nothing. I know Russian businesses that would hire you in a heartbeat and for a better salary.

Pia said, "He's feeding her the notion GSS are exploiting her and, as a consequence, she owes them nothing. It's also the first time money's mentioned."

Scrolling to the next section, she said, "Then, a week later, he won't let her pay for lunch and when she insists, he confesses to having seen her credit card statement. She's embarrassed and explains it away as student debt. She refuses his offer of help, but the fact he knows about her finances will put her under pressure to do something about it."

Pia indicated another highlighted section. "Then, finally, this weekend he drops the bombshell. He tells her that his superiors are unhappy with him and are threatening to send him back to Moscow. She's tearful and begs him to tell her why. He spins her a story that a deal with a British company he was helping to broker has fallen through, meaning his career's in tatters."

Kathryn scanned the transcript although she was familiar with the contents. The entire episode had played out exactly as Pia had predicted, a fact that made her feel great sorrow for Anna Sokolov.

[BALAKIN] We wanted to license their technology. We've been working on this deal for months and at the eleventh hour they pull out. My boss is furious and to save his own neck, he's making me the scapegoat."

[SOKOLOV] Why did they bail?

[BALAKIN] It boils down to the fact they don't want to deal with the Russians. So much for talk of fostering a spirit of collaboration to solve the climate crisis. It's every company and every country for themselves.

Pia added, "It's clear she's very distressed at the prospect of losing him. Here she asks him about the deal with Greenway Solutions and realises it concerns big battery technology and is similar to the project she's working on at GSS." Pia paused and glanced up from the lectern. "And then his plan finally comes to fruition when she offers this."

[SOKOLOV] This is similar to what GSS is working on. Want me to ask if they're interested in licensing the technology?

[BALAKIN] We tried, they refused. They won't deal with us and neither will any other European or American company. Thanks to Putin, Russia's a pariah state. It's hopeless. There's nothing I can do. I've no option but to return empty-handed, meaning I'll be counting paperclips in Moscow for the rest of my days.

[SOKOLOV] I don't want you to leave. What if I could get you what you need? No one needs to know where it came from.

[BALAKIN] I'd never ask that of you, it's far too risky. The last thing I want is you getting into trouble. You could lose your job. Or worse.

[SOKOLOV] I owe them nothing, you said so yourself. I can't bear the thought of losing you. You know I'd do anything for you. I love you so much. Please let me help you.

Pia scrolled forwards. "After much to-ing and fro-ing, he eventually agrees."

[BALAKIN] Only if you let me help you in return. I've a budget for obtaining this technology. I don't see why you shouldn't be compensated for the risk you're taking. It's only fair. That way you clear your debts, and we can start our new life together with a clean slate."

She ended the presentation saying, "I'll spare you the details of how they seal the deal. But, needless to say that after just a few weeks of wooing, she's promised to get him the material he wants in return for his love, and a hundred thousand in cash."

Carl gave a long low whistle which Pia acknowledged with a nod.

She said, "He's not just being nice by insisting she takes the money; he's making sure she's implicated and can't later claim he stole the information from her." Switching off the projector, she added, "And that, ladies and gentlemen, is the power of seduction."

Poor Anna, she's well and truly screwed.

***

Jamie

Jamie rubbed the back of his neck, glanced at his phone and suppressed a groan. Sat on his bed in the squat, he cursed the lack of privacy the paper-thin walls afforded. As the day of the Grangemouth protest drew near, the Climate Warriors had become immersed in logistics. This left little time for anything else, and today Jamie hadn't had the opportunity to call Kathryn.

Wolff and Ethan were also becoming increasingly paranoid and tensions were running high. Since discovering Yaz's phone, Jamie had been extra careful not to give them further cause for suspicion.

Not wanting to risk being overheard making a call, he instead fired off a quick WhatsApp message under his real identity. Aware he was breaking every rule in the book, he no longer bloody cared. What were they going to do — send him home? He needed Kathryn to know he was thinking of her ... even if Fitz could read every word.

Baby, sorry, can't call, been 1 of those days but want u 2 know I luv & miss u so much. Will call 2morrow. J xxx

He waited for her reply. It never came.

***

Kathryn

Kathryn walked Meg along the river bank near to Five's headquarters. The mild autumn evening had drawn others from their offices and homes and she watched as boats puttered by and couples ambled hand in hand along the banks.

She checked her phone for the umpteenth time hoping to see a missed call or message from Jamie. There was nothing. Had he forgotten, was he too busy, or did he simply not wish to talk to her? Their conversations weren't easy but he always made the time, and it was better than nothing. Or was he in danger? Had his identity been discovered? Worry gnawed at her and her empty stomach churned.

Steering the dog away from a kissing couple, she tried to dispel her disquiet, reminding herself Jamie had to send a coded message each evening before midnight to confirm he was all right. Should he fail to do this, his urgent extraction would be triggered. She'd checked today's logs and he'd already messaged Gary, so why the hell hadn't he contacted her?

With her heart full of despair, she returned to the office and settled Meg beneath her desk. She then made her way to the Operations Centre to watch the technical team's infiltration of Grid Scale Systems in Livingston. Concerned Sokolov might attempt to steal the IP before they'd had a chance to swap it, Julien had ordered it to be done immediately.

Fitz and Kathryn's plan had worked and Blue Team had obtained one of the company's secure USB sticks which Kathryn had decrypted. GCHQ provided fake IP with which to replace the real files, and this had been loaded onto the stick ready for the technical team. Operation Alabaster now hinged on that single stick functioning and she prayed it would work.

Despite the lateness of the hour, the Ops Centre was busy. Graham, the Operations Officer, remained calm as he issued a series of clear instructions to the teams on the ground, and directed the support staff in Thames House.

Kathryn exchanged an anxious nod with Fitz and sat at a computer next to him. He'd cast plans of the area where GSS was located onto an overhead screen. Both the surveillance and technical teams were on-site awaiting the go-ahead.

Set amongst landscaped gardens, the company was headquartered in a business park consisting of five modern office blocks centred around a sprawling Victorian pile that housed GSS's sales and marketing division. The Engineering and Research and Development departments, which Fitz had labelled 'GSS Building 1' and 'GSS Building 2' respectively, occupied two office blocks which were joined by a glazed link. Their target, the company's data centre, was housed on the ground floor of GSS Building 2.

The building opposite the target was empty, save for some old office furniture and signage. Earlier that morning, Green Team operatives had taken up position on the ground floor dressed as painters and decorators. From their vantage point, they'd a clear view of the entrance to GSS Building 2. They'd set up a camera, the grainy feed from which showed on a screen in the Ops Centre.

Images from the business park's CCTV cameras also appeared, showing the main access road. The car park was vacant, except for one vehicle which belonged to a GSS software engineer called Tim Frost.

Green team had also positioned a camera trained on the lodge occupied by the site's round-the-clock security guards. Only one watchman was on duty and Green Team reported he'd completed his hourly checks and was safely ensconced in front of the television again.

Operation Alabaster, however, had hit a snag. Late afternoon, Fitz had triggered the fire alarm in the GSS buildings so Green Team could count the number of staff exiting and re-entering the buildings. They later tallied this with the number who left work that evening to discover there was an employee still unaccounted for: Tim Frost was working late on the top floor.

Carl's voice came over the speaker in the Ops Centre. "From Team Leader. Base acknowledge, we've still got company and there's a light on the top floor."

"Base, roger that," said Graham.

Kathryn had observed several operations led by Graham and nothing seemed to rattle him. Late fifties and balding, he'd been in A-branch since his twenties and there was little he didn't know or hadn't seen. Despite the fact he'd an eager technical team waiting to enter the building, several paint-spattered surveillance operators who'd had a long day, and a room full of weary support staff in Thames House, he remained cool and collected. He glanced at Julien who'd already postponed the operation once in the hope Tim would've gone home by now.

Scrubbing a hand over the scruff on his chin, Julien looked at the enormous wall clock and gave Graham the nod to proceed. Kathryn knew her boss was unhappy about the situation but the team were under pressure to swap out the IP before Sokolov stole it from under her employer's nose.

Graham announced, "Stations from Base. STAND BY. STAND BY". He updated Tom, the technical team leader, "Acknowledge, the building is still occupied," and then informed Green Team that Operation Alabaster would proceed as planned.

Kathryn listened as Carl and Tom instructed their teams to get into position.

After a minute, Carl said, "Team Leader to Base, zero three five has control, tech team are good to go."

Tom's voice was deep and baritone as he confirmed they were deploying. Kathryn watched the live video feed from his body camera and listened to the team's communications as the three operators entered the fire exit at the rear of the building. She was astonished at how quickly and silently they gained access through the door and into the stairwell. Fitz had already disabled the building's alarm system remotely and overridden the motion-activated internal lighting. He'd also put the CCTV cameras on a loop so the security guard would see only an empty building.

"Zero three five to Team Leader. Security guard is OUT OUT OUT."

"Roger that zero three five. Let us know if he approaches Building 2," said Carl.

Seconds later, the technical operators had breached the lock and were inside the data centre. Courtesy of the body camera, Kathryn saw a row of server racks and a console. Graham passed comms to Fitz who instructed a technical operator to insert the USB into one of the servers.

Kathryn held her breath as he input the password.

It failed.

Carl's voice burst onto the net. "STAND BY STAND BY. Staff member heading downstairs."

Julien muttered under his breath while Graham calmly said, "Roger that." Turning to Fitz, Graham told him to proceed.

Fitz repeated the password for the technical operator, while Kathryn watched in horror as the feed showed a tall skinny figure descending the stairwell in Building 2.

"Staff member on ground floor," said Carl.

"Base to Team Leaders," said Graham, "If he turns right towards the data centre, we will abort."

"Team Leader to Base, want me to set off the fire alarm?"

Graham glanced at the staff member and security guard on the screens. "Negative."

They'd discussed this possibility earlier but Graham was concerned that the alarm would bring the local emergency services out again, making the teams' extraction difficult.

The password worked and Fitz proceeded to talk the operator through the steps he needed to complete at the console. She detected an edge of panic in his voice as he guided him through a complex set of command-line instructions.

A few moments later, Carl said, "Security guard approaching building 2."

Springing to his feet, Julien swore as he gawped at the monitors. They desperately needed more time and if they failed tonight, they may not get another chance.

Kathryn knew what she had to do. It was risky though and she hadn't mentioned it to anyone, not even Fitz. The idea had occurred to her earlier and she'd already hacked into what she needed. Her fingers flew over her keyboard and a column of coloured text appeared against a black background. Carl's voice informed them the staff member had turned right. They would have to abort.

As Graham went to give the order, Kathryn raised a hand and said, "Wait!"

Heart pounding in her chest, she felt the eyes of everyone in the Ops Centre on her. Ignoring them, she tapped a key and a car alarm sounded, its beeping blaring through the speakers. Heads turned towards the video feed from the car park where a single vehicle's lights flashed in time with its horn. The staff member, a lanky man in his forties, stopped in his tracks and then turned and dashed out of the building towards the car.

"Staff member and security guard in car park," said Carl.

Long minutes passed as Fitz coaxed the technical operator through the remaining steps, while Tim fumbled with his key fob in an attempt to silence his car alarm while the security guard looked on.

Finally, Fitz gasped, "Done. Get them out of there."

Graham instructed the technical team to withdraw and Kathryn watched as the operators left silently from the rear of the building. Not a physical or electronic trace remained to indicate they'd been there.

Every head in the Ops Centre turned to look at Fitz and Kathryn and she felt her face flush.

Julien shook his head at them indulgently and smiled. Fitz turned to Kathryn and they shared a relieved chuckle.

In a calm voice that suggested this was just an everyday occurrence, Graham said, "Good work everyone. All stations CEASE and WITHDRAW and acknowledge down the list."

THE MILITANT

***"Hardly anyone knows just how much money is spent on "Climate research" every year. The cost is spread out among laughably useless study grants, wind and solar farm subsidies, carbon offset credits, "green" building code evaluation and enforcement, salaries for bureaucrats solely dedicated to "climate concerns"... you get the idea, it's a lot of hazy money."*. Mark J. Perry 2019**

***

Jamie

"Their contact's a guy called Stuart McKinness," said Gary. "He's a hard-left militant."

Jamie was sat in his handler's Audi eating a footlong Subway stuffed with every possible filling. There was little food in the squat and he was so hungry he felt lightheaded.

Gary grimaced as relish dripped onto the paper bag on Jamie's lap. "Do you have to eat that in here?" he muttered.

"Piss off, I'm starvin'," mumbled Jamie through a mouthful. "Anyway, why's it taken so bloody long to find this out? I gave you the name weeks ago."

"And I told you I never received it."

Jamie cursed that this was a shithousery operation. "When you say 'militant', what are we talking about?"

Offering him a napkin and a look of disapproval, Gary said, "Usual lefty nonsense." Reading from his notes, Gary rhymed off a series of industrial actions at the plant which McKinness had played a part in organising. "He's been on our radar since the eighties."

Jamie wondered whether being an active member of a trade union automatically put you on Five's grid, a thought that didn't sit comfortably with his working-class roots.

Wiping his chin, Jamie said, "Just because he's a union man doesn't make him dangerous."

Gary explained McKinness had a troubled history with the owners of Grangemouth. About ten years ago, faced with the threat of strike action, the boss had locked workers out of the plant and threatened to shut it down. Rather than imperil the Scottish economy and put all their jobs at risk, Unite members were forced to concede everything: no strikes for three years, no full-time union convenors on site, pay freezes, and an end to final salary pensions.

McKinness had later been made redundant from his job at the plant. As a process engineer, he knew the workings of the refinery inside out, which made him a potentially dangerous ally to the Climate Warriors.

Gary said, "McKinness is bitter about Unite's humiliating defeat and losing his job has only fanned the flames. His motives might be different but that doesn't make him any less of a threat."

Scrunching up the sandwich wrapper, Jamie sighed heavily. Between this, the comms mix-ups, and Gary's intel which had compelled him to continue with the operation, he'd a bad feeling about this protest.

A really bad feeling.

***

Kathryn

Julien's instincts were sound and Sokolov didn't wait long to obtain GSS's intellectual property. She copied the files onto her personal USB stick, just days after promising Balakin the information. Fitz immediately detected the breach and informed Julien who called an emergency briefing.

Kathryn, along with the team in Thames House, assembled in the briefing room while the operators on the ground listened over the air. Yellow team had taken over responsibility for surveillance in Edinburgh since Carl felt his team had reached saturation point and risked being recognised by their targets. Sam, the Yellow team leader, was on the line awaiting instruction.

Kathryn stifled a yawn. Exhausted, she felt as though she could sleep for a week. All leave had been cancelled in anticipation of Operation Alabaster coming to a close and, like her colleagues, she'd been putting in long shifts; not that she minded since there was no one to go home to. Stroking the dog at her feet, she wondered what Jamie was doing at this moment and whether he was also thinking of her. Why hadn't he called or messaged her?

Julien's brusque introduction put an end to her wool gathering. He looked out of place in his suit and tie amongst the bedraggled crew of operators, one of whom looked like a tramp. Julien began by explaining GREY GOOSE was now in possession of the material from GSS and that it was imperative they kept control of both targets around the clock. At no point did Julien mention the IP was fake, and Kathryn wondered who else in the team knew. Julien's first rule of intelligence — don't share what you don't need to — clearly extended to MI5's own.

He explained RED KITE was due to arrive in Edinburgh on an evening flight from Heathrow, and was expected to have the money with him in a diplomatic bag. The plan was for Blue Team to accompany him onto the plane, and then pass control of him to Yellow Team in Edinburgh, a job the operators termed 'an airport run'.

Julien said, "We expect the exchange to take place at GREY GOOSE'S apartment where we'll have eyes and ears. We need proof the material and money have changed hands, and then it'll be a case of watching and waiting to see what he does." He gazed around the room. "We've a lot to do so I'll let you crack on."

Kathryn needed coffee. Badly. She popped to the canteen for an espresso in the hope the caffeine might keep her awake. In front of her in the queue were a couple of middle-aged men in dapper suits who were discussing the Service's latest recruitment campaign targeted at Cambridge University students. One of them remarked how different Five's approach was to MI6's which, he said, still recruited in a clandestine manner.

His comment reminded her of something she'd read in relation to the MP Monty and the PR guru MAM: both had attended Cambridge around the same time.

Kathryn hurried back to her desk and began trawling through Cambridge University's web site. She was unsure of what she was searching for, since Monty and MAM had been in different faculties, but she ploughed on looking for a connection. After exhausting the main web site, she searched sites belonging to the university's various clubs, societies and affiliations. When Meg whined, she took her a quick walk along the riverbank and then returned to her task fuelled with more coffee.

It was after midnight when she finally found it.

***

The following morning, Kathryn knocked on Julien's door and asked if she could have a word. She'd hardly slept, too wired on coffee and excitement about what she'd found. Anxious at the prospect of telling her boss how she'd come by the information and how he might react, she felt sick to her stomach. Julien, however, looked more fraught than herself and she cursed her poor timing.

"Take a seat." He indicated the chair in front of his desk.

Without preamble, she passed him a copy of the photograph she'd discovered. She'd found it buried deep within an archived gallery on the Cambridge University Rowing Club web site. It featured a team of rowers and their coxswain in university colours posing with a silver trophy. Kneeling in the front row of the picture was a young Margaret-Anne McCrae, flanked on either side by Alasdair Montrose and Dominic Shaftesbury.

She said, "Dominic was at Cambridge with both Monty and MAM. They all rowed together. It shows a connection between the publicist, the MP and the MI6 officer."

After scrutinising the photograph, Julien slid a hand down the front of his unshaven face and onto his chin and looked at her. "Could be coincidence."

Raising an incredulous eyebrow, she said, "You really believe it's a coincidence that Dominic's connected to not just one but two people on our grid?"

Placing the photograph on the desk, he said, "It's entirely possible. The intelligence community actively recruit from Oxford and Cambridge. Six still have talent spotters in several of the colleges."

Shaking her head in disbelief, she said, "Okay, but just suppose for one minute they're all in cahoots."

He regarded her carefully, his gaze sharp and calculating. "That's quite a leap but, coincidence or not, we can't investigate Dominic. He's MI6, one of us."

"He could be up to his ears in this and you know it!"

Mashing his lips together, he said, "No, we don't ... and this..." he stabbed a finger at the photograph, "... this proves nothing." He fixed her with a stern look, "And why are you digging around in this anyway? McCrae's not connected to your cases and I made it clear I didn't want you interfering in Jamie's operation."

"What if the cases are linked? If Dominic's involved, Jamie could be in danger."

His voice increased in volume. "You're jumping to conclusions and nothing you've brought me so far suggests a link. You can't go around accusing MI6 officers just because they rowed with someone at university. As far as you're concerned Dominic is off limits. Untouchable. And if we did decide to take a closer look at him, we'd have to do it by the book." He paused for a beat. "There are strict protocols which must be followed."

She matched his volume. "And as soon as you follow them, you'll alert him. At the moment, he's got no idea we know anything."

"We don't know anything," he yelled.

Kathryn paused, unsure of whether to say what else she'd found. But to hell with it, Julien had to be told; her husband's life could be in danger if Six were meddling in his operation.

"Take a look at this." She handed him a transcript of a telephone conversation.

Julien's mouth fell open as he scanned the document. She'd highlighted the interesting parts and it didn't take him long.

He glared at her. "Dear Lord, how did you get this? Don't tell me you hacked the phone of an MI6 officer?" He looked like he was about to burst a blood vessel.

"Of course not, I wouldn't —."

"Do you have any idea what you've done?" He waved the transcript at her furiously. "How many rules you've broken —"

She cut into his tirade. "I hacked the Russian embassy. They're the ones bugging Dominic's phone, not me, so I haven't broken any rules."

Her words silenced him for a moment. Then he stood, leaned over the desk and fixed her with an angry glare. "Kathryn, you will stay away from this. Do you hear me? And need I remind you that you're still on probation?"

She glowered at him.

He slammed a palm onto the desk making her jump. "You will NOT investigate Dominic. Do I make myself clear?"

Huffing out her annoyance, she swiped the photograph and transcript from the desk and stormed out the office.

The Hit

***"The world's richest 10% of people produce half of Earth's climate-harming fossil-fuel emissions, while the poorest half contribute a mere 10%" —* Oxfam 2015**

***

Jamie

With just days to go before the protest in Grangemouth, Jamie drove the van from Salford to Linlithgow packed full of provisions and equipment. Leon accompanied him, leaving the others to follow in Wolff's car or on public transport.

Traffic on the M6 was slow and to pass the time Leon tuned the radio to a music station. When Katy Perry's *Roar* played, they sang along. It reminded Jamie of car journeys with Kathryn and her teasing about his terrible singing.

"My mum loved that song," said Leon when it finished. The adverts came on and he turned down the volume.

Leon rarely talked about his background and Jamie asked about his family, although he knew some details from the brief.

Born in Birmingham to a drug-dependent single mother, Leon had been in and out of foster care from an early age. After his mother died of an overdose when he was ten, he went to live with her sister in Hackney. His aunty didn't want him; she'd enough kids of her own and her husband had left her.

He told Jamie that when he was seventeen, his best mate Yusuf was stabbed to death by a county lines rival. He and Yusuf had grown up together, had gone to the same school, and played for the local football team. That was until Yusuf turned fifteen and started running weed out of the city for a gang to earn some cash. That spiraled into selling heroin and crack cocaine for some heavy criminals.

"He was only 18 when he died," said Leon. "I knew if I didn't get out, I'd be next."

"Why this group? Why here?" asked Jamie.

Leon chuckled. "I blame Lennie. He was a youth worker, an ex-offender, so he knew the score. Spent his life trying to stop kids like me taking the wrong path."

"By introducing you to Extinction Rebellion?"

Leon shook his head. "That came later. Lennie kept on at me and Yusuf to come to the Centre. It was a local group run as a cooperative, a bit like ours really."

Jamie kept his expression neutral. He thought the Climate Warriors more a dictatorship. Or a cult.

Leon continued. "I finally gave in to Lennie's badgering and went. And it changed my life. Started getting involved in all these projects. Arts and drama and stuff. But the one I really liked was the community farm. They let us look after the animals and taught us how to grow vegetables."

"And Yusuf?"

"By that time he was running drugs. We were still mates but we'd drifted." He stared wistfully into the middle distance then, turning back, "After a woman from Extinction Rebellion came to talk to us about the climate crisis, I started going to their meetings. That's how I met the others."

"How did Ethan convince you to move to Salford?"

He gave a mirthless laugh. "Didn't take much persuading. My aunty wanted me out, I'd no job, and my best mate had just been murdered. Ethan said he could sort me out with digs and stuff. No way I could've gone to college otherwise."

"And here you are, living the dream," chuckled Jamie. Then, in a serious tone, "You don't need to go through with this and throw all that away. It's OK to change your mind."

Leon thought for a moment. "Yeah, but Ethan's been good to me. I owe him everything."

***

Kathryn

Kathryn got the call in the early hours, not long after going to bed. She awoke dazed and confused to the sound of her mobile phone vibrating on the bedside table where she'd left it to charge. It was pitch-black and she rubbed the sleep from her eyes as she listened to the message from the Operations Officer. Terror gripped her.

Leaving Meg to sleep in her basket, she sped to the office, her thoughts full of speculation about the reason for the call out. All she knew was it concerned Alabaster, not Jamie, and for that she gave thanks. Feeling lightheaded, she put it down to lack of sleep and too many unhealthy meals.

The mood in the briefing room was sombre. Julien was at the lectern, his face lined with worry. He was dressed in the same suit and tie he'd been wearing yesterday and dark sleep bruises ringed his eyes. Kathryn wondered if he ever slept. She took a seat near the front.

When everyone was present, he began. "Good morning. The reason we've assembled you at this ungodly hour is because RED KITE and GREY GOOSE have been found dead." He paused to let the news sink in.

Kathryn put a hand to her chest, and there were gasps from amongst the team. Julien called for silence before he explained what'd happened.

As planned, the operators in Yellow Team had trailed Balakin to Sokolov's flat. After an hour, when it was clear the couple had gone to bed without discussing the exchange, the team left them and passed control to staff listening remotely from Thames House.

Julien's expression was grim as he reported that at 03:17 hours, a motorcyclist wearing leathers and a helmet with a dark visor was spotted approaching the main entrance to Sokolov's flat. Grainy footage from the internal cameras showed the shadowy figure circumventing the door entry system.

By this point a remote operator had raised the alarm and police were summoned. However, by the time the responders arrived, the motorcyclist had broken into Sokolov's apartment on the top floor. Julien then displayed footage from the hidden cameras in Sokolov's flat. Transfixed, she watched as the figure pulled a pistol from his jacket and crept into the bedroom. Kathryn put a hand to her mouth and held her breath.

Julien paused the video and gazed around the room, his eyes settling on her. "You may wish to look away. The next part is hard to watch."

She couldn't and instantly regretted it because what followed could only be described as an execution. She squeezed her eyes shut after the first muffled shot. At the sickening sounds from the speakers, her stomach roiled and she feared she'd vomit. When she opened her eyes, it was to see the figure fleeing from the flats carrying a hold-all.

Julien explained all available assets in the area were used to track the motorbike, but the police arrived too late on the scene, by which time the bike had vanished. Its plates were false and obscured with mud; a classic countersurveillance trick.

There was a long silence which Julien finally broke. "RED KITE and GREY GOOSE were shot twice at close range, once to the head and once to the chest — a double tap to guarantee the kill. We've searched the apartment and there's no sign of the diplomatic bag or the USB stick. Money, jewellery and other valuables were not taken except for a laptop belonging to GREY GOOSE."

He shook his head and in a low voice, said, "They knew exactly what they were looking for. They were in and out in minutes, and footage from CCTV demonstrates a high degree of skilful driving and a good knowledge of counter."

He let his words settle before adding, "All of this bears the hallmarks of a professional hit."

The Leak

"The IPCC process is related to environmental activism, politics and opportunism. It is unrelated to science." **— Professor Ian Plimer 2009**

***

Jamie

Ethan stormed into the community centre with Yasmine trotting at his heels. "The place is crawling with pigs," he said, "we need to call it off."

The Climate Warriors had settled into the Community Centre in Linlithgow. It was just days before the protest and they'd been taking it in turns to patrol the roads surrounding the petrochemical plant. Jamie had added decals to the sides of his vehicle to make it look like a courier van.

Wolff sprung to his feet, concern furrowing his brow. "What do you mean?"

"There are three police vans positioned around the perimeter," fumed Ethan. "No way can we go ahead if there's extra security. It's like someone tipped them off."

Cursing, Wolff shot a look at Jamie who met his gaze with a challenging one of his own.

"Don't know why you're looking at me," said Jamie.

What the fuck's going on? Gary knows the protest's imminent. There shouldnae be a cop in sight.

"We've got a leak," snapped Wolff glaring at Jamie.

Jamie sought just the right balance of righteous indignation. If there was a time to live his cover, it was now, and he sprung to his feet, the chair making a horrible scraping noise across the vinyl. "If you're gonna make accusations like that, you can just fuck right off."

"Whoa," said Ethan, positioning himself between them as they glowered at one another. "Calm down, both of you."

Alex rose to his feet saying to Wolff, "Hey, that's completely out of order."

Meadow placed a gentle hand on Wolff's arm. "Karsten, no one here's said anything, least of all Jamie. In any case, there are others outside of this group who know what's planned."

Wolff looked at Meadow, his eyes softening. He raised his hands placatingly and turned to Jamie. "Sorry, I'm just pissed off. We're so damn close."

Yaz said, "We're all gutted but that's no excuse."

Jamie gave Wolff a brief nod and said, "We've all got skin in the game but, either way, we've got a problem if the place is hoachin' with polis."

"Jamie's right," said Rose, "We can't risk it. If they're still there tomorrow, we'll need to delay or switch targets, and I'll have to tell our supporters to stay put."

Activists the length and breadth of the country were on standby awaiting a WhatsApp message from Rose to give them the green light to make their way to Linlithgow to join the protest.

Cursing, Wolff scrubbed a hand through his hair. "Impossible. We can't hit another target at short notice."

Yasmine said, "What about plan B, the nuclear power station at Hartlepool?"

There were several gasps. This was the first Jamie knew about a plan B and, judging from the expressions on the others' faces, it was the same for them.

Rose glowered at Ethan and bit out, "And exactly when were you going to tell us about plan B? What else have you been keeping from us?"

With a glare at Yasmine, Ethan said, "We only talked about it, it was never a plan."

Rose snapped, "We? Who is 'we'? We're supposed to be a collective, not a bloody dictatorship. How d'you expect us to trust you when it's clear you don't trust us?"

Before Ethan could reply, Wolff said, "There was always the possibility something like this might happen, but hitting another target at short notice is not feasible. It takes months of planning to pull something like this off, never mind a nuclear facility." Addressing Ethan, he said, "There is no plan B."

Rose clenched her fists by her sides and glowered at Ethan while Yasmine wound a possessive arm around his waist. Rose looked as though she might swing for the pair of them while the others gazed on in stunned silence.

Jamie watched, concerned his months of working undercover were about to count for nothing. He needed to do something, and rapidly. "For all we know," he said, "there might be something else going on in the area that's attracted police attention. I suggest we do regular sweeps and make a decision tomorrow morning."

There was muttered agreement.

He added, "I'll head out later, take another look."

His first phone call was going to be to Gary to ask, "Just what the actual ...?"

***

Kathryn

Still reeling from Julien's shocking briefing, Kathryn returned to her desk and started up her computers. An invite had appeared in her calendar from Robin in Vetting and she groaned. A meeting with the Prince of Darkness was the very last thing she needed right now. It was scheduled for first thing and she wondered if Robin was racing the dawn to get back to the crypt.

"What's up?" asked Fitz.

"Vetting! Need I say more?"

"You been a naughty girl?"

She muttered, "Only in the service of His Majesty."

Fitz approached and perched on the corner of her desk. In a low voice, he said, "I wanted to give you the heads-up there'll be a full-scale investigation as a result of what's happened in Edinburgh." She gave him a quizzical look and he added, "Another team will come in and take over. We can't investigate ourselves."

She gawped at him. "But why?"

Fitz glanced around and then whispered, "There's been a leak. Someone knew Sokolov had that material in her possession and was going to give it to the Russian, and until we find out who the mole is, all of us are under suspicion." When Kathryn gaped at him, he added, "Don't take it personally, it's just procedure. It won't be pleasant though ... just saying."

She exhaled a long breath and looked at him. "Is that why Vetting want to talk to me?"

He shrugged, "Christ only knows. They're a law unto themselves."

Except for those involved in Operation Alabaster, there were few employees in the office early and the next couple of hours passed quickly. Kathryn spent them trawling through terabytes of intelligence about Balakin and Sokolov looking for anything that might hint at a planned assassination.

Only when the reminder on her calendar pinged for the meeting did she become aware the sun had risen and the rest of the city had woken. As she gathered her things, a commotion drew her attention. Four people in suits, three men and a woman, appeared. Julien greeted them with a grim expression and they disappeared into his office.

Fitz glanced up at her and mouthed, "Good luck."

Glancing from Julien's office back to him, she whispered, "Likewise."

As Kathryn made her way towards Robin's lair, she hoped the meeting wouldn't take long. She needed to get home to feed Meg and bank some much-needed sleep. The adrenaline rush she'd experienced during the briefing had subsided leaving exhaustion in its wake. Feeling dizzy and nauseous, she kept picturing Sokolov's face and hearing her laughter as she flirted with Balakin.

Kathryn reminded herself that Sokolov's last weeks had been happy ones and that she hadn't suffered, but she found no comfort, only sadness.

Outside Robin's office, she took a moment to gather her courage before knocking. He kept her waiting a few moments before shouting 'Enter.'

Robin sat at a conference table along with another woman Kathryn didn't recognise. Without glancing up from the thick file in front of him, he motioned for her to sit. The woman cast an unfriendly glance as Kathryn perched opposite and fidgeted with her cardigan, pulling it against the chill in the room. An ominous silence descended, punctuated only by the infernal sound of Robin clicking his biro. Several minutes passed before he deigned to look up at her.

Kathryn met his steely eyes as he slid an A4-size black and white photograph across the table towards her. Although grainy, there was no mistaking that it was of her, despite the hoodie and sunglasses she wore. A time and date stamp in the bottom right-hand corner showed it had been taken on the day her step-father died.

Robin said, "This was taken from CCTV on a bus that runs through Shawlands close to where your stepfather was found dead. We're lucky to get it considering how much time has elapsed."

FUUUUCK! They know. They bloody know!

Gripping the arms of the chair, she battled to keep her expression from betraying her mounting panic. A voice in her head that sounded a lot like Jamie's said, '*The photo's probably fake. He's on a fishing trip.*'

Robin opened the bulging manilla folder and pulled out a wad of paper.

Kathryn heard the voice again. '*Thick file full of blank paper. Classic police interrogation tactic to intimidate a suspect.*'

She glanced at the document Robin passed her; it was a copy of her written statement.

He snarled, "You lied about what you were doing that day. The photograph proves you were in the vicinity of where your stepfather died."

She met his hostile gaze. "I didn't lie. I was simply mistaken about the timing. Like you said, it happened a while ago." The voice in her head instructed her to remain calm and breathe.

He clicked his pen and she wondered if this was another interrogation technique designed to irritate the hell out of suspects and drive them to a confession. She wanted to stab him through the eye with it.

"Nevertheless," he said, "in light of this new evidence there needs to be a full investigation to determine whether you're in the clear or not." He sent her a triumphant look and added, "Until further notice, you're suspended."

She gasped out, "What? But I never laid a hand on him. All this..." she indicated the photograph and statement with a sweep of her hand, "... this proves nothing."

The woman finally spoke, biting out, "Until we've established that, you are not to set foot in this building."

Kathryn gawped at them, "But we're right in the middle of Operation Alabaster."

"Precisely," snapped Robin, "and I hear there's been a leak. Is there something else you'd like to tell us?" His eyes bored into hers.

She gasped in disbelief.

The woman stood and asked her to relinquish her pass. An unseen signal must have been given because a security guard appeared. Kathryn rose to unsteady feet. Noise roared in her ears, the room pitched and she sat again.

This can't be happening.

She slowly removed her lanyard and passed it to the woman.

Robin said, "Our colleague here will escort you."

Kathryn shook her head. "But my team?"

"— will be notified." Robin stood and gathered up the file, signalling the meeting was over.

The security officer ushered Kathryn from the room and led her along a long corridor to a bank of lifts. She stumbled and he caught her arm, his eyes soft.

"Are you okay, Miss?"

She was too stunned to answer. Feeling sick, she nodded and fought back tears.

The guard fixed his eyes on the floor as they rode the lift to ground level and into what appeared to be a loading bay. He politely asked her to wait in a small windowless room furnished only with two plastic chairs. Was this 'the departure lounge'? Not trusting her jelly legs, she slid into a seat.

A few minutes later, the guard reappeared carrying her handbag and coat which he passed to her with an embarrassed nod. She followed him out to the loading bay where a loud buzzer sounded.

"You take care now," he said as a blast door opened onto a cobbled alleyway.

She stumbled out and watched in dismay as the steel door closed behind her with a clang of finality. Tears ran down her cheeks at the realisation of what had just happened.

Arching her back like a cat, she spewed into the gutter.

The Chase

***"Scientific evidence for warming of the climate system is unequivocal"* – Intergovernmental Panel on Climate Change (IPCC) 2009**

***

Jamie

Jamie's phone buzzed with a text from an unknown number.

Phone compromised. New number. Meet 19:00, usual place

His frown prompted Wolff to ask if everything was okay, and he nodded. He assumed the message was from Gary but if so, the eejit wasn't sticking to protocol. Jamie replied.

G?

He remembered how his pithy text messages wound Kathryn up. Although she was adept at text speak, his monosyllabic replies drove her potty and he enjoyed goading her with them at every opportunity. Conscious of Wolff's continued interest, he busied himself on his phone. The reply was immediate.

y

Numpty! Jamie was going to give his handler an earful about this and the fact Grangemouth was crawling with police. This operation was rapidly turning into a clusterfuck.

After dinner, Jamie made his excuses and sat outside in his van sheltering from the rain. He tried Gary's old number only to get an 'unobtainable' message. Sighing, he drove to the back of Linlithgow Cricket Club where he and Gary had met previously. A grey Range Rover Sport followed him under the bridge and into the car park. The lot lay in darkness and it was almost empty except for a red Nissan Micra and silver Volvo estate. The Range Rover parked at the opposite corner but its driver remained in the car. He noted its registration number.

There was no sign of Gary or his Audi and Jamie looked at the dashboard clock which showed he was a few minutes early. He called Kathryn but she didn't pick up. A feeling of unease prickled down his neck. Why wasn't she answering his calls or messages? He desperately needed to talk to her. He checked the time and the car park again.

Where the hell's Gary?

The Range Rover and its driver hadn't moved. Operators were trained to assess a scene for anything that didn't look right. On the surface, there was nothing unusual but he noticed the car's wing mirror was angled such that its driver could watch him. A classic surveillance technique.

What the fuck?

He tried Gary's new number but the phone rang out, and the old number was still unobtainable. Everything about this situation felt wrong and he didn't want to risk sitting there any longer. He gunned the engine and headed for the exit, driving past the Range Rover at a measured speed. He strained to catch a glimpse of the driver but the windows were tinted and all he could make out was a shape. His heart thumped against his ribcage.

Heading back towards town, he scouring his mirrors to check if he was being followed. There was no sign of the Range Rover. He took a detour up the main street, away from the community centre, hyper alert for foot surveillance, cars and motorbikes. He didn't spot anything. After a mile, he pulled over into an empty layby surrounded by trees.

Something was off and he didn't like it.

He called the MI5 Operations Centre, a number he'd memorised. They answered with a bland 'Hello, can I help you?' so as not to reveal who they were. After giving his call sign, he left a message for Gary along with the Range Rover's registration number.

Feeling hungry all of a sudden, he continued to the drive-thru MacDonald's in Grangemouth where he ordered a McPlant burger and fries. He scarfed it and then took a quiet country road back towards the community centre.

Headlights appeared in his rear-view mirror. Telling himself he was just being paranoid, he maintained a steady speed. The last thing he needed was to be pulled over by a patrol car.

The driver rapidly closed the gap.

Rain sheeted against the windscreen and the only thing Jamie could see clearly were the white lines on the road and headlights in his side mirror.

Jamie rounded a bend and eased his foot off the accelerator, expecting the car to overtake on the straight. When it didn't, he slowed again but the driver remained stubbornly on his tail. Peering through the deluge, Jamie gripped the wheel and concentrated on his driving. The road dipped and he veered into the middle to avoid a deep puddle, the water rising up in a wave around him. Just inches from his bumper, the driver flashed his headlights and sounded the horn.

What the hell's he playing at?

He steered back into his own lane and slowed, inviting the driver to move past him. The car rammed his bumper. The noise was deafening and the jolt sent Jamie lurching forward. He battled to control the vehicle and keep it out of the ditch. Heart in his mouth, he stamped on the accelerator and gripped the wheel so tight his knuckles turned white.

The driver matched his speed.

Suddenly, the car pulled out and came alongside him. It was a grey Range Rover.

Panic began to set in. He couldn't outrun the SUV, and there were no turn-offs ahead, only farm tracks, and he didn't want to risk pulling over in case this nutjob was armed. His best bet was to reach the town and pull into a service station where there were cameras.

The SUV inched into Jamie's lane. He dropped a gear and red-lined the engine so hard the rev counter spun to its maximum. That was when he spotted a pair of headlights coming towards them. The Range Rover didn't budge and the car ahead flashed its headlights in warning.

Jamie braked, leaving a gap for the Range Rover to pull in but it remained beside him.

With seconds to go before a collision, Jamie hit the anchors, wrenched on the steering wheel and careened onto the verge, tyres screeching as they left the tarmac. The oncoming vehicle swung into his lane and screamed past him. He fought to keep the van under control as it bounced through gorse and bracken.

The Range Rover took off at a tyre-scorching speed.

Cursing, Jamie slumped over the wheel and caught his breath. When his heart rate returned to normal, he got out and inspected the van for damage. After finding none other than a dented bumper, he drove slowly back to the community centre.

Still shaken, he found the group in deep in discussion about the imminent protest. They were all present. A radio played in the background and they spoke in hushed tones. Wolff glanced up from a map and sent Jamie a brief nod.

Does that bastard know something?

Jamie returned to the office he'd commandeered as a bedroom and paced the floor. He'd join the others soon but right now he needed to calm the fuck down. He considered calling the incident in but with days to go until the protest, he feared Gary might pull the plug. In any case, he'd come to no harm.

Needing to hear her voice, he tried phoning Kathryn again but she still wasn't answering.

Jamie cursed and paced some more. He needed his wife and he prayed this mission would end soon so they could break through this wall of silence and mistrust.

***

Kathryn

Meg woke her.

Kathryn had slept fitfully and the desire to burrow and hide beneath the duvet was almost too much to resist, but the dog needed out.

She'd little memory of returning to the cottage but, somehow, she found herself back home. She'd lain in bed sobbing as she replayed the meeting with Vetting over and over in her mind. Anger and humiliation burned at the memory of how she'd been treated, mixed with anxiety about Robin finding evidence of her crime. Would she be charged with murder?

She ignored the phone when it rang. In no fit state to speak to Jamie, she didn't want to burden him with her worries on top of what he was dealing with, nor could she trust her voice not to betray her guilt. How might he react if he thought her responsible for the death of her stepfather?

Being unable to confide in her husband worried her more. She didn't keep secrets from him. This was the exception and she justified her secrecy as a way of protecting Jamie and his career.

She didn't regret her crime but she had to accept she'd probably done the wrong thing for the right reasons. Knowing her stepfather was grooming another girl for sex was unconscionable. She could never have allowed that to happen to another child and, based on her own bitter experience, she didn't trust the authorities to intervene. Ending Phil's life was the only way to stop him and, if she had to, she'd do the same thing again.

How much had she been motivated by revenge? She'd convinced herself she'd acted purely in defence of the girl but perhaps there'd been a small part that wanted retribution for what he'd done to her? Did that make her a monster?

The guilt was eating away at her from the inside. It was like a wedge driving her and Jamie even further apart. She felt too ashamed to talk to him for fear of seeing the hurt and disgust on his face when she confessed what she'd done.

And even if by some miracle he did forgive her, could she ever trust her husband again? How long before he was tempted into another relationship on an undercover job? Would he, like so many agents before him had done, maintain two separate lives where neither woman knew about the other? She thought of Keith and how this had ended his marriage. Was the same happening to them? She worried about what the future held.

Yet, given her own crime, she'd absolutely no right to judge Jamie, as hurtful as his actions had been. Maybe she deserved this. Perhaps this was her punishment.

Meg barked.

Rubbing sore eyes, Kathryn pulled on the joggies and crumpled t-shirt she'd discarded the night before and dragged herself to the kitchen. After letting Meg out, she shuffled into the bathroom and caught sight of herself in the mirror. Dark circles ringed red swollen eyes. Her hair needed washing but she was too tired and rinsed her face instead, the water stinging her eyes.

After feeding Meg, she searched the cupboards for something to eat. There was little food and she couldn't face shopping. She found a dusty tin of mandarin oranges at the back of the pantry and ate half of it, then vomited into the toilet bowl.

Shambling back to the bedroom, she collapsed on the bed. Smelling the stale sheets, she thought of their bedroom back in Knoydart; the saggy mattress and waking up entwined in Jamie's arms. She ached to be back there, her head full of images of him making love to her. It felt like a part of her had been ripped away and this triggered a fresh bout of painful tears. Meg hopped onto the bed beside her and put her chin on her lap.

Jamie had betrayed her and put their marriage in jeopardy. She felt angry and humiliated but she could not hate him. She loved him still — she'd love him always. And it was a true and pure love she felt, the type that once experienced changed you forever. Love can be both beautiful and dreadful.

She stroked the dog's fur. "What am I going to do Meg? I love him. I love him so much it hurts."

The Hacker

***"Every year, bitcoin mining consumes more energy than Belgium" —* Cambridge's Bitcoin Electricity Consumption Index 2022**

***

Jamie

Jamie's phone woke him. It felt as though he'd only just shut his eyes and he sat up like a flick knife. The caller-id was Gary's usual number which he'd stored in his phone as 'Terry Work'.

Rubbing a knuckle into his eye socket, he tried to keep his voice to a whisper, conscious of the paper-thin walls. "What the hell's going on?"

"Calm down. There was a comms mix up but it's sorted, okay?"

"It's not okay and don't bloody tell me to calm down." Hearing movement in the next room, Jamie lowered his voice. "Where were you yesterday?"

"Listen, I didn't arrange to meet and I haven't changed my number. Fitz is looking into it so if you see weird shit on your phone, it's us. And if I have to switch devices, I'll follow protocol. Understood?"

Jamie huffed out a long breath. "Aye, and what about the presence of our friends? How d'you explain that?"

"Also sorted. We've had a word with the local commander and instructed them to pull back."

"Who increased security?"

He listened while Gary attempted to reassure him everything was fine and that all parties were fully prepared. The more Gary said, the less Jamie was convinced.

He hung up and checked the time, realising it was still early. Knowing he wouldn't get back to sleep, he dressed and crept downstairs. Everyone was asleep and the community centre was preternaturally quiet.

Exiting through the rear door, Jamie walked the short distance to Linlithgow Loch. There was frost underfoot and he zipped up his hoodie against the chill. Waterfowl squawked and scattered in the reeds as he approached the water's edge. Small boats dipped and nodded in the wind-worried loch, and the sun was beginning to rise, illuminating the great hulking shadow of the palace in the blood-red light of dawn.

Beautiful but foreboding.

***

Kathryn

When Kathryn opened her eyes again it was almost lunch time and her stomach growled. Tempting as it was to wallow in a pit of misery, it was time to get up and face what'd happened. All of it.

After showering and washing her hair, she dressed in clean clothes, changed the sheets and put on a load of laundry. She wrote a grocery list and walked Meg to the mini supermarket in the village. Fuelled up on tea and toast, she emptied the bins and tidied the house. Being alone, it was a thankless task.

She missed Jamie so much. Missed his smile, his teasing, his touch. She'd never met anyone like him and never would again. And nor did she want to. How could she entrust her heart to another? Meg rubbed against her calves and she petted her. Kathryn knew she needed to stop moping about and do something to fix this but, until Jamie was home, she knew nothing would be resolved.

Her broken marriage wasn't the only reason for her low mood. Her career was in tatters and if she was right, and Dominic, Monty and MAM were connected, this went right to the heart of government. Her suspicions meant Jamie could be in danger.

Certain the solution to the puzzle lay in the financial trail, she knew she'd struggle to find it without help to penetrate Bitcoin's public blockchain. The technology that made it perfect for concealing funds also made it near impossible to compromise.

Although an expert hacker in her own right, each Grey Nemesis member had had their particular specialism and it was the blend of these skills that'd made the group so effective. While they could all hack computer systems, Kathryn's focus was devices, Pandora's was communications, and Scotty's was crypto. There was little he didn't know about Bitcoin and the blockchain and she needed his help.

But could she trust him? It was one thing to ask for help catching paedos, quite another to share sensitive government secrets. She'd trusted Pandora and she remembered how well that'd turned out: she'd betrayed them all.

What did she really know about Scotty? The first rule of Grey Nemesis had been 'never talk about Grey Nemesis' (which was also the second rule), while the third was 'don't talk about your personal life'. Hackers by their nature were anonymous, hiding behind nicknames and VPNs, and it was considered bad form to disclose personal details. Pandora had always flouted this rule, willingly sharing that she was a young woman from the Midwest. Scotty posed as an American who was interested in Star Trek and crypto, and who enjoyed dishing out cyber justice. But was any of it true?

In cyberspace, you didn't know a person's real name, age, sex or location and it wasn't unusual for females to pose as males to avoid harassment. She recalled the first time she'd entered a chat room as 'Kate', only to be told by one arsehole that if she wished to join, she'd have to show them her tits. Ever since, she'd lurked behind the gender-neutral nickname 'Moniker' and shared little about herself.

Hackers used other methods too, some as simple as Americans avoiding US-spelling, while British hackers embraced it. Some adopted single-letter nicknames, such as 'Z', to render a Google search for them impossible.

Scotty was hardcore and used more sophisticated means to disguise his online identity. He'd at least two computers, each working off a different proxy server that placed him in separate time zones to prevent a location match, and he layered several VPNs to conceal his computer's address. They'd often discussed these tactics and she employed similar ones herself.

MI5 had military-grade technology and, in her work, she used persona management software which allowed her to match different online aliases. Using this tool, she could correlate every login time from different accounts, every piece of grammar used, and every nickname to establish who a person really was. Every scrap of information revealed in the digital world could be used, and she'd once traced a terrorist through the ether based solely on the name of his favourite movie.

She'd used this same tool to glean information about Scotty, confirming he was an American male whose real name was Zachary Cosgrove. He was in his early thirties and, until Pandora's betrayal, had resided in New York. After going on the run from the Feds, he'd landed in the UK. *IntoDarkness* was Scotty.

Using her laptop, Kathryn tracked Scotty down to the lunatic world of 4chan's 'Random' board and invited him to a private chatroom.

[Moniker] *The random board, really? I feel dirty*

[IntoDarkness] *It's my spiritual home :-) I was gonna message you. Remember the wife-beating maggot? Turns out he's wanted for a burglary so he's gonna do time, a long stretch of it. Who knew?*

[Moniker] *Best news I've had in ages! Thank you*

[IntoDarkness] *Happy to help. Anyway, whassup?*

Kathryn explained that she needed help tracing Monty's digital currency transactions, the ones he'd made through his son, which were all in Bitcoin. She didn't mention MAM, eager to see what Scotty discovered on his own.

[Moniker] *Can you find out who the payments are going to?*

[IntoDarkness] *Transactions are not as anonymous as everyone thinks as each one's recorded in the public blockchain to prevent double spending. It's hard to link a digital wallet with a person but it's not impossible. If he's transferred money in and out using a normal bank account, it'll lead me to him as easily as if he'd used a credit card. Gimme a few hours*

After sending Scotty the details, she wound up the chat and poured herself a glass of Riesling. Sipping the wine, she pondered on who the recipient might be of Monty's backhanders. The wine curdled in her stomach and she sprinted to the bathroom to be sick.

She washed her face with cold water. What the hell was wrong with her? She'd been feeling queasy for weeks and had put it down to long days, bad eating habits and her emotional state. She opened the bathroom cabinet and examined the blister pack of contraceptive pills to make sure she hadn't skipped one.

Oh dear God, surely not?

The Gathering

"Population control is very much part of the agenda for many of the most radical green activists..." — **Matthew Sinclair 2011**

***

Jamie

from:	Declan Fitzpatrick < Declan.Fitzpatrick@tacitnet.mi5.uk >
to:	Gary.Singer@tacitnet.mi5.uk
subject:	Operation Monkshood
security:	AES-256 encryption

Gary,

Apologies but we're experiencing some technical issues with the eavesdropping devices in the Community Centre in Linlithgow. Until this is fixed, Jamie's your only eyes and ears.

Will keep you posted,

Fitz

***

Jamie fought his way through a mass of beards, dreadlocks and face piercings.

It was two days before the protest and the community centre was packed to the rafters with volunteers who'd travelled across the country to take part. Many more had turned up than they'd hoped for, arriving steadily in minivans throughout the day with food and sleeping bags. Jamie estimated they numbered around two hundred and fifty.

The Climate Warriors' plea for support had attracted a diverse group, some fitting the new-age stereotype, while others looked like they made jam for the Women's Institute. He recognised a few faces from previous protests and the ICC, and they greeted him warmly.

While Ethan and the others buzzed about like bluebottles, Jamie sought refuge in his van along with Leon. It was filled with equipment the campaigners would need, including bolt cutters, climbing gear, blankets and D-locks. Jamie had hired additional vans to ferry protesters to the site, and another containing enough food to feed everyone for a week, provided they liked couscous. Leon helped with the final checks and Jamie passed him a large first aid kit. The colour drained from Leon's face.

"Just in case," said Jamie.

Leon swallowed and caught his eye. "It's starting to feel very real."

Jamie nodded. "Aye, it is."

"You nervous?"

"Course I am, it's not every day you break into an oil refinery." Then, realising how scared the lad looked, "You don't need to do this, mate. There are other ways you can make a difference that won't land you in jail."

Leon shook his head. "I want to make a stand. Wolff might be a dick but he's right about that. Nothing else we've done so far has made a real impact. But this will."

"You're gonna end up with a criminal record which could scupper your future."

Leon's eyes burned with a furious vibrance. "I won't have a future, none of us will, unless we do this. I mean ... we face extinction man..." Passing Jamie a tube of glue, he added, "Sounds like you're the one getting cold feet."

Jamie chuckled as he waved a hand over the equipment surrounding them, "Nope, but ask me again when I'm half way up a cooling tower."

Leon laughed.

Ethan appeared at the rear of the van and asked if they were packed and ready. Jamie saw Leon rearrange his face into a neutral expression before replying that they would be if given the time and space to complete the job.

Jamie said, "Just need the banner and we're good to go."

Wolff had organised the banner which the climbing team would unfurl down the cooling tower to publicise the protest.

"Karsten has it, I'll make sure he gives you it before we set off," replied Ethan.

After informing them there'd be a meeting at seven, Ethan marched off. Jamie regarded Leon's expression, surprised to see him so riled up. It was unlike him and Jamie often teased him that if he was any more laid back, he'd be horizontal. He asked if he was alright.

Leon huffed out a breath. "Just nerves. But since Wolff pitched up, Ethan's been behaving like a colossal dick. We've always made decisions together but now he treats us like we're his personal army. I'll just be glad when this is over and Wolff pisses off back to Germany."

"Is that his plan?"

Leon shrugged. "Think so. Meadow told Rose he's asked her to go with him."

Jamie shuddered and then reminded himself that Wolff would go to prison for a long time.

Wolff's behaviour wasn't the only thing gnawing at him. His conversation with Gary was playing on his mind and he'd an uneasy feeling the operational gremlins were more than a simple mix-up. Although his handler assured him the police would be gone, he'd made a comment that suggested this wasn't the only fault in the lines of communication. Jamie hoped they'd finally get their bloody act together.

After Jamie and Leon completed their preparations, they went in search of food. As Jamie made his way into the main hall, some new arrivals greeted him. He felt like he was amongst friends and guilt pricked at his conscience knowing they'd likely all be in custody this time tomorrow evening.

The mood in the hall was febrile and Ethan had to shout to call the group to order. A muffled silence descended. There weren't enough seats so people sat on the floor, on radiators and window sills or leaned against the walls. Ethan switched off the overhead strip lights and Wolff flicked on the projector to display the Climate Warriors logo on the back wall.

Ethan welcomed everyone, saying how pleased he was so many had turned up to support them. There were activists from every age range, with as many people over the age of fifty as in their twenties. They were a diverse bunch too and amongst their ranks were doctors and delivery drivers, teachers and builders, and even a retired sailor in his eighties.

"Before we begin," said Ethan, "I'd like to thank those who've already handed in their mobile phones for safe keeping. If you haven't, please do so now to help guard against eavesdropping."

Yasmine collected several phones while Ethan introduced Wolff who was greeted with applause. Wolff warmed up his audience with his presentation from the International Climate Camp which he followed with a tirade about the government's continued subsidisation of the fossil fuel industry.

He tapped a key and an image of Grangemouth appeared. "About six miles from here is Scotland's only crude oil refinery. It produces tonnes of fuel which in turn is responsible for a staggering level of CO2 emissions every day." After a pause, he added, "Which is why we're going to shut it down for several days."

This was met with more rapturous applause, whistles and whoops.

When the crowd settled, he said, "This will be the biggest climate protest on British soil there's ever been, and it will cause ripples here and across the globe as other groups follow our lead." Wolff looked around the room, his expression grave. "If you decide to take part, you can be certain of arrest, maybe even imprisonment. Many of you have families, jobs and commitments. Only you can weigh the risk of this against your conviction to the cause."

There were murmurings as the reality of what he'd proposed set in, and Jamie scanned the faces of the crowd as his words registered.

Wolff continued, "The consequences will be serious and there's no shame in walking away now. No one here will think less of you. However, I do ask you leave the room now before we get into the details so you can truthfully say you'd no idea what we'd planned. You are welcome to stay and help at the workshop tomorrow which is our cover for the real operation."

Jamie noticed an older couple whispering and the man shaking his head. After raising his hands in surrender, he led his partner out as several activists smiled their understanding and patted them on the back. Another young woman followed, and Jamie was surprised more didn't join her.

After the door closed behind them, Wolff thanked those who remained. As he continued his spiel about the need to cut CO2 emissions and end reliance on fossil fuels, Jamie wondered when the riot squad would arrive and make arrests. The community centre was bugged and MI5 were listening, and Jamie had been involved in enough police operations to know that this would be the ideal moment, when all the protesters were gathered in one place with few exits. He strained to listen for movement outside but could hear nothing above the chatter.

Wolff finished and Ethan took his place. He explained that everyone would be divided into groups, with each given a specific role which he outlined in detail. The hardest part would be forcing the plant operators to turn off the processes to prevent the plant functioning for a week. He then introduced Stuart McKinness, the process engineer who'd joined their ranks, and invited him to speak.

Short and squat, McKinness shuffled to the front, appearing uncomfortable in the public glare. He wiped a sheen of sweat from his brow as he outlined the structures the volunteers should target. Using slides, he explained how various valves and levers on equipment within the plant could be operated manually to shut down processes, overriding any signals from the main control room.

Jamie swapped places with McKinness. He explained he and the blue shirts would scale one of the cooling towers and drape a banner over it bearing the Climate Warriors logo. The entire operation would be streamed live to make people aware of what they were doing and their reasons for it.

"Isn't that very dangerous?" asked a volunteer.

He nodded. "But it's the best way to get our message across to the outside world."

"What are our demands?" asked another.

Wolff replied, "We want written assurance the government will stop subsidising the fossil fuel industry with immediate effect and divert all of this money into renewables." This was met with deafening applause.

Ethan and Wolff then spent the next hour fielding questions about the logistics and the plan to hold the site for a week. During the discussion, there were a few mutterings of disquiet and Jamie noticed another couple leave.

Finally, Wolff wrapped up the meeting with, "Tomorrow my friends, we make history."

Tomorrow? Jamie wondered if he'd misheard.

Ethan added, "For operational security we've brought forward the day of the protest. I suggest you all get an early night, we leave at 4:30 a.m. sharp."

Cheering and clapping erupted.

As the volunteers dispersed, Jamie grabbed Wolff's arm and hissed, "When did the plan change?"

"Since I decided it," said Wolff shrugging off Jamie's grip with a glare.

"You can't just change the date at the last minute, we're not ready," hissed Jamie.

"We're ready enough and we risk being caught if we wait any longer." He waved a hand at the main hall, adding, "Look around. You think this number of people won't be noticed?"

Jamie knew he'd a point but he continued to glower at him until Meadow gently tugged Wolff away.

On the bright side, I'll be home a day early.

The Meeting

"By 2030 we could see a 'perfect storm' of food shortages, scarce water and insufficient energy resources which threaten to unleash public unrest, cross-border conflicts and mass migration as people flee from the worst-affected regions" **— Professor John Beddington, UK government's chief scientific adviser 2009**

***

Kathryn

Kathryn did three pregnancy tests – three! – all positive. Based on the dates when she and Jamie had last made love, which felt like eons ago, she calculated she was at least eleven weeks pregnant. She must have conceived when they were on holiday, before he departed for Germany. The realisation shocked her.

Still in denial, she stripped to her underwear and examined herself in the full-length bedroom mirror. She was still slender but now that she looked properly, there were obvious changes. She'd put on a little weight — confirmed by the bathroom scales — but not so much as to be noticeable. Her breasts were tender and there was a delicate swell around her middle.

How had she not realised the changes taking place in her own body? She'd continued to take her oral contraceptives and bled as normal, albeit lightly. The nausea and exhaustion, she'd put down to stress. She'd been so wrapped up in her worries she'd failed to spot what was happening right under her nose. She felt like an idiot.

Flopping down on the bed, she clutched her stomach and tried to process the overwhelming raft of thoughts and emotions. Carrying a child eclipsed everything else, all at once putting her other troubles into perspective, yet making them seem greater. How could she possibly cope without a husband and a job? She didn't feel ready to have a baby, to be responsible for another human being; not while she was a mess and her life was in turmoil. The alternative, however, was unthinkable: after all, this was her and Jamie's child.

She knew she needed to tell Jamie ... but not face to face ... not yet. Not until she knew her own mind. She was certain he'd take one look at her and guess immediately; he'd a radar for these things, which was one of the reasons he was so damn good at his job. Jamie would want the child, of that she'd no doubt. But did she want him?

A pinging sound from her laptop returned her to her senses. She flung on a robe and padded into the spare room. There was a message from Scotty under his [*IntoDarkness*] nickname.

She opened the message and stared at her screen in surprise. Scotty had delivered on his promise and what he'd unearthed intrigued her. His research revealed that Monty's son Rory had amassed a vast portfolio in cryptocurrencies. Consisting mainly of Bitcoin and Ethereum, his investment was worth millions of pounds at current market rates.

With painstaking scrutiny of the public blockchain, Scotty had traced payments from Rory's cryptocurrency account to another digital wallet. He'd also managed to identify or, in Internet parlance, 'dox' the recipient.

`[IntoDarkness]` *`Payments are going to a PR consultant called Margaret-Anne McCrae. We're talking a lot, over a hundred thousand in sterling. From there about 90% of the funds were transferred to a Karsten Wolff. Trail ends there. Hope this helps.`*

So, Monty was the one funding Wolff's climate protest — the same operation Jamie was assigned to — presumably to benefit his renewables company. But the amount of money involved was staggering and far more than that required to fund a peaceful campaign for a week.

It didn't add up.

[Moniker] *Can you access Rory's digital wallet?*

[IntoDarkness] *He's got 2. I can access the smaller wallet but not the other one. It's protected by a 25th word.*

The use of a 25th word was an extra security precaution some investors took to protect their digital wallets. When a wallet was created, the secret keys used to protect it were based on a unique combination of 24 words. Adding a 25th word made the process super-secure because, should the 24 words be compromised, the person holding those words would still need the 25th to access the keys.

Kathryn thanked Scotty and wound up the chat. She needed to warn Jamie and she tried his mobile. When there was no answer, she sent a text asking him to call her urgently. Then she phoned Gary, but again there was no answer.

Something felt wrong and she paced the floor. She was on the verge of calling MI5's main Operations Centre when her phone buzzed. She snatched it up hoping to see a message from Jamie, but it was from a number she didn't recognise.

Wanna meet? Have an idea how to get the 25th but not safe to put in chat.

Kathryn's hand flew to her chest. It was such an unusual request and one that broke all the rules of cyber subculture. Regardless, she trusted Scotty with her life and she wanted to meet him. She tapped a hasty reply.

Yes, where & when?

She held her breath and awaited his response.

***

Jamie

Jamie's social meter had well and truly run out and he returned to his van to escape. He couldn't risk making a call to Gary with so many people around. Instead, he sent an email confirming the protest would take place a day early, although he suspected MI5 had been listening to every word. Gary's acknowledgement came back immediately.

This shit was getting real and he needed to hear Kathryn's voice. He called her mobile but there was no answer. He typed a text, hoping she'd understand his veiled reference to Grangemouth kicking off, adding that he loved her. He pressed send and waited.

Still nothing. He thumped his fist on the steering wheel and swore.

Why wasn't she replying? What did her silence signal? Was she leaving him? Everything was wrong and he felt like he was in a free fall.

Unable to contend with the triumphant atmosphere in the hall, Jamie took himself off to the small room he'd commandeered. It was little more than a cell with one small window which left the place in gloom. A dark utilitarian carpet completed the look.

Sleep evaded him, thoughts of imminent arrest tearing through his mind. He expected to be charged along with the others since his cover had to be maintained at all costs. Guilt licked at his conscience, knowing his mates would likely face prison.

Staring at the ceiling, he wondered what Kathryn was doing at this moment. Without her next to him, he never slept well and his dreams were filled with terrors. He ached to hold her, inhale her natural scent and listen to the gentle beating of her heart. She calmed his mind and soothed his soul.

There was movement in the room next door and he realised Wolff had turned in for the evening and, judging from the grunts and moans of pleasure drifting through the stud walls, he wasn't alone. As Jamie lay there trying not to listen, he worried about Meadow. She was a kind, gentle person who just wanted to be loved and find someone to love, yet she'd gotten mixed up with Ethan and now

Wolff. At least the criminal justice system would take care of Wolff, but at what cost to her?

Stifling a groan, he buried his head inside his sleeping bag and prayed for sleep to claim him.

Or the riot squad.

***

Kathryn

Kathryn didn't have to wait long for Scotty's reply. He suggested meeting that evening and sent a Google maps location. The suddenness of it surprised her. She hadn't been aware Scotty was in the local area.

Nervous at the prospect of meeting him in the flesh, she browsed the rendezvous to discover it was a remote farmhouse several miles from the village of Speen in Buckinghamshire. She thought it an odd place to meet. Then again, it was ideal — in the middle of nowhere and unlikely to have cameras or a phone signal — exactly the sort of place Scotty might hole up.

She wandered restlessly through the cottage, glancing at the clock, willing it to be later. She couldn't settle for thinking about it, wondering what he looked like. Normally, she'd never agree to meet a stranger, especially not a man, in such a remote place. But this was Scotty, a friend she'd known for years who'd saved both her and Jamie's life. Then again, what if they didn't get along or they disappointed each other? Perhaps it was best never to meet and forever remain anonymous? She chewed her fingernails.

Wishing she could talk to her husband, she checked her phone but Jamie still hadn't called or texted. She sighed. It wasn't like him as he always carved out time in his day to contact her. His lack of communication added to her growing sense that things were not quite right. She sent another text to let Jamie know where she was going and that she might be without a phone signal for a few hours.

It was in those moments that she finally knew her mind. She loved her husband and knew that if their marriage was to survive she had to believe in the constancy of the human heart. She needed to trust.

She sent another text:

I love u & I want 2 get back to how it was x

She waited a few minutes for a response but her mobile remained stubbornly quiet. She glanced at the time. It was already dark and rain sheeted against the mullioned windows of the cottage. Deciding she could wait no longer, she left food and water for Meg then gathered her things and hurried out to the car.

Once off the main road, the satnav guided her along narrow country lanes lined with tall hedges. She drove with care, barely able to see much beyond the sweep of her headlights on the slick ribbon of road. She almost missed the turnoff for 'Brodie's Farm' in the gloom and had to reverse to take the tight turn. A rough track continued for half a mile and, just as she was beginning to panic thinking she'd lost her way, it opened into a large farmyard.

On the left was a stone-built farmhouse with red painted doors, behind which lay numerous outbuildings and animal shelters. It looked abandoned. She parked out front but left the engine running.

By now it was pitch black and she could see little through the rain hammering onto her windscreen. She checked her phone. No signal. Still unsure whether she was in the right place or not, she was reluctant to drive off without checking first. She cut the engine, switched on her phone torch and walked across the yard.

She glanced around and behind her as she neared the door to the farmhouse but she could see no one. The air was cool and the place smelled of old manure and decay. She continued on around the house, pausing at each window, but there was no sign of Scotty or anyone else. An owl hooted in the distance which only added to her growing sense of unease. Surely this couldn't be the place?

Drenched, she shivered beneath her light coat. Keeping close to the wall, she headed towards the rear where outhouses and a stable block stood. Thoroughly spooked, she was about to return to her car when she glimpsed a dim light coming from a gap in the door of the furthest away building. She walked towards it, only then spotting a black BMW saloon tucked around the corner.

Pulse racing, she approached the outhouse, unsure of whether to call out or not. A figure appeared and her heart skipped a beat. She froze in her tracks. He was taller than she'd imagined with dark hair that reached his collar. His features were hard to make out in the pouring rain.

"Moniker, is that you?" The accent was American.

"Oh, thank God," she said as she hurried towards the shape.

"Sorry," he drawled, "I never heard the car or I would've come out to greet you."

Smiling, he moved back inside to let her past and she darted inside. When she turned to get a look at him, he bolted the door and spun round to glare at her with eyes like obsidian; cold, hard and black.

The first blow sent her flying backwards into a low workbench. Gasping in pain and stunned, she tried to scramble to her feet, only to catch a second one to her ribs. The wind went out of her and her knees buckled. She cradled her stomach.

She lost count after the third.

THE PROTEST

"Global warming hysteria has a chilling effect on free speech. Those scientists who, on the basis of evidence, have a contrary view are written off as deniers and compared to Holocaust deniers." — **Professor Ian Plimer 2009**

***

Jamie

from:	Jamie Douglas < Jamie.Douglas@tacitnet.mi5.uk >
to:	Gary.Singer@tacitnet.mi5.uk
subject:	Operation Monkshood - postponed
security:	AES-256 encryption

Hi Gary,

The protest has been pushed back a full day and touchdown won't be until Thursday at 5:30 a.m. Please confirm when you receive this and keep the police well clear of the area.

Jamie

***

Jamie scrubbed a hand over his face in disbelief as he slowed the van outside the entrance to Grangemouth. The police had failed to swoop on the community centre during the night and he couldn't understand why. The only communication he'd received was a message from Gary acknowledging the new date of the protest.

So, where the hell were the cavalry? He'd expected to be in custody by now, not sitting outside the refinery's gates with a van full of climbing equipment and two anarchists in the rear. Was there a last-minute change of plan to catch the protesters in the act of breaking and entering? If so, there was no sign of any police presence or additional security. Were they lying in wait in a warehouse ready to pounce?

There'd been so many cockups on this job he worried about the competence of his backup team. If this protest was allowed to get underway, it'd be a disaster. He'd have plenty to say to his handler later but right now he'd no option other than to go through with it.

None of this felt right.

As he approached the security barrier, he swallowed, his mouth dry with anxiety. A sleepy middle-aged security guard emerged from the booth and shuffled towards him wearing a perplexed expression. He was a large man with a gut that strained against the fabric of his black uniform.

Using decals plastered onto the sides, Jamie had disguised the van as one belonging to a regular supplier at the plant. The ruse was completed with a clipboard bearing false paperwork that lay on the dashboard, and a baseball cap embroidered with the same design.

Gripping the steering wheel, he brought the van to a halt and rolled down his window to speak to the man. After greeting him, Jamie made a pretence of checking his paperwork.

"Either you're really early mate or very late," said the guard.

Jamie noted that his older colleague remained inside the booth. He handed over the fake documents. "Aye, I should've been here yesterday but the van broke down in Carlisle."

The guard scrutinised him and then the paperwork, his brow furrowing in consternation. He muttered, "There's nothing on our system about this delivery."

Jamie huffed out a laugh, "Aye, it was the same last time I was here. Thought they might have got their act together especially as they're desperate for the parts."

Pausing, the guard pursed his lips and frowned. "Wait here."

The man ambled back to the booth and spoke to his colleague, and they huddled over a screen. Jamie watched, his heart thumping in his chest. The older guard spoke into a radio handset and then shook his head at his colleague.

Wolff and Ethan lay in wait in the rear of the van and Jamie didn't trust either of them not to let this situation spiral out of control. He didn't want to crash the barriers, not if he could bluff his way in.

The younger man approached the vehicle again and said, "We can't let you through without authorisation. My colleague's checking now." He wandered back to the booth.

Several long minutes passed in which Jamie feigned boredom on his phone as if this was an everyday occurrence. He half expected Wolff and Ethan to explode out the back doors at any second and beat the crap out of the guards.

Is this the police plan? Are they gonnae let us through the barriers and then arrest Ethan and Wolff as the ringleaders?

None of it made any bloody sense.

Suddenly, the barrier lifted and Jamie gunned the engine. The guards rushed from the booth and the younger one stood in front of the van blocking the way with his arm outstretched in a 'halt' signal.

Jamie stuck his head out the window, "C'mon mate, let me through. I'm in a rush."

"Wait!" roared the older guard running towards the van, "there's been no authorisation."

"The barrier's up. What's the problem?" yelled Jamie inching the van forward. The man at the front refused to budge. Pointing to the refinery, Jamie said, "Listen mate, your chief engineer's been on the blower to my boss demanding to know where these parts are. If I don't deliver these pronto, you'll be in deep shit."

The older guard shook his head, thumbed towards the rear of the van and said, "Open the back."

Jamie indicated the barrier, "C'mon, what more authorisation do you need?"

"That's the problem, the barrier shouldn't be up, we control it."

Before Jamie could reply, the rear doors flew open and Ethan and Wolff leapt out. Dressed in khaki with their faces obscured by black balaclavas, they looked like terrorists. They brandished baseball bats.

What the fuck? No one said anything about weapons.

***

Kathryn

Kathryn awoke in dreadful pain. Her entire body hurt.

She lay on her side, the uneven ground cold and hard beneath her cheek. Each breath she drew felt like she was being stabbed. Her hands were tied behind her back, the ligatures biting painfully into her wrists, but these agonies were nothing compared to the twisting, writhing pain in her abdomen. It felt as though her innards were being squeezed through a mangle. She groaned; the sound muffled by the strip of fabric covering her mouth.

Please God, don't let wee bump die.

Tears streamed down her face. Was there a part of her he hadn't beaten? Her limbs felt bruised and swollen, and she trembled in shock. She pressed her tongue against the material of the gag to push it away but it didn't budge. It tasted rank and she fought the urge to retch. She tried rubbing it against the stone floor to slide it off but the effort only hurt her.

She opened her eyes and realised one was almost swollen shut. It was too dark to see anything, but the place smelled of engine oil and damp. She lay shivering for what seemed like hours; she couldn't tell as she drifted in and out of consciousness. Part of her prayed for the blackness to claimed her and end the pain, yet the fear of never waking up again was worse.

I need to stay alive for the baby.

Shaking violently with the cold, the ground beneath her hip felt cold and wet. She smelled a sickly ferrous odour, and realised she was lying in a pool of her own congealed blood. Certain the little life inside of her was dying, she sobbed quietly.

She jerked awake at the sound of footsteps on the boards above and strained to listen. There were angry male voices but she couldn't make out what was being said. Her heart hammered in her chest knowing there was more than one person in this hellhole, and she fought against her bindings but this only caused further searing agony.

And then the screaming began.

***

Jamie

Wolff swung his bat and battered the younger guard across the thigh with it. There was a crack of bone and the man screamed and fell to the ground.

"Do exactly as I say and no one gets hurt," shouted Wolff bearing down on him.

Jamie leapt from the van and roared at Wolff, "What the fuck?"

The guard raised a hand in surrender, his face blanched in fear and pain. Ignoring Jamie, Wolff dragged the limping guard by the collar towards the booth and flung him against the wall. The man slid down clutching his leg. Ethan ushered his colleague in beside him and told him to stand next to him. Shocked, Jamie watched from the doorway.

Wolff spun round and yelled, "Drive!" When Jamie refused to budge, he raised the bat and shouted again, "Move the van, now!"

They locked eyes and Jamie thought he was going to take a swing at him. Wolff lowered the bat and in a moderate tone said, "Bring it inside the gates."

Cursing, Jamie returned to the vehicle and drove it inside the barrier. Back in the booth, the older guard's face had turned a greyish colour. Wolff used his mobile to signal the others who were parked in a nearby truckers' layby. As they waited for them, Jamie asked the older guard if he was alright and suggested he sat down. The man slumped into a chair and wiped beads of sweat from his brow.

Jamie said, "This is a peaceful protest. We're not here to hurt anyone."

"Doesn't look very peaceful to me," muttered his colleague, clutching his leg.

Wolff snarled "Shut up or I'll break the other one." Then to Ethan, "Tie them up."

"Not him," said Jamie, indicating the older guard with a nod of his head.

Wolff snapped, "Both of them. Do it now."

"Fuck's sake, he's not well," snarled Jamie.

Ethan leant the bat against the door frame. He produced cable ties from his pocket, and secured the wrists of both men in front of them.

Glowering at Wolff, Jamie growled, "You're making a huge mistake."

Wolff blanked him.

There was a roar of engines and a convoy of vans and minibuses sped through the gate in pre-planned formation. There were whoops and cheers as protesters disembarked and swarmed into the plant. They wore coloured t-shirts over their outer gear and carried banners and equipment. Wolff pushed past Jamie and began barking orders while Ethan kept watch over the guards.

One of the teams began to chain themselves together to form a human barricade across the entrance, while others started erecting tall bamboo structures which would buy time for protesters to cut through the perimeter fence. Another group shot past shouting and waving their arms and shrieking. Their role was to cause mayhem and create enough of a distraction to enable other activists to target strategic points.

Where the fuck were the police? We shouldn't be inside these gates.

Jamie turned and observed the older security guard. He was sweating profusely and appeared to be struggling for breath. Jamie and Ethan swapped a look.

Crouching beside him, Jamie asked, "You okay mate?"

The man gasped then keeled over onto the floor. Jamie dived and caught his head and laid him down gently. Loosening the man's collar, he shouted, "Need a medic in here!"

His colleague yelled, "You've killed him, you've killed him."

Wolff reappeared with his balaclava rolled up to reveal most of his face. Ethan looked in horror at the man lying on the floor as Jamie manoeuvred him into the recovery position.

Jamie yelled, "Get an ambulance."

Wolff and Ethan gaped at him.

"Now!" When Wolff remained motionless, Jamie pulled out his mobile and dialled 999. Turning to the German, he shouted, "Go, I'll stay with him."

Wolff tried to wrench the phone from Jamie's hands, yelling, "No, you're needed elsewhere."

Glowering, Jamie pushed him away and spoke to the emergency service operator, explaining where they were and that it was a suspected heart attack.

As Jamie described the man's condition, Wolff produced a pistol and pointed it directly at Jamie's head. He snarled, "I. Said. You're. Needed. Elsewhere."

Jamie covered the handset and gawped at him. "What the fuck?" Ignoring Wolff, he crouched beside the guard and felt for a pulse at his neck. Finding it weak beneath his fingertips, he glared at Wolff who looked ready to shoot him and said, "He'll die without an ambulance."

As the two men stared murderously at one another, Meadow appeared. She stopped in her tracks, looking like a startled rabbit as she surveyed the scene inside the booth. Hissing at Wolff to put the gun down, she knelt beside Jamie.

Jamie mouthed 'Heart attack.'

Wolff stuffed the pistol in his waistband and yelled, "We need to go."

He darted from the booth.

As Jamie followed, Meadow caught his arm and said, "Jamie, be careful ... I'd no idea he'd a gun."

He sent her a nod and sprinted towards the van. The sound of sirens floated in the distance as Jamie climbed into the driver's seat beside Wolff and Ethan.

Turning to them, he thumped the steering wheel and roared, "Just what the fuck was that all about?"

The Doublecross

***"What we are talking about is the most important issue humanity has ever had to face up to ... and when I say humanity, I mean all of us. We're all in this boat together."* — Sir David King, former government chief scientist 2020**

***

Kathryn

Kathryn tried to focus on anything other than the pain. Shards of sunlight stole through gaps in the stonework fabric of the outbuilding and she took in her surroundings. It appeared to be some sort of store room. A rickety shelving unit lined with old paint tins and oil canisters ran along one wall, and farming implements along another. A moth-eaten oilskin hung from a peg on a rotten wooden door. Lying on her side, she inched towards it, each movement causing her searing pain. The crotch of her jeans was wet and the floor beneath where she'd lain stained with blood.

Before she reached the door, she heard movement and the man she'd thought was Scotty wrenched it open. Glowering at her balefully, he snarled, "Get up."

She tried raising herself to her feet but couldn't. She looked at him with pleading eyes but, instead of helping her, he grabbed the back of her collar and dragged her across the stone floor as if she were a ragdoll. She howled in agony and fresh blood oozed between her legs.

He dumped her inside what appeared to be a barn that had once stored grain. In one corner sat a copper-coloured cylindrical cereal bin with a long metal auger sticking out of it like an enormous corkscrew. Opposite were two ancient grain mills coated in dust and cobwebs. A set of rickety wooden steps lead to a mezzanine floor that had once fed grain into the mills below.

Pointing to an old wooden kitchen chair, he told her to sit. Using her arms to brace herself, she struggled to her knees. When she took too long, he grabbed fistfuls of her hair and heaved her onto the seat. She shrieked in pain.

He palmed her hard across the face and yelled, "SHUT UP."

Bending forwards, she curled into a ball and shook in terror.

"Enough, we want her alive ... for now." The chilling voice came from a corner of the outhouse which lay in darkness.

It was a voice she recognised, and his words sent icicles down her spine. She squinted through her tears as a shadowy figure approached. It was Dominic. And there was no pity in his eyes. Dressed in a shirt and suit, his appearance jarred with the rustic surroundings.

Glancing at her assailant, he said, "You'll have your fun with her later but for now, untie her hands."

The younger man obliged and she rubbed her wrists which were ringed with red scars from the bindings.

Extending a bottle of water to her, Dominic said. "Drink." His voice was calm, almost friendly.

Hands trembling, she fumbled with the cap and drank. When the water hit her stomach she gagged, the pain almost making her pass out. She put her head between her legs until the edges of blackness receded. Blood dripped onto the flagstone floor beneath her.

Dominic pulled up a stool opposite her and handed her a folded handkerchief embroidered with his initials. She wiped her eyes and blew her nose, covering the starched cotton material in blood. Risking a glance at the workbench beside them which was strewn with pliers, hammers and saws, she felt sick.

"Forgive me, my dear," said Dominic, "I'm forgetting my manners. I ought to introduce you properly." He hitched his chin towards the other man. "Kathryn, meet Petru." After a beat, he added, "Of course, you know him much better as Pandora, your fellow hacker."

Shocked, she placed a hand to her chest as she scrutinised the man looming over her, his eyes ablaze with disdain. And suddenly it all made sense. Pandora's superpower was intercepting and altering digital communications. This explained the muddled messaging and crossed wires that had dogged her investigations and thwarted her attempts to contact Jamie. And now, by posing as Scotty, Pandora had lured her here to reap revenge for the part she'd played in his imprisonment.

In all the years Kathryn had known Pandora, she'd always believed her to be a young woman of a similar age to herself, and she'd accepted her stories at face value. Once considered a friend, there was certainly no trace of that now; there was only hatred in his gaze.

Petru spat, "I've been looking forward to this Moniker. Every day I was locked up, I thought of nothing else."

Gawping, she turned to Dominic. "Why?"

He gave a mirthless laugh. "As soon as I learned you were sniffing round Monty, I knew we'd have to deal with you. You and Scotty. But it takes a thief to catch a thief, so Petru's been helping me."

The wringing pain in her abdomen gripped her again and she felt a trickle of cold sweat run down her back. Fighting down her panic, she said, "What've you done with Scotty?"

"Nothing yet," said Pandora, "you'll meet him soon enough."

"I don't understand," she said glancing at Dominic, "what's any of this got to do with Monty?"

Dominic smoothed out an imaginary wrinkle in the gabardine fabric of his trousers, then met her eye. "Really, I'm very disappointed in you my dear, so many questions. I thought you'd have worked it out by now."

Glancing at the tools on the workbench, she knew her only defence was her words. "I don't know anything. Let me go, I'm no threat to you and neither is Scotty."

Dominic shook his head. "I'm afraid that won't be possible, not now Scotty has traced the funds. Why didn't you back off like you were supposed to when you were suspended?"

Pandora lifted a screwdriver and examined it. She felt terror, overwhelming and immense.

Despite shaking uncontrollably, she tried to keep her voice measured as she addressed Dominic. "I can understand why Monty's funding the protest since it'll benefit his company, but what's in it for you?"

He gave a tight smile. "Monty and I go way back. Margaret-Anne too. We were at Cambridge together and we've looked out for one another since. But this was never about getting Monty the battery technology; stealing that from the Russian was just a bonus. It's far greater than that."

She gawped at him. "You killed Balakin?"

Dominic sneered, "Not me personally, I have people for that."

His matter-of-fact tone sent an icy shiver down her spine. "I don't understand," she wailed, "why are you doing this?"

Pandora swapped the screwdriver for a pair of pliers. Kathryn's heart skipped a beat and she thought she might faint.

Dominic said, "Monty has political ambitions and damaging the oil industry in Scotland will kill an independence referendum dead. If there's no oil, there's no money, and the Scottish people know that."

She tore her eyes away from Pandora and the rusty handsaw he held. "And with Monty in a senior government position, you'll have a puppet?"

"I'd describe it as more of a symbiotic relationship," said Dominic. "If Scotland becomes independent, Defence and Security will be carved up and we'll lose a huge chunk of our military capability and budget. We simply cannot allow that to happen. Destroying Grangemouth will serve both my purposes and Monty's."

She swallowed hard and croaked, "Destroy?"

With a laugh devoid of humour, Dominic said, "My dear, surely you don't believe we've gone to all this trouble just to shut it down for a week? It's going to be far more spectacular than that, and you're going to have a front row seat."

Pandora cleared a space on the workbench on which he placed a laptop. The screen displayed live footage of the events unfolding in Grangemouth. Kathryn watched as hundreds of protesters swarmed over the plant. The news camera zoomed in on climbers scaling an enormous cooling tower.

"Aww look, there's your husband sweetie," said Pandora. He grabbed her chin and hissed, "I can't wait to see your pretty little face when we blow him to kingdom come."

***

Jamie

Jamie paused for breath and risked a glance at the ominous grey sky. The climb up the inside of the cooling tower had been arduous and sweat dripped down his face and back. Adrenaline pumped through his veins and his heart pounded painfully. Sucking in a lungful of air, he took a moment to steady himself and gripped the rope to keep himself steady. His wingman Leon yelled up to him to ask if he was alright, his voice echoing off the walls of the chamber. Leon looked small from this height. Jamie gave him the okay signal.

Slightly below and a few feet to Jamie's left was another climber, a Scotsman in his early twenties called Stephen. Although experienced, Stephen also appeared to be finding the climb up the wooden structure inside the tower challenging. Some of the supports were so rotten and shaky Jamie hadn't dared rely on them to take his weight or use as anchor points. Jamie's ascent hadn't been made any easier by the heavy, cumbersome rucksack containing the banner. He watched as Stephen hammered a piton into the brickwork and tested its hold before continuing.

Jamie estimated he'd only another twenty feet to go to reach the top. Fighting the ache in his limbs, he took a deep breath and ploughed on. As he focused on the task, he could hear sirens and a helicopter in the distance and he wondered how the protesters were faring on the ground. He was still rattled at the fact Wolff and Ethan were armed and he feared for everyone's safety.

Ten minutes later, he pulled himself onto the rim of the tower and saw for himself. It was breath-taking. He'd scaled plenty of mountains but few could rival the view he had across the Forth Valley. He grasped the brickwork as he twisted around to take it all in, fearing a gust of wind might topple him from his perch.

As he caught his breath and waited for Stephen to reach him, he observed what was happening below. Three activists in yellow t-shirts sprinted towards a long thick pipe topped with a manual control valve. One of them, a young woman with curly red hair, produced a large D-ring lock and secured her neck to the valve while the others glued their hands onto the pipe. A couple of security guards ran towards them shouting and waving their arms frantically, and the woman with her neck in the D-lock screamed and kicked at them as they tried to free her.

Deeper within the complex, groups of protesters clad in green ran amok, chased by personnel from the plant. Jamie watched as a purple Volkswagen Campervan belonging to protesters sped along the narrow service roads closely pursued by a security van.

A barrage of noise from the main gate caught his attention and he spun round to get a better look. A line of campaigners had linked arms to form a shield inside the barriers, and another phalanx stood behind them waving placards. Someone had erected a bamboo structure resembling a tepee with a sign proclaiming this was a peaceful protest. In front of the protesters bristled an ominous black wall of riot police armed with batons and shields. A line of vehicles with blue flashing lights waited behind them. Jamie watched as the police thumped their batons against the shields and slowly advanced.

In the distance, along the main access road, the media had gathered and Jamie could see the light reflecting off their camera lenses. He glanced up as a police helicopter swooped into view and hovered above his head, its downdraft washing over him. He gave it a cheeky salute.

Fuck's sake, Grangemouth's in chaos.

Astounded at the scene, Jamie pondered on why this had gotten so out of hand. His intel was supposed to have prevented any of this from happening so there must have been a major cockup in communications between himself, Gary, Thames House and the police. Heads would surely roll for this and he hoped his wouldn't be one of them.

A shout from Stephen brought him back to the present. He'd climbed level with Jamie and sat atop the rim of the tower a few feet away. They exchanged a nod, and Jamie slid off his rucksack and removed the heavy rolled up banner from inside. He unwound a length of thin rope from one end and threw it to Stephen who caught it.

"Ready?" shouted Jamie.

When Stephen gave him the thumbs-up, Jamie double-checked the integrity of his anchor point and swung his legs over the edge. Heart hammering in his chest, he grasped the rope attached to the grigri belay device, and sent a silent prayer to the climbing gods it would hold. Then, pulling the thin rope attached to the banner so it was taut between himself and Stephen, he gave the signal to proceed.

Taking a deep breath, Jamie kicked off from the brickwork and abseiled down the outside of the tower. After twenty feet, he came to a shuddering stop and glanced over to check that Stephen was still level with him. With another nod, they continued their descent until they reached the neck of the cooling tower.

Jamie hammered in a peg to secure one corner of the banner to the brickwork. He followed it with another while Stephen copied his actions on the other side. Once it was in place, Jamie tugged on the rope attached to the banner and it unfurled below. Weights sewn into pockets in the fabric's bottom edge stopped it from being blown around too much. The enormous letters spelled 'End fossil fuels now' and was punctuated with the Climate Warriors logo. At the sight of it, he heard a loud cheer go up in the distance.

With another signal to Stephen, he continued his descent, hammering in pegs every few feet to hold the banner firmly in place.

Drawing level with the banner's lower edge, he paused to adjust its position. It was the first time he'd gotten a proper look at the fabric and its pocket weights. Movement below caught his eye and he glanced down to see a man standing several metres from the base of the cooling tower, frantically punching digits into a mobile phone. He'd a shock of blonde hair and looked familiar.

It took Jamie a few moments to place him and then it struck him; it was Ferdinand Meyer, Wolff's sidekick from the ICC. Cold beads of sweat trickled down his spine.

What the fuck's he doing here?

Jamie paused. Everything about this scene and the man's behaviour was wrong, and every instinct was screaming at him that something wasn't right. Pulling his gaze from Meyer, Jamie examined the banner more closely. Ripping open one of the pockets, he grabbed the weight inside to discover a lump of cream-coloured plastic.

It was C4 explosive.

The Fuel

***"With climate change, the science is driven by computer models and ideology .... Computer models are not data. If computer models torture the data enough, the data will confess to anything."* — Professor Ian Plimer 2009**

***

Kathryn

Kathryn was made to watch as Pandora hacked into the plant's systems and security. His screen displayed an array of graphs, levels and flows, and he gave her a running commentary on what he was doing. By tinkering with automatically-controlled valves and pumps, Pandora was setting up a chain reaction in the refinery's infrastructure.

Pointing to several gauges on-screen, he said, "The hydrocracker exploded in Grangemouth in 1987. I'm simply recreating the conditions that caused the accident." Pointing to a reading on-screen, he added, "Wolff's manually opened and closed a control valve on the high-pressure separator, the liquid has drained away and high-pressure gas has taken its place."

He turned to look at her with eyes of flint. "In a few minutes, the rising pressure will cause an explosion."

An error flashed on the screen and Pandora thumped his fist on the workbench and swore. "Comms are down."

Expecting a blow, Kathryn flinched sending another wave of pain through her.

Dominic said calmly, "It's standard practise. MI5 and GCHQ will have jammed transmissions." When Pandora began to pace like a zoo animal, he added, "Relax Petru, we anticipated this."

Looking at the frozen levels on the monitor, Kathryn realised Pandora was within minutes of achieving his aim. But whatever Thames House had just done, it'd hampered his efforts to control the system and now he'd no way of knowing whether the pressure would continue to rise sufficiently or not. As news channels began to vanish one by one from his screen, he shrieked like a banshee and hurled a spanner across the barn.

Dominic tried to placate him. "It's normal protocol to tear down the news-feeds."

"But I'm blind," screeched Pandora.

"Which is why Wolff and Meyer will take care of the rest," said Dominic in a mollifying tone. "They're our contingency plan."

Pandora stopped pacing and crouched in front of Kathryn. In a maniacal voice, he snarled, "They'll wipe Grangemouth off the map."

Along with Jamie.

***

Jamie

Jamie wrenched the detonator from the lump of explosive, knowing it was the only way to disable it. He glanced at Meyer below whose face was a picture of fury, and then at Stephen suspended on the rope opposite. Showing him the detonator and C4, he yelled to Stephen to disarm the explosive contained in the pocket and get the hell down.

Leon appeared below and called up to him, clearly unaware of the danger. Jamie fumbled with the grigri to aid his descent but the rope jammed in the mechanism. There was a crack of gunfire and the brickwork beside him exploded. Jamie lost his footing and swung wildly on the rope. As he struggled to regain control, he snapped his head around to see Meyer running towards the tower, pistol in hand.

Another shot rang out and smacked into the masonry below Jamie's ankle. Leon screamed at Meyer who ignored him and fired again, the bullet narrowly missing the C4. Jamie knew it couldn't be detonated by a gunshot, and his assailant likely knew it too. Jamie was his target, not the explosive.

He yanked hard on the grigri but the rope stuck fast. Cursing, he tried to free it as another round ricocheted close to his head. Another and Stephen screamed. He'd been hit in the calf and blood poured from his leg. Suddenly Stephen's piton gave way and he dropped like a stone through the air, and jolted to a halt just feet from the ground. Shrieking in agony, Stephen swayed violently as his wingman battled to help him.

Leon's shout alerted Jamie and another sharp crack resounded next to his right shoulder. He wrenched on the grigri and the rope slid through the mechanism, sending him plummeting as another slug thumped into the masonry beside his left ear. Still twenty feet from the ground, it was too high to risk the jump. The mechanism jammed again and Jamie cursed.

As he fumbled with the belay device, Leon screamed at Meyer and ran at him. Meyer shoved Leon aside and took aim at the tower. Jamie kicked and swung to his right as Leon scrambled to his feet and tackled the gunman. A bullet smacked into the stonework close to Jamie's head. Another crack and Leon fell back screaming. Jamie cut the rope and fell to the ground in a crumpled heap.

Wincing in pain and with the sound of Leon's cries in his ears, he glanced up to see Meyer aim at him. Jamie rolled to the side, the bullet striking tarmac. Springing up like a cat, he rammed his shoulder into Meyer's side sending him sprawling backwards. Then he was on top of him grappling like a wild animal for the pistol. A punch landed on the side of Jamie's head, making him reel, but he didn't let go his wrist.

Another deafening blast and the grip on the gun relaxed for an instant, giving Jamie purchase on it. Twisting the weapon away, he kneed Meyer hard in the groin and the man buckled beneath him. Another shot and Meyer grunted. Jamie shifted, realising he was covered in blood. The gun was in his hand. When he felt no pain, he looked at Meyer.

He was dead.

Jamie stuffed the gun into his waistband and ran towards Leon who lay clutching his shoulder. Crouching, he unclipped Leon's harness and tore off his t-shirt to reveal a large bloodstain seeping through the fabric beneath. He crumpled the t-shirt into a ball and pressed it to his wound, making the lad howl in pain. There was so much blood.

"Hold on mate," said Jamie, "just hold on."

He glanced around at the chaos surrounding them. Protesters were fleeing in all directions with security personnel in pursuit. Stephen sat a few feet away clutching his leg, clearly in shock, his young wingman Luca kneeling beside him.

"Get help," shouted Jamie to the lad. "Tell them we need a medic right away." When Luca didn't move, Jamie bellowed, "NOW!"

Startled to his senses, the lad nodded and sprinted in the direction of the main gate. Jamie checked his phone but there was no signal. GCHQ must've jammed communications, which was the reason the C4 hadn't detonated and he was still alive.

Removing his harness, he called to Stephen, "You okay?"

"I'll live," replied Stephen, "how's your mate?"

Jamie glanced at Leon who'd passed out. "Not good. He needs a doctor or he'll bleed to death."

Jamie crouched beside Leon and kept pressure on the wound. As protesters darted past he called for help but no one stopped. Several long minutes passed. Someone released a smoke bomb and clouds of blue smog enveloped them. A klaxon sounded.

From out of the mist ran Meadow, her face a picture of fear.

Spotting Jamie, she raced towards him and cried out, "You need to stop Wolff before he kills someone!" Struggling for breath, she bent over, braced her arms on her thighs and tumbled over her words, "He's in the control room with Ethan .... threatening to shoot the engineers unless they blow the place up."

She dropped her gaze to Leon and gasped, "Oh God, what happened?" She knelt beside him.

"Stay with him," said Jamie, guiding Meadow's hand to Leon's shoulder. "Keep the pressure on 'til help arrives."

Standing, he wiped blood from his hands onto his thighs. He removed Meyer's gun from his waistband and checked the clip. Realising there was only one round left, he cursed.

Eyes wide at the sight of the pistol, Meadow wailed, "What happened to a peaceful protest?"

Jamie sprinted in the direction of the control room, dodging a series of protesters and security personnel on the way. He'd memorised the plant's layout but amidst the pandemonium it took him time to find the block. Outside, he pressed his back against the wall and pulled out his mobile but comms were still down.

Stuffing his phone into his pocket, he poked his head through the blast doors which lay open. The place was eerily empty. He crept along the main corridor noticing that all the keypads for the internal doors had been smashed. Picking his way through debris and glass, he reached a set of double doors marked 'Authorised Personnel Only'. The keypad entry system was damaged and the door splintered.

Ducking beneath the glazed upper panels, he pressed his back to the door and listened. He heard Wolff shouting and there was the sound of crying.

Wolff yelled, "Do it now or you die. Your choice."

"We were supposed to shut it down, not sabotage it. I never signed up for this." It was Stuart's voice, and he sounded terrified.

"You have three seconds." Wolff began counting.

Jamie risked a glance through the glass. The sight beyond curdled his blood. Stuart was sat at a console, his expression one of horror. Wolff stood next to him pointing a gun at his head. At the side of the room crouched half a dozen terrified staff guarded by Ethan who brandished a pistol. One woman appeared to be in the grip of a panic attack.

Ethan yelled at her to shut up.

Wolff reached the count of three.

Stuart shook his head and shrieked, "No, I can't do it, not without killing hundreds of people."

Wolff pulled the trigger.

***

Kathryn

Pandora picked up a claw hammer from the workbench and examined it.

"Let me go," screamed Kathryn.

Dominic gave her a tight-lipped smile. "I'm sorry Kathryn but you know perfectly well you're going to die here." Glancing at his watch, he added, "I hope it's some comfort knowing your husband is already dead."

Dominic rose, signalling the discussion was over. Grabbing her hair, the American dragged Kathryn to her feet making her scream in pain and terror.

"Please," she wailed, "I'm pregnant."

Dominic turned and looked at her. Gathering his coat and briefcase, he said without a trace of remorse, "And for that, I am truly sorry."

Then he left her to Pandora.

She screamed as he manhandled her towards the wooden steps. With one arm protecting her middle, she clawed at Pandora's hand as he tore hair from her scalp. A creeping blackness oozed into the corners of her vision.

Pandora hauled her up the steps and onto the mezzanine floor. She fell painfully to her knees and risked a glance around. The space was approximately eight by ten metres with a rectangular hole in the floor for the auger to transport wheat from the bin below. It smelled of straw and mice. A bundle of jute sacks lay rotting in the corner, on top of which slumped a large man. He was bound and gagged and his face was badly swollen. A deep cut above his left eye had bled down the side of his face and into the material covering his mouth, but he was conscious. His battered appearance and the fear in his eyes made her want to howl in anguish.

"Oh Scotty," she cried, "what've they done to you?"

Pandora responded with a vicious backhand to her face which sent her sprawling backwards into the grain sacks. Scotty tried to mumble something through the gag which she couldn't understand but his gaze was drawn to the spreading blood stain between her legs. Shaking with fear, Kathryn eased herself up to a sitting position and clutched her knees. Tears welled in her eyes as she looked into her friend's terrified, pleading face.

She whispered, "I'm so sorry."

"Shut up!" yelled Pandora. Glaring at them, he began to pace like a caged lion.

The cramps in her gut intensified, each one feeling like her insides were being wrung. Bright crimson blood dripped onto the floor and she began to weep.

For the next few minutes, Pandora seemed to swing between rage and serenity. One minute he was screaming at them, the next talking calmly. He was clearly insane. He left them alone for a minute during which time Kathryn tried to loosen Scotty's bindings. When he returned, he was carrying a canister of fuel.

"No!" she screamed, trying to scramble to her feet as Scotty writhed and bellowed through the gag.

Pandora pushed Kathryn to the floor and doused them both in petrol. The fumes were overpowering and her eyes stung.

Scotty rolled onto his side, struggling desperately against his bonds. When Pandora turned his back, Kathryn clawed at the rope binding Scotty's ankles. She heard the strike of a match and Pandora turned, his face a picture of madness and glee.

Holding a lit match, he snarled, "I'm gonna watch you burn."

The Fire

***"Our livelihoods depend on a planet that is not on fire. We are an arctic people and our culture is written in the snow."* — Henrik Blind, Sami reindeer herder 2021**

***

Jamie

Stuart's head shattered into pieces, splattering the console in bone, flesh and blood. His body slumped onto the desk accompanied by screams from the cowering staff. An ashen-faced Ethan gawked at the corpse and then at Wolff. Wiping his face with his sleeve, Wolff heaved Stuart's corpse off the console leaving a wide smear of blood across the surface.

Jamie ducked back down beneath the glazed panel, barely able to believe what he'd just witnessed.

Wolff shouted. "You. Come here. Do as I say or you're next." A woman wailed.

Jamie knew he needed to act and fast but with only one bullet left, it was a suicide mission. If he didn't, he was certain Wolff would shoot every engineer in that room. Crouching, he flicked the safety off the pistol and eased the door open a few inches. Wolff was dragging a middle-aged woman at gunpoint into the chair where Stuart had been only moments before. She begged him to let her go, saying she'd children.

Ignoring her, Wolff pointed the pistol at her. "Increase the pressure now."

Ethan said to Wolff, "Stop. This is not the way."

"If I don't, we'll all die," snapped Wolff. "Destroying this industry is the only way to save the planet." He began counting.

"The blast will kill everyone for miles around, including us," roared Ethan.

"DO IT!" screamed Wolff at the trembling engineer. He pressed the gun to her temple. Crying, she tapped on the console.

Jamie sprung through the doors into a forward roll and came up in a kneeling position. Wolff swung his aim at him, and Jamie shot him square in the chest. The German dropped like a stone and crashed to the floor. The engineer screamed and her colleagues shrieked in terror. Ethan spun round and pointed his weapon at Jamie.

"Drop it!" yelled Jamie, aiming at Ethan's head. "This ends now. No one else needs to get hurt."

Time seemed to stand still as Jamie waited for a crack of gunfire and searing pain. He prayed his face didn't betray his bluff. His only fear in those long moments was of never seeing his wife again, and at his failure to put things right between them before he died. Eyes fixed on the weapon Ethan held, he awaited his fate and pictured Kathryn. Almost a minute passed, the longest of his life.

An alarm sounded on the console.

Jamie looked at Ethan and said, "Do the right thing."

Ethan slowly lowered his pistol to the ground. Jamie kicked the gun out of reach, then smacked Ethan hard in the face with the butt of his weapon. He fell to the floor in an unconscious heap.

Panic-stricken, the staff scrambled for the exit despite Jamie's pleas for their help. He cursed as he watched the last of them flee. Jamie placed Ethan into the recovery position and used his belt to secure his hands. Ethan didn't stir.

Jamie placed the pistols on top of the console along with his empty weapon, and surveyed the control room. A bank of monitors above his head displayed a range of graphs and levels, all indicating the system was in the critical danger zone. Alarms sounded and symbols flashed red.

As Jamie pored over the array of screens and buttons, a klaxon blared outside and an audible countdown began inside the building, 'EVACUATE. CRITICAL FAILURE.' A timeclock on the main screen displayed a ten-minute warning.

Jamie feared he was too late.

***

Kathryn

Kathryn watched in horror as Pandora extended the lit match.

Scotty kicked out with all his might, catching him on the side of his knee. Screaming, Pandora buckled and fell backwards through the trap door and onto the rusty auger below. There was a horrible thud followed by a gurgling noise.

Then there was a woosh as the jute sacks caught fire and the flames spread. She hastily untied Scotty's hands and feet, and he ripped off his gag.

"We need to get out of here," he rasped.

Rising unsteadily to his feet, he helped Kathryn up. Bent double in pain, she shuffled towards the stairs and descended backwards supported by Scotty who went first. The fire was beginning to take hold above them and the acrid smoke and petrol fumes made her cough.

"Don't look," he said as they passed the threshing machine.

She couldn't help but look. Pandora's body lay face-up, speared through the middle by the metal auger. His black lifeless eyes stared at them and his lips were pulled back in a rictal smile. She led Scotty to her car and fished her keys from her pocket with trembling hands. Shaking uncontrollably, she leant against the door and fought against the tendrils of blackness licking at her vision. Rain bounced off the roof of the vehicle soaking her hair and clothing.

"Can you drive?" she asked, "I don't think I'm able."

Scotty helped her into the passenger seat and fastened her seat belt. As he jumped in opposite, she checked her phone which still had no signal.

"Where's the nearest hospital?" asked Scotty, revving the engine.

The car fish-tailed out of the farmyard and down the long track towards the main road. Although she'd dozens of questions she wanted to ask, she was in too much pain to hold a conversation and merely pointed the way.

After a couple of miles, her phone pinged into life and she called MI5's Operations Centre. Giving her call sign, she blurted out what'd happened.

Scotty yelled, "She needs an ambulance, right away."

"Help's on the way," said the operator calmly, "stay on the line if you can."

"Fuck me," said Scotty braking suddenly on a corner.

The phone fell into the footwell. Ahead was a line of traffic stuck behind a tractor pulling an enormous trailer. It took up the width of the lane and was preventing anything from passing it. Drivers blasted their horns in frustration as oncoming cars were forced to reverse. Kathryn recognised the vehicle four in front as the one from the farmyard.

Pointing, she said, "It's Dominic, he's in the black BMW."

Scotty cursed, pulled on the handbrake and made to get out.

Grabbing his arm, she gasped, "What're you doing? He might be armed."

He thumped the steering wheel. "He left us to die." Then he gazed at her, his eyes drifting to the blood stain between her legs, "You need a doctor."

"Pass me my laptop," she said indicating the back seat. Reaching round, he grabbed the computer and handed it to her. She opened the lid and powered it on.

"What you doin'?" he asked as he peered at her screen.

"Just drive. Once we're past the tractor, follow him."

"No, I'm taking you to hospital," he insisted.

Holding up a blood-smeared hand, she said in voice cracking with emotion, "That bastard killed my baby and my husband. I want him dead."

Scotty merely nodded. The line of traffic inched forward and while he drove, she focused on the laptop, her fingers flying across the keys. A red glow behind them illuminated the car and they watched as the burning farm buildings lit up the sky. She heard sirens in the distance and a helicopter overhead but didn't know if they were for her or the fire.

"Whatever happens, stick close to that car," she said.

Her head swam and she fought to remain conscious. Ten tortuous minutes passed until the tractor cleared the lane and pulled over into a layby. Cars passed it sounding their horns, whether in thanks or frustration. Scotty put his foot down and kept pace with the BMW which accelerated.

"I need you to get as close to him as you dare," she said.

The engine protested and the Volvo sped forwards. Dominic appeared to react and the BMW hurtled along the narrow winding lanes with them in perilous pursuit.

"Closer," she yelled, concentrating on her screen.

Scotty floored it.

When they were mere inches from its rear bumper, she shouted, "When I say the word, brake as hard as you can, okay?"

"Aye aye captain." He gripped the wheel and clenched his jaw.

Two seconds later, she tapped a key. "NOW!"

Scotty braked violently, the Volvo's tyres screaming. Ahead, the BMW veered left off the road and slammed into a tree, exploding on impact. As Scotty swung the car past the ball of flames and twisted metal, she felt the searing heat of the blast. They screeched to a stop several yards up the road.

"Well fuck me sideways," he exclaimed, turning to look at her.

Kathryn passed out.

***

Jamie

Jamie darted back along the corridor in the hope of finding one of the engineers but the place was empty. He was running out of time and he sprinted to the control room. He stabbed a hand through his hair and peered at the monitors, trying to make sense of the information. It was hopeless.

He searched each screen, examining the readings and measurements. They meant nothing. A flashing icon caught his eye.

'EVACUATE. CRITICAL FAILURE.' Eight minutes remained on the clock.

Glancing round the room, he saw a line of A4 binders on the bookshelves lining one wall. Each folder was part of a numbered series labelled 'Operations Manual'. He grabbed the first one and flicked through dog-eared pages of indecipherable diagrams and descriptions. Failing to comprehend any of it, he scoured the other binders as the countdown continued. The manuals might as well have been written in Arabic.

'EVACUATE. CRITICAL FAILURE.' Five minutes on the clock.

In the last folder was an appendix entitled 'Guide to Symbols' and he scanned the tables until he found the icon that was flickering on the screen. Its presence indicated high pressure in the LP separator, whatever the fuck that was, and it gave a numbered reference to another guide. Jamie searched frantically for the appropriate section in another manual.

'EVACUATE. CRITICAL FAILURE.' Four minutes.

FUCK! FUCK! FUCK!

Turning to the page indicated, he quickly scanned the instructions. And there it was: 'Adjusting the LP separator' along with cautionary notes and warnings about the risks of over-pressuring the system. He ran his finger down the numbered list of instructions for lowering the pressure and scoured the console for the controls and dials indicated.

Three minutes.

Hands trembling, he followed the steps and repeated the process for the next warning symbol using the manuals to guide him.

One minute remained. As the seconds counted down, Jamie completed the final instruction and the room fell silent. Only then did he risk a glance up at the bank of monitors to see the flashing warning signs had turned from red to amber. The clock had stopped at seventeen seconds.

Jamie let out a long breath. Raising the Operations Manual to his lips, he smacked it with a kiss and promised never to tease his wife again for reading user guides.

He pocketed the pistols and sprinted across the plant to where he'd left Leon at the base of the cooling tower. Praying help had arrived, he was devastated to find them in the same spot. Surrounded by a pool of blood, Meadow cradled Leon's head in her lap, pressing her hand to the wound on his shoulder. She looked up at Jamie through tears of desperation.

"No one came," she wailed, "Stephen's gone to fetch help but he can hardly walk."

Crouching beside her, Jamie felt for a pulse at Leon's neck, relieved to feel a weak beat beneath his fingertips.

"Help me lift him," he said.

Jamie scooped Leon's unconscious body into his arms. Meadow retained pressure on the wound as they hurried towards the main gate. Leon felt like a dead weight and stared up with unseeing eyes.

Hang in there mate, just hang in there.

Groups of protesters shot past yelling at them to turn back. As they approached the main entrance, they understood why. A line of police armed with batons and riot shields was advancing. An officer with a megaphone called for the protesters to stand down. Dozens of activists lay limp on the ground and hurled obscenities as they were cut free from each other and dragged towards the waiting vans. The noise was deafening but Leon didn't stir. Jamie feared he was too late.

Please God, don't let him die.

Knowing they couldn't risk getting caught in a riot, Jamie skirted around the side of the crowd in search of an ambulance crew. He could see emergency vehicles with blue flashing lights beyond the fencing but no clear path to them.

A protester holding a smoke bomb attempted to outrun one of the 'land sharks', an enormous police dog, and Jamie watched as the animal launched itself at him. The lad screamed blue murder until the handler commanded the dog to release him. Jamie tried to get the attention of officers stationed at the side but they were too caught up in the skirmish to notice him.

As the police line advanced and the protesters pulled back, the crowd swelled against the wire fencing, threatening to trap them. Meadow yelled at a dog handler beyond the gate but her voice was drowned out in the cacophony. An activist wearing a yellow t-shirt collided with her and sent her sprawling to the ground.

Eyes wide with fear and desperation, she looked up at Jamie and wailed, "Do something, please."

Jamie carried Leon over to the fencing and laid him down on the hardpacked earth next to Meadow. Leon was deathly pale and his blood had seeped into Jamie's t-shirt and covered his hands. Meadow cradled his head in her lap and felt his neck for a pulse. Tears spilled over her lower eyelids and she sobbed, "He's going to die."

Frantically, Jamie searched for a route to safety. There was a thundering roar from the crowd as the riot police continued their relentless advance, triggering panic amongst the protesters. Jostled by a man fleeing with a banner, Jamie had to shove him aside. Fearing they'd be trampled, he used his body to shield Meadow and Leon. Bracing himself against the fencing, he was pushed violently from behind and Meadow yelled as activists spilled into the space.

In desperation, Jamie did the only thing he could think of although he was certain it was another suicide mission. Pulling Wolff's pistol from his pocket, he fired two shots into the air.

The Arrest

***"The assertion that humans are causing catastrophic climate change is a lie, and those who insist that the world must take extreme measures to stop climate change are perpetuating a hoax that will itself bring severe damage to the world—especially to the poor."*—C. Paul Smith 2021**

***

Jamie

The crowd's reaction was instantaneous. Protesters ducked, and police crouched behind their shields, then panic set in and people began running.

Jamie stood still, his heart beating furiously. He expected to be shot at any moment. Keeping his hands in the air, he yelled, "Don't shoot! I'm putting the gun down."

"DROP YOUR WEAPON," came the shout over the megaphone.

"Lowering it now," he called, placing the gun at his feet.

He stepped back slowly with his hands extended in front of him. Protesters nearby scuttled away.

"ON YOUR KNEES, HANDS ON YOUR HEAD."

A squad of armed police emerged and ran towards him, their weapons trained on him. Jamie exhaled a hard breath, dropped to his knees and put his hands on his head. He called out to the officer nearest, "My mate's been shot, he needs a doctor." He hitched his chin in Leon's direction.

A member of the squad collected the pistol while another frisked and handcuffed him.

"He needs an ambulance," pleaded Jamie.

Ignoring him, they scooped him up by his arms and dragged him towards a waiting vehicle. Behind police lines, Jamie was pushed into the narrow space between two high-sided vans.

"Fuckin' arsehole," snarled one of the officers, shoving him.

Jamie stumbled, regained his footing and turned to face him, only to be slammed violently against the side of the vehicle. A sharp punch to the ribs followed by one to the gut knocked the wind out of him and his legs gave way. He groaned in pain as the officers hoisted him towards the rear of the van.

He gasped out, "Fuck's sake, my mate's gonnae die if you don't get a doctor." He was rewarded with another punch in the ribs.

Jamie twisted round to face them and, using the back of the vehicle to brace himself, he kicked out with all his might. His foot landed on the younger man's face who swore sulphurously as blood streamed from his nose. This earned Jamie a smack in the face that had him seeing stars. As he was bundled inside the van, Jamie roared at them to fetch help for Leon.

The doors slammed shut plunging him into darkness and despair.

***

Kathryn

Kathryn lay in the hospital bed and stared at the stark white walls. She felt numb as she replayed over and over in her mind the events that'd brought her here.

She'd no recollection of the journey, but an air ambulance had taken her and Scotty to a private hospital in London where the Service reserved rooms. She'd only regained consciousness after they'd pumped her full of fluids. When she'd opened her eyes and blinked them into focus, Scotty had been by her bedside, and she later learned he'd refused to leave until he knew she was okay.

Her room smelled of fresh laundry and disinfectant, and came with an ensuite and a wine list. They'd dressed her wounds, poked her with needles and plastered her in sensors. A bank of monitors displaying her vital signs flickered behind her. The bleeding had stopped and the pain had ceased, and she wondered if this meant her body had finished expelling the foetus.

No one would tell her anything. There was no television in her room, her mobile phone had gone, and her questions were met with blank stares or glib assurances. A tray next to the bed was piled high with food but she'd no appetite. She was exhausted but, each time she closed her eyes, she saw images of Pandora's impaled body with its lifeless eyes, or the fireball that'd engulfed Dominic. Their deaths were cold comfort given that she'd lost both her husband and her baby.

An overwhelming sense of sadness and loss engulfed her but she could not cry. Tears, she realised, would do nothing to salve the profound feeling of despair. Jamie was her life and without him, she didn't know how to go on living. Part of her wished she'd died in the fire.

There was a knock on the door and a middle-aged nurse entered. Short and plump, she'd a brisk manner and a face as starched as her white uniform. She asked Kathryn how she was feeling as she performed her checks and recorded the readings on a clipboard that hung by the bed. Holding her stomach, Kathryn asked if the baby was still alive but the woman merely offered her a professional smile and informed her the doctor would be along shortly.

Kathryn interpreted that as a no. Fighting tears, she pleaded for her phone, adding, "My dog ... she's all I've got left and I need to make sure she's looked after."

The nurse batted away her request, reassuring her everything was being taken care of. With a gentle squeeze on Kathryn's hand, she said, "Once Doctor Lee's made her rounds, there's a visitor waiting to see you."

Her heart leapt. By some miracle had Jamie survived? She asked who it was.

"A mister Julien Tomkins."

Wish I'd died in the fire.

***

Jamie

The noise in the police cells was deafening and Jamie felt grateful to have one to himself, even if it did stink of Lysol and urine. He suspected he'd been labelled as trouble by the arresting officers and the custody sergeant had obliged with a single cell, despite the local station being overwhelmed with protesters.

Exhausted and aching all over, he stretched out on the blue vinyl mattress and bundled the scratchy blanket they'd provided behind his head. He wore a police-issue grey sweatshirt and joggies and he'd been allowed to shower.

The din made sleep impossible and he was too wired in any case. He closed his eyes and replayed what had happened, hoping to make sense of it. Why hadn't he guessed what Wolff would do? Were there hints of the plan he'd missed? But, even so, why had the protesters been allowed to enter the plant and why hadn't they been arrested while in the community centre? As operations went, this one was a disaster.

He wondered if Leon was okay. The police had told him nothing, and he didn't know if the lad was in hospital or in the mortuary. What a bloody waste of a life if he dies, and for what? The protest, he realised, was little more than a vanity project for Ethan who cared more about his reputation amongst campaign leaders than the followers in his group. Had Ethan known what Wolff was really up to? Remembering Ethan's behaviour in the control room, he doubted it. He'd appeared as shocked as Jamie about the escalation of violence.

MI5 had suspected a plot to disrupt fuel supplies and this was the reason Jamie had agreed to remain undercover, although there'd been no indication Wolff was planning to destroy the plant. Why wasn't he stopped before he got within a mile of Grangemouth? None of it made sense.

The hatch on the cell door opened and a pair of eyes met his. When he heard the door being unlocked, he swung his legs over the cot and sat up. The two officers who'd arrested him at the scene entered with a countenance as dark as their uniforms.

Oh fuck, here we go.

"Back to dispense another short, sharp dose of criminal justice?" said Jamie, in a voice laced with sarcasm.

At least there's only two of you.

The younger man approached and cuffed Jamie's hands roughly in front of him.

"Our D.I. wants a word." He hitched his chin towards the corridor, indicating for Jamie to follow.

They led him past the line of cells, up the stairs and into a small interview room furnished with a steel desk and chairs, all screwed onto the floor. Jamie slid into one of them, relieved he wasn't about to get a pasting. The older officer departed, leaving his colleague to stand guard. They ignored one another until Jamie became aware of the man's scrutiny.

When Jamie met his gaze, the man said, "Just who the hell are you?"

Returning a challenging stare, he leant back and replied, "I've already told you. My name's James Douglas."

The guy looked unconvinced but, before he could say something, a woman entered who Jamie instantly recognised. He gawped at her, unable to believe his eyes. Carrying a blue plastic tray laden with food and drink, she asked the uniform to uncuff Jamie and go. After a moment's hesitation and another suspicious glance at Jamie, the officer removed the cuffs and left.

The last person he'd expected to see was his ex-girlfriend, Emma.

"Hello Jamie," she said placing the tray on the table between them. "It's been a wee while."

Jamie rubbed his wrists where the cuffs had left a welt and said, "Uh, hullo Em."

Emma slid into the seat opposite and passed him a cup filled with a brown oily liquid which he assumed was coffee but could have been tea. He took a sip, past caring about the taste as it'd been hours since he'd had anything. Taking the sandwich she offered, he ripped open the wrapper, realising how hungry he was.

"Cheese," she said, "I thought maybe you'd gone veggie."

"Funny," he mumbled through a mouthful, his gaze meeting hers.

It'd been years since he'd seen her and, although Emma was younger than him, she wore the signs of aging more visibly. She'd put on several pounds which made her face look pudgy, and her green eyes were smudged with dark circles. Her hair, once golden, had lost its lustre.

Jamie had often wondered how he'd feel on seeing her again. They hadn't spoken since their acrimonious breakup after she'd dumped him for his best friend. Their relationship had been a car crash and their split had ended Jamie's career in the Murder Investigation Team where all three had worked.

Looking at her, he felt nothing.

After observing him while he ate, she said, "I barely recognised you. It was only when I heard your voice."

Scrunching up the sandwich wrapper, he said, "I no longer require the regulation haircut."

"You look well though," she said, smiling.

"Err ... so do you."

After an awkward silence, they made small talk and reminisced about colleagues they'd worked with in Glasgow. Neither mentioned her new partner; Dean was the elephant in the room, cordoned off with crime scene tape. Jamie detected an air of sadness about her and he wondered what'd happened, only then noticing the absence of a ring on her wedding finger. The last he'd heard, she and Dean were engaged.

Fixing him with her gaze, she asked, "What're you doing here?"

"I'm here because I care about the planet."

Snorting with derision at his glib reply, she said, "Oh come on, at least tell me the truth."

Jamie folded his arms over his chest. "I just did. I genuinely believe we're on the cusp of climate catastrophe."

"Aye right. You were always a good liar."

He shot her a challenging stare. "I never once lied to you Emma."

Ignoring his rebuke, she said, "I've an idea who you work for. Word got around."

He said nothing.

She fidgeted with a napkin and stared at him. "I looked you up ... you know ... a while ago." When he raised an eyebrow, she added, "Your file was blocked."

Again, he said nothing, aware that only officers with the highest level of security clearance were able to view the contents of his police file. A flag would have immediately been raised to the Security Service indicating she'd attempted to access it.

Undeterred, she continued, "And now you pitch up here under a different name." Tilting her head slightly, she said in a low voice, "Are you happy?"

Fearing the conversation was heading somewhere he didn't want to go, he simply nodded and deflected with, "And you?"

She swallowed and gazed at him. "I'm sorry about what happened ... you know ... between us. I never got a chance to say that before, and then ... well, you vanished."

Shit! Don't go there, please don't go there.

When he merely offered her a tight smile, she glanced away and said, "Dean and I ... we didn't ... things didn't work out."

Fuck! She went there.

He kept his expression neutral. "I'm sorry to hear that."

She returned her gaze to him. "Are you?"

Christ, I need to stop this.

Trying to steer her away from the Dean-shaped elephant, he said, "Congratulations on the promotion."

Her eyes filled with tears and she sniffed, "Sorry, but suddenly seeing you after all this time ... it's just brought everything back." She paused as if choosing her words carefully, then stretched out a hand to his. "I might never get the chance to say this again but d'you think—"

"—I'm married." It came out sharper than he'd intended, the words hitting her like a slap.

"Oh." Retracting her hand, she flushed a deep shade of red and managed an unconvincing, "In that case, I'm very happy for you." After a long pause, she asked, "Who is she?"

The person I love more than anyone else.

He sent her a rueful smile. "When do I get my phone call, Em?"

Silence descended, thick and heavy.

There was a knock on the door and the young uniform entered. He shot Jamie a curious look and whispered something into Emma's ear.

Thanking him, she turned to Jamie. "There's a Gary Singer here to see you."

Never thought I'd be so pleased to see that bugger!

Then tendrils of fear crept up his neck at the realisation that something serious must have happened for Gary to risk coming here.

"He's here with CTU," said Emma. "What the hell's going on Jamie?"

When he said nothing, she asked the uniform to show them in. He reappeared with Gary and two plain-clothed officers from the Met's Counter Terrorism Unit.

Oh Christ, it must be bad.

Recognising Simon, a liaison officer who worked closely with MI5, Jamie sent him a nod. Simon's colleague approached and cuffed Jamie's hands in front of him, while Emma and the young constable watched in astonishment. Gary's grim expression sent icicles through Jamie's veins.

"Thank you, we'll take it from here," said Gary leaving them in no doubt he was now in charge.

When Emma and the uniform simply gawped, Gary shot them a look as if to say, "why haven't you pissed off yet?" and they left.

"What the fuck's going on?" said Jamie. "Why you risking a compromise?"

With a sombre smile, Gary said, "We'll explain in the car."

It did nothing to reassure him and a bead of cold sweat trickled down his spine.

"Sorry about the bracelets," said Simon, "it's for the benefit of the furry suits."

Jamie knew they were trying to preserve his cover, although he suspected it'd been well and truly blown. "Is Kathryn okay?" he asked.

Gary put a steadying hand on his shoulder. "Julien wants a word."

Panic set in as they led him from the rear of the station and into an unmarked car equipped with privacy glass. Once safely inside with the doors closed, Simon uncuffed him while Gary dialled a number on his phone. He spoke into it briefly to identify himself and then handed it to Jamie. Julien's concerned voice filled the handset and asked how he was.

Ignoring the question, Jamie said, "What's going on?"

There was a pause, then Julien said, "She's fine but Kathryn's been involved in an incident. She's in hospital but she's going to be alright."

"FUUUCK!" exclaimed Jamie sitting bolt upright, "What's happened? Is she okay?" He stabbed a hand through his hair.

As they drove at an unsafe speed towards Edinburgh airport, Julien told him about Kathryn's escape from the fire, reassuring him that she was alive. He described her call to MI5's Operations Centre and her subsequent rescue along with another male. Julien explained he was on his way to the hospital where she'd been taken by air ambulance, and he arranged to meet Jamie there.

"Call me as soon as you've seen her," insisted Jamie. He hung up and gave a roar of frustration.

"We'll get you there quick as we can," said Gary.

No one spoke as the car hurtled along the motorway. Replaying what scant information Julien had shared, Jamie wondered what the hell Kathryn had been doing in an abandoned farmhouse in the middle of nowhere. And who was the man with her?

He buried his head in his hands as the cruel reality of their situation hit him. Separated by miles and a dreadful misunderstanding that'd threatened their marriage, he and Kathryn were putting their lives on the line on a daily basis.

And for what? The prospect of her injured — or worse — was too much to bear. She was his priority, not the bloody job, so why had he allowed this to happen? Without her, he was nothing and the realisation he might lose her overwhelmed him. Whatever occurred, things could not go on as they were. Kathryn was his world and he would not lose her.

When they arrived at the airport, Simon produced the bracelets again, "Sorry mate, we've got to do it this way."

Jamie couldn't care less; all he could think about was Kathryn.

Please God, let her be okay.

THE TRUTH

***"Somebody needs to step forward and say there has to be a moratorium, draw a line in the sand and say no more coal-fired power stations." —* James Hansen, leading climate scientist 2008**

***

Kathryn

Kathryn awoke to the sound of a woman's shrill voice, and it took her a few moments to orientate herself. The pungent smell of disinfectant, the sound of squeaky footsteps on vinyl and blinking monitors reminded her of where she was. Rubbing sleep from her eyes, she propped herself up against the pillows and listened to the commotion taking place in the corridor outside.

"You can't go in there, the doctor says she's not to be disturbed."

"The hell with the doctor..." said Jamie, bursting through the door.

Kathryn barely recognised him dressed as he was, with his long hair and beard. When his eyes met hers, he paused, as though searching her face for a reaction. Feeling a stab of remorse at his hesitation, she gasped out his name and reached for him. He shot towards her, his relief evident, and enveloped her in his arms.

She buried her face in his chest and wept. He held her and whispered her name over and over. A nurse appeared, took one look at them and left, closing the door quietly behind her.

"I'm so sorry," he rasped, "Julien told me what happened." He pulled away and looked at her, running his fingers gently down her unbruised cheek. "God, I nearly lost you." His face was lined with worry and his eyes were glassy.

Relishing the feel of his touch, she drank in his features. "Well, you didn't ... and I'm fine."

He looked unconvinced as he scrutinised her injuries.

Welling up, she said, "I thought I'd lost you too."

"I'm also fine," he chuckled.

Grinning, she reached for his hand and guided it onto her stomach. She whispered, "And so's our baby."

Jamie's mouth fell open and his eyes filled with tears. In a voice thick with emotion, he said, "A baby?"

She smiled and nodded, her own eyes filling up. "You're going to be a father."

With a sob, he clutched her to him and wept unashamedly. They held one another, her tears mingling with his, and then he covered her face and hair in kisses which made her giggle.

Beaming at her, he said, "I love you so much. I can't even begin to tell you how happy I am."

"I love you too." Then, after a beat, "And I'm glad you're happy ... I mean, we didn't exactly plan it."

His eyes sparkled and he laughed. "It's the best news I've ever had." Then his expression turned serious. "I'm never leaving you again Kathryn. I'm done with the job."

With a rueful smile, she said, "We both knew what it involved when we signed up."

He shook his head. "I made this decision before I knew about the baby, but this reinforces it." He placed his hand on her stomach. "I want to be with you and see my child grow up." He gazed into her eyes, concern lining his brow. "I know we'd problems before ..." When she tried to say something, he shushed her. "But I need you to know there was never anything between me and Meadow."

Swallowing back emotion, he said in a low voice, "Since meeting you, I've never wanted anyone else ..."

Tears falling, she touched his lips with her fingertips. "I believe you."

"But I feel responsible for causing you this heartache. I should never have allowed the situation in the first place."

It was her turn to silence him. "You and me, we've been through so much together. We're stronger than just the two of us."

Smiling through his tears, he said, "And now we'll be three."

She grinned, seeing her own joy reflected in his face. "Daddy," she giggled.

Wrapping her in his arms again, he murmured, "I'm never gonna be apart from you again. Ever."

When he finally let go, she stretched over and pressed the call buzzer. When he gave her an inquiring look, she said, "There's someone I want you to meet. He saved my life ... for a second time."

A nurse appeared and Kathryn requested her to fetch Mr Scott. After the nurse left, Jamie asked if this was who he thought it was. Before she could reply, there was a knock on the door and Scotty limped in. His bloodied Star Trek T-shirt had been replaced with a draughty hospital gown, and the only unbruised parts of his face were covered in white gauze and plasters. He looked like he'd been hit by a truck.

Kathryn smiled and said, "Jamie, I'd like you to meet my best friend Scotty."

Jamie sprung up and shook Scotty's hand which made the big man chuckle and wince. Apologising, Jamie fetched another seat and helped Scotty get settled.

"Hey, what did the doc say?" asked Scotty. He spoke with a strong Brooklyn accent.

Smiling, Kathryn reached over and gently squeezed his arm. "The baby's fine. You saved two lives."

"Oh man, I'm so happy to hear that." Then he shook his head, "But I'm such a fool. I should've realised it was Pandora..."

Placing a hand over his, she silenced him with a look, "Neither of us did. We couldn't have known. This isn't on you."

They took it in turns to explain to Jamie how Pandora had intercepted their communications and lured them to the farmhouse to meet. Jamie seemed as stunned by the revelation as them.

Jamie said, "That explains some of the weird shit on my own job." He glanced at Scotty, appearing to make his mind up he could trust him, and described the mix up in messages between himself and Gary. Kathryn also realised Pandora had been interfering with the personal messages between herself and Jamie.

She told him about the links she and Scotty had discovered between Monty, Wolff and MAM. She omitted to mention she'd been suspended from work, fearing how Jamie might react when he encountered Julien. For now, that conversation could wait.

Shaking her head, Kathryn said, "How did we not know *she* was really a *he*? All those years, Pandora pretended to be a woman, and it was never mentioned once when he was arrested and jailed."

Jamie said, "The Feds kept a tight lid on the whole thing because of the embarrassment he caused the US government when he hacked their spy satellites." Jamie didn't mention that he knew Scotty was responsible.

"How was Dominic able to free Pandora and bring him here?" she asked.

Shrugging, Jamie said, "Guess that's a question for Julien and the powers that be."

A staff nurse appeared and politely suggested it was time for the men to leave and let Kathryn rest. Scotty shook Jamie's hand, gave Kathryn a gentle fist bump, and limped out.

After he'd gone, she said, "I'm worried about what'll happen to him. He risked everything by staying with me until the paramedics arrived. I wouldn't have blamed him if he'd fled. The Feds are looking for him, and he could go to jail for a very long time."

"Aye, it doesn't seem fair." Jamie perched on the side of the bed and placed a tender kiss on her lips. "I'll be back tomorrow," he murmured, "I'm not due in front of the beak 'til Monday."

To preserve his cover and execute a graceful extraction, he explained he needed to appear in court along with his fellow Climate Warriors to face charges although he expected to be freed on bail.

Smiling, she addressed her tummy, "Should we take him back wee bump — your daddy, the notorious eco-warrior?"

Chuckling, he kissed her again. When he finally broke away, she reminded him to look after Meg and he reassured her he'd take care of their dog.

"You'll be a great mother," he said, beaming.

"Ask if Scotty can go home with you. He needs somewhere to stay and he can dog sit while you're away. It'll solve two problems."

He rolled his eyes and chuckled. "Yes Mummy."

The nurse reappeared, hands on hips, looking stern. With a final kiss, he told her he loved her and she repeated his words back.

As Jamie rose, she said, "Can you ask Julien to pop in before he goes." When the nurse objected, she pleaded with her.

Jamie left with a spring in his step which made Kathryn smile. Shortly afterwards, there was a knock and Julien entered carrying a large bunch of flowers with the price tag still attached. He looked worn out, as though the last few weeks had put years on him. She thanked him for the bouquet which he placed in the sink. Perching awkwardly on the chair by the bed, he asked how she was feeling.

"I need your assurance that Scotty will have immunity from prosecution."

When he voiced an objection, she silenced him with a finger, "Here and in the US. He also needs a job and somewhere to stay."

Julien blew out a breath and looked at her with a mixture of amusement and annoyance. "Anything else?"

"That'll be all for now," she quipped.

Chuckling, he shook his head. "Dear Lord, at this rate, our cyber team will be staffed with the entire Grey Nemesis collective."

"At which point we will assimilate you into the hivemind."

He smiled and then his expression turned serious. "I want you to be part of that team Kathryn. You can return to work whenever you're well enough."

She shot him an incredulous look. "Have you forgotten I'm suspended? Vetting not only believe I murdered my step-father, but they also think I'm your mole."

Julien looked down at his feet and then slowly met her gaze. "Only because I told them you were the source of the leak."

She gawped at him and tried to say something but no words came out.

He added, "Which is utter nonsense, of course, but I needed you off the team and free of all legal and procedural constraints so you could investigate Dominic."

When she remained speechless, he went on. "You see, I suspected Dominic's motives from the start. There was something odd about the whole Russian business and then when the comms started getting mixed up ..." He shook his head. "But as an MI6 agent, we couldn't take a closer look, not without approval from the Home Secretary and we didn't have enough to go on." With a contrite look, he added, "I'm sorry but it was the only way. I knew you wouldn't be able to leave it alone."

She gasped, "You set all of this up?"

He nodded sheepishly. "And you didn't let me down. But I miscalculated how far you'd go. If I'd thought for a moment you'd be in danger, I'd never have done it." He scraped a hand through his mop of hair, "Christ, he almost killed you and I never meant for that to happen. I'm truly sorry Kathryn."

Shaking her head in disbelief, she whispered, "Jesus Julien, I don't know what to say."

Yet it all made sense. Julien was right; his team could never have scrutinised Dominic's work or probed into his personal affairs. As part of the circle of intelligence agencies, MI6 officers were considered beyond reproach. However, once free of such constraints, she and Scotty had been able to trace Dominic's links to Monty, MAM and Wolff and uncover the nefarious plot they'd hatched.

She gazed at her boss in astonishment. She'd always known he was clever but this, she had to admit, was brilliantly cunning. She wasn't sure whether to be impressed or furious, and her inner turmoil must have shown on her face.

He raised his palms placatingly. "I'm sure you'll have plenty to say to me when you're feeling better, and I'll deserve to hear it at full volume. But you have my word, I'll never put you at risk like that again. You or Jamie. And, as far as your suspension goes, we know Dominic was the mole. He used Pandora to intercept our communications and..." He hesitated, then added. "And the thing with your step-father ... well, you can forget about that. It was clearly a lot of vindictive nonsense."

"Robin might not see it like that."

"You'll be pleased to learn Robin's been redeployed elsewhere. He'll not be bothering you again."

Placing a palm on her chest, she said, "Really? I'm in the clear?"

Julien nodded. "As far as Five are concerned, the matter is closed."

It felt like a huge weight had been lifted from her shoulders and she couldn't help but smile. However, before she could say anything further, there was rap on the door. The nurse entered, her expression leaving no room for negotiation.

Julien rose and in a low voice said, "I can't promise anything, but I'll see what I can do for your friend. We'll talk again in a few days." Pointing to her tummy, he smiled. "And congratulations by the way."

As he walked away, she heard him mutter, "Dear Lord, I'll have three of you to deal with."

The Family

***"Climate change is big business ... around the world companies are making billions out of the schemes governments have put in place ... There is little evidence that those policies are an efficient way to cut emissions"* — Matthew Sinclair 2011**

***

Jamie

Jamie sat in the hospital canteen with Scotty, sipping mugs of instant coffee. He was so happy he couldn't stop smiling. Not only was Kathryn fine, but she'd just given him the best news ever. He was going to be a dad. Nothing else bloody mattered.

Scotty stared at the dregs of his coffee. "Guess I'll have to get used to lousy coffee. Don't suppose they serve the good stuff in prison."

Jamie glanced up at him, "Doubt it'll come to that."

"Feds have been on my ass for months, man. They're probably on their way now, and this time tomorrow I'll be bunked up in a cozy cell with a bloke who wants me to call him Angela."

Jamie laughed and shook his head. "This time tomorrow, you'll be bunked up with me and the dog ... and if you call me Angela, I'll shoot you."

Scotty gawped at him. "Really? Hey, thanks man, I don't know what to say."

Jamie took a last swig of coffee and pulled a face at the bitter taste. "You can thank Kathryn; it was her idea. Reckons you'll make a good dog-sitter."

"I've never had a dog."

"Once you meet Meg, you'll never want one. Kathryn's fond of her though, and she doesn't bite ... much."

"I'll be sure to take good care of her, for as long as you need."

"As for what happens to you next, I've no idea, that's way beyond my pay grade."

Julien appeared at Jamie's shoulder accompanied by Fitz.

Having overheard Jamie's remark, Julien cast Scotty an appraising look and said, "I'll see what I can do."

Scotty's face lit up in a smile.

Fitz extended a hand. "I wanted to thank you personally for saving my colleague."

Scotty shook his hand, and Jamie glimpsed the spark of interest that passed between them. He knew that look.

Addressing Scotty, Julien said, "That's twice you've saved my agents. I reckon Her Majesty's Government owe you a favour." Then, turning to Jamie, he said, "Debriefing's tomorrow, 08:00 hours. Go home. You look like shit."

That may be, but I'm on cloud fucking nine.

***

After spending hours in a stuffy room in Thames House being debriefed by Gary and the team, Jamie had returned to Scotland to salvage what remained of his cover and execute a credible extraction. As part of the charade, he'd endured an uncomfortable night in the cells ahead of his court appearance.

He yawned and rubbed his knuckles into his eye sockets as he awaited his turn in front of the magistrate. The holding cell was sparse and stank of despair. The last few days had taken their toll and he was exhausted.

The clerk appeared and summoned a young woman with green hair, black lipstick and face piercings who'd been part of the protest. Jamie sighed loudly, wanting this over quickly so he could return home.

Almost an hour later, Jamie was called and with the help of his solicitor—a young woman from Extinction Rebellion's Welfare team—he pled not guilty to the multiple charges against him, knowing all would be expunged. After being freed on bail, he collected his personal effects, thanked his brief, and wove his way through a throng of activists and their legal representatives.

Still dressed in police-issue grey sweatshirt and joggies, he trotted down the steps of the courthouse, and nearly collided with Alex coming in the opposite direction. The lad was barely recognisable; gone were the dreadlocks and piercings, replaced by a short haircut and clean shave. He wore a tailored grey suit, white shirt and sober tie. Accompanying him was an equally well-dressed woman in her early fifties sporting a lawyer's briefcase and a scowl.

"Bloody hell," gasped Jamie, "you scrub up well. I almost didn't recognise you."

Laughing, Alex extended a hand and introduced Jamie to his mother who offered Jamie a tight smile that failed to reach her eyes.

"How was it?" asked Alex indicating the courthouse.

Alex looked nervous, and Jamie assured him he'd be in and out in no time. His mother's lips wrinkled in annoyance and she reminded her son he was due in court any minute. Ignoring her, Alex asked for news of the others. Feigning ignorance, Jamie grumbled the police had told him little, only that Leon was stable in hospital.

Glaring at Jamie, the mother tugged on her son's sleeve, insisting he'd be late. With an apologetic look, Alex let himself be pulled towards the doors, calling "Stay in touch, yeah?"

As he disappeared into the courthouse, Jamie knew it'd be the last time he saw him. Alex was home, back where he belonged.

Jamie collected his van and drove to the community centre in Linlithgow. The place had been boarded up and secured, but he recognised several protesters milling around outside. He parked up and approached them.

"Jamie!"

He turned to see Meadow running towards him.

She threw her arms around his neck and gasped, "Oh thank God, I've been so worried. No one knew what'd happened to you. Where have you been?"

Peeling her off, he explained he'd just come from court. Meadow told him she and the others had been processed earlier that morning, and had returned to collect their possessions.

"What happened?" she asked. Before Jamie could reply, she grabbed his hand. "Wait, let's find the others, they're inside."

Noticing the back door of the community centre had been jemmied, he allowed her to lead him into the building. The power was off and the corridors were in darkness as they picked their way through broken glass into the main hall. The place had been ransacked and clothes and belongings were strewn across the floor. Jamie spotted Rose and Yasmine among a small group gathering up their things. Meadow called to them and they turned.

Rose marched over, closely trailed by Yasmine, and stood in front of him, hands on hips. "What the hell happened to you?" She cast wary eyes up and down his length, clocking their clasped hands.

Jamie released himself from Meadow's grasp. "I'll explain later. Is there news on Leon?" he asked, although he knew the answer already.

Meadow turned to face him and took his hand in both of hers. "He's fine thank goodness, and is expected to make a full recovery." Her eyes brimmed with tears and she sniffed, "But if you hadn't done what you did, it would've been a different story."

Rose said grudgingly, "You probably saved his life."

Shaking his head, he said, "None of this should've happened." He fixed his gaze on Yasmine and asked, "And Ethan?" Again, he knew the answer.

"He was arrested trying to board a ferry to France," said Rose, visibly upset.

Yasmine reached for Rose's hand and the two women shared a look, appearing to acknowledge each other's pain.

There was the sound of a commotion outside and Jamie suggested they leave before the police arrived. After finding his beloved yucca plant, he helped carry their belongings to the van. In the car park, two security guards were remonstrating with activists who were carting bedding and bags to a camper van, and he was reminded of the security guard at Grangemouth. Gary had broken the news the older man had died. He hoped manslaughter was added to the list of charges against Ethan.

As Jamie gunned the engine and headed south towards Salford, no one spoke. Like the others, he was lost in his thoughts.

Several miles passed before Rose broke the silence. Staring at Jamie, she said, "Care to tell us exactly what happened?"

He relayed what'd occurred in Grangemouth, and they took it in turns to quiz him about the climb, Leon's shooting, and what he'd witnessed in the control room. His story was met with anger and disbelief and a host of questions about Wolff, his accomplice Meyer, and how they'd managed to smuggle in guns. Jamie had learned from Gary that Meyer had climbed aboard a goods train headed for Grangemouth the night before and lain in wait inside the plant, but he didn't share this with the others.

"How the hell did things get so out of hand?" wailed Yasmine.

Rose ignored her and addressed Jamie. "D'you think Ethan knew what Wolff had planned?"

Jamie shrugged. "Hard to say, all I know is he was shit scared and wanted no part in those peoples' deaths."

"Will you vouch for him?" pleaded Yasmine. "Wolff's the one to blame, not Ethan."

"Already did." Knowing his evidence would put Ethan behind bars for decades, Jamie felt like a double-crossing bastard.

After an hour, they stopped at a motorway service station to refuel. Over sandwiches and coffee, Jamie asked what they planned to do now that Ethan was likely facing a lengthy prison sentence.

"The group's finished," said Rose, "at least in its current form. We still support the cause but we're done with direct action."

Rose explained she and Yasmine had plans to expand the gardening business. Jamie asked Meadow what she intended to do, but her emotional wounds were clearly too raw and he immediately regretted the question.

Grasping Meadow's hand, Rose said, "We're hoping Meadow will join us. We're going to clear out of the squat and rent a flat. We need a fresh start and, in any case, I'm getting too old to live like this."

"Me too," whispered Meadow smiling at her.

Rose added, "Meadow's planning to hire a treatment room at the Ubuntu Centre where she can use her skills."

"That's a brilliant idea," said Jamie.

Meadow rewarded him with a watery smile. Jamie then told them about his encounter with Alex and his mother on the courtroom steps.

Rose gave a mirthless laugh, "Doubt we'll see him again now his mother's got her claws in him. She's been giving Ethan money for years in return for keeping Alex clear of trouble, so I guess she finally got what she wanted." Then, after a beat, she said, "And what about you? Will you stay in the area?"

Conscious of Meadow's gaze, he stuck firmly to his extraction story and explained he was returning home to his wife. "She's agreed to give it another go," he said, "I leave tonight."

Meadow glanced away but he could see the pain written on her face. But, as hard as the events of the past few days had been on the women, seeing the fondness that existed between them, he knew they'd be alright. Although they'd a peculiar relationship, they were a family of sorts.

And family was everything.

The Confession

***"But the facts do not lie. And we know that our emperors are naked."* — Greta Thunberg 2021**

***

Kathryn

Kathryn listened as Jamie told her about his extraction and how difficult he'd found it to say goodbye to his friends. He sat in the chair beside her hospital bed. He'd yet to shave, having come straight from the squat in Salford to visit her.

"Hey, what's wrong?" he said, "You tired?"

"I'm fine." She smiled but he seemed to sense it was forced.

He moved to the edge of the bed and took her hand. "Talk to me Kathryn."

Under his gaze, her eyes brimmed with tears. "I can't stop thinking about what happened. Every time I close my eyes, I see Pandora's body or Dominic's car in flames. Last night I woke up screaming after dreaming I was the one in the car."

Tucking a stray lock of hair behind her ear, he said, "And if you and Scotty hadn't acted, Pandora would have killed you both, and Dominic and Monty would've been free to plot another attack."

She cried, "Dominic said they planned to go after you."

"Even more reason to believe you did the right thing." He held her and she sobbed against his chest with great heaving breaths. When she calmed, he pulled away and fixed her with his gaze. "Kathryn, you need to talk to Pia about how you're feeling. If you don't, well ... you saw what bottling it up did to me."

She nodded. "I will ... but it's not just that. I deliberately caused a man's death. I drove his car into a tree and watched it turn into a fireball." She sobbed again.

"Aye, because he tried to kill you and he'd have gone on killing. He'd turned rogue, and a rogue MI6 agent is a very dangerous beast. You did what you had to and I'm proud you'd the courage to do it." After a pause he added, "You've no reason to feel guilty."

She swallowed hard, unsure of whether to share the secret she'd been carrying around like a dead weight for months. By confessing, she knew she risked losing him; if she didn't, it would fester and poison her and their relationship. She exhaled a long, shuddering breath and whispered, "He's not the first man I've killed." Desperately, she searched his face for a reaction.

He looked at her for a long time then, after a pause, said, "Your stepfather?"

She nodded.

He cupped her chin and looked into her eyes. "Kathryn, I know what that bastard did to you. I probably understand better than anyone how he almost destroyed your life, and he'd have done it again to another kid if you hadn't stopped him."

Her mouth fell open. "You knew I killed him?"

"I guessed."

"You never said."

"I needed for you to tell me."

She stared at him and swallowed. "You're not angry or disgusted?"

He shook his head. "Sometimes we have to do the wrong thing for the right reason. I'm glad you did it." He paused, then in a voice choked with emotion, "Because if you hadn't, I sure as hell would have."

She gawped at him. "You'd have done that for me?"

"And anyone else that tried to hurt my family." He drew her mouth to his and kissed her, then pulled away and murmured, "Promise you'll not keep secrets like that from me again. Carrying something like that around on your own's hard. It eats away at you."

She wiped tears from her eyes with the back of her hand. "I didn't want you to hate me for what I'd done."

"Kathryn, I could never hate you. You're my wife and I love you."

Then he scorched her with a kiss.

***

After three weeks in hospital, Kathryn was allowed to go home provided she rested. Doctor Lee had explained she'd suffered a small separation of the placenta due to the beating which had caused the extensive bleeding. The baby, however, was fine and the pregnancy expected to be normal, although Kathryn would require careful monitoring.

Kathryn had been ready to go for over an hour, bag packed and forms filled out, but she needed the consultant to sign the discharge papers. She stood at the window gazing over the grounds, massaging the small of her back while Jamie paced up and down behind her. He seemed as anxious as her to be home.

"Any longer and you'll be in labour," he grumbled.

A few minutes later, a nurse popped in to apologise for the delay, telling them Doctor Lee had been delayed in theatre.

Jamie closed the door behind the nurse and turned to Kathryn. "I was going to wait until we were home to tell you this but I've news about the Monty situation." He took her hand. "You'd better sit down."

"That bad?"

He led her to the bed. "If Doctor Lee catches you on your feet, she might keep you here. You're supposed to be resting."

She perched on the edge of the mattress and he sat beside her, taking her hands in his. He explained that a meeting had taken place behind closed doors in Whitehall between the Home Secretary and the Director General of MI5 to slug it out. The result was that no charges were to be brought against Monty so as not to embarrass the government and risk losing another seat in Scotland. From now on though, the MP would be kept on a tight leash and forever be a puppet of his masters.

Her mouth fell open. "He's getting off scot-free? But he was financing an act of terrorism."

Jamie nodded. "He denies knowing anything about Wolff's plot to blow up Grangemouth."

"Well of course he'd say that."

"Aye, a lot of people are angry at the decision, me included."

"So, he just carries on as before?"

"He won't be appointed to the Defence Select Committee, and he's stepping down as CEO to make way for his son."

She gasped out, "Who's also up to his ears in tax evasion and God only knows what else. Where's the justice in that?" Shaking her head in disgust, she added, "The pair of them ought to be in jail, and if Monty wasn't part of the establishment they would be."

He squeezed her hand. "Please don't get upset or you'll not be allowed home."

Exhaling slowly, she asked, "How did Julien take the news?"

Rolling his eyes, he said, "You know Julien and his schemes. He sees it as an opportunity as he'll have Monty and his son exactly where he wants them. The evidence against them can be used as a lever at any time."

Kathryn shook her head. "Julien's a sly fox."

"Aye, sleekit as the day is long. But there's some good news too."

He explained that, as part of the deal, all charges against Scotty would be dropped in the UK and US. While the details were being thrashed out, Scotty was being transferred to a property owned by the Service in London.

Laughing, she said, "I'm so happy for Scotty."

"I'm just grateful he's moved out."

She asked what he meant and he explained that after Scotty had had a run in with the neighbour's son, he'd hacked Darren's WIFI so every time he accessed the internet it redirected him to a web site called 'Goatse'.

When she gave him a questioning look, he said, "Err ... it's full of images of unnatural acts with ... ugh, trust me, you really don't want to know."

She rolled her eyes and laughed.

"That's not the only good news," said Jamie. "Julien's approved my transfer. From now on, I'll be working out of Thames House as an intelligence officer overseeing investigations, so no more long spells away."

"That's not just a transfer, that's a promotion!" she squealed.

His face broke into a smile, "Guess I must've done something right." Placing his hand on her tummy, he said, "And the extra money'll come in handy."

She threw her arms around him, "I'm so proud of you."

Their celebrations were cut short when Doctor Lee bustled into the room, apologising for keeping them waiting. After a quick check of the paperwork, she announced everything was in order and they could go home.

She fixed Kathryn with a stern look and in a soft Chinese accent said, "Remember, lots of rest. Any problem, you come straight back here. Understood?"

Kathryn nodded.

Dr Lee said, "Any question?"

"Uhm..." said Kathryn. She felt her face flush pink, "Can we ... err ... you know ... are we okay to...?"

When the doctor looked perplexed, Jamie chuckled. "I think what my wife's asking is can we still make love?"

Certain she'd turned a deep shade of volcanic red, Kathryn gawped at Jamie who laughed at her, his eyes sparkling with amusement.

"Ah, yes of course," said the doctor matter-of-factly, "You should make a lotta love." She pointed at Kathryn's belly. "Good for you. Good for baby." Then she wagged a finger at Jamie. "But no acrobatic."

With a smile, she wished them luck and bustled away.

Jamie waved a finger at Kathryn and sniggered, "Remember, no acrobatic."

She thumped his shoulder which only made him laugh more.

"Come on Mrs Denton, time to get you and wee bump home." Then, in a ridiculous attempt at a Chinese accent, he said, "Gonna make a lotta love."

***

Jamie

Back home, after following doctor's orders and doing a lotta what was good for mother and baby, Jamie pulled the duvet over them and wrapped Kathryn in his arms. Burying his face in her hair, he inhaled her heady scent and delighted in the feel of her warm skin against his. He'd been dreaming of this moment for such a long time and didn't want it to end.

Their lovemaking had felt different, imbued with an intensity after such a long absence, and coupled with a tenderness because she was pregnant. She'd been even more responsive to his touch than usual, and he already noticed the subtle changes in her shape. He'd taken his sweet time exploring them too, worshipping every inch of her.

Stroking her face, he whispered, "You okay?"

She smiled at him, "Better than okay. I'm so happy Jamie."

"Me too. I love you so much," he murmured, the words moving from his lips to hers.

The kiss deepened and somehow they found the strength to make love again. Without acrobatic.

The Resignation

"We are facing the greatest global threat ... it is not global warming. It is the threat from policy responses to perceived global warming and the demonising of dissent." **— Professor Ian Plimer 2009**

***

Kathryn

"I refuse to accept your resignation," said Julien tossing the letter disdainfully onto the desk in front of him.

Kathryn sat opposite. It was her first day back at work after getting the all-clear from her obstetrician. Jamie had insisted on driving her to Thames House and he'd escorted her into the office, much to the amusement of her colleagues. After he'd stopped fluttering about her like a mother hen and left, Julien summoned her to his office.

Kathryn slid the letter back towards her boss. "I'm not giving you a choice. I quit."

Tutting, he leant forward. "Nonsense. We simply cannot have a situation where your husband works for us and you're on the other side of the fence."

"I'm not going to return to hacking if that's what you're worried about."

He fixed her with a steely glare. "That's exactly what I'm worried about. Kathryn, it's what you do, it's who you are." His expression softened. "And that thing you did — hacking the Russian embassy to spy on Dominic — that was really quite brilliant."

He picked up the letter and tore it in two. "No, resigning is out of the question. In any case, there's maternity leave, subsidised childcare, flexible working and the like to consider."

She harrumphed, "I failed my probation. I'm not the right fit for this role."

Julien folded his arms over his chest. "I disagree. As I said before, you're one of the best cyber-analysts we have and I do not wish to lose you." He sat back and regarded her for a few moments, then added more evenly, "The nature of the threats we face nowadays has changed. We're fighting a hybrid war in which cyberspace is a battleground and information is a battlefront. I need your skills Kathryn."

"But half the time, I'm working with two hands tied behind my back with red tape, and the other half I'm blindfolded."

Raising his palms, he said, "It's true and there's little I can do about it because we have to operate within a strict legal framework." He paused and in a low voice said, "Which is why I've proposed to the DG we trial a new model of working."

When she threw him a questioning look, he steepled his hands and said, "As we've learned, there are some jobs where we need specialist resource with a more flexible approach."

"You're willing to give me free rein?"

He frowned. "Certainly not. I can't have one of my cyber-analysts going rogue. However, there are occasions where it might be prudent to outsource some of our work to ... err ... more agile operators." The corner of his lips tugged into a smirk.

After the Synergistico application had been identified as the vulnerability that Pandora had exploited to gain access to MI5's communications, Harriet had been reassigned to GCHQ.

Kathryn said, "If I didn't know better, it sounds like you're suggesting a Black Ops cyber team."

Julien sighed. "You've been watching too many movies Kathryn and I would never describe it in those terms. I prefer to think of it as what some might describe as 'efficiency savings'."

"And you're telling me this why?"

"I'd like you to act as the main point of contact between us and —"

Kathryn cut in, "Black Ops."

Julien scowled. "Don't use that term or the DG will have a purple fit. Remember this is a massive step for us. We've always kept things inhouse but I believe that for some work, it'll be possible to use carefully vetted consultants."

"Ooh, I've someone in mind," she grinned.

He gave her a wry smile and she realised he'd been a step ahead of her the whole time, and this was Julien's way of bringing Scotty into the fold without violating any rules.

She laughed, "You won't regret it. Just wait til you see what he can do..."

He gave her a stern look. "I'm relying on you to keep him on a tight rein."

She assured him that would be the case, knowing she'd have her work cut out. This was Scotty after all.

Julien rose and, almost as an aside, said, "Before you go, I've something for you." He unlocked his desk drawer and produced a small black leather box no larger than a drinks coaster. Handing it to her, he told her to open it. Inside was her Security Service badge.

With a broad smile, Julien extended his hand. "Welcome to MI5 Kathryn."

The 25th

"As of now, Earth is our only shareholder. ALL profits, in perpetuity, will go to our mission to 'save our home planet'." **— Yvon Chouinard, Patagonia Founder and Billionaire 2022**

***

Kathryn

2 months later

"You want us to do what?" said Kathryn, gawping in disbelief at her boss. It was so ... 'un-Julien.'

They were sat in his office surrounded by plastic packing crates ahead of Julien's move upstairs. In the aftermath of Grangemouth, a restructuring at Thames House had been announced resulting in his promotion. Kathryn hoped his meteoric rise through the ranks might compensate in a small way for the breakup of his marriage; a fact she'd gleaned on the office grapevine.

His lips curled in amusement as he repeated what he wanted her new cyber crew to do.

"Seriously?" she said. "And after, what d'you want done with it?"

"I suggest you dispose of it responsibly," he said. Then after a pause, he gave a wry smile, "Something fitting though."

She grinned, "Ooh, they're going to love this."

"I'm sure they will but remember, if they're caught, they're on their own."

"Understood."

He slid a copy of the Telegraph towards her. "Thought you might like to see this."

Kathryn unfolded the newspaper. The headline read, *PR Guru Charged with Tax Evasion* and beneath it was a picture of the publicist Margaret-Anne McCrae leaving court. Kathryn looked at Julien in askance.

He raised a shoulder. "One of the chaps at Revenue and Customs owed me a favour."

They shared a laugh.

When Julien rose, she used both hands on the arms of the chair to slowly push to her feet. Almost seven months pregnant, she felt like a zeppelin as she waddled out. Julien fluttered around her, handing her files and opening the door. She smiled; he was almost as bad as Jamie.

"Let me know how you get on," he said.

She said, "I seriously doubt pond life like me are allowed upstairs."

Chuckling, he shooed her out and she returned to her desk where Fitz was busy taking apart a laptop.

"Having fun?" she asked.

He grinned in reply and she smiled, knowing his happiness had nothing to do with dismantling computers and everything to do with the relationship blossoming between him and Scotty.

"I'm off to Wycombe." She cocked an impish eyebrow and added, "Anything you'd like me to take for Scotty?"

"Thanks, but I'm seeing him tomorrow. There's a Star Trek exhibition in London."

Fitz had it bad.

"I'll see you tomorrow," she said, smiling.

She left Thames House and drove to High Wycombe in Buckinghamshire where her cyber crew had set up shop.

The innocuous-looking office was set above an estate agent on a busy street lined with shops and takeaways. Squeezed between a dry-cleaners and an insurance broker was an ordinary looking door bearing a tarnished plaque with a list of businesses.

She pressed the entry buzzer and took the steep, winding staircase to an opaque glazed door on the 2nd floor, stopping to catch her breath on the way. She tapped on the glass which was etched with the name 'Denebian Computer Services'; the closest thing to Deniable Cyber Ops that Scotty could get past Julien.

A large blurry shape approached and the door opened. Scotty greeted her with an expansive smile and she followed him past the small reception area towards the rear. The only visible sign of high security was badge-access was required to enter the room at the back. Lined with server racks and desks overflowing with computer equipment, it looked like a regular repair shop. In reality it was a classified sanctum developing military-grade digital hacking tools. Deniable ones.

Another man sat at a desk and he swivelled round on his chair and said hello. Although only in his late twenties, she'd known Jake for many years under his hacker name, Grey Lady. Tall and slender with a mop of unruly black hair, his angelic features concealed the fact he was a demon in cyberspace. From his teenage bedroom on the Isle of Skye in Scotland, Jake had headed up the Grey Nemesis hacktivist collective of which Kathryn, Scotty and Pandora had been part.

While still at school, Jake had orchestrated some of the most notorious cyber-attacks on corporations and individuals across the globe. However, after Pandora's betrayal of the group, the police had only been able to pin lesser charges on him, and he'd spent time in an open prison and under house arrest. That was until Julien tracked him down and offered him a deal. Like Scotty, Jake was employed by a fictitious company as a freelance computer consultant with a vague contract.

Jake leapt up to fetch Kathryn a chair and hovered over her as she settled herself into it. He asked if he could get her anything, speaking in a soft Highlands and Islands accent which she found pleasant to the ear.

"Oh, don't you start," she laughed, "I'm not used to people fussing over me like this."

Scotty said, "I'd offer you coffee but caffeine isn't good for the baby so I'll make us herbal tea." When Kathryn rolled her eyes, he added mischievously, "How about a foot rub?"

As Scotty shuffled off towards the kitchenette, she cast her eyes around the chaos of computer hardware and cables. Turning to Jake, she said, "I like what you've done with the place."

They chatted about the new digs he'd moved into in Loudwater village close to High Wycombe, and how much he was enjoying London and the South East.

Over mugs of camomile tea, they discussed the configuration of the computer network that was not connected to the internet, and progress on a new digital weapon; tasks that'd kept them busy since moving into the premises. Scotty said they'd already had a walk-in customer from the office downstairs who'd pitched up with a faulty laptop. When Kathryn frowned, Jake said he'd fixed the machine and invoiced the customer so Denebian appeared legitimate.

Scotty winked at Kathryn and said, "Nah, the reason he fixed it was because she was cute."

Jake grabbed a Nerf gun and fired a volley of foam bullets at Scotty and they shrieked with laughter.

"Bet you put a timebomb in the software so she has to come back," chuckled Scotty.

Jake smiled but didn't deny it.

Kathryn looked from one to the other and rubbed her hands together in glee. "So, we've got our first assignment."

They wheeled their chairs closer and leaned forward.

"Yeah, so what're we hackin'?" asked Jake.

She grinned. "Monty's millions."

Jake gave a long low whistle and Scotty's jaw dropped.

"No shit?" said Scotty, "We're allowed to do that?"

She explained that Julien had given them the green light to hack into the MP's cryptocurrency wallet. If successful, she said they could give the money to charity and good causes. This prompted a heated discussion between Scotty and Jake as to what constituted a worthy cause, which she'd to prevent escalating into a Nerf gun war.

Kathryn had chosen Greenpeace as one of her beneficiaries, knowing Jamie would approve. Since his stint with the Climate Warriors, he was a convert to the campaign, to the extent he wanted to design an eco-friendly home for his growing family. He'd already discussed solar panels and storage batteries with his brother-in-law Ross who'd decided to diversify his business into the renewable domestic energy sector.

Scotty's statement jolted her from daydreaming about her new home.

"Without Monty's 25th word," he said, "we've as much chance as a Tribble on a Klingon Battlecruiser."

Scotty was right — without the secret password, they'd be unable to access his crypto wallet.

"Which is why I've brought this," said Kathryn, rifling through her handbag. She produced a USB stick. "It's footage from when the tech team took a first look at Monty's home. It contains photos of all the documents in his safe and office desk, as well as pictures of all the rooms."

When Scotty and Jake looked sceptical, she added, "Most people choose a memorable word or phrase as their 25th word, something they're unlikely to forget. Often, they write it down and store it in a secure place." She pointed to the USB stick, "If Monty's done that, the answer's in here."

Jake blew out a breath. "The odds are stacked against us."

"We've got to try; we cannae let Julien down man," said Scotty taking the USB.

Several hours, pizzas and failed attempts later, they'd failed to guess the 25th word and Kathryn took a break. She was tired, her back ached and she knew she'd have to call it a day soon since she still had the drive home.

The offices around them had emptied, their occupants having gone home for the evening. She sat in the small reception area and phoned Jamie to tell him she'd be late and not to worry. He offered to drive over and fetch her but she declined. He said he'd make dinner, a vegan dish he thought she'd like. After reminding him of how much she loved him, she re-joined Scotty and Jake.

Jake thumped his keyboard. "Dammit, we're running out of ideas."

They'd tried every word, phrase and combination they could think of based on possible keywords in the paperwork in Monty's safe, without success. They used variations with different capitalisation and number sequences. Jake had also tried Monty's known passwords and he'd examined a list of these for patterns such as favourite special characters and numericals. Nothing yielded results.

Kathryn had printed copies of the photographs the tech team had taken of Monty's home office and she spread these out on a table. They'd already tried using the titles of the books and DVDs on Monty's shelves but to no avail.

She paced the room and rubbed her lower back, convinced the answer was staring them in the face.

"Ah Jesus," said Scotty, wheeling his chair away from the desk in frustration.

She squealed, "That's it! That's it!"

Jake and Scotty looked at her as if she'd gone mad.

Scotty raised an eyebrow. "Jesus is the answer?"

Kathryn picked up a photograph. "Look at the birthday card on his desk. It's Superintendent Ted Hastings."

Neither had the faintest clue what she was talking about, so she explained that Hastings was a character from the popular British TV police procedural *Line of Duty*. Monty had DVD box sets of the series on his shelves and his son had sent him a birthday card featuring a stern-looking Hastings on the front.

She said to Scotty, "Hastings has a catchphrase, 'Jesus Mary Joseph and the Wee Donkey'."

Snorting with amusement, Scotty's fingers flew across the keyboard as he input it.

It failed.

Kathryn held her breath and Jake hovered at his side as Scotty tried different capitalisation combinations.

Leaping out his chair, Scotty scream-laughed. "It worked! It bloody worked!"

She peered at his screen. It had worked and they'd finally cracked Monty's crypto wallet, the balance of which was worth just shy of three million pounds.

Laughing, Scotty wrapped her in a suffocating bear hug which Jake joined in with.

Squealing with delight, she said, "Jesus, Mary, Joseph and the Wee Donkey."

— THE END —

A Note to the Reader

Dear Reader,

I hope you enjoyed reading *Wolff's Bane* as much as I enjoyed writing it. I welcome feedback from my readers, and I read each and every one of your reviews. So, if it's not too much trouble, please leave me a review on Amazon.

If you'd like to find out more about me, please visit: https://hjrussell.co.uk/

Thank you,

H.J. Russell

Acknowledgements

I want to thank my family for putting up with me while I wrote this novel, especially my partner in crime, Alasdair, without whose support I'd have gone off the rails. I also want to thank my tutors at Edinburgh Napier and my wonderful band of beta readers in helping to shape this book. I've a number of good friends and neighbours to thank too: Brian for your stunning book cover design; Gail and Pauline for sharing your police knowledge and experience; Declan for your cybersecurity expertise; Corrine and Helen for listening to me ramble on during our dog walks; Alice and David for showing me your barn which inspired the grisly denouement.

If you think I went too far with Darren's misogyny, I'm sad to say it's based on fact. Laura Bates in *Men Who Hate Women* provides chilling examples of the violent ideology espoused on Incel platforms. She also reveals how this dogma has spilled over into the real world resulting in attacks on women, many of them fatal.

Also By H. J. Russell

HELL'S GLEN

Please visit: https://hjrussell.co.uk/

Printed in Great Britain
by Amazon

39468503R00185